They were surely but a dream, a terrible dream, and they had killed his beautiful son, and now he would die, and when he died, he would awaken, and with his son and all those who went before, the earth and the sun would go on forever. And so he chanted, and as he chanted, he pulled his blanket over his head, and the soldiers at the side of the road could not help but laugh at the quaint old Indian whining a loud but muffled chant into his blanket.

Beneath the blanket, he was gnawing flesh from the heels of his hands to make them smaller, and slick with blood, so he could slip his manacles. Then let them laugh. He would die as Kaitsenko would die, killing the enemy . . .

AUTUMN THUNDER

MICHAEL KOSSER

St. Martin's Paperbacks

AUTUMN THUNDER

ISBN: 0-312-96560-5

Printed in the United States of America

St. Martin's Paperbacks edition/December 1997

St. Martin's Paperbacks are published by St. Martin's Press, 175 Fifth Avenue, New York, NY 10010.

10 9 8 7 6 5 4 3 2 1

For David and Francine

Chapter 1

"**Y**ou!" shouted White Bear to a young, snake-lanky warrior. "Are you coming with me to Texas to kill Texans? Or are you still peeing from your mother's cradleboard?"

The young warrior wilted under the laughter of his friends, but not for long. The great Kiowa war chief wanted the youngster to fight alongside him, and that was what the boy wanted to hear.

White Bear was making his way around the camp, boastful and boisterous. Stocky and deadly, he could be counted on to stir up the warriors when the raiding season began. "What are we waiting for?" he asked in a thunderous voice. "Our brothers the Comanches have been running free in Texas since the last new moon!" The young warriors were gathering around him, excited. He was pleased to see that he could still pull a crowd with the crook of his finger. He picked out another young man from the crowd. "Have you seized the pack strap instead of the arrows?" he asked. In other words, have you decided to save your life by playing the part of the woman?

There had been plenty of rain in the spring of 1871. Kiowa bands were camped for nearly a mile along the north fork of the Red River, along with bands of their cousins, the Kiowa-Apache, and a band of Comanche.

There was good grazing for their ponies and lots of red meat for the camp. The day before, a large hunting party had returned from a foray north, carrying the meat and hides of thirty buffaloes. So much for the white man's boast that the buffalo would soon be gone. Chief Au-sai-mah assured the people that his hunters had culled their buffaloes from a herd so big they never saw the end of it during the two days they lurked along its edges.

Autumn Thunder was enjoying the seventeenth spring of his life. He had reached his full height, a slender five-foot-ten, which made him tall among the Kiowas. His long black hair was braided, and his dress was typical of a Kiowa warrior: leather breechcloth and moccasins, gold hoop earrings, and little else except rawhide strips, wound three times around each bicep and knotted. It was part of his medicine.

He cared tenderly for his rifle, accumulated a few horses, and made shrewd trades so he would have plenty of ammunition to fire. There was always ammunition to be had from Caddo George the trader.

"And you! Quiet boy with the noisy name! Is this the year you tear yourself away from your grandmother's tepee and follow me to strike our enemies?"

This time Autumn Thunder was the target. He feigned indifference, but the observant war chief saw him shift his weight uneasily from his right to his left foot, and the chief laughed.

No young man could sit still under the scornful gaze of White Bear. And no young man could resist the look of fierce pride he would throw at any young warrior who would step forward and say, "I will go with you, Set-tainte."

As he spoke with Autumn Thunder, who was one of his younger recruits, White Bear felt the tall shadow of Kicking Bird behind him. For the moment he forgot about Autumn Thunder as he whirled around. "Ah, Tay-nay-angopte," he said. "You are here to worry me, as always, I see." White Bear would have loved to dismiss Kicking Bird with a hand wave and a nasty remark, but Kicking Bird was a revered figure among many of the Kiowas, in spite of his eternal insistence that they must find a way to get along with the white men. Even White Bear respected the man who so often opposed his adventures. He had seen Kicking Bird in action, a formidable force on the battlefield. How could one so soft and pliant in camp be so tough and strong on the warpath? White Bear did not understand. Either a man was young and tough or he was old and spent.

Look at old Sitting Bear, he thought. Not the most pleasant of men, but what a man! His enemies were *enemies*. He could count nearly seventy summers, and yet his force was not spent. His right arm was still strong; his eye still held the stern fury of a born warrior. White Bear would not say so, but if he feared any man, it was old Sitting Bear, whom the Kiowas called Set-ankeah. Not for his might; even in middle age White Bear was among the strongest of Kiowas. Thick-waisted, with a barrel chest, arms like the old cottonwoods along Medicine Creek, and a heart strong as iron, White Bear feared the might of no man. It was Sitting Bear's implacable will that made White Bear step carefully around the old chief, who would not retire to his pipe and his tepee and his grandchildren. Only death would still his will to do battle.

Now this Kicking Bird—he was more like a white man— no mighty speechmaking to the many as a real man would do, but soft words in the ear of one then the other; not honest emotions but words that played with a man's thoughts and could make him doubt his own beliefs. The white men loved Tay-nay-angopte, and no wonder. He had the right soft words for them too! And now he wanted his Kiowas to sit around in their camps like women. What next? To scratch up the ground and grow watermelons like the Wichitas?

White Bear's Kiowas would not be staying home this year. Texas awaited him, just as Texas had always awaited the war cries of the real Kiowas.

"You must not raid this year," Kicking Bird said.

White Bear stuck out his mighty chest and looked up into the face of Kicking Bird. "My medicine is strong," he replied. "We will raid this year, and we will return with many horses carrying wonderful things."

"My friends among the Americans have said that they have a new war chief. He will be angry if you raid into Texas."

"If he is angry let him find us and fight us."

"He need not find us. He will find our villages. Then our women and children will suffer."

"If he kills our women and children, we will kill his women and children."

"But he has many more women and children than we do. I do not want to see our women and children suffer for the sake of our honor."

White Bear thought for a moment. "Good," he finally said. "Tell your friends that White Bear will not raid the Americans. He will only raid the Texans, and the Mexicans.''

"The Americans have said that we should not raid the Texans and the Mexicans.''

There it was! Try to understand the white man. Texas was not America, no matter what the Americans said. Texas was full of evil people who loved to kill Indians.

And Mexicans! Even Americans hated Mexicans. Why was it all right for Americans to go down to the shallow river and kill Mexicans but it was not all right for the Kiowas to do the same? "What do they want us to do, fight the Utes?" he asked. "Fighting Utes is fine but they do not have enough plunder to take. Texans, even Mexicans, have many fine things.''

"I have told you before,'' said Kicking Bird. "The Texans and the Americans are one people again. And the Americans are at peace now with the Mexicans.''

White Bear laughed from deep in his chest. "Then let the Americans not raid the Texans and the Mexicans. I will not make them raid the Texans and the Mexicans. All the more for us to kill. But as for me, in three more dawns, my braves will cross Red River and the Texans will be sorry for their bad behavior.''

By this time at least a dozen grinning young braves had surrounded the two chiefs. They liked White Bear. Unlike most of the other older men, he still loved the tomahawk and the coup stick. He was not always counseling them to have patience. Where White Bear was, there were always bold words and action. Kicking Bird was smart, and he loved his people, but he dreamed of peace and the young men dreamed of war.

One of the young braves had grown bored with the dialog. A great young pony rider, his Kiowa name meant "passes like the wind,'' but he had gained such a reputation for excessive rhetoric that the Fort Sill post interpreter had privately renamed him "Passes Wind.''

"Ah,'' he said in Kicking Bird's face. "If you don't want to go, don't go. You afraid, uncle? We're not afraid. When I come back from Texas my pony's mane will bear the scalps of many Texans.''

Kicking Bird wore the sour expression of a man who had just eaten an underripe melon. This boy was new to the camp.

He did not understand who Kicking Bird was. But the chief kept his patience. It would be a relief to cease his eternal debate with White Bear.

"My young brother," he said. "For many summers I have held the white man's hand. There are many bad white men, but also some good ones and we must heed what they say, for they have great power."

"Great power, hah!" the young brave cried. "Last summer we fought them in Texas. I killed one whose hair hangs in my mother's lodge."

"How did you kill him?" Kicking Bird asked, though he knew the answer.

"With one shot from my rifle. I can shoot a rifle better than any white man."

"But can you make a rifle, my little brother?" Kicking Bird asked. "When it stops shooting can you fix it so it can shoot again?"

The young warrior did not care to argue further with Kicking Bird. "You are afraid of them. But I am not. I—"

Kicking Bird raised his hand with such grace and dignity that the young brave stopped his chatter.

"Last summer I did a bad thing. Some bad birds were chirping like you are. 'Kicking Bird is a coward,' they said. 'Kicking Bird is a child to the white man, and does as he is told.' A leader must lead or he receives no respect. So I told them I will lead. A hundred warriors followed me. We went down to Texas. We fought the soldiers from Fort Richardson. We chased them all the way back to the fort and killed some of them without them doing anything to us. I killed one of them myself, not from far away with a rifle, but with my lance. Is that not so, Tsen-tainte?"

Tsen-tainte, or White Horse, was a noted raider of army horses and mules. The young braves respected him.

He had been attracted to the group of young braves standing around White Bear and Kicking Bird. Experienced as he was, he could smell a raid in the making, and he had wandered over to see if it was worth being a part of.

"My brother Kicking Bird is a great war chief," he said, simply, and walked away. He did not want to give the young braves any satisfaction, but White Horse was disgusted with

Kicking Bird. "White men hate horse thieves!" he had once scolded White Horse.

White Horse had scoffed at Kicking Bird. "Kiowas honor good horse stealers!" he had retorted. Now, he walked away without further comment.

White Bear had had enough discussion. They would be riding in three days and he still had not finished his preparations. "Leave us, Kicking Bird," he said, quietly. "Or will you try to stop us from going?" He turned away from Kicking Bird and looked around at his young followers, but his hand gripped the arm of the great chief. "Or will you ride to Fort Sill and betray us?"

Kicking Bird stepped away from the grasp of his old cohort. "I am Kiowa," he responded. "We have always raided south. It is no longer good to do so but I will not stop you and I will not tell the soldiers either. But I warn you, bad things will happen if you do this thing."

"I hear your warning, my brother," White Bear said, walking toward his big tepee. Then he turned toward the young braves. "There are others who will be joining us when the sun is close to the mountains there." And he pointed north toward the Wichita range. "I will show you how we will destroy the horse soldiers at Fort Richardson if they try to save the Texans."

Autumn Thunder's spirits soared to the sound of hoofbeats over the spring grass of the southern plains. He looked around him at the young men who, like him were on their first raid into Texas. Among them were his close friends Hau-tau, Ko-yah-te, and Po-lan-te. Also among them were some of the great Kiowa warriors. Kicking Bird was not with them, but White Bear was there. So was Tsen-tainte. And the great young chief Addo-eta, or Big Tree. Autumn Thunder did not count the number of braves in the raiding party. He believed it was bad medicine to count Kiowas, though it was all right to count horses.

They had been riding south along the valley of the north fork of the Red River all day, but ahead he could see the tree line that marked the course of Red River itself. He looked forward to fording the river. On the north side of the river he behaved himself, but like other Kiowas he believed that south of Red River he was bound by no promises or treaties.

He glanced to his left for a moment, then quickly focused his eyes straight ahead and kept them fixed on the tree line, which was still more than a mile away. He did not want Maman-ti to know that he had looked at him.

Maman-ti, the Owl Prophet, had a look that could wither the stoutest of spirits. He was both a war chief and a great medicine man. When he said that something would happen, it always happened.

Autumn Thunder had talked to Maman-ti just long enough to be certain that the medicine man knew the hour of his— Autumn Thunder's—death. Maman-ti did not tell Autumn Thunder when it would be, but he did tell him when it would not be. Not today. That was good enough for Autumn Thunder.

The sky was cloudless and endless, like the string of Autumn Thunder's life. In the new spring grass there was little dust. It seemed to Autumn Thunder that never had the greens and golds and purples of the plain been as bright as they were this day. He felt no sense of foreboding, dread, or fear. Not now. This was what he was born to do. Some day he could tell his children that he went to war against the Texans with Set-tainte, and Addo-eta and Tsen-tainte and Maman-ti the Do-ha-te. He remembered the stories he had heard from the ancient warriors who had ridden with the great chief To-hauson—not the To-hauson that he had seen in the village on Cache Creek but an earlier To-hauson, the legendary To-hauson, last chief of all the Kiowas. He felt the pull of the great Kiowa warrior tradition that went back long before the first Kiowa climbed on the back of a horse and became one with it.

The ponies drove on in an easy trot. Far behind the warriors a half dozen younger boys drove a herd of spare ponies, one or two for each warrior. None left their best behind. This was to be a raid that would never be forgotten. It was as if the chiefs who had planned the raid knew that their years as raiders were numbered. But they knew no such thing. Not then. To them the days of the Kiowa warrior stretched as endlessly into the future as in the past.

They dismounted and walked their ponies down the north bank of the Red River. They were determined to spare their

best mounts early in their journey, at least until they had en-
larged their herd with horses stolen from Texas corrals. Once
the ponies were in the water, the Indians mounted up and
forded the river. Riding beside Autumn Thunder was Hau-Tau.
Hau-Tau had promised Autumn Thunder that when the fighting started, he would be the first of the Kiowas to count coup.

Once they crossed the river, Maman-ti had them hide their
saddles in a rocky crevice and hobble their spare ponies. The
young boys were left with the herd while the warriors pushed
on toward the Butterfield Trail, where they hoped for action.
After a long day's riding even these well-conditioned warriors
were pleased when the Owl Prophet finally called a halt and
let his warriors make camp.

Camp for a warring Kiowa was not much: a campfire; a few
mouthfuls of corn and buffalo jerky; a few pulls on the wa-
terbag; a pipe or two; and a few minutes of talk before it was
time for them to wrap themselves in their blankets and ease
on down into the prairie grass for a night's sleep. ·

This night, after they ate, they watched as Maman-ti walked
up a hill and vanished into the night. They listened in silence,
but heard very little—the quiet hoot of an owl in the dark; a
low moan; the rattling of dried beans in a gourd. Then silence.

In the evening stillness, with the earth lit by a nearly full
moon, Autumn Thunder was transfixed. He looked to the sky,
at the big bright moon and he saw drops of blood fall earth-
ward. He felt a gentle calm take a warm hold on him. His
heart was at peace. The Owl Prophet could conquer death itself, and he had conquered Autumn Thunder's death. He had
said so. What a blessed thing, to live on, secure amidst danger!

He heard the drums. They had been beating all the time,
softly. And he heard a soft toot on an eagle-bone whistle. He
looked away from the bleeding moon toward Hau-Tau, and
his heart fell. Hau-Tau was not protected. In the soft light of
the brightly glowing moon, he could see the face of his friend,
a mask of death itself. Hau-Tau turned toward Autumn Thunder and smiled. The smile grew into a harsh grin acknowledg-
ing and rejoicing in his own death.

With great relief he saw the spare figure of Maman-ti appear
from the gloom. The medicine man chief walked over to the
fire and with a few motions of his slender right hand summoned all the warriors to join him. When the great chiefs were

seated around the fire and the lesser warriors gathered in a standing circle behind them, he motioned for them to listen.

For a few dramatic moments he stood silently and stared at the young faces flickering in the firelight, and from the blackness of his eye sockets peered into the soul of every warrior present. He raised his hands high, and spoke.

"When the sun is overhead," he said, pointing straight up, "a small group of Texans will pass along the trail. You"— and he looked toward where some of youngest, most eager braves stood—"you will see how easy it would be to defeat them. But you *must* let them go." His eyes drilled right through them. Many a good ambush had been ruined by young glory seekers. Maman-ti would have none of that. "If you attack the first group, then my medicine will be no good. I will die, and many of you will die." As if in agreement, a distant owl hooted in the night.

"We will wait, and later another group of white men will come. They will be bigger. Some of you may be afraid that they are too powerful. But it is they we will attack. It will be a hard fight, but we will defeat them. You will win many honors and as for the Texans, many of them will die.

"Now, there must be nothing more said." He kicked at the fire, scattering a few sticks. It was the signal that the fire should be extinguished. As he rolled up in his blanket, Autumn Thunder felt a warm surge of excitement—not from fear, but from anticipation of great deeds to be done the following day.

Chapter 2

Nobody needed to awaken Autumn Thunder. The paling of the night sky was enough. In a winter camp a warrior might lie abed as long as he pleased, but on the warpath the sleep left his eyes long before sunrise.

As he welcomed the dawn, his eyes spotted Maman-ti on his spotted pony slowly reconnoitering a nearby hill. With him were Addo-eta and a Kiowa-Apache whose name Autumn Thunder did not know. The hill looked down on a broad valley of sparse grass and little else. Through that valley, far from any cover, traveled the road where Maman-ti prophesied the enemy would appear.

The Owl Prophet placed scouts on the north end of the hill and the rest of the warriors in the scrub oak toward the opposite end of the broad valley. Then they waited, their ponies tied up behind them.

Autumn Thunder looked around him. Veterans like White Bear and White Horse sat quietly in whatever shade they could find, not particularly interested in the windblown flat below. They had made their medicine. They were prepared for the conflict to come.

Hau-tau tapped Autumn Thunder on the shoulder. His eyes shined. "I am ready for this," he said. "Everything is right. This day is right. When today is done you will look at me in a different way."

"I look at you as my friend," Autumn Thunder said, simply. "Why would I want to look at you in a different way?" Hau-tau grunted in disgust and eased on down to another young warrior. How could Autumn Thunder explain his anxieties to his friend? How do you tell a friend that for all his courage he will die this day, while you will be wise and cautious and you will live?

So Autumn Thunder sat quietly, like the older men, and he watched the warm spring sun begin its journey across the sky. He felt a tap on his shoulder. He turned and his eyes met those of his closest friend Ko-yah-te. Today's fight could be an important one for Ko-yah-te. He was pony poor. His animal was an old plug not up to great deeds, so he would have to struggle along behind the leaders and hope that he could gain something valuable that he could trade for a good pony.

"It is a good day to live, my brother," said Ko-yah-te, whose sunny disposition made him a favorite among the young people of the village. Autumn Thunder nodded, but said nothing. On this day he and his friend would not be fighting side by side. "Take no chances," he told Ko-yah-te, simply.

The morning came and went. Occasionally a swirling breeze blew a twist of dust from the plain below into the air, but otherwise the land below lay still. The youngsters began to fidget and mutter to themselves. "Why are we lying here like panthers? We are men. We should be traveling toward Mexico burning farms and stealing horses as we go."

Maman-ti ignored the young complainers. The more experienced warriors, like White Horse and Big Tree, did not deign to reply to them. Only White Bear arose from his hiding place and stood above them. "The Do-ha-te has spoken," he said. "I would not have him angry at you. He can kill a man with his thoughts." Then, just for a moment, his hard eyes twinkled. "If he says they will come, then do not worry. We will have our fight. And you will fight like the great Kiowas of old."

In the village White Bear attracted young warriors to him. Out on the warpath he was a primal force. Young men all knew the legends about his power in battle. He feared no one, so when he warned people away from a man, they took him at his word and backed off. They went back to lying concealed in the brush, waiting while the sweat rolled down their bodies and into the parched dirt. Maman-ti lay as still as the rest, but his eyes and ears were attuned to the sights, the smells, the rhythms of the great plains. Maman-ti knew. He didn't know how he knew, not really. But he knew.

The sun climbed to the top of the sky and stood there, an angry white ball drawing the life from those beneath it.

Still no one came.

And then from the north end of the hills came a mirror flash, and another. The Owl Prophet caught the flash. And he spoke softly.

"My young brothers, take care. We are here to kill *Tai-bos*, not to make stories for our grandchildren. You wait and listen for what I will tell you. If you do not, I promise you, you shall surely die."

A small group of men on big cavalry mounts appeared on the road, trailing a cloud of dust that hung in the afternoon heat then settled slowly to earth. Behind them appeared an army ambulance pulled by four matched black horses. As the distant ambulance made its way closer to them, the young warriors began whispering to each other, checking their weapons and their paint.

Eager to attack, Autumn Thunder's moccasins began to itch him. He and some of the others ran back to their horses and untied them from the scrub trees that held them. "I will count first coup before you make it down the hill," Hau-Tau told him.

Autumn Thunder leaped on the back of his pony and kicked at his sides. It flinched but did not move. A stony-faced veteran warrior named Tabenanica had grabbed the reins. "You don't go," said Tabenanica. "Not until Maman-ti says you go."

Autumn Thunder looked around him and saw some of his friends with expressions of grim purpose on their faces. In front of them stood the medicine man with a piercing gaze that stopped them in their tracks. Hau-tau clucked to his pony, but before the animal could vault forward Maman-ti took his quirt and whacked her on the nose, then did the same to the bare ribs of Hau-tau.

"You will move when I tell you to move," said the Owl Prophet.

Even young Kiowa warriors were not accustomed to being ordered around so imperiously by their elders. They grumbled, but White Bear rode up and said, "Listen to Maman-ti. It is his raid and I will sink my knife into the ribs of any pony that moves forward.

"Listen to Maman-ti," White Bear repeated. "He knows."

The young warriors climbed down from their ponies not because they were afraid White Bear would make good on his threat, but because they were impressed that White Bear was following the medicine man. If he was in thrall to Maman-ti, then Maman-ti must have some powerful medicine.

"We will wait," said Maman-ti, calmly. "Soon others will be along. They are the ones we will attack."

So the young men settled down again to wait, peering through the scrub into the bare valley below. The ambulance had passed out of sight, leaving a long dust cloud to linger over the entire length of the road as far as they could see. They almost hungered for that wagon, so anxious were they to strike a blow.

Some drank a small quantity of water. Others slept. But mostly they lay still, ignored the flies and bugs, and watched with their eyes and ears for a force that would surely come along, as the Owl Prophet had said it would. The iron sun crept across the sky hour by hour and the road remained empty.

Forward along the trail, in the ambulance, rode a gaunt, red-bearded general who went about with fury in his eyes even when his mind was on his next dinner. On this afternoon, his mind was far from dinner. He stared out from the ambulance at the low arid hills that rose in the near distance. The soft spring wind stirred the sparse new grass, and that was all.

Bam! The ambulance hit a rut and both left wheels sprang into the air, to land on the road with a crash.

"Damn!" he cried out, moving his jaw around as if to check for missing teeth.

He shared the coach with another general and two colonels. "Marcy," he said, addressing the other general, "I'm not sure I believe all this garbage we've been hearing about the Indians. You look around, what do you see? Little families here, little families there. Women, children, milkin' cows and plantin' gardens. You'd think they'd all come to the forts if they was scared of Indians."

One of the colonels scoffed. "General, if you was a woman would you feel safer out on the plains where you can see a rider comin' in from five miles off, or in some fort where a love-starved corporal can come up behind you and—''

"If I was a woman!" growled Sherman. "How in hell would I know what I'd think if I was a woman? You ever wake up in the morning and say to yourself, 'Now, how would I feel about watchin' the sunrise or plowin' a field if I was a woman?' Hell, if I was a woman I'd kill myself before I get in bed with an ugly-lookin' bastard like you."

The colonel did not want to do battle with his boss. "Yes, sir," he said, subdued.

"Look here, General," said Marcy who respected Sherman but was not awed by him. "During the war I spent a heap of time in Texas. I tell you, a dozen years ago there was more people out here than there are now. Something's been driving them away."

Sherman returned Marcy's respect for him. If Marcy said something, then it was so. Still, he was a bit skeptical.

"Well, I ain't seen a solitary Indian in a week," he said. "Still, when we get to Fort Sill I intend to ask Grierson if he knows where his Indians are. The rangers claim the Indians raid, then they cross Red River and lay around Fort Sill with halos dancin' over their heads until the horse-stealin' mood comes up again. If Fort Sill is just a rustlers' refuge, then we've got some major work to do."

Two of the younger braves walked over to where Big Tree, who was aptly named, was sprawled in the grass, his dark eyes studying the dark clouds that were appearing in the sky beyond where the road appeared. Big Tree was a warrior not much older than themselves, a man who craved action like themselves.

"Addo-eta, if we started now, we could catch up with that wagon before dark and wipe them out," said one of them.

"I think Maman-ti is too cautious," said the other. "The scalps of the soldiers should have long been hanging from our belts. Perhaps in the wagon was a soldier chief. I have heard that their chiefs ride in such wagons. You lead us, Addo-eta."

Big Tree was a down-to-earth warrior, not as religious as some of the others. He took Maman-ti's rituals with a grain of salt. And yet, like White Bear, he feared and respected the power of the Owl Prophet's will.

"Do-ha-te knows much," he said to the anxious young

men. "And his anger is great. He has told you what is to come. If his prophecy does not come as he said it would, we will know that he has lost his medicine." He smiled, and his squinting eyes turned from the horizon to them. "All of Texas is ours to take. Winter is gone. Our ponies are ready. It is not only the summer of the earth, it is the summer of our lives. Wait, my young brothers. Wait, for the summer stretches out before us, warm and good." His eyes flickered and focused on the road. "And now, you will not have to wait long," he said. "To your ponies. Check your rifles. They are coming."

They turned around to look at the road, and could not believe what they were seeing. A line of white-canvas-covered freight wagons was rumbling from the east, heaving into view like clumsy little ships, pitching and yawing as they followed their mule teams over the rough-rutted dirt road. One after another they appeared from behind a rock outcropping until the braves began to wonder if the wagons would be too much for them to handle. But after ten, none followed. There were horsemen riding on either side. The battle might not be easy, but if they fought well they could win. Maman-ti's prophecy had been true. Here was a prize far more precious than the one lone ambulance.

Quickly the braves ran to their mounts and untethered them. Maman-ti nodded to White Bear, who was inordinately proud of an old, dented cavalry bugle he owned. He raised the instrument to his lips, but before the first sour note a hundred warriors were galloping headlong down the open slope.

There was no formation. This was a downhill race, pure and simple, a quest for honors and damn the consequences. In the lead was a seasoned, ambitious warrior named Yellow Wolf, and immediately after him rode Big Tree. There were several Kiowa-Apaches close behind, and then came Hau-tau and Autumn Thunder.

Autumn Thunder's spirit thundered down the hill even faster than his pony. This was what he had been born for, to race for the enemy and strike him. He felt no fear, only exhilaration, for had not Maman-ti promised him safety, and had not Maman-ti proved his medicine to be great?

Autumn Thunder cried his war cry: "Strike hard! Strike hard!" And the others yipped and howled like a pack of ferocious wolves certain of their kill. The wagons began to draw into a circle, with the mules facing toward the center, but they were slow and the Kiowas were swift. They closed quickly. Puffs of smoke began to blossom from the wagons. Two braves jumped from their horses to one of the wagons. One fell dead and the other limped off, blood pouring down his left leg. Several teamsters were also lying still on the ground, killed by gunfire during the initial charge.

Autumn Thunder rode for the gap between the first and the last wagon in the broken circle, drawing heavy fire, and quickly fled through the circle, excited but now more wary. The teamsters had made their point with well-aimed rifle fire. While several warriors removed the dead warrior, Autumn Thunder rode in close and caught the wounded one onto the back of his pony. The other warriors were riding in a wide circle around the wagons. Some of them were watching to see if Autumn Thunder could make his escape. His pony was laboring hard under the weight of two warriors. Bullets kicked up dust around them. One clipped a feather that decorated the pony's mane. Another creased the shoulder of the wounded warrior, who lay doubled over the pony in front of Autumn Thunder. The wind caught the blood and spattered Autumn Thunder's chest. The pony labored on, down into a ravine, and there Autumn Thunder left the wounded warrior with a friend and dismounted to give his pony a quick breather.

The teamsters continued to fire at the circling Kiowas. Another Kiowa-Apache slid from his horse. Two of his cohorts grabbed his legs and pulled him bouncing over the rough ground until they found cover in a dry creek bed. The rest of the warriors drew further back, but they continued to circle, still shouting their war cries, few of them bothering to return the teamsters' fire.

The distant storm clouds that Big Tree had first noticed before the attack were now nearly overhead, breaking the sunshine into narrow beams. The teamsters had recovered from their panic and surprise. The Kiowas knew that they would have to break the will of the whites. Big Tree gathered a half dozen of them, including Hau-Tau, Autumn Thunder, and Ko-yah-te. They sought out one wagon that was a bit more isolated than the others, and from three hundred yards they charged it, suddenly, in a swift, downhill run.

For a few moments the teamsters held their fire, as if they

could not believe what they were seeing. Then those at the isolated wagon, and others whose wagons faced in that direction, began to fire as fast as they could, perhaps too fast to be accurate. Ko-yah-te's pony stopped suddenly, reared up, and toppled over. Ko-yah-te leaped free, but he did not flee. Instead, he lay prone, reloaded his rifle, and searched for a target in the wagon.

Led by Big Tree, the others rode in until they were fifty yards away, then they divided in two and rode around the ends of the wagon. Autumn Thunder could see one of the teamsters, his body draped face-down over the front of the wagon, his arms hanging limply toward the ground.

Big Tree's target was not that wagon, but the wagons on the other side of the circle, whose teamsters were so preoccupied with the Kiowas circling in front of them that they had no idea that a hell-riding clutch of Kiowa warriors was about to ride right over them. There were no war cries from Big Tree and his men, only the clatter of Kiowa hoofbeats lost in the rattling gunfire. The six warriors leaped from their ponies onto two of the wagons, seized the surprised teamsters and quickly, competently disposed of them with the flashing blades of their knives or trade hatchets. They then took cover in the wagons and began firing at the wagons closest to them. The teamsters fired back and although neither side was scoring many hits, the issue was close and hot for awhile.

Gradually the pressure of gunfire from within their midst destroyed the will of the teamsters to resist. Several of them noticed a gap in the circle of Kiowas and broke out of the wagon circle. Hau-tau, Autumn Thunder, and Big Tree spotted the fleeing teamsters, caught up their ponies, and rode hard in pursuit, firing as they rode. One teamster fell, then another. The rest ran for their lives, and would surely have lost them then and there had not Hau-tau reined up suddenly.

"Why are we chasing them here?" he asked. "The booty is there!" He pointed back toward the wagons. "And we will have none if we chase those men."

"But should we not count coup on them?" Autumn Thunder asked. "The honors are here."

"Those honors are yours, my brother," Hau-tau growled, and off he rode, back to the wagons.

In the meantime the Kiowas had closed with the wagons.

The firing from the wagons had nearly ceased. Between those killed in the exchanges, those killed by Big Tree's attack, and those who had fled, all resistance appeared to have ceased. Or perhaps the Kiowas had caused them to use up their ammunition firing at the circling riders. Autumn Thunder had followed Hau-tau back to the wagons. His hungry young friend broke through the circling warriors and slowed his pony down to a wary walk.

Yellow Wolf cried out to him. "You are too close. It's dangerous there."

Hau-tau moved in closer. There was no movement around the wagons. The silence made him nervous. White Horse rode up to him and grabbed at his reins. "Come, my brother," he said calmly. "They may be waiting for you."

Something made Hau-tau laugh then. "Waiting for me? Their spirits may be waiting for me, if white men have spirits. You may roost out there like buzzards, but it is I who will make the carrion for you and"—he pointed toward the closest wagon—"I will have what is in that wagon."

Having convinced himself that only phantoms remained with the wagon train, he urged his pony into a trot toward the nearest wagon. As the clouds gathered blackly overhead, the young brave lifted the canvas flap of the wagon to see what it contained.

What he saw was the muzzle of a Spencer rifle, the last thing he saw on this earth. A flash from the muzzle and a bullet tore apart his face. He fell backward, without a sound, his blood darkening the earth where his head lay. Through the short silence came the grumble of distant thunder.

White Horse let out a chilling screech, which echoed in the throats of a hundred warriors. No more circling now; they rushed for the wagons, dismounted, and immediately made corpses of four of the five men left alive among the wagons. They fired arrows and bullets into the corpses and took hold of the one surviving teamster who, wounded and frightened, had fired point blank into the face of Hau-tau. They had great adventures in store for this one.

Po-lan-te was a close friend of Hau-tau. He was less than twenty yards away when he saw the brains and blood explode from the head of the young adventurer. He led the charge into the center of the wagon train, waving his tomahawk, then he went from corpse to corpse, smashing their skulls to pulp.

"Come here!" Yellow Wolf called to Autumn Thunder. "Find some rope for that white man."

White Bear had his knee on the back of the neck of the surviving teamster. Autumn Thunder glanced quickly at the face of the man, windburned, heavily bearded, great lines of fear etched around his mouth and widened gray eyes. His breath was coming in horrified gasps. Autumn Thunder could find no rope but Ko-yah-te discovered twenty feet of chain coiled up in the back of one of the wagons. Yellow Wolf had cut the mules free from the wagon. He and White Bear tilted up the wagon tongue and backed the teamster up against it. The man was so frightened that he let them do so without resistance, as if he were an obedient child. They stripped his clothes from his body, and still he did not resist.

"Iron rope. Good," said Yellow Wolf. "Tie him to the pole, tight."

Autumn Thunder wrapped the chain around the man and the pole, as tight as he could, and found a way to secure the chain so it would not slip. While he was so occupied, White Bear built a fire a few feet away. Now Red Arrow, Yellow Wolf, and three others grabbed hold of the wagon tongue and lowered the teamster slowly, face-down, toward the fire. As he felt himself coming closer to the fire his mouth opened wide in horror, then when he was so close the scorching pain became unbearable, he screamed a long, shrill scream, and his body jiggled like a palsied puppet.

The Kiowas close to him laughed, and some of them jiggled in grotesque imitation. They lifted the wagon tongue until the screams had subsided to moans, then they lowered it again. Again came the screams and the jiggles, so desperate this time that the chains rattled furiously, and the screams grew more and more hoarse, until they were pained, terrified, whispered cries.

Again they lifted the wagon tongue up from the fire. Autumn Thunder wished to see no more. While most of the men were plundering the wagons, the young man decided that he wanted mules. They had all been cut from their traces and were wandering around the valley individually or in pairs. He mounted his pony to pursue them. Just before he rode away he took a last look at the teamster who was being barbecued.

His face was seared red, his whiskers had burned away. His body was twisted to avoid the fire. His tormentors were again doing their jiggling dance in sadistic mockery. He was screaming again. He had gotten his voice back. Someone must have given him a drink of water.

Chapter 3

$\mathbf{G}$athers The Grass heard the tiny splash just five yards down the creek from where she was washing her father's leggings. Quickly she dropped the leggings on the big rock, took five running steps along the bank and three into the water, reached down, grabbed a slippery leg, lost it, grabbed it again, this time at the ankle, and pulled out a tiny boy who could not yet have seen two summers.

He was a husky little boy but not too big for her to throw over her shoulder, walk up to the rock, grab the leggings, and carry him back to his parents' dome-shaped grass house a hundred yards farther up Buck Creek.

The house was empty. The family was out looking for Wild Henry, as they called the young child after a drunken sergeant they had once known at Fort Cobb. Scarcely a day went by without the boy roaming. Sometimes he simply toddled over to a neighbor's hut, ate their food, and fell asleep in a dark corner. Other times he'd take a jaunt wherever the maker of the heavens led him, and when that happened, mother, grandmother, father, aunts, uncles, and cousins would scour the local countryside for the sight of a naked little boy on a serious journey.

It never occurred to the mother or the father to tether the child. Indians, even Wichitas, did not like to put limits on their children as long as they did not annoy others. Far from annoying others, when Wild Henry set off on a jaunt, his stealth was so natural that others generally did not take note of his presence or his absence.

She set the child down and looked around to see if any of

his family was in sight. Gathers The Grass had many chores set for the day and she could not spare much time to wait for a responsible adult to return. She supposed that she would have to keep the child with her while she did her chores. There had been a heavy thunderstorm the night before and Buck Creek was surging. Wild Henry's next watery adventure might be his last.

Her father needed a new pair of moccasins and she had the perfect hide for it, leather from a young buffalo cow. She took Wild Henry in tow back to her mother's house, picking up a large rock and a sturdy stick on the way. She drove the stick into the earth and with a long piece of rawhide tethered Wild Henry by his ankle. Sooner or later a member of his family would come around and take charge of him. Meanwhile, the child had taken a keen interest in one of her mother's dogs.

She was grateful for the sharp knife her father had received in trade at Fort Cobb. It made the pattern work easy. It was the decorating that would be difficult and tedious, but she didn't mind because she adored her father and she wanted the young Wichita men to notice how clever she was with quills and beads.

A breeze stirred up the dust on the main street of the village. She blew the dust off the leather and continued with her cutting. At fifteen she was ready for a man, but there were few suitable candidates in the village—in fact, no suitable suitors for her if she were to be honest with herself. But soon they would be coming around. She was too honest with herself to deny that she would be attractive to other men, especially in a small, peaceful village where there were not many girls for young men to choose from.

Because Wichitas lived outside during the warm months, not just her mother's grass hut but the village itself was her home. As she began the first cutting of the moccasin pattern, she could hear the sounds of the village around her: the soft buzz of a nearby conversation, the barking of a dog, the shouting of boys playing a game in a nearby field. Among all the familiar sounds, she was content, not restless. A young man would come in time—more than one. She would have a choice.

She was deep in her work, too deep to notice that Wild Henry had lost interest in the dog and was now playing with the rawhide thong and the stake that held him in check. The stake would not come up, but he was able to work the thong free and crawl off behind the house of Gathers The Grass's father.

Almost immediately she felt the child's absence. She took a quick look inside, then dashed behind the house in time to see his little figure disappearing into the tall grass.

Agile as a deer, she sprinted after him, gaining on him with every step, but he had a long head start on her. It wasn't hard to follow his path through the long grass, which ended at the edge of a garden of early melon plants. Beyond the field was the Fort Cobb road.

"Why is it always me?" she asked herself as she raced through the watermelon field avoiding the new plants, but she knew it had to be her because she cared, and everybody knew she cared. She never stepped in where she wasn't wanted, but she always knew where she was needed and even at this early age, she was always there. Her very name came from her ability to harvest rapidly the bunches of long prairie grass that her people used to make their distinctive, beehive-shaped homes that were so cool and comfortable in the summertime. Gathers The Grass did not know it, but the adults considered her a village treasure.

There was a horseman riding full gallop along the dusty road. Gathers The Grass redoubled her effort to catch up with Wild Henry before he could make it to the road. Although horses sometimes had enough sense to shy away from approaching children, she could not take the chance, but she was still five steps behind the boy, and he seemed determined to cross the road in front of the pony.

Trailing behind him was the long rawhide thong she had used to tether him. She dove for it, missed it with her right hand, grabbed it with her left, and pulled the child's right foot out from under him. The boy gave a grunt as he went down, then an incoherent shout. The pony reared up and nearly threw its rider, who hung on expertly with his thighs and knees.

Kiowa! They had been raiding south of Red River, everybody in the village knew that, and now one has to come here, probably with half the horse soldiers from one of the forts trailing him and thinking that the Wichitas were sheltering murderers.

The rider was talking softly to his pony, who was still jumpy. Slowly, with his voice and with the touch of his hands, he soothed the animal until it stopped jumping around and stood in the road shaking its head and swishing its tail. For just a moment she had to admire the young man's way with his mount, but then, she thought, this savage probably sleeps with his pony. She could still see traces of war paint on his face!

Clutching Wild Henry's hand in a viselike grip, she stood beside the road and stared up at the rider. "Why are you here?" she asked.

He did not understand her Wichita tongue. She knew no Kiowa, but she did know Comanche. Many of the tribes near Red River knew some of the Comanche dialect. "Why are you here?" she repeated, this time in that tongue.

He smiled when he heard familiar words, even though she said them funny. Kiowas spent much time with Comanches, and often became fluent in the Comanche dialect.

"I am hungry," he replied.

"And you have come to take?" she asked. "That is what Kiowas do, they take, is it not true?"

"We take from our enemies," the Kiowa said. "The Wichitas are not our enemies, even though they scratch at the ground like women, and hold tight to the hand of white men."

"Someone must grow the food that you—take!" she spat. It was the Kiowas and the Comanches that kept this part of the country in a constant uproar and made the white men suspicious of the Indians. Worse, it was the Kiowas and the Comanches who kept the young men of the Wichita village yearning for the free life. Every once in a while one of the young men and his pony would disappear, then the village would know that they had lost one of theirs to the others, at least for a while.

"In our village when a stranger comes we dip into our kettle and feed him," remarked the Kiowa with an edge to his voice.

"We know what hospitality is," she answered. "But if you have led the soldiers to our village I want you to know that we will not hide you."

He laughed. "There are no soldiers following me. The men of the Kiowas have scattered to the winds leaving many trails so thin that they have faded into the wind."

His words were hard, but his voice was not. Unlike some of the Kiowas, he did not carry his rifle in his hands at all times as if it were stuck to him. He was proud but did not seem arrogant. He was Kiowa, which meant he was nothing but trouble for the Wichitas, but she would see to it that he was fed.

"Come then," she said.

"Who is this?" he asked. "Your little brother?"

"No," she said, as she pointed her feet toward the village and he followed close behind, still sitting in his saddle.

"Your child?"

"I am not married."

That was the extent of their conversation as they walked toward the village. The closer they got to the grouping of grass houses in the village, the more people stopped what they were doing to get a look at the young Kiowa on his well-muscled gray war pony. They remembered not so very long ago when some of their men had war ponies, but they had been stolen one night.

Probably by Kiowas.

As she walked she could not help but notice his lean muscular body. She studied his face, looking for a trace of softness, but what she saw was hard eyes and fierce pride, the face of a warrior. She hated and feared what she saw, but the strangeness of it attracted her as much as it repelled her.

Not that she wanted to be dominated by such a man; she would never allow any man to be her lord in more than a ceremonial way. But Gathers The Grass feared the white men, and she saw in her own people no will to resist them.

The Kiowas were different. This man was different.

On the way to her mother's house she spotted Otter Chaser, the mother of Wild Henry. Gathers The Grass said nothing, she just smiled and handed the rawhide thong to Henry's mother and let her lead him away. Then she led the Kiowa warrior toward the fire in front of the entrance to her mother's house. Her mother was there, stirring an iron pot. She looked up and saw several women staring at the entrance to the circle of houses. She followed their gaze to her daughter, then to the fierce stranger who was tying his pony to a tree just outside the circle.

Gathers The Grass walked toward her mother without looking back at Autumn Thunder. "My mother," she said, "this Kiowa wishes to eat."

"Does this Kiowa have a name?" her mother asked.

"He has not said," Gathers The Grass replied.

"I am called Autumn Thunder, and I am hungry."

"I can see that," said the mother of Gathers The Grass. She studied his face and saw the not-quite-obliterated war paint. "From the look of you, you have been too busy killing white men to eat."

"It is not wrong to kill Texans," Autumn Thunder said proudly. "Kiowas have always killed Texans."

"I see," said the older woman, dishing out a steaming bowl of jackrabbit stew and handing it to the young warrior. "And have you led the Texans across Red River to the village of the Wichitas?"

"If I have, then the Wichitas should fight the Texans and drive them off. Do not worry about the Texans. I left no trail for them to follow. Besides, the white peace chiefs do not let the Texans cross over Red River. So you see, the white peace chiefs must not care what we do in Texas."

He had already finished his stew, and was looking at the empty bowl with longing.

"If I were a chief," Gathers The Grass's mother said, "I would serve you twice more than I have, but food has been scarce lately and I must be careful in the summer lest we starve in the winter."

"Then I must go," Autumn Thunder said, arising suddenly and walking toward his pony without looking back. In one fluid motion he mounted the animal and rode it slowly toward the road.

Her mother eyed Gathers The Grass with a look of wry amusement. "That is a Kiowa," she said. "Like a wild animal, with no manners at all. These young warriors of theirs, they are vicious people, and they will bring the whites down on all of us, you will see!"

Gathers The Grass did not disagree with her mother. She was too stunned by Autumn Thunder's sudden departure. She was clever at reading people's feelings. From the corner of her eye she had caught him studying her. And then no sooner did he empty his bowl and belch, when he was clip-clopping away on his war pony. Perhaps he was crazy. The old women in the village said that many Kiowa men were crazy.

She shrugged her shoulders. At least she was rid of Wild Henry, which meant that she could devote her entire attention to her chores.

She sat cross-legged in front of her mother's house working on her father's moccasins. As she shaped the leather she pictured in her mind the patterns she might create from porcupine quills. Then the quills vanished from her mind as she thought about the young Kiowa.

The sun dipped down until it stood atop the distant hills, and then it began to dip below them. She worked on the moccasins until the light grew too dim, then she began to gather up her work to bring inside the house. Without sunlight to cast a shadow over her shoulder, she was caught by surprise when a young man's voice spoke from behind her.

"I have some food," the voice said, simply.

He threw down a deer quarter, and a sack of flour. The deer quarter raised dust and the sack expelled a great puff of white powder as both hit the ground in front of Gathers The Grass.

She sat staring up at him with her father's moccasins in her hands. In the twilight she could barely see his face, but she could see the smooth outline of his upper body against the darkening sky.

"Thank you for the deer meat," she said, quietly, rising to her feet. In the light of the dying campfire, the white flour sack seemed to glow. "Did you steal the flour from the Texans you killed?"

"I stole the flour from Texans who would kill every Kiowa they could find, and if a dead Kiowa turned out to be a Wichita, that would be fine to them too."

His words entered her and for a few moments they stood silently staring at each other in a quiet village.

"Thank you for the flour, then," she said. He turned on his heel, and walked slowly to his pony. Slowly he untied the reins from the tree, then slid onto its back. He turned the pony around and looked back at Gathers The Grass. He noted that she held the heavy flour sack effortlessly in her arms. From where he was he could not see her face, but he had already memorized all of its features.

Chapter 4

Lieutenant James Leroy Sweeney awoke irritable and angry in his room in back of the post trader's shop.

Barely conscious, sitting at the edge of his bed, his big bare feet flat on the splintery floor, he reached beneath the unbuttoned top of his long johns and scratched his hairy chest. A man shouldn't have been wearing long johns on hot nights, but if he didn't, he knew he'd awaken with bedbug bites up and down his legs.

He rubbed his ankles together. The bugs had done double duty where the long johns had left off.

Oh jeez! Out of habit he started cursing as soon as he opened his eyes and let the bright shafts of sunlight that streamed through the windows hit his sedated pupils. He shouldn't have been a drinking man. None of his family were big boozers. But he had a right to be a boozer. Every brevet major had the right to be a boozer after six years as a first lieutenant with no imminent hope of promotion.

When you're an old lieutenant, every day brings new humiliation. Yesterday had been a long, unending succession of humiliations. Early in the morning, while he was at mess, the adjutant had come to see him. A new officer had arrived on the post late the night before, a captain.

Lieutenant Sweeney knew what that meant. Officers were assigned quarters on the basis of rank and seniority. Sweeney had plenty of seniority but little rank. For the third time this year he would be bumped from his comfortable stone house and would have to find accommodations where he could until the next officer vacated his house. Then all the other officers in the houses would move up to a better house and he would take the least of the stone houses on officers' row.

Some of the men were on police detail when they saw him and several privates leading mules bearing his belongings across the post to the room behind the trader's store. Broken down mules they were too. White Horse had stolen all the good mules from the post the year before and the stock still had not been completely replenished.

The men who were walking around picking up trash and replacing displaced boundary stones paused to watch the rag-tag procession. They had seen it before. The old lieutenant was still junior to enough old lieutenants and captains to get bumped out of his house yet again.

They were too far away for him to hear their comments, but he could see their shoulders shaking. They were probably being pretty funny. He liked the humor of his black troops. In fact, he liked his black troops. It was the Indians he despised.

Which was why Captain Rhem had chewed him out in front of his cohorts just before officers' mess that night. He had caught a Caddo named Tobacco Sam sneaking out the back door of the room he had taken behind the trader's store. In the Caddo's hand was a bottle of Peruna's Tonic. Hidden in his blanket were two more bottles.

When whiskey was hard to find on post everybody bought Peruna's Tonic because it was loaded with alcohol and Evans the trader ordered it by the case as a medicinal item. It was medicinal, all right, a cure for the doldrums for half the sol-diers on the post. The Indians, who were by nature observant, soon found their way into Evans's medicinal stocks them-selves, but then Evans took extra precautions to secure the tonic, and the Indians had to create other ways to get it.

"Sam, what the hell are you doin' here with my Peruna's, ya red hellion?" he asked. The Caddo hadn't even bothered to close the door to Sam's room.

He looked up at Sweeney, who at six feet even towered over him by five inches. "Not your whiskey. Mine," said the Caddo. The bottle was almost empty and Sam was drunk enough that Sweeney knew he had probably spent the last ten minutes sitting at the edge of Sweeney's bed, his feet dangling, pouring the tonic down as quickly as he could.

"Damn it, that bottle was for *me* to get drunk on tonight, not you!"

Tobacco Sam looked at Sweeney through unfocused eyes but said nothing. Sweeney was sure that the Caddo was about to pass out, but instead he threw up on the lieutenant's boots. As he did so the two hidden bottles slipped out of his blanket and fell to the ground. There was no grass, it had all been cropped or trampled by horses. The bottles clanged on the hardpan, and on each other, and broke. Sweeney stood in silence and watched the tonic he had counted on to get him through the night soak into the thirsty earth.

"Sorry," the Caddo belched, and started to walk off, but Sweeney grabbed him by the scruff of the neck.

"Sam," he said, "I'm gonna kick your ass for stealin' my tonic."

The Caddo was not impressed. He was so drunk he probably didn't understand a word Sweeney was saying, so he said nothing, just continued to stare in Sweeney's general direction. The lieutenant's temper rose another notch. He squeezed Tobacco Sam's neck and began to lift him. Drunk as he was, Sam did not enjoy dangling by the neck so his feet bent down till he was standing on the tips of his toes.

By now two other lieutenants who lived nearby had gathered round, grinning. Life on Fort Sill after hours was so boring that it didn't take much to amuse them.

"Sam sure is gettin' tall," said one.

"Specially at the neck," said the other. Sweeney was so angry he paid no more attention to the other lieutenants than Tobacco Sam did.

"Sweeney!"

The voice belonged to Captain Rhem, battalion executive officer. Sweeney hated Rhem because he had more service time than Rhem yet Rhem outranked him and still had his stone house on the post quad.

"Captain?" Sweeney's voice was controlled, barely.

"Put him down."

Sweeney let loose his grip. Tobacco Sam belched again and walked away, a little more sober than before he'd been dangled.

"I have told you, Lieutenant, that I don't want you abusing the Indians."

"That Indian stole my tonic."

"Knowing you, you probably have three or four more bottles hidden around your quarters."

"He stole them too, damn it."

"I don't care if he stole your horse, I especially don't want that one abused. Do you understand me?"

The other two lieutenants were enjoying the confrontation. They hoped that Sweeney was angry enough to take a punch at Rhem.

"Why that particular Indian . . . Captain?" Sweeney asked. His voice was insolent, insinuative.

Rhem sighed in disgust. "Because, Lieu-tenant, if you must know, we think Caddo George is the reason some of the Kiowas have repeating rifles. I never thought I'd see the day that we were bein' outgunned by Indians. But we are, or haven't you heard? This sorry specimen that drank up all your booze has promised to help us nail Caddo George, if we pay him enough."

"If you're payin' him, why can't he buy his own whiskey?"

"How in hell should I know? Because he'd prefer to steal it, I guess."

"Well, you care to reimburse me for the three bottles of tonic he stole from me?"

"Hell, Sweeney, the army ain't gonna reimburse you for the alcohol you didn't get a chance to run through ya."

The two lieutenants snickered and walked away. Sweeney headed for his room, angry. The room was hot and stuffy, which did nothing for his disposition. "If I ever get that damned Caddo alone," he muttered, "I'll take him apart feather by feather."

It wasn't that he had grown up hating Indians. In Ohio, where he'd been raised, it had been so long since the Indians had had their land stolen that all that was left of them was the names of places—like Kinnickinnick, and the Ohio River.

It was just that Indians made life inconvenient for Sweeney. If they weren't stealing his Peruna's Tonic, they were stealing vegetables from the post trader before Sweeney's sergeants had a chance to steal Evans's vegetables. Or they were going raiding in Texas. Every time the Kiowas went raiding in Texas the Texans came running up to Fort Sill claiming that the fort was giving refuge to murdering, thieving Indians.

Well of course Fort Sill was giving refuge to murdering, thieving Indians, but Sweeney had no desire to hear it from a bunch of ill-tempered ornery Texans. Sweeney didn't like Texans any more than he liked Indians, but the way he figured it, it was the fault of the Texans that Fort Sill was a redskin refuge.

"Look," he had said to one of the biggest, meanest Texans he had ever met, a ranger who had no business on this side of Red River. "If Texas hadn't a-seceded from the Union, then General Grant would not be president today. If General Grant was not the president today, then nobody would've put the Quakers in charge of the Indian Bureau. If the Quakers were not in charge of the Indian Bureau, we'd be out there killin' Indians like the good Lord meant us to do instead of pattin' them on the head and beggin' them to behave."

The Texan had just shifted the tobacco in his mouth and spat a brown stream at a rattlesnake that had wriggled up close to make his acquaintance, having recognized one of its own kind. He'd hit the rattlesnake too, and the snake had run off as if he'd remembered that he had an important engagement elsewhere.

And now, speaking of inconveniences, Colonel Grierson had told his adjutant to send out a company—not to engage hostiles, just to pick up their trail and try to figure out whether they'd come back to the reservation. Sweeney's company had been selected because everybody figured it was a wild goose chase and they wanted the best troops to remain on the post, in case White Horse decided to come in and steal any more mules, or worse.

Rhem had almost smiled when he had told Sweeney that the job would be his.

"How in hell am I supposed to find Indians three rainy days after a raid?" he had asked.

"Don't bother lookin' for a trail," Rhem had responded. "Start by going to some of the Wichita villages and ask around. Or the Caddo villages."

Sweeney had a washbasin full of lukewarm water sitting on top of his chest of drawers. He plunged his hands into them, and splashed his face to get the dust off. He splashed behind his ears, then he took off his yellow bandanna and splashed all around his neck. The water dripping down his back felt exactly like the sweat that had been dripping all day long.

He looked around his room, at the chest of drawers, and the coathooks on the walls, and the bed with the strawtick mattress that sagged in a "U" shape over the grid of ropes. The best thing you could say about it was that the rats wouldn't run over your belly while you tried to sleep on it because it smelled too bad.

He had counted on the tonic to get him through the grim first night in the field. After only one night in the room behind Evans's store he'd be thrilled to be sleeping in a tent across the river.

He reached into the pocket of his britches and found a few greenbacks and about two dollars' worth of change. He could go to Evans and pick up a couple of bottles of tonic, but it was weeks till the next payday.

The first smile of the day creased his sunburned face. A couple of poker games generally went on every night in the trader's store. He was a good poker player, but in the past he had avoided the games because he preferred getting drunk alone.

He grabbed a ragged towel and dried his face and neck. He smacked his hand against his shirt and drew a cloud of dust. That wouldn't do, he decided, removing the shirt and throwing it in the corner. A fresh shirt might bring him fresh confidence, and he needed all the confidence he could get. He buttoned his shirt, tucked it in, ran a brush through his thick dark hair a couple of times, and walked out into the still hot, dry air. First a little food at the officer's mess, then over to Evans's.

There were two games going on in the store when he walked in. One was the officers' game: Rhem, Major Rice, the post surgeon, and three lieutenants. Veterans of the last war, veterans of many an isolated post, poker geniuses all. Vain as he was about his poker skills, Sweeney normally would have loved to trim Rhem and company. But not with five dollars in his poke.

The second table looked much more promising, a small stakes game with three heavy-drinking civilians and Corporal Peretti, the post sucker. He sat and watched the four men play for awhile. The more he watched them play, the more promising his opportunities appeared. After half an hour he was certain that by the end of the night he would have enough cash to last him through the month and fill his saddlebags with tonic bottles for the entire Texas patrol.

The civilians were Seamus O'Brien, a freight contractor, Jeremy Barlow, who did a little of everything, and a stranger who looked like a buffalo hunter to Sweeney. He introduced himself as Tuck, and he showed a mouthful of rotting teeth when he smiled.

They were the worst poker players he had ever seen at one table, and when Marv Mapes, procurer of horses and mules for Fort Sill, and possessor of a brain to match, sat down to play, Sweeney was convinced that his ship had come in.

And yet, cautious as he was, he waited a while longer before jumping in. Barlow was a bit better than the others. He could be trouble.

So when Barlow got up, stretched, and walked away from the table with fifty dollars, Sweeney took it as a sign that he should come in.

He should have stayed out. O'Brien, who was dumb as a box of rocks, immediately got a streak of cards so good that even he couldn't lose with them. No sooner did O'Brien get cold than the cards started coming to Mapes, and then it was Barlow and the buffalo hunter, battling for pots left and right and shutting out everybody else.

The net result was that a wave of money passed around the table, from player to player, except that it somehow passed Sweeney by. Playing carefully, with all the skill his years could muster, he slowed the dwindling of his small stack of money to a trickle, sometimes dropping out early, sometimes taking in a small pot, playing with an ever smaller stake, until he had only a dollar and a half left. His ears were red as his long johns with embarrassment. How could he lose to his bunch of misfits? he thought, and when finally the buffalo hunter accused him of palming a card on a seventy-five cent bet, Sweeney stood up and started to call the shaggy giant out.

"Let me get this straight," he roared across the table. "You're sayin' I'd risk my good name on this post for a lousy seventy-five cents?"

"Lookin' at your stack there," said the hunter, who was sweating clear through his buckskin and was drinking some kind of straight whiskey, "looks to me like seventy-five cents ain't no small matter fer a man of your means."

The fire-eyed look on Sweeney's face did not intimidate the hunter at all, and suddenly the situation seemed so ridiculous to Sweeney that he started laughing.

"Think I'm a funnyman, Lieutenant?" the shaggy hunter asked. "I'll show you how funny I am outside that door."

Sweeney shook his head while he kept on laughing. "Not you, you old wolf-bait. Me. And if you think I'm gonna bust my knuckles on your head and probably lose an eye or an ear in the bargain over seventy-five cents, then you are crazier than I am."

"Crazy am I?" said Tuck, reaching for Sweeney with a huge right paw. Sweeney simply grabbed the hunter's arm and with a quick jerk pulled him onto the table, scattering cards and money everywhere. Strong as a bull buffalo, he grabbed Tuck's arm and started twisting it.

"Listen here," he hissed at the hunter. "I started out with very little money tonight and lost most of it to four of the sorriest poker players I have ever seen. I am going out tomorrow to look for wild Kiowas and it strikes me that fightin' you over seventy-five cents is a damned stupid way to spend the night before a campaign. Now I have vowed to get drunk on this night and thanks to you men I don't have enough money to do the job proper.

"So I will go to Mr. John Evans there and purchase two bottles of Peruna's Tonic with what little money I have left in this world, and I will go home and try to get as drunk as I can on those two miserable little bottles. Do you have a problem with that?" he asked the hunter even as he gave the arm an aggressive little twist.

The hard look on the face of the buffalo hunter softened. "Let go of my arm, Lieutenant," he said, in a soft, raspy voice. Sweeney turned his arm loose.

"Seamus, you ugly Mick, gimme half a buck."

"Half a buck! The hell you"—

"You too, Peretti. This man's goin' huntin' for redskins tomorrow and I know you ain't goin' with him since they never let you off the post, ain't that right?"

Peretti and O'Brien each put fifty cents on the table, to which the buffalo hunter added fifty cents of his own.

''There,'' he said. ''That'll be good for two more bottles for you. I'd advise you to save one for the trail so you won't feel it as bad when they start to peel the scalp off your head.''

''You're a right fair man—what's your name again?'' said Sweeney.

''Name's Tuck. I can clean out fifty head of buffalo in an afternoon and I keep three skinners workin' the whole season. When I ain't huntin' buffalo I'll sometimes hunt a Kiowa or two, just to keep in practice,'' he said.

Sweeney took the last remark as a bit of braggadocio. His first impression was that Tuck was a likable gent, though maybe a bit on the crude side. He missed the spiteful gleam in the keen, squinty eyes of the buffalo hunter.

The two men shook hands, hard. Sweeney, not a bit proud, took the change, walked over to Evans and bought himself four bottles of Peruna's Tonic. He intended to take Tuck's advice and hold three bottles back for his saddlebags, but once he got to his room, pulled off his boots and shirt, and lay back on his bed, he knew he'd need every drop of alcohol he could get in his veins to sleep on this night.

Chapter 5

The last two bottles of his Peruna's Tonic were gone the first night out from the post. Like a miserable miser he walked away from camp in the dark, found a dry creek bed, wrapped a blanket around him and drained the bottles dry, quickly, hoping for a buzz.

The next two days he went through the hell of life without booze. By the third day out he had sweated all the poison out of his system and he was still grouchy as a bear. The trouble was, the trail of the Kiowa warriors wasn't just cold, it was washed out of existence. Nobody Sweeney and his troops visited had seen a Kiowa. Nobody had ever seen a Kiowa in his entire life. They stopped at a farm. Nope, never seen no Kiowas not like to two year, now. That was probably true.

They stopped at a Tonkawa Village. Nope, no seen no Kiowa three, maybe four moon now, maybe longer. That was probably not true. Kiowas and Tonkawas had no love lost for each other. The Kiowas persisted in believing that the Tonkawas were cannibals and the Tonkawas were furious that the Kiowas should say such terrible things about them. Still, in this Tonkawa village, the people were silent.

The plan was to ride due south, cross the Red River, and begin a wide swing that would take them first west then north, stopping to question whomever they ran across and for God's sake keeping their eyes peeled for Kiowas war parties. It was a small patrol, Sweeney and fewer than a dozen black soldiers, all Grierson felt he could spare at this time, because the Wichitas were bringing in rumors that the Kiowas and Comanches were planning an attack on the fort itself.

Grierson doubted the truth of that bit of intelligence but he was bound to be cautious. "If you see, say, half a dozen Kiowa warriors you can skin 'em alive if you want to because they got no business on that side of the river. On the other hand, you see forty, fifty of them, you ride on out of there or they'll be the ones doin' the skinnin'," Grierson had told Sweeney before the patrol had left Fort Sill.

The trouble was, there was nothing interesting to see: day after day, gently rolling plains, the grass long and lush and green from the thunderstorms that had been lashing the land all spring. Every so often a long meandering row of cottonwoods would appear and then Sweeney would groan because that meant another creek or river to ford. Once across the creek it was back into the sea of grass, one rise after another in the hot, hot sun.

After five days without alcohol Sweeney was a new man, but he was a tired new man, like the rest of his tiny command, maybe a little too tired to see a solitary figure on a horse far off to their right, definitely too tired to register the danger of a rock outcropping coming up on their right. Like a ghost troop they sat their horses quietly, their heads nodding with the rolling gait of their animals, their eyes half—or completely—closed, their senses shut down, victims of their own boredom and fatigue.

Maybe his horse was in its own kind of trance. Or maybe it just stepped on a rock that was hidden in the long grass. Whatever it was, its next step was a misstep that jarred Sweeney into wakefulness, but still he thought he might be dreaming.

Emerging from behind the outcropping on his right was a long curved line of Kiowas, their faces and ponies brilliantly painted, blankets tied around their waists, bodies leaned forward as their ponies swiftly closed the distance between themselves and Sweeney's patrol.

"Here they come, Lieutenant," said his sergeant evenly. Sweeney gave a rebel yell—how do you wake up a sleeping patrol?—and commanded them forward at the gallop to close quickly with the enemy.

But something was wrong. The Kiowas continued to stream out from behind the outcropping until there were nearly thirty of them. Too many to handle. Sweeney had the men dismount.

Eight of the men handed their horses over to horseholders and took aim on one knee.

"Aim for the horses, boys!" he shouted, then yelled, "Fire!"

They fired—and missed everything.

The Kiowas stopped only long enough to fan out in a line across the land. By the time they had started surging forward again, the troopers had reloaded.

"Fire!" shouted Sweeney. The soldiers fired and hit two ponies, none seriously, but making it hot enough to get the warriors thinking about their own mortality.

The Kiowas halted their advance and moved out of range. Sweeney gave the order to remount, and the troopers rode down the valley, followed by the Kiowas, who kept their distance for nearly two miles until they reached another place where the valley narrowed. Now there were more Kiowas riding out from behind a hill, cutting off Sweeney's line of retreat.

Sweeney had a quick decision to make, and he made it correctly. He was a much better officer than the single silver bars on his epaulets indicated. He pointed his saber north, up the road, charging the second, smaller party of Kiowas, surprising those who had thought that the little patrol might go to pieces in panic.

The men had faith in their lieutenant, and they rode hard, some firing their carbines at the Kiowas who came closest, other keeping their weapons aimed at those who came too close. The Kiowas poured a heavy fire at the little group of galloping cavalrymen, but they were keeping their distance; most of them still had old weapons, and they, like everybody else, found it difficult to draw a bead on a target while galloping over the uneven grassland.

The gunfire echoed off his hills like distant cracks of thunder. The men rode hard and they broke through the line. Sweeney's snap decision had proved to be adequate, if not brilliant. The first group of Kiowas merged with the second, joining in the long chase. But all the troopers had made it through.

Except for Sweeney.

One Kiowa had loitered a little too long over his prayers and war paint, and he almost missed the show. On his little gray pony, one of the swiftest in the herd of his village, he galloped out whooping and brandishing his feathered lance. His horse's hooves found dusty road and they charged directly toward the head of the patrol.

Sweeney fired his revolver six times at the lone, crazy, approaching warrior. Each shot missed so he holstered the pistol, adjusted his grip on his sword, and prepared to meet his foe hand-to-hand. Like knights of old, the two mounted men closed with each other, one with lance, one with cavalry sword. The distance closed to a hundred yards, then fifty, then twenty.

Sweeney saw the lance and extended the sword as far ahead of him as he could, then changed his mind and prepared to swerve his mount just before impact, and slash at the Indian's neck as he rode past.

He never had a chance. Even before the two horses crashed together, Sweeney felt the lance sink into his shoulder, hit bone, and dump him from his saddle into the prairie grass. The rest of the men thundered by, pursued by more than forty hollering, whooping, screaming Kiowas.

The Indians had seen something magnificent. In another day they would have stopped to take second and third coup and do honor to the courage of Autumn Thunder, but they had been told by their aging leader Set-ankeah that this was a war to kill whites, and for once they were determined to obey. They thundered down the valley, in pursuit of Sweeney's patrol. Both groups were riding weary, jaded horses, but on this day the cavalry mounts had a little more stamina left in their bodies, and gradually they pulled away from their shrieking, whooping pursuers.

That left Autumn Thunder alone, climbing down from his pony and walking over to where Sweeney lay with the broken stub of the lance protruding from his shoulder, dazed from the fall, barely conscious enough to know that his time had come.

The young warrior put his knee on Sweeney's chest, took hold of his thick dark hair and prepared to make the first incision for taking the scalp.

"Cut away, you damned heathen," said Sweeney, quietly, trying to focus on the blurry vision before him. "Your time'll come soon enough, and then I guess I'll see you in hell."

Sweeney's calm words made Autumn Thunder stop, even though he understood not one word of English. There was a better way, he thought. This man is mine! Instead of taking a scalp back to his village, why not bring back an entire prisoner. Imagine, an army officer as his very own slave!

Every day since they had picked up the trail of the patrol just ten miles south of Red River, he had thought about Gathers The Grass, and what it would take to gain her favor. Maybe if he returned to the Wichita village with a live, trussed up army officer he could gain her attention, even her admiration. Before the dust on the road had settled, he had pulled the point of the lance out of Sweeney's shoulder, poured water all over the wound, and shoved the lieutenant's yellow neckerchief into the wound to slow the loss of blood.

Sweeney was back on his father's Ohio farm. It was early morning and he could feel his bed being lifted and dropped. Bump! Bump! Bump!

"I'm up! I'm up!" he cried. Anything to stop the bumping and shaking. His dad would always be shouting, "Rise and shine!" as he let the foot end of the bed drop on the wood floor. Funny, he had never hurt like this before in the morning, even when he was suffering from a moonshine hangover. His body was aching all over. Must be getting old. Time to slow down.

"Slow down," he mumbled to himself although he knew nothing was happening very fast. Gradually his senses returned. He opened his eyes and found himself upside down staring at the belly of his horse. The horse was in a fast walk. Every time a hoof struck the ground his body twisted in pain. His wrists were tied so tightly behind his back that his hands felt numb. His legs were tied together, and his body was bound to the saddle of his horse.

He could see a pony on the other side of his horse, in a slow trot to keep up with his horse's fast walking steps. He could see a moccasin and a bare calf down the side of the pony. He turned his head each way as far as he could but he could neither see nor hear any other horses. Apparently he was captive of a single warrior.

He was terribly thirsty. The dust from the horse's footfalls was clogging his nose, his mouth, his eyes. And as if he didn't have enough problems, he was nauseous from his pain and the jouncing of his horse. For a few miles he tried to hold in the contents of his stomach but finally he belched, gagged, vomited.

The pony and his horse stopped. A figure crouched by his horse and a face came close to his. He gagged and heaved again.

The Kiowa laughed and said something Sweeney could not understand but he figured it probably had something to do with the mixture of blood and vomit that coated his face. What the irreverent Autumn Thunder said was, "Very pretty paint." Sweeney could feel himself losing consciousness, and as bad as he felt, he did not mind.

As Autumn Thunder led his unconscious captive north, he thought about Fort Sill, and the sacred Medicine Bluffs nearby, places so familiar to the Kiowas from the days before the white soldiers came and started telling the Kiowas what to do. The thought made him angry. He would take this officer to his village and there the women would work him over until his screams turned to feeble whimpers. He would see to it that the lieutenant was well enough rested to beg on his knees for his death and then, maybe then, he would drive his tomahawk through his skull.

He wanted to see the lieutenant's face as they rode and he could not see it as long as he was draped over the horse like a slain deer. He dismounted, untied the lieutenant, and watched as Sweeney slid to the ground with a groan and a thump. He cleaned the muck off his face with water and watched closely as Sweeney regained consciousness. He cut the thongs that bound Sweeney's legs and pointed to the saddle. Sweeney tried to mount but with his hands still bound he did not have the strength to lift himself up into the saddle.

Autumn Thunder helped him up.

"Water!" Sweeney croaked once he was in the saddle.

Autumn Thunder did not understand. Sweeney opened his mouth and showed his tongue, then made sucking sounds with his lips, then Autumn Thunder did understand. With the white man facing him, bloody, weak and defeated, it did not enter the Kiowa's mind to refuse the soldier's request. He grasped Sweeney's canteen, supported him as he leaned over in his saddle, and let Sweeney take five swallows.

"Enough," he said in Kiowa speech that Sweeney did not

know, but he understood. He straightened up and said, ''I'm ready.''

''Good,'' the Kiowa responded, creating a dialogue between the two, accidentally, since neither understood the other.

They crossed the Red River late the following day, without Autumn Thunder having made up his mind what he would do with his prisoner. He had fed and watered Sweeney, sparingly, and had also spared him any further pain. In this he surprised himself. Although he was still very young, like many other Kiowas he suspected that the white men meant to take the land for themselves if they could. It was Autumn Thunder's opinion that these white men could not, because they were so much more white than they were men. Take away their rifles, and the big guns that shoot twice, and what do you have? Big fools with bad medicine who do not know where the center of the earth lay.

Oh, every so often some Indian who called himself a chief would come and tell the Kiowas that he had seen the city of the Great Father, and that there were more houses than they could count, and more people than they could imagine. But Autumn Thunder and others, like Set-ankeah and Addo-eta and Gui-pah-go would call the Indian a liar and a blowhard, and he would slink away in shame.

The only way an Indian could come up with stories like that was if the white men told him to tell those stories and promise to give him things if he did. That's what white men did best, make promises. And then after they make their promise, like promising Black Kettle peace, they would wait until winter, when any real man would be snug in his lodge with his woman, and they would ride down on the village and kill. Kill everybody they could.

To go west once they had crossed the river meant that he intended to reach his home village, where he would be celebrated and praised. To go east would mean the Wichita village, where people would revile him for bringing a white captive there. Why would he wish to bring the wrath of the soldiers down on them? Did they not treat him well the last time he had come?

But he wanted to honor Gathers The Grass, and what greater honor than to bring her a white army officer?

They crossed the river.

He turned east.

Five miles west of the Wichita village was the farm of a Wichita family that lived like white men. It was there that he had left the four mules he had captured during the attack on the wagon train. He allowed the man to use the mules to break up the land while he was gone, but pointed out that when he came back the mules had better be there and well or he would burn down every building on the place.

At the end of a long valley he found the farm, and his mules, as he had left them.

"Towakani!" he shouted. "Look what I found in Texas!" The Wichita farmer had been standing in front of his house, which was not the traditional grass beehive that Wichitas preferred, but the abandoned cabin of a white man. The short, squat Wichita, who could speak and understand Kiowas, Comanches, Caddos, and white men, walked over to the young Kiowa and his white captive. He folded his arms and squinted up at the cavalry officer.

"So you let this boy catch you, hah?" he said. "Well, you watch him, he will feed your pieces to the camp dogs, you will see."

Sweeney was still feeling so bad didn't care all that much about his future. His head swiveled slowly toward Autumn Thunder. He studied him for a moment through slits of eyes. Then he turned back to Towakani.

"Tell you what," said Sweeney, feebly. "I'm lucky he didn't just spit me and slow-roast me over a fire."

Towakani shook his head. "He a Kiowa, not Tonkawa," he said.

"Well, for a boy, he's a hell of a man."

Autumn Thunder wanted to know what the Wichita and the lieutenant were talking about. Towakani told him, and he was pleased, but he was old enough to know that captives sometimes tried to flatter their captors to make things easier on themselves.

"You tell this old soldier chief that I *will* roast him if I want to," said Autumn Thunder. Towakani relayed the news and Sweeney nodded.

"I'm glad to know that," Sweeney answered. "I hate surprises."

*   *   *

When Autumn Thunder entered the Wichita village he seemed less like a visitor than a procession. It was the height of a hot summer afternoon. Gathers The Grass was sitting in the shade of a cottonwood tree, cutting strips of meat off a side of deer and placing them in a clay bowl. Next to her was another clay jar filled with dried wild berries.

The shadow of a pony appeared just outside of the cottonwood's circle of shade. She looked up, saw Autumn Thunder and smiled a quick smile that faded as soon as she noticed the stranger behind him in the dusty blue uniform, his hands tied behind him, his face twisted in pain, his body tilted forward in his saddle.

For a moment she said nothing as her eyes shifted from the stranger to Autumn Thunder and back again. Autumn Thunder's face bore the look of the conqueror's pride that she had seen before on the faces of Kiowas, Comanches, and even sometimes on the faces of Wichitas.

Sweeney gave a soft moan.

"Get him down!" said Gathers The Grass, suddenly. "Don't you see he is badly hurt?"

"Of course I see—I hurt him!" said Autumn Thunder, dismounting. "Do you see my mules?"

She took a quick look at the four mules behind him, beautiful, well-kept teamsters' mules. "You hurt him bad," she said.

"He is a warrior soldier. He will be fine, I think. I give him to you," Autumn Thunder smiled. He reached out quickly with his right hand and pulled Sweeney out of the saddle. The lieutenant toppled into the dust with a suppressed grown. He tried once to get up and fell over, struggled to one knee, and waited there while his head cleared and his dizziness subsided.

Slowly, reluctantly, he sank to both knees, then his body tilted forward, and finally, he lay full, length in the dust.

"Get me water, you oaf!" she said sharply. She looked up and saw that a number of her neighbors had come by to stare. On their faces were a mixture of curiosity and fear, but she didn't notice their expressions. With her knife she cut the thongs that bound his hands behind his back, and turned him over. His breathing was rapid and shallow. His eyes were open and unfocused. Over the years she had watched her mother care for sick and wounded men who came to the village after battles and internecine squabbles that seemed to pop up in other villages. They always came here, to this village of peace, and she had learned her mother's healing arts, which were a combination of Wichita lore and a little bit, though not much, of white man medicine.

She laid out a blanket and rolled him onto it, then sat him up and stripped his shirt off. The only open wound she could find was the large gash in his left shoulder.

"You did this?" she asked, glaring at Autumn Thunder.

"I sure did that," he replied. "You like my mules?"

"The soldiers will be coming here, sure enough," she said. "You're lucky the wound did not get infected." He handed her Sweeney's canteen. "Lost much blood, this one." She washed out the wound and washed his face with water from the canteen, till his eyes focused a little better, then she let him drink the last few drops.

"Go fill this in the river," she said, handing Autumn Thunder the canteen and pointing toward the creek. "You almost killed him."

"He sure would have killed me," Autumn Thunder said, pulling Sweeney's Colt from his sash and fingering it significantly.

She stared into his face, wondering what it was that made him so appealing to her. "I'm glad he didn't," she said. "Water. Hurry."

Chapter 6

General William Tecumseh Sherman's face was even redder than his hair. He had heard too many reports from furious Texans that Kiowas were raiding well below the Red River, then returning to the Fort Sill reservation with halos on their heads. The reservation was their sanctuary. They could not be pursued there no matter how hot their trail.

If the story about the wagon train fight was correct, then those devils had been there watching the road when he rolled by in his ambulance on the way to Fort Sill. Did that mean they knew there was a supply train on the way north? If they did then how did they know?

As he sat rocking on the porch of his temporary quarters at Fort Sill, he imagined them atop that bare hill overlooking the rutted Texas road, their beady little dark eyes following the ambulance as it bumped its way north, salivating over the prospect of spilling the blood of white men onto the Texas plains.

He had been dealing with these sons of Satan long enough to know who the probable leaders were: Satank, Satanta, Lone Wolf, Big Tree—one, some, or all. If they hadn't done this one then they were bound to have done something else, so it wasn't as if he might arrest an innocent man by mistake.

The worst part was having to deal with the damned Quakers. What had Grant been thinking when he had turned the Indian Bureau over to them? Grant had been such a sensible man when Sherman served under him during the Civil War. You could pretty much count on Grant in those days to make the right decisions. You could always count on him to fight. What could have happened to him to turn him into such a fool? Sherman could only guess, but buried deep inside him, so deep that no one else knew it existed, was a whimsical side that thought maybe the Temperance people had gotten a hold of Grant and made him stop drinking.

That was it! The fool had taken the pledge.

But no, General Hancock had been to Washington to visit the White House, and he'd seen old Hyram polish off half a bottle of Kentucky bourbon without any help.

So the Indians belonged to the Quakers and the Quakers were bound to love them right down to the last Texan. Sherman, who had peeled the hide off many a subordinate during his incomparable military career and feared only the Almighty, felt his stomach burn at the prospect of having to deal with the Quakers and their Indians.

"This Tatum is a very different sort, General," said Colonel Grierson as they rode their horses along the path that took them from the post to the office of Lawrie Tatum, Indian Agent. "I know how you feel about them, but some of them are a lot tougher than you might think."

They knocked on the door of the building and were greeted by the agent himself, who wore a somber suit in the heat of late spring and was bald as an egg. The agent asked the two officers to be seated and offered them some lemonade. They declined. Sherman was impatient and a bit brusque.

"Mr. Tatum," he said. "I know how you feel about your Indians. It's your belief and your job to take care of them. But they have the blood of civilians on their hands and they want to have more. It's my job to protect the civilians. Do you understand me?"

Tatum smiled. "General," he said. "I'm afraid *you* misunderstand *me*. Whatever my superiors might say or think, I do not believe that my Indians have the right to go marauding in Texas then come back to Fort Sill for refuge and annuities. Tell me what you need from me. I will do my best to help you."

Sherman's eyebrows lifted. He had worked himself into a seething anger and was looking forward to doing battle with a Quaker. Don't tell me this one is going to love *me* to death too! he thought.

"I need to know who has been off the reservation," he said,

sternly. "Have you any information to that effect? You must not hold out on me."

Tatum did not smile, but the severe lines on his forehead may have softened a little. "I think Satanta was probably off the reservation. Maybe Big Tree. You never know about Satank, but wherever there's trouble and Kiowas, that's where you'll find him. He's one of the really bad ones, I must tell you, General. While it is my desire to cooperate with you, my superiors do not agree with me on this and so you must work with me or they'll send someone out to replace me."

"I understand," Sherman said. Tatum's words were convincing him that he might have an ally among the civilians, and civilian allies he dearly needed. He had had a belly full of easterners preaching to him about how to deal with his red brothers. Tatum was a westerner. He understood that plains Indians were not angels in breechclouts.

She had been afraid that Autumn Thunder would never leave. Then she had been afraid that he would leave Sweeney with her. Then she had been afraid he wouldn't.

He had spent two days and nights with her family, and he complained about everything. Living in a grass house was for women, he told them. Real men lived in houses made from the skin of the buffalo. Real men lived in a village that moved. Real men did not tend the fields with the women. Real men were not Wichitas.

"You are a rude man, Autumn Thunder," Gathers The Grass told him. "You bring me mules. You bring me a white officer—so that I will see you are a mighty man and want to marry you. But I think you are a cruel man and I would never marry a cruel man."

"I will show you that I am a good provider too," he said. "Inside a day I will have more fresh deer meat for you. Or perhaps I will hunt a buffalo and bring home his tongue."

"Only his tongue?" Gathers The Grass asked him.

"And the hump. Or maybe I will take one of your mules and bring back much more of the buffalo. I know you can use some fresh meat in your village, and I cannot stand Wichita food."

"You cannot understand what I am telling you," she insisted, breathless. "You are like the wolves or the mountain lions."

He smiled. "That is true," he said proudly. "We are not deer who flee from man. We were born to fight. We are the wolves. We are the great cats. We take what we want. It is what men do."

"You will not take me."

"If I want."

"I would cry out. And I would fight back. The warriors of the village would come, and by nightfall your scalp would be drying in the lodge of a warrior of the Kiddykadish."

"They would not dare to lift up a hand against a Kiowa brave."

"They would and they have," she replied. "We have *men* in this village, Kiowa. And our women are not afraid to fight. It has been many moons since an Osage or a Ute or a Comanche has come to strike our village. That is because we are like a snake lying in the sun. If you do not step on us we will do you no harm. But we know how to strike at those who would harm the Wichita."

Autumn Thunder was angry. He had liked Gathers The Grass when he met her because he thought she was quiet and peaceful and hardworking like his mother. He did not care to argue with a woman, especially a woman who lived in a grass house.

"Do not underestimate us," he said. "We have our way with the Wichita."

Now it was her turn to be annoyed. This boy had some nerve to receive the hospitality of the village then make threats.

"I see your lips flapping like the wings of the hummingbird," she told him. "I hear your voice. But you say nothing. I see you are leaving us this morning. Will you take your prisoner with you?"

"You know he is too sick to travel. I will be back in two days. Do not allow him to escape or the Kiowas will be angry with their brothers in the grass houses."

She turned her back on him then, and knelt over Sweeney, who was feeling better than the day before but was still very weak. Autumn Thunder wheeled his pony around and headed out toward his home village.

"What is your name?" she asked Sweeney first in the Wichita tongue, then in Comanche. Each time he shook his head. She repeated in Kiowa, this time signing along with her speech. Again he shook his head.

White men are so stupid and arrogant, she thought. Indians learn each other's tongues so they can talk to each other. White men think they are too good to even speak to Indians. She sighed. She knew some English, but she hated to use it. As a language it made so little sense.

"Your name?" she asked.

He smiled at the familiar words, and nodded. This woman seemed kind.

"Sweeney," he answered. "Swee . . . ney."

"Very good . . . Sweeney," she said. "How do you feel?"

"Why do you care?" he asked. "He's gonna come back and carve me like a buffalo rump, isn't he?"

She smiled at him, the first time in his ten months in Indian Territory that he had seen an Indian smile. He hadn't thought they knew how. "He gave you to me," she said. "Along with some mules."

"That's very nice," said Sweeney, dryly. "Doesn't that mean you have to marry him?"

"I did not accept the mules. And I don't want you around here either. White men bad luck for Indians."

"I suppose we are at that," Sweeney replied. "I'll try to get better quickly as I can. Do you have something to drink?"

She nodded, went into the house, and brought out a white man's glass jar filled with creek water.

He took a big swig and spit it out. "This is water!" he growled.

"That is what we have to drink, soldier man."

Sweeney sighed with disgust. The Indians must be the most confused people on earth, he thought, and it's the white man's fault. First we give them booze and teach them how to use it to get stupid drunk like we do, then we send out preachers to tell them that if they drink, they're goin' to hell.

"Got no whiskey?" he asked, almost plaintively. His mouth felt dry in a way that no water could make wet.

"No whiskey in this village, Captain," she said.

"I'm not a captain, I'm a lieutenant, and I need a drink."

She pointed to the jar of water. "You might not like the

cold way it goes down,'' she said, ''but it will help you feel
better. Drink.''

He drank, and he did feel a little better.

She sat down beside him with the moccasins she was bead-
ing for her father.

For a time they were silent. When she looked up from her
work she did not turn to him but watched the noisy children
across the dirt path as the big ones chased the little ones, then
let the little ones chase them for awhile. She was sorting glass
trade beads by color, and he was lying on his back, watching
her from the corner of his eye.

She had been very kind to him, yet he was not impressed.
He thought that she and other Wichitas played up to the white
men because they knew the white men were powerful, and
they wanted to be with the winning side.

For all his hatred of the Comanches and Kiowas who raided
into Texas and killed women and children, he had more respect for them. Kiowa warriors were like soldiers. Wichitas
were just ignorant farmers with a red skin who lived in houses
made of grass instead of sod.

''What will you do with me when I am better?'' he asked
her.

''I do not do nothing with you. You do with yourself—
when you more better, but must do it quickly or someone kill
you sure.''

He fixed his eyes on her. ''You mean I'm free to go?''

''You free all right. But you go nowhere yet if you want to
live.''

''Do you know if they killed anybody in my patrol?'' he
asked.

She thought for a moment. ''Big mouth Kiowa he say nothing, but I think he would a-told me about all the dead white-
eyes in Texas. But he didn't. He didn't say nothing.''

''Then I was the only fool in my patrol who didn't make it
back?''

''You say fool, lieuten'n. Must be so then.''

He smiled at her, a smile that was also a grimace of pain.
He couldn't help but like this young girl. He had been wrong.
She was not afraid of him, not now. She was pretty, and she
hadn't begun to spread out around the hips like most of her
older cohorts did. To young girls like her, army officers were

rich men. If he wanted her for a wife, surely he could have her.

The thought that she would be so easy made him like her less. Still, it would be good to have a woman to do for him. He put his hands behind his back and closed his eyes and daydreamed of a woman who would cook his food, keep his clothes clean, and warm his bed in the wintertime. It was a pleasant daydream. It made him drowsy, and his weakness made him crave sleep that much more. The daydream merged easily into a sleep dream that seemed very real, and very domestic.

Except he could not have been more wrong about her thoughts of him.

Chapter 7

Colonel Grierson and General Sherman had planned their next step as carefully as if it were a major battle. They knew how independent and unpredictable the Kiowas could be, yet they were certain that if they could separate the three worst ones from the rest of the tribe, then the Kiowas would be much easier to manage.

Who were the three worst ones was a matter of opinion. White Bear loved public acclaim. He loved to be recognized by the white men. Sitting Bear's hatred of the whites was so obvious that he was surely a man to separate from his people. As for the powerful Big Tree—he had been there, he had to be taken.

But they didn't know that their shortage of mule stock was due to the talents of White Horse, and they had no idea of the powerful presence of Maman-ti, the Owl Prophet.

Grierson's house was a simple white one-story frame dwelling with a large front porch that caught the evening breezes sometime after the nighttime meal. When the moon was right, the guard duty could see the colonel, the post interpreter Horace Jones, the post surgeon, and another officer or two, their boots up on the porch railing, sharing after-dinner whiskey and cigars, endlessly reliving the Civil War, wondering how their lives could have degenerated from the momentous events of that horrible time to the petty frustrations of dealing with handfuls of savages whose idea of a good time was killing and looting Mexican peasants.

On this warm spring afternoon, the doors and shutters of the house were shut tight. Inside, sweating fiercely in uniforms too warm for the weather, were a dozen soldiers armed with carbines. Agent Tatum had told Lone Wolf to tell the chiefs that the great American army general Sherman had arrived and wished to parley with them.

Lone Wolf had his horse at a trot along a wet weather creek west of Fort Sill when he ran into White Bear, who was peering anxiously northward.

Although he was in a hurry, Lone Wolf saw worry on the face of his old cohort. "You better get to the fort," Lone Wolf said. "There is a big soldier chief there, much bigger than Grierson." White Bear brightened quickly. "Big man, big presents, always, don't you think?" asked White Bear.

"I think you better think about something else," said Lone Wolf.

White Bear grabbed the reins of his pony. "Gui-pah-go, does it seem that there are not so many buffalo now as there were when the whites were still fighting their big war?"

"I think you have been hearing too much from the mouth of white men."

"They have said the buffalo are going."

"We have been here since the beginning of time, White Bear. They come here not so long ago and they talk the big talk about the buffalo. Never mind the buffalo. They number like these grains of sand. It is the whites we must worry about."

A few moments of dead silence passed. A sudden breeze made the cottonwoods hiss.

"I will go to see the big soldier," said White Bear. "I must find out why they want me."

Lone Wolf laughed. "Everywhere there is a general, you expect big presents. That is what you want, big presents. Well, just you get there quickly. Maybe you should wear your soldier suit when you go."

White Bear gave a grunt of dissent. "I will go as a warrior," he said. The peace people are afraid of warriors, he thought. They laugh at us when we wear soldiers' uniforms. They will not laugh at me. Pride and dignity were more important to him than presents, even more important than his life or his freedom.

He rode his pony along the old Indian path to Fort Sill. As

he rode he did not dream. His eyes were forever searching the rolling plains around him and the hills beyond, still green with spring rains. The sky was a light spring blue, not the deep blue of winter, and a few sparse clouds were scudding along like Utes fleeing for their lives from pursuing Kiowas.

His anxieties left him and his spirit soared. Take away the fort, and the land is as it has always been. Buffalo gone? More white lies. Some years many buffalo, other years fewer. The way it has always been. Buffalo are sacred. As long as there are earth and life, there will be buffalo. For these puny white men to think they can send the buffalo away—white men's lies.

A buffalo hunt would be a good thing. After this meeting he would take the new ammunition they gave him back to his village and talk to the other chiefs about a big buffalo hunt. That would get his people away from the whites for awhile. It was good for his people to be away from the whites.

He arrived at Fort Sill full of hope. How long would this talk take? Three, four days? The big white chiefs loved to spend time making much big talk, he thought. He loved the bread the army baked. Maybe for awhile he would have some bread to eat. He rode directly to Colonel Grierson's house. Everything seemed quiet but not bad. There were a few soldiers walking around the dusty streets and paths of the post, but none even seemed to take notice of him. Horace Jones was sitting on the steps of the porch when White Bear dismounted and tied his pony to a side post of the porch.

"Go on up," he told White Bear, cordially. The warrior chief walked up the stairs and took his seat on a rocker. There he rocked back and forth for awhile, staring out across the post. Times like these, White Bear did not mind Fort Sill sitting there right in the middle of Kiowa country. Times like these he felt as if he belonged, as if it were not Colonel Grierson's headquarters, but his. He could come to the fort, get a little food, a little drink, some ammunition, then go out and hunt some buffalo, raid south across Red River, and come back north to spend a peaceful, prosperous, well-fed winter. Not a bad life at all, easier than before the whites came.

But they had to be watched, these whites. You turn your back, they'll ride in on a cold morning and bite you. Kill your wives and children.

A breeze crossed the porch and stirred his unbraided hair that fell freely below his broad shoulders, as he rocked; as an uneasy thought or two crept through his mind.

The shutters and door behind him were shut tight. Was that strange? He wondered. The Wichitas had dark houses. A tepee could be dark when it was closed up. Maybe the white men sometimes made their houses dark. White Bear did not know. He was not all that familiar with many white customs.

He liked the rocker. As he sat on the porch, looking out over the post and rocking, post life continued to seem normal around him.

He could see several officers approaching from the trader store nearby. One of them was Colonel Grierson, and two others were officers whom he had seen around the post but did not know by name. Then there were two civilians. One of them was Matt Leeper, the other was a man who seemed familiar to him. He was certain that in spite of the unmilitary clothes, the man was a soldier. He had heard that when they put fine civilian clothes on an old soldier chief it meant that he had become an even bigger soldier chief. This, then, must be the man who wanted to talk to him.

A pair of soldiers with bayonets on their rifles joined the officers as they neared the house. Now White Bear began to get nervous. Why men with guns for a little powwow among chiefs? He stepped forward from his rocker to greet the officers but one of the soldiers blocked his way. The other felt under White Bear's blanket for any weapons and, finding none, pushed the chief back toward his chair.

Now he knew that the whites were up to something, and he was glad that he had hidden his knife and pistol in his leggings. The officers were speaking to each other in urgent English that he could not understand. Why had he been so foolish as to come here alone? He struggled to keep his emotions under control, and succeeded.

Then came a pair of familiar horses around the trading store up the path to the colonel's house. Tay-nay-angopte and Set-imkia, not necessarily two of his favorite people, but at this moment he was glad to see them. The whites liked Kicking Bird and Stumbling Bear. If they were here, maybe there was nothing to worry about.

They were walking their horses slowly, too slowly to suit

White Bear. "Come here, quickly," he shouted, and the two chiefs kicked their horses into an easy trot. They dismounted a few yards away from the house. One of the officers came down the steps to greet Kicking Bird in the white man fashion, right hand shaking hands, left hand slapping him on the back.

That was Kicking Bird, White Bear thought, always in favor with the whites. Still, he was glad Kicking Bird was there, and he came down the steps to greet him, but once again the soldiers pushed him back onto the porch. The veteran chief would have loved to pull out his knife and slit the soldier's throat right then and there, but he knew that he would have been killed, because all of the officers in uniform wore sidearms.

The two chiefs joined the white men already on the porch, and soon all were sitting except the soldier chief in the civilian clothes. Sherman was pacing up and down on the porch, impatient. "Where are the rest of them?" he asked Grierson. The colonel didn't know. Neither did Kicking Bird.

"Why don't you go to the camps and round up all the chiefs?" Sherman said to Horace Jones, who translated into Kiowa for Kicking Bird.

"I'll do it!" said White Bear, suddenly, but when Jones translated, Sherman shook his head, and the two soldiers with bayonets stood a little closer to White Bear. Kicking Bird descended from the porch and rode off.

"Why are they holding you back with guns?" Stumbling Bear asked White Bear.

White Bear did not answer. He had been in situations of great danger before, but never had he felt so completely trapped. Desperately he tried to figure out what to do to avoid death, but he could not because his long memory of dealing with the whites convinced him that his death might not be necessary.

The afternoon wore on without much conversation between the soldiers and the two Indians on the porch. By the time Kicking Bird returned with the principal Kiowa chiefs, not only was White Bear worried, Stumbling Bear was convinced that the white men had brought the chiefs together to kill them all, and even Kicking Bird was nursing feelings of dread.

But if the men he had brought with him shared his apprehension, they were hiding it beneath a series of running comments in Kiowa concerning the officers who were sitting on the porch. "Shhh," cautioned Kicking Bird. "That one understands our tongue."

"That one looks like he has a lodgepole stuck up his rear end," said White Horse. Among those who had come with Kicking Bird was one young man with no chiefly status, but his recent exploits were such that he was considered a candidate for leadership among Kiowas. He was Autumn Thunder.

Kicking Bird did not stand on ceremony. This youngster had made a name for himself in battle. He was fearless. It might not be bad to have him along in case of trouble.

Sherman now had a hard time finding room to pace up and down the porch, it was so crowded with soldiers and Indians. So he stopped pacing and studied the Kiowas, a thin dead cigar clenched in his teeth.

"Which of you were there when the teamsters got massacred?" he asked through interpreter Jones.

White Bear was still worried, but he was a warrior first and a worrier second. He stepped forward from the ring of lieutenants. "I was the leader of that raid," he said.

Kicking Bird walked over to White Bear and talked to him, loud enough so it didn't seem like a secret but soft and fast enough that the interpreter Jones could not quite catch what he was saying. "Say no more," he told White Bear. "They are looking for reasons to take you away."

White Bear knew that Kicking Bird understood the white man's ways, but he hated him for it and was jealous of him. That, and his audience of admiring cohorts, were too much for his vanity.

"You are not the only people that have good leaders in battle," he said. "I gave orders to my braves by blowing my bugle, hey?" He looked toward the gaggle of chiefs, who stopped admiring him once they realized that his glance in their direction could incriminate them. They stood expressionless, giving away nothing.

White Bear was now into his speech. "I would never have my braves raid on this side of the river," he said. "Here there is a treaty, and Kiowas always keep our word. But we are men. Our enemies are Utes, and Texans, and Mexicans. It is these that we strike, with a fist of stone!" Here he made a downward striking motion with his fist.

Autumn Thunder watched the great Kiowa orator weave his spell, but he saw the concern of his elders and he mimicked their demeanor.

"You are warriors, like us. You had a war and you fought your war. I heard about it from some of your officers. It was a great war. You won many honors. You are great warriors. But your war is finished, while our wars go on. You would not deny me my honors as long as I keep my peace with you. This I know, for you are men of honor yourselves."

This last bit of flattery did not escape even Autumn Thunder, for he knew that White Bear did not trust any army officers, especially the big chiefs like Sherman.

"I have heard that one person in that raid was supposed to have been tied to a wagon wheel and burned alive. Whoever did that was a bad man that I do not know about. It was a bad thing and I would not have allowed it. But as for the rest, it was my battle, and my victory."

Jones rendered White Bear's speech word for word as faithfully as he could. Sherman stood staring at the Kiowa chief as he listened, without expression. Once or twice he glanced at the other chiefs to see how they were reacting, and once he took in the looks of mild amazement and amusement on the faces of his officers. He was pleased to see that several of them had their hands close to their sidearms, just in case White Bear attempted to whip his cohorts into a fighting frenzy right then and there.

There were a few moments of silence, while Sherman waited to see if White Bear had anything further to say. Then he asked White Bear if he had anything further to say. The stocky chief listened to the tense silence. He took a quick glance at the sagacious Kicking Bird, whose eyes told White Bear everything he needed to know.

Sherman was working his mouth as if he had a chaw of tobacco in it. If the army arrested and punished every Kiowa who had been out raiding over the last few years he might as well extinguish the tribe, and he knew that the Quakers and their do-gooder friends back east would never stand for that. Over the past few months he had heard from many people in the Indian Territory, particularly members of other, more tractable tribes. He did not know everything, but he knew something.

He cleared his throat, and spat off the porch into the dust.

"Satanta—" he began, and White Bear waited to hear what the big soldier chief had to say to him. "—Satank and Big Tree will be arrested. The governor chief in Texas will see to it that all three are tried for murder." White Bear could not believe what he was hearing as Horace Jones translated Sherman's words into Kiowa. The chief raised his hand and began to step toward Sherman, but one of the soldiers armed with rifle and fixed bayonet stopped him.

"Then there's a little matter of forty-one mules." White Horse pricked up his ears.

"We understand that you like to steal livestock but from now on anybody who steals any more livestock will be punished. For this time it will be enough that the mules be returned. Good mules too! You understand?" Kicking Bird started to say that he understood, but White Bear interrupted.

"Why would you send me to Texas? I murdered nobody. I just sat on my horse and watched the fight and blew my bugle and led my young braves. You know young men. They must fight and they asked me to lead them, to show them how. Three of my young men were killed in this battle. That is how battles are. The Texans lost lives. My men lost lives. It is sad that good lives are lost, but that is war. We should call it even and take each other by the hand and it will never happen again."

"Never again?" growled Sherman to the sweating Horace Jones but eyeing White Bear as he spoke. "Too many have already died from your raids. If you want a real battle, I have just the men to give it to you!"

"Then let it be right now!" shouted White Bear. "Now is a good time for the both of us to die!" Horace Jones was still on the job but before he could translate the chief's last outburst White Bear had flung his blanket aside and reached for his revolver.

Sherman shouted something short and sharp that Jones did not have to translate. The shutters of the house flew open and carbines were thrust out the windows in a row of steel.

"Don't shoot!" cried White Bear, who had decided that now was perhaps not such a good time to die.

Kicking Bird knew he'd better step in or there would be blood spilled on the porch and that would just be the beginning. "You know me," he said to Sherman through Jones. "I have done the best I could to keep the braves at home. I ask that you not arrest these chiefs who are my brothers, and I will see to it that the mules are returned. There will be no fight about that."

"I know of you and your good work, Kicking Bird," the general replied. "Even the president knows who you are. But I have made my decision. These three men are going to Texas to stand trial for murder."

Kicking Bird was not pleased. He was trying to hold his people together and the general seemed to be doing his level best to start a war. "If you take these men you will kill them, this I know," he said. "I will not let you do it. Try it and the sun will set on the dead bodies of you and me."

Words had been flying thick and fast, maybe a little too fast for Horace Jones. He had had a few drinks before this council and when the shutters had flown open he had been certain that his hour had come. And he knew that if he quoted Kicking Bird word for word the bullets would surely fly.

"Do not harm my people," was what Jones told Sherman.

"Don't worry," Sherman said soothingly. "We would not harm you and Stumbling Bear."

There is no telling what this bit of miscommunication might have led to, had they not been interrupted by the sudden sound of broken glass down by the trade store. The men on the porch looked across the open space and saw an Indian covered with a blanket, picking himself off the ground in front of a broken window. He dropped his blanket and ran through a large vegetable garden, followed by half a squad of soldiers all firing their weapons at him.

"Addo-eta!" exclaimed White Bear, and the argument ground to a halt as the men on the porch looked on with interest. Big Tree was a big bull of a man but his foot speed was more than the equal of the booted soldiers who were attempting to surround the garden before he could make good his escape. He might have made it had there not been a single armed gardener hoeing weeds.

Men went armed on the post wherever they went, and the gardener was no exception. He picked up his rifle and fired. Big Tree immediately decided the game was up. He flung his rifle aside, dropped to his belly, and raised his hands so the soldiers would not fire again. The soldiers surrounded him and seized hold of him, and dragged him up to Colonel Grierson's porch to join his fellow chiefs. He was coated with garden soil. Sweat was glistening on his bare chest, which was heaving violently from his futile sprint.

In the midst of the excitement, some of the chiefs had jumped off the porch and attempted to flee. Soldiers had appeared from inside the house and from the stone corral nearby. They surrounded the Kiowas and drove them all together on the porch. Every one of them thought his end was near. Autumn Thunder was stunned by the sight of all the great men he had ever known submitting to the despised white men.

Now a small group of mounted Kiowas, including White Bear's father, To-quodle-kaip-tau, arrived on the scene, riding past the guardhouse, on the way to Grierson's house carrying weapons under their blankets for the chiefs. Loitering in the area, awaiting with interest the outcome of the meeting, they had heard the gunfire and knew they had better do something fast. They could think of nothing better than to mosey up to the house with weapons under their blankets and somehow get those weapons in the hands of the chiefs on the porch.

But the officer of the day with a small detachment intercepted them, and it was then that things really went wrong. As the Kiowas rode deliberately away from the soldiers, one of them could not resist pulling back his bowstring and firing an arrow back at the soldiers, and his arrow wounded one of the troopers. In return the soldiers fired a volley and one of the Kiowas tumbled to the ground. The soldier had a flesh wound, the Kiowa was dead.

Up to this point there may have been some doubt among the Kiowas as to how the day would come out. They had been sparring, playing the waiting game, but that one volley from the soldiers destroyed the dream of the safe reservation. The warriors kicked their ponies into gear and rode out toward their camps, alarming everybody on the post as they galloped off. Any other Kiowas, including women and children, who happened to be hanging around the post, as they often did, also headed for the outlying villages.

Afraid that they might have an uprising on their hands, the mounted troopers rode over to the house and more or less surrounded it. It was over, thought Autumn Thunder, staring into the muzzles of the carbines and rifles pointed from all directions at the chiefs.

He was not frightened, but he was disappointed. How sad, he thought, for the great chiefs to be lured into a trap by such a lying, deceitful enemy.

But from within came one last glimmer of hope. Beneath his blanket in his waistband was a very sharp knife. The great soldier chief was not close, he was still in motion, walking from one end of the porch to another, but Colonel Grierson was within reach. If he could strike the enemy before he died, then death would not come as a stranger, but as a friend.

Chapter 8

Sitting Bear was at an age when most Kiowas were either dead or spent their days warming their bones in front of their tepees.

This old man still burned with the fire of the warrior, and he did not fear death. He could remember back to when there were no white men to sully his days and grab at the land that was his to roam at will. While the other chiefs stood packed together on the porch agitated and undecided about what to do next, the old chief seated himself cross-legged on the rough wooden floor of the porch and pulled out his pipe. Some of the chiefs were beginning to sway, and sing their death songs. Others looked wildly around at the prickly thicket of rifle barrels pointed at them.

Sitting Bear took no notice. He packed his pipe with trade tobacco and lit it with a trade firestick.

He sucked in the smoke and his old wrinkled face creased with enjoyment. I am ready to die now, he thought, and his mind began to drift away from the commotion that was going on around him. He did not notice the soldiers on their horses crowding closer to the porch; he was oblivious to the black soldiers peering out the windows with their rifles ready to execute. A gray smoke cloud rose from where he sat, as he awaited the final act of treachery from strange men he had learned to hate above all others.

And then, amazingly the encroaching horses in front of the porch gave way to a single Indian pony, ridden by Lone Wolf. His quiet dignified presence foreclosed any possibility of interference by the soldiers. When his pony was right next to the porch, he slid down to the ground. From beneath his blanket came a pair of Spencer repeating carbines, better weapons than the soldier had. These he laid on the ground in front of him. He had a bow and a quiver full of arrows too, and these he laid next to the carbines.

He took his blanket from his shoulder and tied it around his waist, as Kiowas did when they were preparing to ride into battle. He had a Navy Colt revolver too, in excellent condition. Where did these men get such fine weapons? Sherman thought as he made his way from the end of the porch toward where the Kiowa was arranging his armory.

Now Lone Wolf gathered up his weapons and began to distribute them to his cohorts on the porch. The soldiers and officers watched, fascinated, waiting for the general to give an order. But Sherman possessed a cool nerve, and he believed that he had broken the will of the chiefs who stood with him on the porch of Colonel Grierson's house.

To his surprise, Autumn Thunder received the revolver. Lone Wolf handed out the bow, and one of the Spencers, then took the other Spencer for himself and sat down on the floor next to Sitting Bear. The soldiers crowded in ever closer, but General Sherman turned his back and walked away as if nothing unusual were going on.

The sun was reflecting red off a thin film of clouds on the horizon. It seemed to Autumn Thunder as if the day of the Kiowas would end right there along with the sun. Stumbling Bear had strung his bow and nocked an arrow. Sherman and Kicking Bird were exchanging urgent words that the young brave could not understand. He could hear the loud clicking sound as Lone Wolf cocked his Spencer. Autumn Thunder cocked the revolver without checking to see if Lone Wolf had even loaded it.

Stumbling Bear dropped his blanket onto the floor of the porch and told those near him that he intended to shoot Sherman. Autumn Thunder knew that Kicking Bird's cousin was working himself up so he could do the deed without caring about his own life. Without thinking he gave a loud whoop in tribute as the chief pulled back the string and raised the bow.

"No!" shouted White Bear, grabbing Sitting Bear's arm. The arrow flew harmlessly away. Grierson acted next, grabbing Lone Wolf's Spencer before he could pull the trigger.

Reds and whites alike were shouting as Grierson and Lone Wolf struggled with the gun and fell in a heap. Sherman hadn't been a war hero for nothing. He gave a single sharp command. Autumn Thunder closed his eyes and waited for the bullets to strike, but instead the commotion began to die down. He looked around and saw that the soldiers had all raised their gun barrels into a vertical position. For several moments, it seemed, nobody took a breath. Then, gradually, bodies began to relax.

Lone Wolf and Grierson looked at each other warily. Lone Wolf uncocked his weapon and sat down next to Sitting Bear, who had never stopped smoking his pipe while all around him seemed about to burst into open warfare. Stumbling Bear saw that the soldiers were not about to shoot anybody. Feeling foolish, he unstrung the bow and returned the arrows to their quiver.

Slowly everybody's breathing returned more or less to normal. The Kiowas sat down on the porch and the officers resumed their seats. Perhaps now there would be a council after all.

"You must surrender Satanta, Satank, and Big Tree to us," Sherman said in English and Jones said in Kiowa. "And tell them I want forty-one good mules back and I want 'em back inside of ten days."

Jones told them, the best he could.

"You, Tsen-tainte, you have plenty mules," said Kicking Bird. "And Set-tainte, I believe they will set you and the others free if we give them back their mules." He looked at his cousin, Set-imkia, who simply nodded. Lone Wolf pledged some mules, and so did the others, except the implacable Sitting Bear, who had finished his pipe and was surprised to be still alive.

"Why should we give back the mules?" he asked.

"Because if we do the big soldier chief will free you and Set-tainte and Addo-eta," Kicking Bird replied.

"Is that what they said?" asked the wily old chief.

"I think that's what they said."

"Might be," said Addo-eta, who was busy scraping mud off his brawny body.

"Jones," said Kicking Bird. "Tell the soldier chief that the chiefs have promised to return to him forty-one mules." Although Kicking Bird could speak a little English, he knew his own people would not trust him if he did, so he spoke to Sherman through the interpreter.

"You understand that you must leave Satank, Satanta, and Big Tree with us, Kicking Bird?" asked Sherman.

"You will treat them well?" asked Kicking Bird.

"As if they were my babies," Sherman replied with an acidity that was lost in translation.

"Stay with the soldiers now, Addo-eta," Kicking Bird said to Big Tree and the other two. "I will have the mules in camp before the sun sets twice more."

"As fast as you can," said White Bear, who could stand nearly anything but the idea of being locked up behind walls.

There was no pipe passed around to close the council. There was barely a good-bye. Both sides were still shaken from the near-war that had occurred on the porch of Grierson's house.

The free Kiowas scrambled for their horses, leaving Big Tree, White Bear, and Sitting Bear on the porch of Grierson's house. They were gone too quickly to observe the post black-smith riveting manacles on the three chiefs' wrists and ankles, and nobody remained to watch them being led into a basement cell.

Kicking Bird and Stumbling Bear rode west toward their villages to outrace the rumors. Seeing them ahead of him Autumn Thunder raced his pony to catch up.

"Where are you going?" he asked them.

"To get to our villages before the others so they will not pack up and ride west," Kicking Bird replied.

Autumn Thunder rode with them in silence for awhile, deep in thought but backward about questioning such great men. What should he do? Try and keep his village from fleeing? Why would they listen to him?

"Maybe they *should* flee," he said to the chiefs, finally.

Kicking Bird gave Autumn Thunder a long look as the horses continued their steady gait along the plains.

"No," the chief said, and nothing else.

The young warrior rode with the two chiefs until they reached the parting place on the Sweetwater Branch. The night had cooled off the plains enough that he could urge his pony into a steady gallop.

Hills and creeks familiar to him since his youth hove into view then passed to his rear as he galloped on, and he asked himself if he would ever again see Set-tainte, Set-ankeah, or Addo-eta. Why would the bluecoats so treacherously take three of their great chiefs captive, unless it was to leave the Kiowas leaderless while they attacked the western villages, just as they had attacked the Cheyenne village on the Washita three summers before.

He kicked his heels against the pony and she responded with a little more speed. He had time to wonder then, as he rode north along the Sweetwater, why he could outrun the hills and the creeks, yet he could not outrun the stars and the moon. Surely it meant that they were his brothers, riding along with him. But no, he knew that if he and Hau-tau rode in opposite directions, the stars and the moon could ride along with both of them. They had tried it, once, as young children, and had returned to a meeting place to argue over which one the stars and moon had really followed.

When each insisted that the heavens followed him, they got into a long dispute in which they called each other liars. Autumn Thunder invited Hau-tau to ride along with him awhile and see that the stars were truly following him, Autumn Thunder, but once they had ridden a few miles together, Hau-tau declared that the moon and stars accompanied Autumn Thunder only because Hau-tau accompanied Autumn Thunder.

They were sitting on their mounts shouting at each other in the dead of night when Autumn Thunder heard a whisper.

"Be still!" he said sharply to Hau-tau, and something about Autumn Thunder's tone cut off Hau-tau in midsentence.

"Is it not possible that the stars and moon could go with both of us?"

Hau-tau thought for a moment. "That could not be," he said. "Stars always travel alongside the same stars. They would not split up just so they could follow each of us."

"I don't mean that," Autumn Thunder insisted. "I mean, could not all those stars, up there, at the same time, follow you, and follow me, even though we are riding away from each other?"

Hau-tau was not a fool. "I cannot see how such a thing could be," he said. "But I do not know everything, so I must admit that it is possible."

"You are my brother forever," said Autumn Thunder, elated that his friend had tried to understand what he was feeling. But just a little while ago his friend had died, his face shot off in the wagon train battle. The stars suddenly lost their appeal. He thought only of his village, not a place, but a wandering circle of tepees where he had once lived with his mother. He still had many relatives in this village, whose chief was Au-sai-mah, the brother of his father.

He rounded a final bend of the Sweetwater Branch and rode down a path through some scrubby cedars until he found the clearing where the village should have been, but there was no village. In the ghostly light of a three-quarter moon he could make out the tracks of a village on the move, lodgepoles dragging in the dust behind their ponies. They had been in this camp since early spring, so the circles of the tepees were clear.

But there were no tepees.

He stopped and dismounted. He knew they had crossed the Sweetwater Branch and were heading west as fast as they could to put as much distance as they could between themselves and the white soldiers, who had to be plotting a horrifying strike on the women and children of the Kiowa villages.

He stood in the moonlight, his head cocked to one side listening—for what, the echoes of a once-happy people now fleeing west in misery and fear?

Scattered around the encampment were pieces of firewood, food scraps, circles of rocks, and an occasional bit of leather or cloth. He waited yet another few moments, listening for the bark of a camp dog that might have been left behind.

There was nothing else to be found but a single cornshuck doll, a shadow Autumn Thunder nearly missed as he started to mount his pony. He picked it up and slipped it inside the blanket he was wearing around his shoulders. Then he mounted his pony.

It had been a long day, and he was tired, but he had to find his people. When he did, what would he tell them, that Kicking Bird did not believe the soldiers would attack? Kicking Bird was a good chief, but Black Kettle the Cheyenne had been a good chief, and he had thought the white men would not attack a peaceful village. Twice he had thought that the white men would not attack a peaceful village, and twice his people had been slaughtered.

Autumn Thunder decided that he would not go after the people of his village. Something or somebody had told them to run. Perhaps that something or somebody was right. He longed to talk to the quiet young Wichita woman who seemed to know things that the men did not. He turned his horse east and slowly, sadly set his course for the village of Gathers The Grass.

Chapter 9

Sitting Bear sat on the dirt floor of his cell late the following night, rocking back and forth, tears running down his wrinkled old face, silently keening.

The tears were not for himself, though he was utterly miserable. To put a Kiowa in a stone-walled basement, away from the sun and the air and the wild plains grass was like putting a great big hand over his face and smothering him.

All day long he had paced, first back and forth, then around the cell, until the soles of his moccasins were nearly worn out. He had checked every square inch of the walls, had tugged on the barred windows until his arms felt numb. He beat on the stones with his bare hands, and he tried to dig under the walls, not methodically, like a man bent on escape, but frantically, like a man about to lose his mind.

When he heard footsteps his self-control returned to him. He would never let the white men see him lose his self-control. Oho! He could use a taste of rum all right, and he hated himself for needing the white man's drink. The night arrived with him in such deep despair that he began to bang his head against the bars on the windows, not to break the bars but to split his head open and spill his brains out.

He was crying for his son, whose name he would say no more. Sitting Bear had watched proudly as the boy grew into an unconquerable Kiowa warrior. Like all great Kiowa warriors, when the weather warmed and the springs ran bright and clear, the young man rode south with his cohorts to raid the Texans.

There was nothing his son could not do with a horse. He

was strong and wiry, skilled with the lance, the bow and the rifle, triumphant in the buffalo hunt, good for a deer or an elk in the hungry days of winter. He was a future chief, worthy to carry the name Sitting Bear himself. Someday.

There were a dozen of them, riding out of their village with extra ponies, sure of their medicine, leaving early so they could make it across Red River before dark. Sitting Bear wished to go with them, but these young men were determined that it would be a first great strike for their generation, and the older men agreed that this was right. There was already experience among them, and new leaders must always emerge, to keep the people strong.

Three days out from their village, in search of white settlers thinly scattered across the north Texas plains, they found a solitary farmhouse flanked by cultivated fields and a barn that promised livestock. There were no whites outside to take warning from their approach, and the sharp eyes of the young Kiowas detected no activity within. Boldly they rode forward toward the house.

A hundred yards away the young warriors left their horses with the even younger apprentices who had come with them, and walked forward in a crouch, spreading out as they came closer. They were cautious, but not very cautious. They were always fascinated by the things they could find in white men's houses, and they were determined to make their raid and leave before the whites came back. If there were whites there, fine, let them cringe under the knife.

Then suddenly, in the still air a puff of smoke arose from a window opening, followed by the sound of the rifle shot. All of the young Kiowas dropped low into the grass—all except the son of Sitting Bear. He sat down, suddenly, a dazed look on his face, blood spilling down his bare chest.

Two windows were now belching a steady stream of gunfire. The grass was not long. The warriors were vulnerable. All sprang to their feet and ran low to the ground, for their ponies. All except for the son of Sitting Bear. As the hoofbeats of his friends receded into silence, he sat for a few seconds more until the sun's golden light turned to gray and then finally black. Silently he settled on his back into the grass, breathing rapidly, shallow, painlessly until his heart pumped one last time.

So stunned were the young braves by the death of Set-ankeah's son on the first raid of their journey that they decided their medicine was bad and headed back to the reservation. But first they waited till nightfall, came back to the farm and found the young man's body, hid it in a crevice and covered it with rocks.

When they arrived home and told the old warrior of his son's death, Sitting Bear ordered them from his tepee, then sat alone, inside, in the dark for a very short time. He felt as if his old body would burst with the grief growing up inside him.

But even at the age of seventy he was an elite warrior of the Kaitsenko, the society of the ten bravest warriors, a man of action, and as the weeks went by it came to him that he must retrieve the body of his son. So he and three of his friends journeyed south to the place where his son's remains rested, a place he knew, for he had raided across Red River so often that he knew most of northern Texas like the back of his wrinkled old hands.

He found no body. He found only bones. The carrion birds had done their work. Tough old Sitting Bear stared at the bones that were once his beautiful son, and he began to weep. While his friends watched, he pulled his knife from his waist-band and began to slash at himself, then stabbed directly into his chest, only to be thwarted by the bone chestplate that he wore.

One of his friends grabbed him and held him, the other tied him with a rope until he calmed down. Even then they would not trust him enough to untie him until they were certain that they had taken all his weapons away from him. They watched as the old man laid a blanket flat on the ground, washed the bones in a stream, put them on the blanket and folded the blanket into a secure bundle.

His emotions once more under control, he never again went anywhere without the bones of his son on a pony that he led wherever he went. The pony even went with him on the wagon train raid, though he left it a few miles away from the raid with the pony herd. Beside his own tepee he always erected a tepee for the bones of his son.

Never the most sociable of Kiowas, who were a sociable group, he now spoke to almost no one. Most of the time his eyes burned with fierce anger but sometimes, when nobody else was with him, they softened into dark pools filled with lonesome sorrow. He would fill a bowl with water, and another bowl with meat, and place it in his son's lodge, sustenance for his spirit, though his earthly remains now required none.

It was early morning for the white civilians on post but mid-morning for the Kiowa chiefs when their captors came to them and checked to see that the manacles on their wrists and ankles were secure. Their ankles numb from a night in irons, the three chiefs clumped up the stairs from the dark basement and out into the bright sunlight. They stood squinting at Lieutenant R. H. Pratt and the interpreters, Horace Jones and Matt Leeper, who were there to tell them what was happening to them. Also there was George Washington, the Caddo chief who was the principal arms merchant in the area, several soldiers, and Colonel Grierson.

Sitting Bear still had a knife secreted on him. Where he kept it so it had not been found when he was searched, nobody ever figured. With a smile that looked like a grimace fixed to his face, he stumbled toward Grierson in his heavy chains, hands outstretched as if he wanted to shake hands and say good-bye. White Bear and Big Tree, his fellow prisoners, knew what he was about. Afraid that they would be blamed for any damage Sitting Bear did, they grabbed him and pulled him back.

He struggled for a moment, then realized he would have to wait for another moment to strike, but strike he would, quickly, because his son's bones were tied to the back of a pony less than two hundred yards away from him and he was not about to leave the reservation for any reason without those bones.

Two wagons filled with shelled corn drove up and stopped by the little group. White Bear and Big Tree shuffled quietly over to the second wagon. The soldiers lifted them and deposited them on the loose corn, and the two chiefs did not resist. Sitting Bear stood rooted to a spot ten yards away from the wagons and he refused to follow his cohorts' example.

So four soldiers were detailed to lift the old Kiowa and carry him to the wagon. His body was stiff and straight, all his muscles rigid. He wasn't making it easy for the soldiers to carry him and they retaliated by tossing him into the lead wagon as if he were a sack of feed grain.

Humiliated and brokenhearted, he moved into a sitting position on the loose corn, his back up against the wagon seat, and began to chant his death song.

Kaitsenko ana obema haa ipai degi o'ba ika.
Kaitsenko ana oba hemo hadamagagi o ba ika.
O sun, you remain forever but we Kaitsenko must die.
O earth you remain forever but we Kaitsenko must die.

The song made him feel a little better. The whites were just another tribe scoring a temporary victory over the people, but the sun remained forever and the earth remained forever and so did the people, though the Kaitsenko must die. The song came back to him from his youth, when there were no white men on the Canadian River or the Washita or the Red or anyplace else.

They were surely but a dream, a terrible dream, and they had killed his beautiful son, and now he would die, and when he died, he would awaken, and with his son and all those who went before, the earth and the sun would go on forever. And so he chanted, and as he chanted, he pulled his blanket over his head, and the soldiers at the side of the road could not help but laugh at the bad old Indian whining a loud but muffled chant into his blanket.

Beneath the blanket, like a wolf who would gnaw off his leg to free himself from a trap, between choruses, Sitting Bear was gnawing flesh from the heels of his hands to make them smaller, and slick with blood, so he could slip his manacles. Then let them laugh. The driver and the guard were facing away from him. He would die as Kaitsenko should die, killing the enemy.

The wagons passed through the gate of the fort and out into the open plains, and still Sitting Bear pulled with his teeth at the flesh of his hands. He felt the pain as he pulled his hands against the manacles and the pain felt sweet as honey when one of them slid free.

His free hand found the hilt of his knife. With the other hand he pulled his blanket down from his face and glared at the smirking soldiers at the side of the road. He continued to chant his chant until he spotted Caddo George, riding beside the wagon, with a Tonkawa scout and his woman riding just behind him.

In Comanche he said, "Tell my people that they may find my bones at the side of the road. Tell them to gather them up and carry them away."

Caddo George said he would do so.

Sitting Bear looked at the cloudless blue sky. No buzzards were flying overhead. They would be flying soon, to bear his flesh away.

He craned his neck around the seat of the wagon and spotted a pecan tree along the side of the road a hundred yards distant. "Do you see that tree?" he asked the Caddo gun trader.

"I see it," George answered.

"When I reach that tree I will be dead."

Caddo George nodded and let his horse fall back.

"My scalp may not be much," he said to the Tonkawa scout, "but when I am dead you may have it."

One last time he looked at the sky and spotted a single hawk.

"Summon your brothers," he said to the hawk, then he stopped singing, and stood up, his knife raised above his head.

The knife came down and the guard yelled. Sitting Bear snatched at the guard's carbine but the soldier held fast to it and the two men tumbled backward, into the wagon bed then over the tailgate onto the dusty road. The guard landed on his head and Sitting Bear had his carbine, a carbine of a type he had never worked before. He rose to one knee and struggled to cock the weapon.

The soldiers watched, stunned, and did nothing until the officer in charge, gave the order to fire. Instantly three carbines discharged, followed quickly by five more, and Sitting Bear fell backward into the dust.

Sitting Bear was not dead, but his time was short, and the other chiefs had a date with Texas justice. The soldiers left the old warrior at the side of the road, sitting up, his back against the pecan tree, blood pouring from his mouth.

The scout rode up to the officer. "The old man told me I could have his scalp," he said.

"No scalp," said the officer, who was afraid that when the Kiowas retrieved Sitting Bear's body they might think the soldiers had scalped him and then Colonel Grierson would have a rebellion on his hands. "You can have his buffalo robe."

The wagons rumbled on. Sitting quietly, their backs against the wagon seat, White Bear and Big Tree watched their old comrade-in-arms dying at the side of the road. And the moment Sitting Bear died, the old way of life for the Kiowas began to die too. White Bear's thoughts were of his future in Texas so he didn't notice. But Big Tree knew, and he left a part of his mighty heart by the side of the road with the last of the great Kaitsenko.

Chapter 10

Tuck hated skinners. They stank from rotting buffalo flesh, dried buffalo blood, and their own sweat.

He could remember a time when he had first started hunting buffalo, when he was his own skinner. He recalled how the end of the day would find the skin on his arms stiffened with a thick coating of hard, coagulated buffalo blood. The memory made him hate skinners that much more.

Now he supported two skinners with his steady shooting eye, men with hides nearly as tough as a bull buffalo. One drove a wagon half full of lead ball ammunition and powder, and the other a wagon half full of food. Tuck had just bought himself a brand new Sharps .45 caliber rifle that accommodated a five hundred grain ball. He had carefully calibrated the sight in a field outside of Fort Cobb then headed south for a bit of summer shooting in north Texas.

At the Brazos River he found a small herd of about a hundred buffalo grazing quietly on the green grass that grew along the south bank. He turned his horse around and headed back toward the wagons.

"We got ourselves a herd," he said to one of the skinners. "Now pull your wagons up about a half a mile, to those rocks up yonder and no further. See to it your knives are sharp cuz you got a heap a cuttin' coming before this day is over."

The men were listening, not saying much, which would have seemed strange to Tuck had he been paying attention. But that little herd was just the right size for breaking in a couple of new skinners.

"Now, you just keep your horses still while I clean out that there herd. We want to be quick about this. I don't want any stray Injuns comin' down on us before we're finished with the skinnin'. If there's any around, that shootin' might draw them thisaway and we want to be long gone by the time they're here, understand?''

They understood too well. One of them was a skinny old ex-soldier named Rayburn. He may have been new to Tuck, but he'd lived for years on the Texas open range and he knew plenty about survival.

"Tuck," he said, "while you was scoutin' along the river I took a look from that hill and I saw about fifteen, twenty bucks headin' south.''

"Who were they?''

The skinner studied the gray eyes of the irritable Tuck. Rayburn wasn't afraid of the big buffalo-runner, but he was a man who loved peace in his life and generally was glad to skirt trouble. There was always an angry glint in the corner of Tuck's eye, so Rayburn always chose his words carefully. Here, however, the stakes were too high to soft-pedal the news.

"Don't rightly know who they were," he said, "but . . .''

"Hell, you gotta know something. Kiowa? Tonkawa? Comanche? What?''

"They were kinda far to tell, Tuck, but some of them had rifles, that I could tell.''

"Damn!'' he muttered. As much as he hated skinners, they were his bosom buddies compared to Indians. He and Rayburn crept to the top of the nearby hill and watched as the mounted Indian riders turned directly south, their horses loping along at an easy ground-eating canter.

"We'll wait an hour or so and by then they'll be out of hearing range, understand?''

Rayburn understood, and he did not like it one bit. He wanted out of the area, quickly, and he certainly did not want to take the slightest chance that the warriors might hear the shooting and stalk them like hungry hunters stalking winter meat.

Tuck was not exactly sensitive to other people's feelings, but he could tell something was troubling Rayburn by the way he was chewing on the ends of his mustaches.

"Don't worry," he said. "They won't attack buffalo hunters."

"Why not? asked Rayburn.

"Cause I can shoot," Tuck replied. "And they don't want
to die."

The previous summer, alone on the plains, he had done some
shooting when he had found a family of Tonkawas camped
by a spring. Mother, father, two young boys. They possessed
several Indian ponies as well as an old wagon that looked to
be in good condition. No telling what he might find among
people like these.

With no more compunction than if he'd been killing buffalo,
he laid his telescope sight on the father of this little group and
pulled the trigger of his old Springfield. At more than three
hundred yards he hit the Indian dead center and laughed at the
way he jumped in the air and flopped to the ground. Hell of
a shot.

The man's wife made it easy for Tuck when she heard the
shot and saw her man hit. Instead of hiding she ran directly
to where her husband lay still and struggled to help him. Tuck
chambered another round, aimed carefully, and drilled her in
the chest. She fell on top of her husband.

The two boys came next. They were very young, maybe
three and four, and had never seen violent death. He watched
the two boys as they tugged at the arms of their parents, trying
to awaken them. This was simply meant to be, he thought, but
he decided to move in a little closer, because the children
presented such small targets.

At a hundred—no, he made it eighty yards—he chambered
first one round then another, and made his kills quickly and
easily.

He walked in on the camp, warily, lest there be someone
else there that he hadn't accounted for. He walked around the
camp looking for some worthwhile possessions, but he was
bound to be disappointed.

These people owned nothing! Three broken down Indian
ponies; a Kiowa-style tepee with a raggedy old buffalo hide
covering; several worn-out blankets; an oft-patched iron kettle
that still simmered over a fire; a few threadbare items of cloth-

ing; and other worthless odds and ends. Viewed from close-up, the wagon proved to be a rotted-out relic.

The buck's musket was so worn and hopeless that Tuck wasn't surprised to find a quiver full of arrows. The gun could have had no function other than to bluff someone into leaving them alone.

He spat into the dust. They were better off dead, he muttered angrily, offended that there wasn't a single item these people had that could be of any use to him. How he hated Indians!

It was his custom to leave his skinners far behind because he was convinced that the buffalo could smell the stench of death on them even when the skinners were downwind.

He walked about half a mile with a heavy pack full of ammunition. When he reached a spot about four hundred yards away from the herd, he dropped his ammunition, laid down his rifle, and set up for business. He had a rest for the rifle, made out of wood, that stood about thirty inches high once he had stuck the end of it deep into the ground.

He knelt behind the gun rest and looked through the telescope sight on his rifle. The buffalo looked big and juicy in the crosshairs.

He chambered a round and selected a big young female to start out on. He cocked the hammer, and studied the herd through his telescope sight. There was a light wind coming from the west. Almost as if by instinct, he adjusted the weapon to allow for the cross wind.

The "lady," as he called females, (he was not fond of women either) was right where she was supposed to be. He took a deep breath, let a little out, and pulled the trigger. The rifle cracked and bucked, the bullet ripped and the buffalo settled quickly to the ground and lay on its side, still in sudden death.

He loaded another round and chose another buffalo that presented a good side shot. Another cow. He was in no hurry. He had found that if he fired too fast the barrel heated up too much and lost its accuracy. He wanted to kill every animal in the herd, starting with the young adults and working his way down to the calves, who would be staying with their dead mothers, just as the Indian boys did.

When the fourth one went down a big bull walked up to the carcass and started to nudge it with his great head. "Get up," he seemed to be saying. "What's the matter with you?" Tuck hated it when buffalo started to prod their dead. It angered him, and he always went after the prodders next. When he fired, the big bull fell over hard, raising a big dust cloud.

He worked slowly and confidently in the warm morning sun. Periodically he had to clean the powder residue out of the barrel with cold water and a rag on a stick. He hated to interrupt the rhythm of the killing, but he had no choice.

Now half the herd was down and the rest of them still hadn't caught on. Their stupidity filled him with perverse delight.

Aiming at buffalo number forty-seven the rifle misfired. Tuck cursed softly, pried the old round out of the chamber and inserted a new one. He loaded these shells himself, using lead that he melted and molded to his own satisfaction. Once again he laid the rifle on the gun rest, cocked the hammer and squeezed the trigger.

While killing number sixty-one his bullet deflected off a bone and the animal let out a bellow of pain. It sank down to its knees but then rose again. Quickly Tuck fired another round and finished off the young bull before he could alarm the animals around it.

His ears were ringing from the loud bangs of his rifle and maybe the heat was disturbing his aim a bit. Number seventy was a mother with a calf close by. He was certain the bullet meant for her had hit precisely where he had intended it to, but the cow did not fall. Instead she crowded up against her calf, trying to protect it. His second shot at her went through the mother and into the calf, killing them both.

Number eighty-four would have been the last standing adult, who was grazing some distance behind the rest of the herd. Tuck decided to ignore him for awhile. There were a dozen calves out there with soft hides that commanded a premium. One after another he gunned them down without ever needing a second shot.

Until the last one. Tired, maybe a little careless, he pulled the trigger a little too quickly and the bullet went off to the right. The young beast didn't notice, and he didn't move. Tuck loaded again and fired. Number ninety-six.

The lone buffalo left was spooked by something, what Tuck could not guess, but the creature had drifted beyond a swell, nearly out of range. Tuck had no desire to go running over the plains in pursuit of a lone buffalo, so he decided to chance a long shot. If he missed him, no big deal, he had plenty of hides. Besides, he was in a hurry to get his skinners skinning before the hot sun turned the buffalo carcasses evil-odored and fly-infested.

The buffalo stopped running and started nibbling the grass nervously. Tuck took a long time aiming before he finally pulled the trigger. And missed! The bullet ricocheted off a rock right under the animal's nose and set it running toward the north.

And then, abruptly, for no reason, he turned around and began to run south, heading straight for Tuck's position.

Smiling grimly he loaded, replaced the gun on its stand, and took dead aim. Then he waited, as the buffalo's shambling gait led him closer and closer to him.

He waited for the buffalo to turn sidewise but the animal was still heading straight for where Tuck was silently kneeling behind his Sharps rifle.

At about eighty yards Tuck cocked the hammer, sighted the animal, leaned into the stock, and drilled the buffalo neatly in its forehead.

With death in its eyes the buffalo lay down on its belly and fed its blood into the earth one heartbeat at a time.

Tuck pulled out his big old Walker Colt and fired three times into the air. In a short time the wagons rolled into view, and within a few minutes they had passed him and were rumbling toward the field where nearly a hundred bison lay. Two or three were still kicking feebly. The rest were all dead.

Tuck knew how to skin a buffalo, but he never did so anymore. His job was quick and clean, to level a herd from a distance. The skinners' job was long and dirty and smelly, to cut the hides off dead buffalo—big, cumbersome hides that weighed as much as a hundred fifty pounds apiece. Once the hides were removed—and that process took hours—they were staked to the ground so the sun could dry whatever blood and tissue clung to the skin.

Feeling privileged and special, Tuck mounted his horse for a better view, raised his field glasses and watched his skinners do their hot, disgusting work.

First they ran their wagons in among the carcasses, then they pulled out wooden boxes of knives that they had honed to a keen edge the night before. They worked from opposite edges of the herd toward the center, cutting away the main part of the hide and leaving the rest of the animal to rot in the sun.

They worked long in the hot sun, cursing Tuck for his privileged indifference. Either one of them could have been the man with the rifle, and a lowlife like Tuck should have been out on the plains elbow-deep in gore. The flies quickly found the bloody bodies of the buffalo and soon they were attacking the arms and hands of the hiders, which were steeped in the blood and tallow of the beasts they were cutting.

They sweated, and cursed, and slashed, and hauled the skins to the vicinity of the wagons. There they dropped them on the ground and staked them away from the carcasses, which were already beginning to bloat and stink in the hot sun.

In the meantime Tuck the hunter was running cold water down the bore of his rifle and cleaning it out very carefully. If he could somehow get the cargo to market without colliding with a bunch of thieving redskins, he could make out a little for the day's work.

Before he got into it, he hadn't realized how tough a business killing buffalo was, and the Indians just made it all that harder. One of these days, he thought, it would be a pleasure to lay his sights upon a party of Comanches and Kiowas, and teach them who was the real master of the plains.

Chapter 11

Autumn Thunder couldn't believe it. He wanted his captive back, and Gathers The Grass would not let him have Lieutenant Sweeney.

Sweeney's recovery had been swift. Within a week he was tottering around the village, and asking the young woman to let him go back to Fort Sill.

"You are not fit to travel yet," she had told him. "When the time is right I will have my cousin Three Wolves take you back."

That was the day before Autumn Thunder arrived at the village filled with hatred toward the soldiers who had given the Kiowa chiefs over to the despised Texans and demanded the return of forty-one mules, three of which he still possessed. He would have to give back the mules to help ransom his chiefs, but nobody except the Wichitas knew he owned an army lieutenant. He was not about to let loose of Sweeney until he was good and ready.

"I want him now!" Autumn Thunder demanded, the fury in his voice and the fire in his eyes telling Sweeney what Autumn Thunder's fluent Comanche speech did not.

"And what would you do with him?" she asked, smiling.

"What would I do?" He pondered the question for the moment. "I'd cut off his eyelids and stake him out in the sun, that's what I'd do with him."

"He is a good man," Gathers The Grass said, quietly. "The two of you could be friends."

"Friends? Me and a soldier? Soldiers are here for Kiowa braves to kill, don't you know that? When they are all dead and the army gives up trying to take everything we have, then maybe I'd make a friend of one. Fetch me this, friend! Fetch me that, friend! That's the kind of friend I want him to be. Don't you see? He is my enemy. Besides, look at him. He is so pale and thin I do not think he will last the week.''

Gathers The Grass appraised Sweeney for a moment. ''You are right,'' she said. ''I do not believe he is well,'' she said.

They were both right. That night fever came to Sweeney.

''We must get him away from the village,'' she told Autumn Thunder.

''Why should we do that?'' he asked.

''Don't you know anything?'' she asked. ''Sick white men come to Indians. Then the white men get better and the Indians get sick but then they die.''

''Indians? You mean Kiowas? Comanches?''

''Indians to the north. Mandans. Hidatsas.''

''I do not know Mandans and Hidatsas. I know Kiowas and Comanches and Cheyenne. They are strong. Don't get everybody's sickness. Indians. That's what white men call Kiowas?''

''What they call all red men.''

''You mean Utes and Osages too?'' He began to laugh. ''They think we are like Utes and Osages?''

''I think we are too.''

''You might think that,'' he replied. ''You are not us. You think there is something called 'Indians.' Let me tell you something. The Utes and the Osages are not my brothers, you understand? They are very different from us.''

She looked at him with sadness, and with tenderness that he had never before noticed. In spite of himself his own feelings softened.

''Now let *me* tell *you* something,'' she said. ''I know you Kiowas think you are the mightiest of men, and that Wichita men are nothing. But you better know that the white men are the mightiest of men, and they would see us all dead, were there not a few good men among them.''

''Wahah!'' snorted Autumn Thunder. ''If they are so mighty why did they send the soft peace chiefs to us?''

Gathers The Grass smiled. ''Have you ever watched white men with the yellow metal? What are they like with the yellow metal?''

"I have spent very little time inside the forts," Autumn Thunder said proudly. "The strong Kiowa bands stay away from the forts. The ones who stay around the forts get fat and drunk and smell bad. But I have seen the *Tai-bos* enough to know that they will kill to get the yellow metal and kill to keep the yellow metal."

"The ones who kill to *keep* the yellow metal—that is how white men are. They have so many men to spend in battle but they do not want to spend them. Instead they send the soft peace chiefs to you to make you weak—"

"It is as I said!" he interrupted, eyes blazing. "That is why the strong Kiowas keep away from the forts."

"Listen to all I have to say," Gathers The Grass said, patiently. "That is the easy way for the white men. But when the peace chiefs have had their time, then they will send the war chiefs with many more soldiers."

"We have whipped the soldiers before."

"Many more soldiers," she repeated.

"How do you know all this?" he asked.

She inclined her head toward Sweeney, who had fallen asleep.

"But you do not speak his tongue."

"And the men at the forts," she added.

"But you do not speak their tongue."

She smiled a funny little smile, and suddenly Autumn Thunder knew.

"You *do* speak their tongue," he said, excitedly.

"I do not speak their tongue," she answered. "Maybe few words. Enough. But I understand many of their words. We must take him away from the village."

"Tell me all else you know about them."

"After we take him from the village."

"Do you have a travois?"

"How do we have such a thing?" she said. "We don't go anywhere, and we have no lodgepoles."

"Then I will tie him on one of the mules."

The two of them did just that and Autumn Thunder could not help but notice how gentle she was with the soldier as she helped knot the ropes. Sweeney was now in about the same position as he had been the day Autumn Thunder had brought him in.

Quickly Gathers The Grass assembled some provisions and told her family she and Autumn Thunder were taking Sweeney away from the village. Since she had been doing as she pleased for several years they did not say much other than, "Watch that Kiowa, they're worse than white men."

Autumn Thunder mounted his pony and Gathers the Grass climbed atop another of the stolen mules and they rode northeast for about twenty miles until they found an abandoned cabin.

The Kiowa did not want to stop there. "I will not live in a wood house," he said.

"The house is not for us, it is for him," she replied. "We will stay outside, mostly stay away from him."

Gathers The Grass spent the next few days caring for Sweeney and sent out Autumn Thunder to hunt deer and wild birds. At first he objected, saying that, in the first place, he had intended to kill this man in battle, and in the second place, if she was so certain that the whites were mightier than the Indians, then why save one more soldier so he could help with the killing?

She answered only that this man was a good man and that there were not many good men so it was wrong to let a good man die.

"He's a white soldier," he said. "How could he be a good man?"

She just shrugged her shoulders and repeated, "He's a good man."

By the third day Sweeney was sitting up, able to hold his own cup to drink the broths and teas she was brewing for him. Autumn Thunder watched as Gathers The Grass and Sweeney held conversations that he could not understand, Sweeney talking slowly, in long sentences while Gathers The Grass listened, and she answering in single words and short sentences accompanied by hand gestures.

He took to brooding over the situation, staying away most of the time and coming back in early evening only because he was curious as to what was really going on. It was obvious to him that the white man liked Gathers The Grass, and Gathers The Grass was attentive to Sweeney.

He spent most of his time ranging the hills, hunting and wondering why he cared about a young Wichita girl who had learned the tongue of the white men. He had given her gifts, but he did not know the customs of the Wichitas, and she did not seem to acknowledge any commitment to him.

And yet he felt a pull from her.

One late afternoon he came back to find Gathers The Grass and Sweeney walking together. He was leaning on her as he walked, and the Kiowa decided he had had enough. After she took Sweeney back in the house, Autumn Thunder took her by the arm and led her outside, to a creek that ran about a hundred yards from the house.

His face was a mask but she could feel his arm tense with emotion, so she allowed herself to be led there without a word. Once he had stopped walking she took two quick steps away from him and looked at him, her arms folded.

"What do you want?" she asked.

He laid his hand upon the sharp knife he kept in his waistband.

"Tonight I am going to kill that white man," he said, "and if you try to stop me I will kill you."

She didn't tremble. She didn't flee. She didn't even flinch.

"Why would you do such a thing?" she asked.

He did not have the words at first. His jaws worked without a sound for several moments. Still she waited, arms folded over the light blue cotton dress her father had once received in trade for corn.

"You stay with him," he said. "You speak his tongue. You want to be with him—with them. That I cannot bear."

She sat on the edge of the bank of the creek and let her legs dangle down the side. "It is too bad that you do not speak his tongue," she said, looking up at him.

"Why? So that I may become part of them?" he asked. The thought of betraying his people to be part of the strange, evil ones made him dizzy.

"No," she answered. "So you would understand how much of his talk was a cry for whiskey. Whiskey!" she croaked in a voice hoarse with emotion. "He needs whiskey. He only needs whiskey.

"I don't want a man who craves whiskey. I want a man who craves freedom. I want you. Now, do you want to live in a grass house with me, or will you take me to your village to live in a high house of skins?"

He sat down beside her and looked earnestly into her face to see if she was making fun of him.

"You would live in a Kiowa village?" he asked in amazement.

"I would live in the desert—or anyplace else—with you," she replied.

The following afternoon, when he brought in several birds for Gathers The Grass to cook, he stayed in the house, sat down on the floor of the main room, facing Sweeney, and stared fixedly at him. Sweeney stared dully back at Autumn Thunder. Although he had regained enough strength to sit up for several minutes at a time, he obviously was not yet well.

Autumn Thunder studied Sweeney's narrow, hollow-cheeked face—light blue eyes—dark, almost black hair, slightly curly—whiskers as long as his captivity, reddish black flecked with gray. He tried to read Sweeney's character in his face, but he could not.

Gathers The Grass watched as the two men stared at each other, minute after minute, without speaking. Sweeney spoke first.

"Thank you," he said.

Autumn Thunder squinted his eyes as if squinting might help him hear better.

Gathers The Grass translated the English words into Comanche for Autumn Thunder.

"Why does he thank me?" Autumn Thunder asked.

"For taking care of him. He knows you have been bringing in the food."

"But—" Autumn Thunder suddenly understood. "He does not know that I was the one who almost killed him?"

"He remembers nothing from the fight till the time he woke up in my father's lodge."

"You did not tell him?"

"It was not for me to tell him."

Autumn Thunder was astonished. He studied Sweeney's face again, flickering in the light of Gathers The Grass's cooking fire. This time he thought he could detect smile lines on either side of his mouth, and vertical fret lines between his eyes. Autumn Thunder thought that maybe Sweeney was not a bad man. Never mind. He was a white soldier. Autumn

Thunder had pierced him while he and the black white men had been down in Texas looking for Indians to kill, that much was certain.

He smiled at Sweeney, and Sweeney gave a weak smile back.

"I will kill you if I get the chance," he said, conversationally.

Sweeney obviously did not understand. He leaned toward Autumn Thunder, and the Kiowa found himself shaking the officer's right hand.

Chapter 12

The winds of late August hissed through the dry yellow plains grass that rolled on and on in ever-undulating swells. A single Kiowa on his nervous war pony, followed by two figures clinging to patient mules, rose and fell with the swells as they made their way toward the eastern edge of the reservation.

Sweeney was still weak and he didn't like the way Autumn Thunder was looking at him. He reminded Sweeney of a time when he was seven years old on his father's Ohio farm, where his father had a big old hound that salivated for the goats his father kept. One cold winter night his father brought a newborn billy into the house and nursed him into a pet. The young goat followed his father around like a puppy. The dog was aware that his father loved the little billy, and tried not to harm it, but every so often his predatory nature would get the best of him and Sweeney's father would catch the hound stalking the little goat. When that happened he would catch the attention of the dog by smacking him on the side of his head, hard. The dog always knew why he was being smacked and eventually he stopped stalking the goat.

His father was not fooled. He could still see the dog eyeing the goat from time to time as if the animal were barbecued and laid out on a platter. His father loved the hound and the goat, so there was nothing he could do but keep an eye on the dog and whale away on him if he stepped out of line.

The day came when his father had to go to the courthouse on a legal matter. He could not take the dog with him, he could only hope that the dog knew what was good for him.

So he was not surprised that when he got home three days later, the goat had disappeared and the dog was keeping himself on the other side of the world from Sweeney's father. If his father came inside, the dog went outside. When his father stepped outside, the dog went into the barn. The dog did not behave normally for nearly a week.

Sweeney's mother was so angry at the dog that she urged her husband to get rid of it, but Sweeney's father just looked sadly at her and reminded her that the dog, after all, was just being a dog, and it shouldn't be punished for that.

Autumn Thunder had not yet threatened him, but Sweeney had learned long ago that though a Kiowa could be very sociable on the reservation, out in the open country he was a killer. One Kiowa had almost done him in, that he knew, though he could not remember the event itself. Autumn Thunder must have been there. He was the kind of fellow who wouldn't stay home when there was action to be had with a Kiowa war party. No, Sweeney did not quite trust the young man. So he convinced Gathers The Grass to bring him back to Fort Sill before Autumn Thunder decided to make a trophy out of the top of his head.

But Gathers The Grass could not get him back without Autumn Thunder's approval.

She knew how to get that. One night as they stood talking quietly outside the cabin, she told him what she was thinking. "I will go with you to your village," she said, "if you will leave the soldier at Fort Sill on the way."

"He is mine," came the predictable reply.

"Then I am not," she had answered.

"Why does his life mean so much to you?" Autumn Thunder asked.

"He is a good man," she said, as she had said before.

"He is a white man."

"It is good to have the friendship of a white man in these times," she insisted.

"Kiowas do not need white men," Autumn Thunder said. "Addo-eta has told me what happens to people who take the hand of the white man. I have seen for myself what happens to men who take the hand of the white man."

"I am not asking you to take his hand," she said. "I am asking you to let him live."

"So he may come back and kill me the next time we fight?"

"I have spent much time with him," she said. "I know his heart. He is not a warrior like you are a warrior. He does not want to kill you or any other warrior. If you had heard some of the things he has told me, you would know that soon will come the hardest fight the Kiowas have ever had, and he has told me you cannot win."

"We have talked of this before. Why should he be telling you the truth?"

"It is not that I believe his words because they come from his mouth," she said. "I am very young and it is hard for me to tell truth from lies. But his words fit with what I have seen."

"What have you seen?"

"I have seen your new rifle."

"*My* new rifle?"

"The one you took in the wagon fight."

"What about it?" he asked.

"It is a much better rifle than any you ever had before, is that not true?"

"Yes it is," he said proudly. "It is a finer rifle than any I have seen in my village, better than what most of the soldiers have."

"Tell me," she said. "Have you ever seen a warrior come into your village from another village with a bow that is a better bow than any you have ever seen?"

He thought for a moment, then he laughed. "Of course not," he said. "A bow is a bow."

"That is how white men are different," she said. "To them a rifle is not just a rifle. Everybody in my village has to take a stick and push a bullet down the front of the rifle to load. Your rifle is not like that. I have seen how you do it. You push one bullet in and then another, and another and then when you shoot it you shoot one, then another, and another."

"Is that not fine?" he asked. "Think of how many whites I could kill in a battle with a fine rifle like this?"

"But don't you see? They will always have a newer rifle that shoots faster, or farther."

"We will just buy them from Caddo George."

"Did you buy your new rifle from Caddo George?"

"Of course not. You know I took it off a dead white man in Texas."

"And you think you will always have a dead white man in Texas to give you his new rifle?"

He thought about it, his brow furrowed with the seriousness of his thoughts. Then he smiled. "Yes," he said. "There will always be a dead white man with a better rifle. But I understand what you are telling me. We will take the man to Fort Sill."

But as the walls of the stone corral began to appear beyond the next rise, Autumn Thunder began to have second thoughts.

"I have heard from other hunters that the bluecoats have been out trying to force the Kiowas and Comanches to come back to the reservation. I have heard that Au-sai-mah is down near Red River and that is where we will go."

He turned to Sweeney, who was slumped over in his saddle, still far too weak to fend for himself.

"Tell him that we will wait for nightfall before we go in."

"Why?" Gathers The Grass asked.

"Just tell him," Autumn Thunder answered, annoyed, and when she did she was surprised to see the lieutenant nod his agreement, or at least his understanding without objection.

They ate cold deer meat and drank creek water and waited for dark. When it came Autumn Thunder led the other two in a wide sweep that ended nearly a mile south of the post. Then they moved directly north toward the twinkling lights of the officers' houses and Evans's trading store.

When they were a quarter of a mile from the post, he had them stop. Quietly he put an ear to the air, to listen for the hoofbeats of any patrols in the area.

"Ask him if he feels strong enough to make it to the post alone," Autumn Thunder said.

She complied. Sweeney looked at Autumn Thunder and nodded.

"Good," he said, walking his pony up to Sweeney's mule. He patted the cavalry lieutenant on his wounded shoulder and Sweeney winced.

"Good, good, you go soon," said Autumn Thunder, using nearly his entire English vocabulary in the process. Strange, Sweeney thought, the Kiowa's eyes still seemed to blaze with hatred, and yet his voice was gentle. For the first time in his tains experience, he wondered what was on the mind of an Indian.

Later that evening, when the moon ducked behind the clouds, Autumn Thunder led Sweeney's mule as close as he dared to the post. "Can you go from here?" Gathers The Grass asked.

Sweeney nodded, but he seemed so feeble that she thought he might not be able to make it.

"Let me go in with him," she said.

"You will not go," Autumn Thunder said. "I do not trust them."

"It will be all right," she insisted, but he was adamant.

"No," he said, simply.

"Can we at least stay and see if he gets to the gate without falling off his mule? If he does not make it and dies, they will say that the Kiowas killed him."

Autumn Thunder thought for a moment. Then he agreed.

They waited again, this time for the moon to come out from behind the clouds. They rode part of the way with him, then they sent him toward the gate. It was a bright moon, almost full, so they still had a glimpse of him as he approached the gate. When they heard a sentry call out, and heard the weak response from Sweeney, they felt it was all right to go.

As for Sweeney, waves of dizziness were beginning to wash over him as his mule walked quietly through the gate and turned of its own accord toward the stone corral.

"Halt!" cried the sentry, and Sweeney pulled on the reins just hard enough to bring the animal to a stop.

He felt nauseous, a feeling to which he had become accustomed since he had been launched from his horse and onto his head during the fight with the Kiowas. He felt hands help him down from the mule. He heard a cry for the post surgeon, and heard the sentry exclaim that it was Lieutenant Sweeney all right, that everybody had assumed he'd been killed, and that he looked as if he had come mighty close to dying.

Strong hands helped him into the post infirmary, helped him undress, and helped get him between clean sheets for the first time since the last time he had been in a hotel in St. Louis.

The fever was not quite gone, not then, not for the next week. While his fellow officers tried to imagine what kinds of torments he might have endured to reduce him from his robust if boozy hundred and ninety pounds down to the sparse, emaciated remnant spread across his six foot frame, he dreamed a lot. The dream was always the same, with annoying minor variations—of him being unhorsed by a warrior with a long, feathered lance.

Sometimes the warrior came in the form of a young child on a huge cavalry horse. Sometimes the warrior rode a mule and his face was seamed with lines of great age, and sometimes he was in the prime of life riding a dappled Indian pony. Sometimes Sweeney was able to empty the cylinder of his Colt at the warrior—*bam-bam-bam-bam-bam*, five quick shots that left his pistol hot and smoking, and useless; sometimes the gun would jam after one or two shots; mostly he would raise the pistol and pull back the hammer but his horse would not allow him to bring the barrel to bear on his adversary before the lance would pierce his shoulder and he would go flying from the back of his horse onto the hard earth, headfirst.

When he was awake, he was forever calling for water and they were forever giving it to him, which did not help him very much, because the infirmary was located on a creek a quarter of a mile downstream from where the cavalry units watered their horses.

But he had an iron constitution that pulled him through in spite of the army's best efforts to kill him.

He thought about the dream a lot, and only gradually, as his mind cleared and his body healed, did it begin to dawn on him that the man who had almost killed him might possibly have been the same as the one who joylessly saved his life, then set him free.

He thought about Autumn Thunder, the fierce and angry look that softened only occasionally, always in the presence of Gathers The Grass. Both the Kiowa brave and the Wichita girl seemed so young and yet not at all children. The young man in particular seemed so wise and yet so impenetrably stupid.

Even Gathers The Grass seemed to lack the ability to grasp the things he was trying to tell her. She was a lovely young woman, in an Indian sort of way, and at one point he thought he had been on the verge of talking her into his bed, but then the fever had overtaken him again, and when he had next become conscious of the world around him, the Kiowa had moved in on him and she had lost interest.

It was probably for the better, he had thought. For one thing, Indian woman were always spreading venereal diseases among the soldiers—or so he had heard—for another, it was. obviously Gathers The Grass who had won his freedom from Autumn Thunder. Perhaps she had even given herself to the Kiowa in return for his—Sweeney's—life. She had so much as told him so, he had thought, but then, it was hard to understand what either Gathers The Grass or Autumn Thunder were really thinking.

Indians were just different from whites. They were undeniably human, he thought—not beasts as some of the officers and men believed—but still, different. And yet, ragged and poor though they were, they had a pride about them, a belief in their own ability to survive and triumph, that so defied logic that he wondered who was the fool, they or he?

As his vision cleared and he became more sensible to the white sheets and the words of the surgeon and the orderlies around him, he remembered where the superiority lay. But from now on he would always regard the red men more as puzzles than contemptible beasts. And he would never forget the long conversations he had had with Gathers The Grass, conversations that had led to greater respect between them without leading to anything like real understanding.

Their minds had come so close to each other in passing, but had never really touched.

Autumn Thunder and Gathers The Grass camped a mile west of the fort and with the first slender pink fingers of dawn on the eastern horizon rode west toward the north fork of Red River. There, a day's ride hence, he knew he would find his band's tall, majestic tepees thrusting upward through the early morning mist of the river.

And they were there all right, together with the delicious smells and happy sounds familiar to him all his life. His spirits rose as they came down over the last long rise that led to the village, but he could not help wondering how his friends and family would take to the young Wichita woman he was bringing with him.

He wished his mother were there to welcome them. What-

ever he did had always been fine with his mother. She would
have made Gathers The Grass feel comfortable. She would
have understood Gathers The Grass, and the strong, spirit, independent and yet loyal, that had attracted Autumn Thunder
to her. She had always told Autumn Thunder to find a woman
with a strong proud spirit.

"A strong woman makes a great warrior greater," she had
said. "When life is bad," she said, "the strong woman will
stand beside you and help you through it, but a weak woman
will look for a warrior who is having better days, and she will
go to him, and feel protected and secure.

"That is a foolish woman," his mother had said. "The life
of a warrior can be so short. No warrior can protect a woman
forever. She must protect herself and her children. And if she
does not need a warrior to protect her, then she can find a
man who is good to her. A good man."

A good man. Gathers The Grass was always telling him that
he was a good man. She had said that Sweeney was a good
man, though Autumn Thunder could only see a white man.

As they made their way through the grove of cottonwoods
that led to the village, he was proud to see how tall she sat
her mule, not looking to him for reassurance, but looking
straight ahead, strong and calm. A fit woman for a strong
warrior, that was what he thought, and he did not doubt that
his friends and his relatives would accept her. And if they did
not, he did not doubt that she would be fine anyway.

The first tepee they passed belonged to Seven Doves, the
young wife of Ko-yah-te, who was his friend since childhood,
more precious to him than ever since their friend Hau-tau had
been killed in the fight with the teamsters. And it was Ko-yah-
te who spotted them first as they rode in.

"My brother!" he shouted boisterously. "And—"

He was about to make some sort of inappropriate remark
about Wichitas in general and Wichita women in particular,
but there was something in the look of Gathers The Grass that
stopped him cold.

"Aho!" he said, and then his mind struggled for more carefully chosen words. "My brother has much to tell me, is it
not so?" he said.

Chapter 13

It was the sweetest winter of Autumn Thunder's life. Gathers The Grass adapted quickly to the Kiowa way, even though she did not like the Kiowa contempt for the more peaceful tribes, such as her Wichitas. She was a strong woman in both mind and body, and he was drawn to her strength and her ability to think for herself. Yet he was not a weak man, he was simply a man who wanted a partner, and not a child to take care of.

By this time the Kiowas had settled down from their panic over the arrest of the three chiefs. They didn't like it, but Lone Wolf and Kicking Bird had convinced them that the soldiers would not attack, and that if they behaved, the chiefs would be returned.

During their courtship, Gathers the Grass's behavior had always been correct according to the strict ideas of her parents. This was the side of Gathers The Grass that Autumn Thunder had seen. He had pursued her in spite of her reserved behavior. But then they were married, and the full tide of feelings that came with their first night together in their own tepee swept aside all boundaries that remained between them.

It was the sorriest tepee he had ever lived in, with an old outer lining donated by Ko-yah-te's mother after she had finished stitching together a new one out of twenty-one buffalo skins. The lodgepoles were worn out sticks of wood collected from families that had recently gone north to cut some new lodgepoles for their tepees.

Many of the young women in the village came by to watch Seven Doves try to teach Gathers The Grass how to put up the tepee. The two of them struggled, and the tepee went up slowly, with many a slip that made the young women first snicker, then laugh until tears ran down their faces.

Leave it to a Wichita woman to be so stupid that she could not even put up a tepee. A number of the young women who had been interested in Autumn Thunder got particular satisfaction out of seeing her struggle first with the poles then with the heavy old tepee cover.

"He'll leave her lodge inside a year," they told each other. "No Kiowa warrior could be satisfied with a Wichita girl. After all, Wichitas aren't really even people."

The lodgepoles were too short so the old tepee covering sagged on the ground. The bottom of the covering was so rotten that the wind ripped the skin off the pegs and the cold crept through like an evil miasma. The smokehole poles were so short that they could not control the flaps. Gathers The Grass built the fire outside and promised Autumn Thunder that their first night together inside their new home she would keep him so warm that they would not miss the fire.

She was true to her word. Without the fire inside he could barely make out her trim young body as she stepped out of her cotton trade dress and came to him. Deep in the cold gloom of the lodge, her curves and angles stirred a passion in him that he had not known during his days with her in the Wichita village.

She reached her hand to him and let him pull her down onto the soft buffalo skin that was their bed. They lay down together and pulled several more buffalo skins over them, and waited for the heat of their bodies to fill the space around them. They did not have to wait long, and soon their hands were exploring. They were both shy that first night, and their shyness made them slow and patient.

But gradually patience gave way to passion. The caresses became firmer, surer. He was amazed and thrilled to find that her feelings could equal his.

When his body moved toward her she rose to meet him, gave a soft cry that might have been pain, but repeated her movement, first gingerly, gently, then with greater and greater desire until time and place dissolved into feeling and motion and desire.

When they were both spent, they clung to each other, each

feeling tenderness toward the other such as they had never felt during their courtship.

Gathers The Grass saw a great difference between the Wichita way and the Kiowa way. The Wichitas stayed in one place and planted fields of melons and corn. They were sensible savers, and if the summer was good, there was plenty of food to last them through the winter.

The Kiowas often did not have much food in their lodges. They were hunting nomads. If the game did not come to them, they folded their tepees, hitched their lodgepoles behind their horses, and off they went, in search of a better place to hunt.

The snow was on the ground but not deep when they crossed the Red River into Texas, not to raid, but because some of their hunters had found buffalo, lots of buffalo, down on the Brazos. It was good to get away from their winter camp, good to move out into the open Texas plains where their tough, wiry ponies could crop the yellow grass beneath the snow.

Men, women, and children all rode. Those without good mounts borrowed from those who had spares. Some of the wealthier Kiowas had many spares. Autumn Thunder's three mules saw service, bearing some of the heavier and poorer people, people too poor to even participate in the hunt.

The wind howled in the faces of the children, but Kiowas were used to hardship, and in their world a hundred-mile jaunt in the face of a winter wind was no cruel twist of life but merely a thing to be done. Gaunt, wolflike camp dogs tagged along effortlessly, sometimes halting their progress to chase each other in circles, then running to catch up with the moving village. Only the old suffered terribly, and eventually it was decided to erect a small group of tepees along the way for them to stay until the hunt was over, then the band would collect them on the way back to the reservation.

Ahead of the main body and the large herd of spare ponies that moved with them traveled a half dozen scouts fanned out toward the west, searching for signs of the sacred beasts. The fifth day out, when the sun was directly overhead, a warrior called Pone-audle-tone guided his pony down a low hill until he had nearly reached the level plain, then he eased his pony into a slow gallop, back and forth, back and forth across the snowy slope.

Excitement spread through the long parade of mounted ponies. Pone-audle-tone had found the buffalo. Immediately the group changed direction from southwest to directly west, until they had reached Pone-audle-tone. They followed him over the hill and found themselves riding over snow trampled and flattened by the big buffalo hooves. All knew the herd was near, so nobody was surprised when chief Au-sai-mah ordered them to stop and set up camp.

Women paired off and quickly erected the tepee village among the sheltering cottonwoods and oaks that grew along the river. Many of them had brought all the comforts of home with them on their travois, including inner liners, backrests, buffalo robes, woolen trade blankets, and camp kettles. The older children walked along the river gathering fallen boughs, which they piled in old buffalo robes and dragged back to camp with them. Then they trudged back up or down the river for another load, again and gain, until the women were certain there was enough wood gathered to last the day and night.

Soon thin white smoke could be seen rising through the smokehole of one tepee, then another. The lodges were erected close to each other, and the smoke from each tepee spread out and joined the other smokes to create a sheltering white cover. "There," the smoke seemed to say, "you are now all together under one roof."

The women and their families gladly sought refuge in their cozy lodges, and as the sun sank below distant hills, the lodge fires cast a glow through the skins that made the tepees glow like warm lanterns in the cold dark.

Autumn Thunder stepped out into the cold and looked back at his tepee, which had undergone numerous improvements since the first day after their wedding. Gathers The Grass had made them a beautiful home within, though she had never before lived in such a dwelling. She was tough and resourceful, as he knew she would be, but more, she loved him, and showed it, and he drank up that love as if he had been wandering in a desert for many years.

The glow of his lodge echoed the glow he felt within him, the most complete satisfaction of his life. She had felt ill when they had risen at dawn for what they knew would be the last day of their outbound journey, and he felt fear for her future. Women died young sometimes, he knew, especially in giving birth, and the briefest thought of losing her was enough to send tears to the edge of his eyelids.

But she had shrugged off her dizziness with a smile, swallowed hard to hold down her breakfast, and mounted her pony with easy strength to begin the day's journey. The spell must have passed, because she felt in high spirits the next morning as he left the lodge and headed for the ceremonial tepee that had been erected farthest downriver.

Inside, Chief Au-sai-mah lit his ceremonial pipe, blew a great puff of smoke, and opened the council more quickly than usual. The main herd was spread along the river for several miles, but one group of several hundred were in a valley with two hills beyond them. If they moved out quickly they could do a surround and kill many buffalo, Au-sai-mah said.

"You, Po-lan-te," he said, sternly. "You like to go your own way, but we cannot do this now. To survive this winter we must have a good buffalo hunt, and kill many buffalo. We have chosen the men who will preserve order in the hunt. Whoever disobeys them will be whipped in front of everybody. It is never good to have to say such things but this is not for honors. This is not for coups."

Po-lan-te laughed at the idea of him counting coup on a buffalo. Nobody else laughed.

"This is for the food and shelter of your women and your children. It will be a terrible winter for us unless we kill many buffalo this day." The chief looked around the tepee into the faces that flickered in the dancing flames. "Do you hear me, Po-lan-te?" he asked.

The big, burly, troublesome young Kiowa whom the chief had chosen as an example growled a rough, reluctant assent. Then the chief gave his instructions as to how he wanted to carry out the hunt. The Kiowa men listened. Most of them had done a surround before, many times and they knew what was coming.

He took them all outside. "When the sun is there"—and he pointed toward a place in the sky where the sun was due in less than two hours—"I want you there." He pointed to a level field not completely covered with newly trampled snow.

The marshals of the hunt, Tsein-kop-te and Tau-ankia, inspected the weapons of the younger braves and gave last bits of advice to the men they felt needed it. Tsein-kop-te threw a final warning at Po-lan-te. More than two dozen braves mounted their best ponies, even though they knew that they were risking them to the horns of the great shaggy beasts. Every man, including the youngest, most glory-hungry of the braves, understood that the lives of their loved ones depended upon their performance this day.

In two columns they walked their ponies up the long, slope ahead and spread across the skyline when they reached the crest. In the distance, a rugged bluff to their backs, were nearly two hundred buffalo with their matted, shaggy winter coats, a wonderful sight for the hunters. They reformed into the two columns and rode easily down the hill so that one column was well to the left of the herd and the other column was well to the right.

If the buffalo were aware of the presence of the men, they gave no sign, but continued to nibble at the winter grass beneath the snow. So far, so good. The herd was now hemmed in on three sides.

The chief raised his feathered lance. When he brought the lance down the warriors from both sides converged on the herd at full gallop, waving blankets and shrieking their war cries.

The herd began to run east, toward the open end, out of their trap, but the riders closest to the lead buffalo outflanked him and rode straight for him. Nostrils flared wide with panic, he turned suddenly to flee from his tormentors. The buffalo closest to him also turned, which drove them head-on into the rest of the herd, some of which turned, some of which did not. The result was a huge mass collision that sealed their fate. Without leadership they could not drive in any one direction. The collision in the front ranks had the effect of throwing up a great wall. Succeeding ranks of the beasts plowed into the animals in front of them, bringing them to a halt and confusing them to the point where they just milled around aimlessly, bellowing in terror while the Kiowas began their bloody work. Some used their lances, driving them deep into the buffalo, often piercing their hearts with the first thrust.

Others rode close enough to touch the buffalo, then pulled back their bowstring and drove a shaft so deep into the crea-

tures that not much more than the feathered ends stuck out.
Still others, like Autumn Thunder, had enough ammunition
left to fire their rifles point blank into the buffalos.

Some of the animals sank to their knees, rolled onto their
sides, and lay still. Others had enough left to turn and charge
their slayers, attempting to sink their horns into the side of a
horse even as the lifeblood poured from their bodies onto the
heavily trodden white snow.

The frightened, stubborn, stampeding buffalo stirred the
white dry powder snow into the air in feathery geysers. Many
of the shaggy creatures were screaming with pain and outrage
as they dashed and thrashed about in their final moments of
torment before their hearts ceased to beat and they lay still in
the snow.

In ones and twos and sixes they died, but one mighty bull
with a heart so tough that even a direct hit from an arrow
would not still it sank its horns deep into the side of Ko-yah-
te's pony. The animal cried out in mortal terror, reared up and
threw Ko-yah-te from its back.

Autumn Thunder had just levered a cartridge into the chamber of his rifle, ridden into the herd until his left knee was up
against the shaggy coat of a great beast, pressed the barrel of
his rifle into the animal's back, above the heart, and pulled the
trigger. He felt the buffalo shudder, then watched its running
gait degenerate to a shamble followed by a heavy fall into the
snow. Autumn Thunder looked up to see if anybody had witnessed the kill, but what he saw was Ko-yah-te dodging
among the milling buffaloes, striving desperately to stay out
from underneath the hooves of the frightened animals.

"*Heyah*!" he shouted, and used the stock of his rifle to prod
the animals and get them out of his way. A large cow knocked
Ko-yah-te sprawling into the snow, end over end, but the ath-
letic young brave rolled right into a standing position, his eyes
searching wildly for a safe place to go.

Autumn Thunder forgot about his own kill as he turned his
pony and raced for his trapped friend. From the opposite direction came a big dappled gray horse. Po-lan-te! Neatly as if
they'd rehearsed it, Po-lan-te grabbed the downed warrior under his right arm and swung him onto the back of his mount.

His pony sensed a gap between two large bulls and headed
for it. For a moment it seemed as if the pony would win free,

but a young cow, maddened from the pain of a lance thrust deep into her, bumped the pony on her blind side. The pony shied to her left, ran into a buffalo calf and still managed to keep its feet, but the wounded cow was still coming, smack into the pony, bowling her over and knocking the two young warriors off her back.

Autumn Thunder rode in quickly and pulled Ko-yah-te up behind him, but Po-lan-te was left to his own resources, on his feet amidst a half dozen huge, frightened, milling, buffalo. Dead game, he dodged among the creatures, looking for a way out, but he was caught in a vortex of lowered horns and stomping hooves.

Agile as a ceremonial dancer he avoided the horns of the bellowing bulls and even grabbed hold of the matted fur of one of them, trying to leap on its back. But the fur was wet and his hands slipped, just as the animal was bumped hard by one of its neighbors.

Seeing the struggle of Po-lan-te, Autumn Thunder did not ride clear of the herd, but plunged deeper into it, as Po-lan-te lost his footing in the snow and went down under the hooves of the herd. For a moment he disappeared, but Autumn Thunder did not give up.

He charged his pony between and around the buffalo until he caught a glimpse of his downed cohort, and headed straight for him. As his pony passed the downed figure, Ko-yah-te reached down and fastened an iron grip on Po-lan-te's ankle. Autumn Thunder's tough pony slipped for a moment in the churned up snow, then pulled hard, in a labored gallop at first, then with greater speed, toward the outer edge of the herd.

Po-lan-te's body slid easily over the snow, and soon it was bouncing over the plains as the pony worked to put distance between herself and the bellowing, dying, blood-scented herd.

Ko-yah-te slid down off the back of the pony and knelt beside Po-lan-te who, miraculously, was still alive. Autumn Thunder did not linger but moved his weary pony back toward the herd, watching for any animals that might escape the surround.

By now, nearly half the buffalo were down. If one was wounded enough to be disabled, the Kiowas did not finish it off but ignored it, knowing that the animal was too badly injured to get away. To them it was not a massacre but a harvest, a winter's worth of food, blankets, tepee coverings, bowstrings, pillow stuffing, sewing needles, and hide scrapers.

Autumn Thunder's pony recovered rapidly from her exertions. He checked that his rifle was loaded, picked out a cow and calf that had become separated from the herd, rode close up to the cow and dispatched it with a single shot through the heart. The calf did not try to run away. Frightened and confused as it was, it remained with the still body of its mother until Autumn Thunder killed it with a quick, merciful shot.

The young Kiowa spotted a large remnant of the herd disappearing into a draw beyond the slaughter, but he declined to chase it. There were many carcasses lying in the snow, surrounded by great bloodstained circles, and those that still survived within the killing area were so confused and traumatized that they stood still or walked slowly, head down, while the warriors finished them off.

Already the people who had not been in the hunt, older men as well as the women and the older children, were approaching, knives in hand, singing their praises for the warriors who had made the hunt such a great success. But first the hunters surged forward and sank their knives into the animals, cut out their livers, and began to devour the organs raw, blood dripping down their chins and their arms.

The women started their bloody work on the animals, spreading out old worn buffalo skins on the ground. They removed the hides from the animals, cut out the organs and placed them on the old skins, then began to cut up the steaming, bloody, raw chunks of meat.

A lone angry spectator crouched behind a rock on a distant hill, staring though a pair of binoculars. The great white hunter Tuck crouched behind a rock. This was supposed to be his herd. He had been tracking it for two days.

Tuck hated hunting buffalo in the winter, but he had experienced a bad run of cards at Fort Sill, swelling the purses of Sweeney, Evans, and Horace Jones, among others. He was hunting because he was broke. He had been out for two weeks without spotting a single buffalo. One of his skinners had deserted him, leaving him with a skinny old asthmatic named Weaver, surely the worst skinner in the territory but one of the few who would brave the cold and the Kiowas at this time.

They had no luck until they spotted the tracks of the herd, and after tracking it more than ten miles, they heard gunshots, which told them that someone had found the herd first.

He left Weaver behind and galloped over several hills before he found a peak where he could observe the hunt and its aftermath. He was furious. Those were his buffalo! He'd found them first! Damn them! he thought, watching the deadly efficient Kiowa assembly line turn a small herd of wild, live buffalo into bundles of flesh and bones.

Damn them!

The women would be working through most of the day removing every bit of every carcass that was useful to them. They did not shiver in the gloomy cold. Since it was not extreme they were used to it and did not consider it a hardship or a cause for complaint.

In the meantime, Po-lan-te lay against a rock, pale and silent. He was bruised from head to toe, woefully sore, but the licks and buffets he had received from the buffalo would have mattered little to him had not one great bull stepped on his forearm and broken it.

"My brother Po-lan-te, I saw that you went into the hunt today with your hair loose," said Tsen-aut-te, the village healer.

Po-lan-te nodded his head but could not speak, so great was the pain. Nor did he groan.

"You know that one of your taboos is that you must tie your hair behind you before you go into battle or the hunt. Why then did you not do it?"

Po-lan-te would not answer. He was not the most religious of Kiowas and he did not want to be nagged into answering questions about things he did not care about. The sacred man continued:

"You know that your taboo demands that you go into the hunt or battle with your hair tied behind you by a black ribbon."

Po-lan-te nodded his head impatiently. "I forgot," he said through clenched teeth. "You must fix my arm. Give me some water."

In the light of torches the hunters helped the women to complete the work. Before long the carcasses had been reduced to little more than bones and bits of muscle and tendon. The rest had been wrapped in bundles, tied to horses, and brought back to the temporary village by the Brazos River. Autumn Thunder laid claim to three hides that would go toward the new tepee covering Gathers The Grass would make when he had accumulated eighteen more.

Quietly, wearily, the people stoked their homefires and pulled their robes and blankets around them. Autumn Thunder and Gathers The Grass lay in each other's arms watching the flames cast flickering shadows on the walls of their lodge, which Gathers The Grass had worked on patiently. She had also found enough odds and ends of skins and cloth to create a liner for the lower part of the dwelling walls.

The wind no longer whistled through a dozen holes and cracks. Autumn Thunder found it to be a snug, pleasant home, a home that would be even better when he rode north toward the big mountains and brought back tall, sturdy new lodgepoles, and when he had amassed enough new buffalo skins for Gathers The Grass to sew into a beautiful new tepee cover.

For a while they lay in silence listening to the night sounds. Other than the wind, the night seemed especially silent.

Now came the biting loneliness in his chest, pangs like fangs. On this night he held Gathers The Grass closer to him to ease the pangs, but they only made him worry. Like a bridle on an unbroken pony, the whites were squeezing in on them, closer and closer, pushing them into smaller spaces. Go here! Don't go there! Stay on the reservation! Don't go to Texas! Don't go to Mexico! Do not search for the buffalo. Stay home and plant corn like the Wichitas! It made Autumn Thunder choke to think about it.

Tay-nay-angopte had said that they would somehow have to learn to live with the whites, because some day the whites would be everywhere. The other chiefs hated Tay-nay-angopte when he said such things. But suppose he was right? What is the use of learning to live with others if the others are so murderous that they won't let *you* live?

As they lay together, Gathers The Grass felt his worry. She knew what was on his mind. They had spoken of it only the night before. Tonight was a night to think about being a Kiowa *now*.

"As we were cutting the hides," she said, "the women were talking about the hunt. Some were watching from the hill. They saw you rescue Ko-yah-te and then they saw you both as you saved Po-lan-te. They say that at the ceremony tomorrow you will be given a new name."

"I do not want a new name. My father gave me my name. It will always be my name."

"I am glad. You are Autumn Thunder to me and I would not want to learn to live with somebody of another name. And yet you will be called by another name and you will be pleased to answer to it."

"I will never answer to another name," he replied stubbornly.

"You will answer when your child calls *you* father," she said, and in the flickering light of the fire, he could see her beautiful white teeth as her lips curled into a smile. The pang vanished from his chest. He had no more room there for pangs. Not now. When one child came, another soon followed. Unlike some other braves who remained dedicated sporting warriors until they died a glorious death in some distant scrap with the Utes or the Pawnees, Autumn Thunder knew that his first thoughts must be of his family.

Nobody knew where his father's bones rested. The same must not happen to him.

Chapter 14

Tuck may have been good at wiping out isolated Indian families, but he had no desire to do battle with a band of Kiowa warriors. He had noted the escape of a small remnant of the buffalo herd, slim pickings for a big-time buffalo hunter like him, but he was desperate to kill and skin something. He and Weaver could even use the meat.

He had to wait to see which direction the Kiowas would be traveling so he could go the other way. He was a man of much action and little imagination, but slowly it dawned on him that if by some chance they were able to discover him on his distant ridge they would stake him to the ground and dismember him joint by joint.

But he was obsessed by the handful of buffalo that had escaped the Kiowa's hunt, and the only way for him to find them was by picking up the trail from the site of the hunt and following it. Surely they would be leaving soon. They weren't supposed to be hunting south of Red River. If the army caught them down on the Brazos there would be a fight.

He wrapped himself in two of his warmest buffalo robes and watched and waited on his hill, while his skinner Weaver whined that they had best be going home if they didn't want to be spitted and roasted.

"Shut up," Tuck said in a very soft voice although the Kiowa camp was nearly a half mile away. "They're packing up. They're finally gettin' the hell out of here. I swear we'll get those buffalo. Tell you what else we'll do. After we get the buffalo we'll pick up their trail and if any of them lag behind we'll kill 'em and take their skins. Their women cut a hide a hell of a lot better'n you do, I'll tell you that.''

A single snowflake landed on his nose and melted. Another soon followed. There were more, then many more. His spirit sank.

''Get the hell out of here!'' he cried, inwardly, toward the Kiowas, who were packing far too slowly to suit him.

In fact they had stopped packing. Their chief was staring at the sky watching the snow thicken minute by minute. Tuck focused his binoculars on the trail of escaped buffalo that led through a notch in the hills on the other side of the valley. The trail was still there but he knew that within an hour's time it would be gone forever.

''Get my horse ready, Weaver!'' he commanded. ''As soon as they've left the valley, we're ridin' down there to get to that buffalo trail before it's completely covered.''

Weaver shook his head. This man is crazy, he thought, but because Tuck frightened him even more than the Kiowas did, he did not argue. Tuck had put down his binoculars and turned a deadly glare on Weaver to make the man obey quickly. But when he faced the valley again and raised his binoculars, Weaver saw him stiffen. Lodgepoles were being reset on the ground. The women were climbing on each other's shoulders to re-cover the lodgepoles with buffalo skins. Men were unburdening the ponies, and children were spreading out across the valley looking for old buffalo chips for the fires.

There was no question about it. The Kiowas were staying.

The sound that issued from Tuck's throat was soft but raspy and guttural with squelched emotion. Weaver thought it sounded like a combination of a cougar being strangled and a sawmill.

His eyes grew wide with disbelief as he saw Tuck pick up his buffalo gun and check it to see if it was ready for firing. Either Tuck was going to take his anger out on the buffalo skinner or he was going hunting for Kiowa meat. Either way, Weaver did not want to be around. Slowly at first, he crept down the back side of the hill then he picked up the pace, and soon broke into a dead run to hitch the team to the wagon. If he had turned around then, he would have seen that Tuck had left his observation point on the hill.

*　　*　　*

Autumn Thunder was not displeased when he heard Au-sai-mah give the command to rebuild the camp. Not that he disliked traveling in the snow. He didn't mind at all. But he was glad for any excuse that would keep them in Texas, far away from Fort Sill. Sometimes the sight of Fort Sill gave him an ache in his belly. There lived the men who thought they had the right to tell Kiowas what to do and where to go.

"Ko-yah-te!" he shouted to his friend, as they left the pony herd and walked back to the circle of tepees on the north bank of the Brazos. "Come to our lodge tonight. Gathers The Grass has a special way of cooking buffalo, like her mother learned from the Caddos."

Ko-yah-te smiled. "I like the way my woman cooks food like my own mama did like her mama do. Why try food like the Wichita? Suppose I don't like it. Have to eat it anyway or Grass's feelings be hurt, then you get mad at me and I lose a friend. No-no. I stay home tonight with my woman and eat Kiowa food."

Autumn Thunder smiled good-naturedly. Every man should have a friend as good as Ko-yah-te. "Man should eat what he wants," he said. They had stopped walking, and were looking at each other, when suddenly Ko-yah-te's chest gushed red. His friend opened his mouth wide to cry out, but no sound came.

The breath ran out of Autumn Thunder as he saw his friend fall. Thinking they were being attacked by soldiers, he looked around, but all he could see was the pony herd in one direction, and the village in the other. Swiftly, he knelt by his friend, but death had arrived there first. He glanced at the distant hills, but saw nothing. Men and women were running over from all directions.

"Come with me!" he cried, and four young warriors ran with him to the ponies. There was no time to lose if they were to catch a killer. By now the snow was blowing in so thick the hills were disappearing behind a falling sheet of white. Quickly the men mounted up. With the wailing of women ripping through the cold air behind them, they rode off toward the nearest hills, intending to make a wide circle around the camp, hoping to pick up a trail.

At a swift gallop they made their way around the encircling hills, heedless of the slippery snow and the limited vision. By bad luck they started on the wrong side of the valley, and by the time they reached the place where Tuck had dropped behind a large rock, rested his rifle on top, and fired a single round at the most exposed Kiowa warrior, the snow had nearly wiped out his tracks.

When he saw the depression in the snow Autumn Thunder immediately understood what had happened. In his hurry to leave the shooting place, Tuck had failed to retrieve the spent shell from his rifle. Autumn Thunder's keen eyes quickly found the near-buried piece of brass, and knew that it was a big, high-powered buffalo hunter's shell.

Only Autumn Thunder had dismounted to investigate the site. He leaped atop his pony and pointed downhill at a barely visible set of footprints leading to a less visible set of hoofprints. A short distance farther the hoofprints joined a set of wagon tracks. The wind was blowing a frigid gale in their faces. Desperate to overtake the enemy and make him pay, they cut through the gale only to find that the wind had blown drifts across their path and obscured the tracks completely.

They did not give up. Frantically they surged forward against the wind for another two hours hoping against hope to get a glimpse of the assassins through the thick, blowing snowstorm. At last, a young warrior named Talia-koi shook his head. "We'd better go back," he said, "or we'll never find our way home."

"You men go back," Autumn Thunder responded in a shaking voice. "I'm not quitting till I find them!"

Talia-koi seized at Autumn Thunder's bridle. Autumn Thunder swiped at his hand with his quirt.

"Come, my brother," said another of the young warriors, "It is no use. They probably turned off from this way a long time ago."

"Go home!" Autumn Thunder shouted. "I must find them!"

"You will die out here alone. Then how will your woman and your child that she'll soon have survive without you?"

Autumn Thunder kicked his pony, hard. It broke free from the grasp of Talia-koi. "You go home!" he shouted, as he and his pony vanished into the snowstorm.

"We cannot follow him," said Talia-koi. "He is crazy with grief."

Reluctantly they turned for home.

Alone, riding around in the snowstorm, his anger and grief cooled enough for his reason to tell him that finding the killer of his best friend in the snowstorm was impossible. He turned his face to the sky and let loose an incomprehensible scream, which was lost in the roaring gale. Then he turned his pony around and let it find its own way back to the village, where he hoped to catch a last glimpse of his lifelong friend Ko-yah-te.

Chapter 15

A warm wind had been blowing through the camp for a week. Green shoots were popping through the old yellow grass, and young men swore they could smell the spring coming. They had planned to hold a horse-stealing dance, but Au-sai-mah and Tsein-kop-te insisted that the time was still too early. "You always forget that after the first thaw always comes the last freeze," said the old chief. "And you will be out on your pony in the middle of a snowstorm with icicles dripping off your nose wishing you were back in your warm lodge smoking your pipe and eating your wife's buffalo stew. Why do young men have such short memories?" he asked.

The young men had been through enough winter to see the sense of their chief.

And he had much more to say. "We can stay here," he said, "only if we have our men out always, looking for soldiers and rangers. I will not let the army do to us what they have done to the Cheyennes."

"Why not go back to the reservation?" asked Tsein-kop-te, who was almost as old as Au-sai-mah, but who still held his muscled frame straight and tall, and had little gray in his sleek black hair. "That is where we are supposed to be and the soldiers will not attack us there."

"That is what the soldiers say," answered the chief. "But there are many faces of soldiers. This one is peace chief and says that we are safe. That one is a war chief and he comes down on us and kills our women and children. Then the peace chief says that a new piece of paper tells him that his way was wrong and the way of the war chief is right, and he feels very bad about our dead women and children.

"We are supposed to love him because he is sorry that the war chief burned our village and killed our people. I will tell you, my brother Tsein-kop-te. We will not move back up to the reservation until the real thaw comes, then we will do it quickly and be there when the peace people come out to ask us if we have been good Indians."

"I do not wish to be a good Indian," said Po-lan-te from a place close to the fire. "I wish to be a very bad Indian." He shifted his position and grimaced, for his arm had not healed well and was still painfully swollen.

"My very young brother," Au-sai-mah answered. "I want you to think less about counting coup over dead white enemies and more about saving your people. The whites want us back on the reservation so they will know where we are when they want us dead."

Po-lan-te laughed derisively. "My wise old grandfather," he said. "Is it not true that the bald-head Tatum is still the big man among the whites? He prays the *Tai-bo* prayers for us and says he loves us. I hear he cannot even shoot a gun. He gives us words. What do we have to fear from him?"

Au-sai-mah had to laugh in spite of himself. "Young Po-lan-te, we have nothing to fear from any white man," said the chief. "But we have much to fear from all of them. They have strong weapons and are dangerous. If we are to survive, we must be clever as our brother the coyote."

"What would you have us do," Po-lan-te jeered. "Cower in our tepees all winter?"

"I fear that your injury was not only to your arm but to your head, Po-lan-te," the chief responded. "Our young men must spend less time in their tepees. They must be out on the land, watching for the soldiers. Soldiers move slowly. If we find them before they find us, we can always escape them."

"Why don't we ambush them?" asked Autumn Thunder, to everybody's surprise. Autumn Thunder seldom spoke up in council. Everybody liked him because his deeds were so much greater than his words. For one so young, he was well respected.

Au-sai-mah smiled at him. "We cannot ambush them because we are at peace with them."

"If we are at peace with them," Autumn Thunder asked, "why would they come down on us?"

"Because we are supposed to be on the reservation."

"But we are not on the reservation because we are afraid they might find us there and attack us."

"This is so. If it seems crazy, it is because I fear that white men are crazy. They make wonderful weapons and yet they never seem to know what they are doing. They say one thing and do another—all the time—and then they promise in their god's name that they didn't do it, or that somebody else did it—or that it was really our fault that they did it."

Tsein-kop-te spoke then. "I believe that someday I will awaken and they will be gone, all of them, and the maker of the heavens will tell me that it was all a dream he gave us to convince us that we should no longer make war against the Utes or the Pawnees or all these other people that the white men call Indians."

The others around the council fire gave grunts of agreement, not because they thought the whites would turn out to be a dream—they were *much* too real to be that—but because the idea was so appealing to them that many would have settled for a dream of a world without white men.

"What we will do," Au-sai-mah said, "is send out scouts every day in all directions. If we find a large column of soldiers, we will move west, to the Llano Estacado. If they are a small patrol—then maybe we'll kill them all. But I warn you, if we decide to fight them, we must not let one of them escape."

Winter was like a prison to Autumn Thunder. He was growing tired of the cold plains wind in his face, and his ponies all grew scrawny and weak nibbling at the thin winter grass. Game was often lean and hard to find, and his body craved the fresh vegetables that the women grew in their gardens. Eating away at him was the death of his friend, and the need to find and kill the man who caused that death.

It pleased him to see the colors of spring coming during their daily patrols. The smells of spring also, starting with the damp earth that promised lush grazing for the ponies. Au-sai-mah saw to it that they were split into many small patrols, both to cover the most territory and to make sure that the young men were not tempted to do battle with any soldiers they encountered.

Autumn Thunder and five other braves rode a section to the northwest every day, until they knew every draw, every hill, every creek, wet or dry, in their area. He was pleased to be with Po-lan-te, whose arm was finally healing properly, his friends Talia-koi, Yay-go, and Kone-bo-hone, and steady old Tsein-kop-te. He had three ponies that he considered good running mounts, and he rode each one as often as he could in order to get them all in shape for the summer raiding season.

And he had no doubt there would be a summer raiding season. There had always been a summer raiding season.

Long days on horseback when the air was sweet and mild were a touch of paradise for Autumn Thunder. They would ride several miles from the village then fan out at a slow trot or even a walk over likely approach routes.

The eyes of the younger men were so keen that from the back of a pony they could spot a blade of grass out of place. When they examined the spot more closely they generally found a deer footprint, or maybe the print of an elk. Sometimes they could not figure out what had caused it, and then Tsein-kop-te would say, "Must have been a jackrabbit." After awhile it came to be a standing joke among the young warriors, and one afternoon, when a young warrior called Wounded Deer found the trail of a single buffalo, he fluffed up the grass of three or four of the huge prints, then partly fluffed up another, leaving the next two of the large prints as he found them.

Tsein-kop-te was on the other side of the valley, searching for other possible approaches, when Yay-go called to him. The older warrior came across at the gallop.

"What could this be?" asked Yay-go, deadpan.

Tsein-kop-te studied the half edited depression with great seriousness, while Yay-go went forward as if to continue his search.

After a few moments he saw the old warrior's face relax. "Must be a jackrabbit," he said.

"Must be a very big jackrabbit," Yay-go answered, still deadpan. He, Autumn Thunder, and Po-lan-te had dismounted and were standing by two large buffalo footprints and a buffalo chip that seemed as big as a camp kettle.

Nobody laughed. They didn't have to.

"I want to cover this valley all the way to Blanco Mountain," huffed Tsein-kop-te, clutching his dignity like a blanket in the wind. And he rode back across the valley.

Day after day they found no signs of soldiers. Once they saw a lone rider on a mule off in the distance but before they could go after him, Tsein-kop-te reminded them that they were out there to find soldiers. They would have ignored him but sharp-eyed Po-lan-te quickly made out the figure to be a Caddo who usually hung around Fort Sill. They followed the Caddo for awhile, until they had convinced themselves that he was just a lone Indian trying to get from one place to another.

Sometimes on the way home after a long, tedious, fruitless day of trailing, they'd be feeling frisky enough to hold riding contests. While the others watched, one of them would go galloping across the plain with his body suspended from the far side of his pony, and just a single moccasin and hand on top to present a target.

If the pony stumbled the rider might slip enough to expose the lower part of his body beneath the horse and then he would lose. The three friends gambled various possessions on their contests, but Autumn Thunder was so much the superior rider that at first it seemed as if he would strip his three best friends to abject poverty by the time spring came for good.

But once it had become obvious that these contests were no contest, he began to slip up on purpose so that within a few days they were almost even again. Far from discouraging the contests, Tsein-kop-te watched with interest, his mind going back to a time when *his* pride centered on his horsemanship.

One day he said, "It's just a lot of foolishness, you know. White man can't kill you, but he can sure kill your horse, and a good horse is more valuable than you are, anyway."

This time they all laughed.

One afternoon at the end of the second week of patrolling they found themselves in a valley they had not seen before. They followed along a dry creekbed for several miles then crossed over a saddle between two hills and found themselves looking down into a valley turned snow white by the biggest buffalo kill they had ever seen.

All the way down the valley as far as they could see lay the bleached white bones, many scattered by the flocks of buzzards that must have descended on the valley by the thousands.

Buffalo bones, from one end of the valley to the other! For a moment Autumn Thunder's imagination put hides and sinew back on those bones and sent them thundering across the plains. Each buffalo was so vulnerable to the rifle or the bow. And yet the herds, by their numbers of powerful, massive animals, seemed unending and invincible.

The rumbling buffalo turned back into scattered bones, and suddenly he knew that if the Kiowas did not fight back, some day the bones of his people, all his people, would be scattered over the plains like the bones of this ghastly herd.

Kiowas did not make a practice of sitting astride their horses silhouetted against a skyline, but for once, shocked by what they saw, they forgot about their security.

"They must have had several hunters," said Wounded Deer, quietly. Nobody had to say that white men did it. The bones told the story of thousands of animals left skinned on the plains, their carcasses rotting in the sun, the powerful stench of decay drawing scavengers from miles around to tear hungrily at the flesh and organs of the dead creatures and scatter the bones helter-skelter from one end of the world to the other.

Slowly they descended into the valley with a sense of dread and horror that they ascribed to the souls of the dead buffalo, but it was not only that.

Tsein-kop-te spoke what the others were thinking, or at least feeling. "I once knew a white man," he said. "A hunter of the buffalo. He was full of drink on this night and told me he had killed some great number of buffalo. He said the men in the villages where many people live give him gold for the buffalo skins.

"I asked him why he would kill so many buffalo and he said he must kill buffalo now and get the gold while there are still buffalo on the plains. I asked him if he thought the buffalo would go away from the white man and he laughed—that cruel *Tai-bo* laugh—and he said the buffalo will all be killed.

"I told him that Great Spirit would not allow the white men to kill all the buffalo. He laughed again with his whiskey breath in my face. He said the buffalo will all be gone, and I did not believe it. But when I see this"—he swept his hand across the valley below, with its bones from end to end—

"when I see this, then I think maybe the world of the Kiowa is going away."

"You must be getting old and sad to believe such things," Po-lan-te said. "Remember our buffalo hunt? The buffalo were at the salt lick—right where you said they would be. This winter has been like many others before. And soon we will cross Red River from our home valleys and leave our women and children here while we raid the Texans and the Mexicans. We are Kiowa. We are men. What are the *Taibos*?"

"A bad dream," Tsein-Kop-te answered. They climbed their horses out of the valley and turned to look one more time at the ghastly sacrilege.

Chapter 16

Colonel Grierson knew that some of the bands had left the reservation, but he feared attacks on the post by the Kiowas and Comanches if he dared to send half his slim garrison in pursuit of them. Still, he was determined to find at least one band and punish them, and the Quaker Indian Agent Tatum had seen enough Kiowa disobedience to agree with the post commander.

So he sent out a patrol to look for straying Kiowas.

North Texas is a big place. For days and days the Kiowas and the cavalry played blind man's bluff and could not even manage to run across each other's trails, though the troops crossed the trails of hunters from other bands and tribes. And then, finally, one March noon, cold enough that the horses snorted frost, Tsein-kop-te and his young men thought they saw a wisp of dark white man's smoke beyond one of the many shallow ridges that they crossed on every patrol.

They picked up their pace but the fire was far away, and by the time they reached their destination all that was left were the ashes of three small campfires. About a dozen sets of horse tracks were headed east, along the Brazos River. They had passed each other an hour earlier, and only a row of ridges between them had prevented them from meeting.

"They're headed straight for the village," said Tsein-kop-te. "If we do not do something, they will find it, and then they will go back to the fort and lead many soldiers here to kill our women and children."

To Po-lan-te the solution was simple. "Let's ambush them," he said. "There is a place where the valley narrows and the banks of the river are steep: We can kill all of them."

Tsein-kop-te shook his head. "There are too many."

Yay-go had an idea. "Why don't we show ourselves to them and let them chase us so we can lead them away from the village?"

The older warrior shook his head. "Their ponies are in better shape than ours," he replied. "In a long chase they might catch us. There are many more of them, and they have better guns."

Autumn Thunder had been listening without a word, which was often his way, but now he spoke up. "Some of them are smart," he said. They will understand that we are trying to lead them in a different direction and then they will know where the village is without having to get there themselves."

"We have to do something," Po-lan-te insisted.

"We will," said Tsein-kop-te. "But first, we will wait."

They watched until they were certain the soldiers would continue their route along the river, then they dropped below the ridgeline and rode slowly in a direction parallel to the river. Every hour or so Tsein-kop-te would ride near the ridgeline, dismount, and climb to a spot where he could look down on the adjoining valley. The soldiers were always there.

"There are ten soldiers," he told them, "and two Tonkawa scouts. They are tired of riding. They are not paying attention."

At dusk the warriors dismounted and went up to take a look at the soldiers they were shadowing. From three hundred yards away they watched the cavalrymen as they tethered their horses in the cottonwoods and set up their tents. Soon the smoke was rising from the campfires and the smell of real coffee brewing was having its effect on the Kiowas.

"I'd rather have their coffee than their horses," said Yay-go.

Autumn Thunder felt the same. These white men never seemed to run out of good things that the Kiowas always had to struggle to acquire. He wondered why the Kiowa women couldn't grow their own—the real coffee that smelled so heartbreakingly delicious.

Among the men he saw several figures he thought looked familiar, including a Tonkawa scout, but one man he was certain of. Along with the enlisted men was a lone figure in an officer's uniform, with broad shoulders and massive mustache and a white broad-brimmed hat like that which had tumbled from his head when Autumn Thunder had unhorsed him with his lance.

For a *Tai-bo* Sweeney was not a bad man, but he was the enemy and if he had the opportunity, Autumn Thunder would certainly kill him this time. That's what a little kindness will do for you, he thought. Let a soldier live and sooner or later he will be back leading more soldiers against your village. For the life of him Autumn Thunder still could not understand why he hadn't just ripped off Sweeney's scalp and his right ear and left the rest of him to the buzzards and coyotes.

There was nothing special about Sweeney. He was just a white man in a blue uniform out to kill redskins. It made Autumn Thunder feel restless and frustrated that Tsein-kop-te's plan was to run off the horses and the pack mules and see to it that Sweeney and his men had to walk home.

"We just want to keep them away from our village. If we kill them the soldier chief will send an army down after us."

"Let them come. They can't fight against real men," Po-lan-te said.

"No, but they are good against our women and our children," Tsein-kop-te responded. "We must keep them away from our villages and the only way to do that is to not get them too mad at us. So this night, we steal horses; we don't kill soldiers."

To their right the sun got bigger and redder as it floated down to the horizon, balanced on the skyline, then by stages dipped into purple darkness. In spite of their determination to be fearless, the young men were nervous as they rode their ponies down the valley, crossed over the ridge and then rode back up through the cottonwoods along the river.

A quarter mile down river from the dying campfires they dismounted and led their ponies. They could approach the soldier camp more quietly on foot, and they had to make sure the soldiers' horses were unguarded before they made their move.

There were no guards, just big bay and gray cavalry mounts that smelled them approaching and did not like what they smelled. The braves counted the horses and mules; every one of them was there, tethered on two picket lines. The Kiowas retreated back downriver, mounted up, and walked their ponies up toward the camp.

When they arrived at the place where the horses were picketed they undid their blankets and cut the picket lines. The horses began to shift uneasily, but they did not wander off.

''Now!'' said Tsein-kop-te. All six Kiowas fired their rifles almost in the ears of the army horses, waved blankets, and shrieked like banshees. They were trying to get the horses to break across the river so they could round them up on the other side and run them out of sight before the soldiers even got their boots on, but instead the terrified animals bolted out of the woods and ran right through the camp. The Kiowas had no choice but to follow them, howling and shooting all the way.

The troopers awoke cursing, scrambling for their boots and their weapons. One or two were knocked down by the passing herd as it ran through the ashes of the campfires. The animals scattered coffeepots and kettles, flattened a pair of tents, and headed for the nearest ridge, followed closely by the Kiowas, who were determined to drive the horses and mules all the way down the valley to their village. There the mares would help improve the blood of the band's herd.

They could hear whole choruses of white man profanity. Several of the soldiers fired their weapons harmlessly into the night but by then the Kiowas and the horses were long gone over the ridge.

As quickly as they had appeared, they had vanished. Sweeney looked around at the wreckage of his camp, looked at the drunk of a sergeant who should have posted guards but didn't, cursed himself for not having made certain that the guards had been posted. He looked around him and saw that none of his men had been killed or wounded. That, at least, was a blessing considering that the hostiles had taken them completely by surprise.

He stared at his two Tonkawa scouts, eyes blazing with anger. But he knew that, ultimately his debacle was not the Tonkawas' fault, it was not the sergeant's fault—the fault was his because he was in charge. Beyond the ridge he could hear faint whoops of the Kiowas as they continued to drive the horses.

He walked up to his most reliable Tonkawa, a short, wiry old campaigner called Sharp Knife. "How many were there?" he asked the scout.

"Five, six," said the Tonkawa. "No more."

"Good," Sweeney said, turning away from the Tonkawa.

"Sergeant," he said, "we can't track them on a night like this, but as soon as dawn breaks, I want us out on the trail of those horse thieves, understand?"

The sergeant understood. "It is not easy for Indians to hold white man's horses," he said, with a thick German accent. "We're gonna get them horses back, that I swear."

On the rare mornings when he was not hungover, Lieutenant James Leroy Sweeney generally awoke in a good mood, especially in the field, away from garrison life. On this morning he woke with a smile, which quickly turned to ashes when he realized he and his men were now afoot, and had a long hunt for his animals before he could continue his patrol—*if* they found the animals.

The Tonkawa scouts followed the easy trail made by the herded animals, but to their surprise the Kiowas had had very little trouble keeping the horses together. After about three hours of hot walking in his riding boots, Sweeney conceded that the warriors had successfully stolen all his horses and mules. He'd have a terrible time explaining the theft to his superiors, and he would be lucky not to get thrown out of the service.

In fact, he realized, he would be lucky to get his men back alive. The countryside was crawling with Indians. They had crossed dozens of tracks made by unshod Indian ponies. Now they would have to defend themselves, on foot, against the best light cavalry in the world.

Just then a Tonkawa ran up to him, so excited that Sweeney thought surely the first attack must be beginning now, but the Tonkawa explained that he had seen a four-footed animal in the distance, and maybe another.

Sweeney's spirits rose. If two of the horses were out there, did that mean that the Kiowas had lost the entire herd? He ran to the top of the ridge, right behind the Tonkawa, raised his binoculars and peered across the valley.

Two mules.

He was terribly disappointed, but at least they would have animals to haul supplies. In camp were sacks of biscuits, bacon, and coffee. They could keep their minds on the journey home. They wouldn't have to waste time and energy hunting food. But would the Kiowas and Comanches lurking in the grass and the rocks allow them to make it home?

Chapter 17

It could have been worse, but this was bad enough. Cavalry boots were not made for walking.

They loaded as much food as they possibly could on the two mules and hid the rest among the trees and rock shelves by the river. Maybe someday they could return and reclaim their saddles. They loaded their blanket rolls on their backs, slung their canteens and carbines over their shoulders, and headed north for the Red River according to Sweeney's compass.

It was a cool day but sunny, and soon the sweat was rolling down their backs as they made their way across the endless plain that stretched between them and Red River. Flat as these lands looked from a distance, they were actually a succession of rolling ups and downs broken by dry and wet creeks and rivers. Except for the riverbanks where the cottonwoods grew, there were virtually no trees to throw a little shade their way.

The Tonkawa scouts spread out in front of the troopers, their sharp eyes peeled for anything that they said "smelled wrong." They made four miles the first two hours they walked, but then Sweeney had to call a rest because some of the soldiers were complaining that their feet hurt.

Already their soles were blistered and burning. Sweeney explained to them, slowly, that if they fell behind the rest could not wait for them so they had better take care of themselves. He personally saw to it that they changed their socks, pulled them on smooth so the wrinkles would not cause further blistering, and he actually did a little light cobbling work on boots that were worn inside, improvising ways of hammering nails back below the leather and bandaging feet where they might come in contact with the nails or the leather uppers.

With the exception of Sergeant Schnitzer, a German immigrant, his troopers were all ex-field slaves, all strong, all courageous and used to hardship, but to Sweeney's way of thinking, slow-witted as the buffalo. Schnitzer, he decided regretfully, was similarly strong, courageous, and slow-witted, and after an entire day traipsing across the sun-baked plains, so was he.

The rest of the day proceeded without further problems. His message about leaving them had taken hold. The soldiers were careful about their feet and Sweeney took frequent breaks. They made camp at sundown, ate and slept early, and were on their feet at first light.

Swells and troughs, valleys and ridges, occasional streams and rivers, and cloudless blue skies were their scenic menu. Some of the soldiers tried to take their boots off and walk barefoot for awhile, and Sweeney declined to order them back into uniform. At any rate, the ground was considerably rougher than they had thought and the boots quickly went back on.

As they made camp that evening, the other scout, Standing Elk, sat down with Sweeney and spoke to him in halting English.

"Somebody watching us out there," he said, sweeping his hand across the horizon.

"You saw them?" Sweeney asked, knowing how the Tonkawas, Wichitas, and Caddos feared the more aggressive plains tribes.

Standing Elk shook his head and touched his nose.

"You smelled them?" Sweeney asked, dubiously.

Standing Elk shrugged his shoulders, shook his head and said no in such a way that Sweeney knew he meant, not exactly, but he sensed their presence. Sweeney did not make light of Standing Elk's concern. He had seen this Indian in action and did not doubt his courage or his skill. If Standing Elk sensed that they were being watched, then they were being watched.

"Who do you think?" Sweeney asked, and the scout shrugged again.

"Maybe Comanche," he said.

Sweeney had been out on the plains for three years. He knew how the predator tribes worked. They were hunters, patient men who could lie still and watch for hours or days until the time was right to attack.

But he knew that they could be lazy and overconfident. He looked around him. Many of his men had eaten quickly and fallen asleep where they had eaten, their heads pillowed on their still-rolled-up bedrolls.

He called Schnitzer to him. "You and Standing Elk will sleep for an hour," he said. "Then Sharp Knife and I will sleep for an hour. When I wake up we push off. By the time it's light, I want us five miles away from here, and I want our trail covered too."

Standing Elk nodded his approval. "Yes, sir," said Schnitzer, and headed immediately for his bedroll.

A little more than two hours later Sweeney had the men on the move in a column of twos. Canteens were carefully tied down so they wouldn't rattle, and a nighttime wind that hissed through the grass was welcome. The men felt desperate enough to maintain total silence and all had their eyes wide open for hostile silhouettes in the light of the quarter moon. To their surprise and gratitude, the two mules were as silent as the men.

At first they headed east because they knew that if they were being followed, their pursuers would expect them to continue their trek directly north. After walking for about a mile they found a creek that wound along a broad valley first north, then northwest, then northeast, then doubled southward before heading northeast again. They waded along the creekbed for about two miles before they found a broad rock shelf. There they climbed out and walked east some more with the Tonkawas doing their best to hide any signs of the patrol's exit from the river.

At dawn, a full six hours after they had begun their nighttime flight, they turned north again and headed directly for Red River, which Sweeney figured at two or three days' march, depending on the terrain and the men's stamina.

Sweeney was pleased to find himself feeling strong and confident in a way he had not felt since the end of the Civil War. Garrison life had always brought out the worst in him. He

dreaded inspections and parades more than he had dreaded
battles, and he hated himself when he cringed in front of pom-
pous inspecting bureaucrats.

They hit their next creek around ten A.M. and only then did
Sweeney call a halt to the march. There was a stand of cottonwoods so deep surrounding this part of the creek that the
men could hide themselves among the trees and brush, nibble
on cold biscuits, and pretty much sleep concealed from anyone
who didn't know they were there.

He let them sleep until nearly sundown, then had them up
and walking. They needed their rest so badly that Sweeney
almost let them sleep a while longer. But the men were strong
and desperate to get home.

They had come to some rugged country, where the footing
was treacherous and so tiring that after three hours of marching
he let them make camp early. They would get a start in early
daylight.

Breakfast was water and biscuits. The coffee that the Kiowas had coveted had been cached in a rock crevice the day
before to lighten the load of the smaller mule. Sweeney was
convinced that Indians could smell a pot of fresh coffee from
fifty miles away, so the soldiers would taste no more of it until
they reached Fort Sill.

The sun was just below the horizon when Schnitzer, looking
pale and blue in the pre-dawn light reported to Sweeney that
the men were ready to start.

"They're well rested, Sergeant," Sweeney said. "I aim to
push 'em all day, do you understand that? We've got the jump
on those Indians and I don't want them catching up and am-
bushing us while we're waist deep in the Red River."

"*Ja*," Schnitzer replied laconically as he moved to the head
of the formation, consulted his compass, and had them step
off in a northerly direction.

Sweeney's men may have been stepping lively, but he could
hardly step at all. The day before, the toes in both his boots
had been rubbed raw by the leather and nothing he did seemed
to help. Not only did he have to fight through the pain, he
couldn't even allow himself to limp, lest he remind his troops
of their own aches and pains.

By the time the sun had climbed atop the horizon he felt as
if some unseen carpenter was dragging a ripsaw across the

tops of his toes with every step he took. He decided to take the point, alone, a hundred yards behind the Tonkawas and forty yards ahead of the troops, not to inspire his boys but so they wouldn't hear him grunt with pain every time his foot hit the ground.

The day would be unseasonably warm. With every mile, with every step, he wanted to give up and lie in the grass and wait for God or the Comanches to come and take him. What did he have waiting at the post but a court marshal for allowing a group of flea-bitten Kiowas to steal a dozen expensive cavalry mounts? That White Horse had stolen forty-one mules from the post would only make the colonels in Washington that much more determined to stop their people from losing stock to the Indians even if it meant court marshaling every lieutenant and captain in Fort Sill.

By the time the sun was directly overhead, his knee joints were aching like an abscessed tooth. Change in the weather? he asked himself, feeling detached for just a moment. He opened his eyes and noticed that his path had wandered about five degrees from the rocky outcropping he had focused on as his destination point. He must have been walking with his eyes closed. Perhaps he had even fallen asleep. His toes felt numb—no, they weren't numb, they had stopped throbbing with every heartbeat. They were just a hard, steady pain now.

He looked back and was pleased to see that his men were still forty paces behind him. He could grunt if he wanted to, and he wanted to, with every step. To take his mind off the pain he decided to scan the horizon all around him, in search of something that shouldn't be there. Not that his eyes could add anything to those of the Tonkawas who were still wandering over the plains a hundred yards ahead of him.

He pulled the cork from his canteen, threw his head back, and took three big swigs. He wanted more—in fact he wanted to sit down, scoop out a little hole, empty his canteen into it, and shove his feet into the puddle. He imagined the feeling of cold water on his fiery toes.

Toes. Always the toes. He was a weak man, he thought. What he really needed was to make it to the fort, buy a bottle of good whiskey and go to bed with it.

"Sir," came a voice suddenly, three or four paces behind

him. "The men really need to stop and take a rest. They're flat worn out!" Schnitzer insisted.

"Another mile or so and that's just what we'll do. See that little hill over there? That's where we'll take our break."

They were continuing to walk as they spoke. Now Sweeney was aware of the approach of Standing Elk. The lines on his forehead, always prominent, looked deep enough to hide a prairie dog.

"Tenan," he said in a voice straight from the sepulcher. "Comanche."

"Where?" Sweeney asked. Standing Elk patiently pointed to a swell to the left that could hide an army.

"You're sure?" Sweeney asked. The Indian nodded ferociously. "They're out there, many of them."

"Too many for us?"

"Much too much," was the reply.

"Then we'll try to make that hill yonder," Sweeney said, pointing not with his hands but with his eyes, lest some skulking Comanche spot the gesture and anticipate Sweeney's next move.

It wasn't all that much of a hill, but it sloped down in all directions and all the old tall grass was gone. The top was no more than thirty yards in diameter and there was a slight depression in the center. But they had to deviate from their line of march to reach the hill, and there must have been one smart Comanche chief keeping watch because as soon as he saw the troops change their direction he knew what was happening and suddenly men and horses were spilling out over the big hill like blood from a bucket.

"Come on, boys!" Sweeney shouted. "Double quick!" His last words were unnecessary. Once they heard the chilling whoops of the Comanches, once they saw their leader break into a gimpy sprint, they broke ranks and sprinted forward, gaining on Sweeney with every step, and passing him. The Comanches were urging their ponies on to cut the troopers off from the hilltop, but they had a long way to go, and the soldiers were so desperate that they forgot they were nearly worn out from their long day's march.

There was no way to tell whether they were prepared to stop at the top of the little hill, but fortunately there was a corporal, a man named Greer, who was one of the quicker

men. When he got to the top he turned, flopped on his belly,
and pointed his carbine in the direction of the horsemen, who
were closing rapidly on the little hill. Gimpy as he was, Sweeney managed to make the hilltop before the men who had
charge of the mules, or the portly Schnitzer.

The men were snapping off shots at the distant horsemen
and ammunition was one thing they did not have to waste.
"Hold your fire until I say fire!" Sweeney cried between
wheezing gasps. Pumped up by excitement that verged on
panic, he forgot completely about his feet though his legs were
so weary they barely held him up. Running from man to man
he arranged them in a circle small enough to provide covering
fire for each other but large enough for the mules to fit in the
middle, in the depression. He did not want to lose the mules.
They were carrying a lot of precious water, and he knew that
if the Comanches chose to play a waiting game, the water
would be as important as the ammunition.

And they *would* play a waiting game.

His throat went dry. There must have been fifty warriors
below, so close he could see the patterns of their warpaint.
His first thought was that if they decided to rush the little
patrol all at once they would ride right over it and a dozen
scalps would be drying in their tepees by nightfall.

But they weren't rushing up the hill. For the first time since
the big war had ended, Sweeney had been either very good or
very lucky. The hill had wonderful fields of fire in all directions and although it wasn't terribly steep, the slope was steep
enough, and long enough, to slow the horses down if they
attempted a frontal attack.

The Comanches had surrounded the hill, and it was obvious
that the leaders of this group were assessing their situation.
Sweeney decided that he had enough time to assess his. He
choked down his fear and called Standing Elk and Schnitzer
to join him for a conference.

"We're in better shape than it looks," he said. "Most of
them have bows rather than rifles and from up here our carbines outrange their bows. They can't charge and we can't
panic and run. We've got water and food, maybe more than
they've got. And you know Comanches don't have the stomach for a long siege." Standing Elk nodded. Neither did Tonkawas.

One of the troopers fired off a fruitless shot.

"Just a moment," Sweeney said to Standing Elk and Schnitzer. The Comanches were spreading out around the hill now, and those with rifles were trying a few shots at the hilltop. Two more troopers fired down at their besiegers.

"All right, boys," said Sweeney, standing tall and walking into the center so all the men could hear what he was about to say. He was presenting a clear target against the skyline, making a calculated gamble. Most of the Comanches had been keeping their distance from the whites and Fort Sill. He was betting that their rifles were old and worn, and that they did not have enough ammunition to practice with to make them decent shots. He estimated that they were about three hundred yards away, a hard shot for him if he had a rifle, a near impossible shot for them.

He looked around at his troopers, all former slaves, all young, few veterans among them. He could see the lines of tension around their mouths, the tension in their hands as they held their carbines in grips of iron. It was a simple problem with a simple solution, he thought.

"Men," he said, watching the smoke drift from several more muzzles. He cleared his throat. "Men, don't waste your ammunition. Where they are, they can't hit us, and we can't hit them." From below came four more shots. He wanted to duck or at least sink to his knees to present a smaller target, but what he had to say demanded a fearless appearance.

"This is a good hill," he said. "You men all know how to shoot. If we do not run, if we stand, and we make our shots count, we will win and we will live." Now he began to walk around the circle, in front of them, so they could all see his face as he passed them. "But if we panic, if we run, we will all die. Now I want you all to look at the man next to you." He said that mainly to see if they were listening. They did as they were told. He had their attention.

"You see the face next to you? If you don't do your job, you'll be letting him down. Letting everybody down. And you'll die too. Now, sooner or later they're gonna charge, or at least pretend to charge. There'll be plenty of time to take aim, plenty of time to remember how to hit a target. You'll be able to hear me give orders like you're hearing me right how. If I get hit, you'll hear orders from Sergeant Schnitzer here. Just follow orders and we'll be all right.

"One more thing. The next man who fires his carbine without my order will get a kick in the head from me. You hear?"

There were nods and "yessuhs" around the circle.

A number of braves had made their way up the beginning of the slope. "Don't shoot, boys, they're still too far away," Sweeney ordered.

The braves had bows; they pulled back hard on their strings and shot, but an unpredictable, swirling wind took the arrows every which way and deposited them everywhere but on top of the hill. All fell far short. The hill, distance, and wind were too much for them.

They tried once more, with each warrior making what he considered an adjustment, but the results were the same. One of the Tonkawas whooped and fired his rifle at the closest bowman. The bullet kicked up dirt close enough that the Comanche moved down the hill and out of range.

"That's it," Sweeney said to Schnitzer. "The Tonkawas have rifles. They're better armed than we are. Standing Elk, let me borrow your rifle."

Sweeney, like many officers, thought he was a far better shot than he was. "Watch this, boys," he said, bringing Standing Elk's rifle to his shoulder and sighting in on the closest horseman. He got a good sight picture and squeezed the trigger. When the smoke cleared The Comanche and his horse were still there.

"Good shot there, Lieutenant!" shouted Corporal Greer, with a big grin on his face. The other men laughed.

"Must be the wind," Sweeney said, and they laughed again.

"Anyway," said Corporal Greer, "I'd sooner be layin' here on my belly waitin' for them to try and come up, than trampin' on back to Fort Sill."

"You fool," said a private next to him, a man the rest of them just called Shug. "Sooner or later we gonna have to get back on our feet and head for home."

"Yeh," Greer agreed. "But when we do I'll be so grateful to still have my hair on my head that walkin'll seem easy, right?"

Some of the men laughed, but others were paying attention to what the Comanches were doing at the bottom of the hill.

They were beginning to ride around the hill in a continuous circle, whooping and screeching, sitting upright on their ponies, defying the guns of the troopers on the hill.

"Steady, men, hold your fire. They can't hurt you from down there. I'll tell you when," Sweeney said. The panic was gone, and the pain was gone, replaced by a majestic feeling of calmness.

Slowly they were tightening the circle, drawing closer to the soldiers on the hill. The warriors were crouched a bit in their saddles now, expecting to draw fire, and they did, from two or three of the troopers.

"Damn it, don't fire until the lieutenant gives the order!" shouted Schnitzer.

"They're still out of your range, boys. You wait till I tell you when to shoot and what to shoot at," said Sweeney. His voice was so calm he might have been talking to Evans in the trading store about a new shaving mug. His poise was catching. He could feel the men settling down around him. No nervous jokes now. No desperate gunfire. It was as if survival had become a matter of business rather than an emotional issue.

The Comanches were circling closer now, much closer, only now they were hanging from the far side of their ponies.

"Okay boys, get ready," said Sweeney, and a pair of itchy trigger fingers fired useless rounds.

"Now then," said Sweeney. "They're giving you nothing to shoot at, they think. You've got single shot carbines and if you fire and miss they might try to rush you while you're loading. Boys, you can't expect to hit their heels, but you can hit their horses. I want to see horses go down you hear? At my command . . . fire!"

A dozen weapons blazed almost at once and three ponies reared in pain. Two went down, the other was out of control.

"Again boys, fire as you load and hit those ponies!"

The Comanches with unwounded horses moved closer, firing their rifles and bows from under the bellies of their horses then moving down the slope about fifty yards, but at least two more shots from the hill found their marks. Three horses lay dead or badly wounded on the slope and the troopers watched while the Comanches tended their wounded animals.

None of the men on the hill were thrilled by this form of

warfare. They were cavalrymen, and they all loved their horses. Some of them were carrying a load of grief over the mounts that had been stolen from them. But the sight of the dreaded Comanches this close and this determined to kill them focused their attention on their own survival.

"Anybody hurt?" Sweeney asked.

Schnitzer and Greer looked around and said no, but a private named Davis said he thought that one of the mules had caught a bullet in her flank.

"How bad?" Sweeney asked.

"Can't tell yet," answered the private. "Ain't bleedin' much and the mule she ain't complaining."

The Comanches quickly figured that unless they wanted to chance a frontal attack that could cost them many warriors, then there was no sense in pressing the action. The chief was a tough, aggressive man named Parra-o-coom, who had fought many battles in his life. Parra-o-coom knew that this war was not sport for honors, but life and death for Comanches. He did not desire to spend warriors when the prize was so small.

There were others who felt differently, and desired to argue the point with Parra-o-coom. While half the Comanches remained surrounding the hill well out of range of the carbines, the other half retired to a nearby creek to debate the issue. Through his field glasses Sweeney could see the animated gestures.

"What do you think, Standing Elk?" he asked his chief scout.

"We very lucky," the scout responded. "We didn't kill any of them."

Sweeney nodded. "If we had," he said, "they wouldn't rest until they had revenge, I know them that well."

In fact, for all the shooting not a single two-footed combatant had been wounded. But the sky was turning pink and purple. What would the night bring?

"No clouds, bright moon," said Sweeney. "And we have plenty of water. My friend, I think our medicine today has been very good."

"Long way back to the fort," said Standing Elk.

"We'll make it," said Sweeney confidently. After this day, he felt as if he could conquer the entire Comanche nation with a hundred men and one light howitzer.

But he had no desire to try.

Chapter 18

The successful buffalo hunt had made the winter a good one for Autumn Thunder's village out on the Texas plains. When the warm weather came they rode north of the Red River to avoid the Texans and came together with some of the other bands. Some of the men had tried to whip up a revenge raid against the whites for the imprisonment of the three chiefs, but neither Au-sai-mah nor Kicking Bird would hear of it.

"If we want the chiefs to be returned to us safely, you had better behave yourselves," both of the chiefs insisted, and then they would send their warriors away grumbling.

Not that Au-sai-mah completely trusted the whites. He would be no Black Kettle, massacred with his people by Custer, like a buffalo run off a high bluff because the white men decided to break their word without bothering to tell him.

Autumn Thunder had over the past two summers gained considerable status within the band. His mother had been *kaan*, that large part of the tribe who were poor and without much status, though not the lowest level on the Kiowa social ladder. He had not helped his stature within his band by marrying a woman of the Wichitas, especially since he purchased her with mules instead of stealing her.

But his wounding and capturing of Lieutenant Sweeney in battle had become an event of some note in the annals of his band. If two Kiowas were visiting Fort Sill and they spotted Sweeney, they would wait until they were within earshot of the lieutenant and then one of them would say to him, in Kiowa, of course, "Good morning, Autumn Thunder's soldier," or "I hear Autumn Thunder traded you for a Wichita wife. Is that all you were worth?" Then the Kiowas would continue on their way, without changing the expression on their faces, but bursting inside nevertheless.

Sweeney noticed that a number of Kiowas he didn't know would greet him on the street, but since they never followed this routine in front of a Kiowa speaker like Horace Jones or Matthew Leeper, Sweeney never caught on.

At this time, he would not have cared very much anyway, because his own stock had risen considerably since he had limped through the gates of Fort Sill with a leaner Sergeant Schnitzer, two Tonkawa scouts, and eight very footsore black cavalry troopers. Somehow a dozen lost horses did not matter very much once Colonel Grierson realized he would not have to write a letter to General Sherman trying to explain how an entire patrol had disappeared on the Texas grasslands.

The men told the story of how they had held off the Comanches for two entire days without any of them sustaining a scratch. At the end of the second night, Standing Elk and his scouts had nosed around and found that the Comanches were hiding behind a distant hill, pretending to be gone to entice Sweeney down off the hill. Sweeney had, by the light of a lucifer, consulted a map and in the dead of a cloudy night led the men into a creek and walked *south*, farther into hostile territory but away from the route the Comanches expected them to take. They followed the creek sixty miles as it snaked its way east, then north, where it emptied into Red River.

"We didn't dare leave a single footprint in Texas," Sweeney had told an admiring group of officers at the trading store later, when he was giving his own personalized version of their long trek.

"Let the Comanches jes' run you out of Texas, di'nt you?" said Tuck, who had stopped at Fort Sill to refit his wagons. "D'ya kill any?" he asked, with a vinegary expression on his face.

"Not unless some of them wore out ridin' round our hill," Sweeney answered. The officers and trader Evans laughed, but Tuck sneered.

"Is that how you protect us civilians?" he asked. "I thought your job was to keep the peace on the frontier. Way to do it is to kill the varmints every chance you get. That's how I do it.''

"What do you mean, 'That's how I do it'?" Sweeney asked, staring at the buffalo hunter through narrowed eyes.

"Zac'ly so," Tuck replied. "You wouldn't understand, because soldier boys can't hardly hit nothin' with a bullet futher'n you can throw a rock. When I see an Injun I just draw a bead on him with old Red-Killer here and let him have it—or her, if that's the case."

"I thought you was a buffalo hunter," said Sweeney.

"Injuns, buffalo, same thing. Dirty, filthy, stinking—'cept I make money killin' buffalo. The Injun killin' is just pure pleasure. Course, now, if you soldier boys would just start payin' bounties for injun scalps, I reckon folks like me 'ould solve your Injun problem in one long, happy summer."

"Tuck, just who have you been hunting down this year?" asked Sweeney.

The buffalo hunter shrugged his shoulders. "This year? Couple a Caddos, one a them Tonkawa maneaters. Hard for me to tell. I don't classify 'em. I just shoot 'em."

"Tell you one thing, mister buffalo hunter," Sweeney said, tilting back a mug of beer that had been going flat while he'd been listening to Tuck and growing angrier by the minute. "If I ever catch you in Texas throwin' your sights on a lawful Indian, I'll hang you from the nearest cottonwood right there if it takes me a week to find one."

"Well look who's turned into the Injun lover, hey?" said Tuck, growing red but watchful of Sweeney from their past encounter.

"Who appointed you to decide who lives and dies?" Sweeney asked. "I notice you're awful hard on the Indians who ain't hostile. Ain't heard you mention goin' up against Kiowas, or Comanches, or Cheyenne, or Arapaho. Come to think of it, I ain't heard you say a word about goin' up against anybody. Heard a lot about you sneaking around and back-shootin' folks."

"That what you call Injuns? Folks? Last I heard they were more like a bunch of horse-stealin' murderers than 'folks.' " Tuck almost bragged about the Kiowa he'd killed, but decided not to.

"And what kind of murderer are you?" Sweeney asked.

The red flowed out of Tuck's face. A look of beatific calm came over him. "Let me explain something to you, mister oldest lieutenant. While you was over in Tennessee during the late war you was killin' Christian white men. I hunt buffalo for a livin', I hunt Injuns for pleasure. I do my huntin' in Texas, and the Texans got no say in it."

Sweeney laughed and turned to Evans. "That's what the Kiowas say," he said. "Seems to be a whole lot of people who believe anything goes in Texas."

"I don't suppose you heard, Mr. Tuck, that the colonel has put Sweeney in for a medal for gettin' his boys home safely from Texas," said trader Evans.

"Ain't that tender," said Tuck.

As a result of his battle with Sweeney, and his courageous action during the buffalo hunt, Autumn Thunder was now regarded as part of the *Ondegup'a*, not exactly the aristocracy like the *Onde*, but a status that commanded some respect within the tribe. He still had an extra mule or two, and an extra horse or two, which he traded for more buffalo hides.

Gathers The Grass had her own garden, one considerably finer than any of the other gardens in Au-sai-mah's village, because Wichita women were better farmers than Kiowa women. But as she grew bigger with child she felt she must cut down on the long hours of cultivating and weeding, so she got to work on making a new tepee cover that was worthy of a young brave who was coming up in the world. Not to be outdone, Autumn Thunder and Talia-koi rode off to the northwest to cut some lodgepoles tall enough and strong enough to support Gathers The Grass's fine new tepee cover.

At the last minute Po-lan-te decided that he wanted to come along. They took extra horses and rode long and hard for three days before they found a stand of pines that would provide them with the wood they needed. Using saws they had borrowed from the Indian Agency, they cut all the lodgepoles they needed in two days, and the second night they gathered around the campfire and celebrated.

They smoked and talked about what a good raiding season they would be having over the summer, ate some jerked deer meat and a couple of cans of peaches that the post trader had given them in exchange for some rabbit skins. They loved the sweet syrup that trickled down their chins as they drank it directly out of the cans. Then Talia-koi produced a single bottle of liquid and said it was fine whiskey. He had stolen a bottle from Evans when the latter's back was turned, he said.

"Not a very big bottle," muttered Po-lan-te, who did not drink often, but when he did, he didn't want a taste, he wanted oblivion.

"You want me to pour it out on the ground?" asked Talia-koi. "Or maybe I should run off in the woods and drink it by myself. I'm sure one man could get to feel right if he drank down the whole bottle." He was miffed at his friend's lack of appreciation and he said so.

"Well, I just wish the bottle was as big as a whiskey bottle," said Po-lan-te. "Let me just have it first."

Talia-koi laughed. "You think I would trust you with this bottle?" he said, producing a little tin cup. "I'll pour some for you to drink, then I'll pour some for Autumn Thunder to drink, and then I'll have the rest."

"You'll get more than we'll get," said Po-lan-te.

"I'll try to give you as much, but just remember, I could have gone off into the woods and drunk it all myself," said Talia-koi. He poured out portions big enough to convince the other two that he was being fair, and then he drained the rest of the bottle himself, and that's how the three friends managed to get a little drunk, very little drunk, on their way back from Colorado.

When Autumn Thunder arrived home he found that the new tepee cover was almost finished. Gathers The Grass was thrilled by the beautiful, tall lodgepoles. But Autumn Thunder had traded much for the additional buffalo skins and he felt the need to recoup his fortunes. Kone-bo-hone, one of the band's more active raiders, announced that he was going to Texas on a horse-stealing expedition and specifically asked Autumn Thunder to join him and ten of his friends, including five from the *Semat* band of Kiowa-Apaches that he occasionally ran with.

Autumn Thunder agreed eagerly, but when he told Gathers The Grass she became angry with him for the first time in their marriage.

"Kone-bo-hone is a big fool," she said. "He will get you killed and then your child will never get to know his father!"

Autumn Thunder surprised Gathers The Grass by raising his voice to her for the first time. "Autumn Thunder does not need permission from his woman," he said with a knifelike edge to his voice. His eyes narrowed dangerously. "We will speak of it no more."

"At least go to A-do-te before you make up your mind," she said.

His eyes widened and he nodded. "You are a Kiowa woman," he said. "I will go see A-do-te, but if he does not object, I do not want to hear sharp-tongue from you."

A moment later he was on his way to the tepee of A-do-te the Owl Doctor. It was A-do-te's talent to tell a warrior if his medicine was good enough to keep him safe during a fight. Smart warriors in Au-sai-mah's band simply did not strip down and head off to war without visiting A-do-te.

Two hours later he was back home, sulking silently in a far cranny of his lodge.

Gathers The Grass went about her chores and did not speak to Autumn Thunder. He would speak to her when he was ready.

Three days later Kone-bo-hone and his warriors rode off on what everybody in the village said would be the biggest raid of the summer. With him were half the young men of the *Onde*—the top caste of the village. Autumn Thunder had been the only one invited to go who had declined. He watched the rest of the village as they saw the raiding party off with ceremony, and shrill whoops of support from many of the women, and he seethed with resentment that he had allowed his wife and the medicine man to talk him out of going.

But he could not help noticing that A-do-te was not present to see the warriors off, and he wondered if maybe this raid did not have the support of the entire village. Au-sai-mah was standing in front of his lodge with his arms folded, his face the kind of mask he usually reserved for the white man. Maybe, he thought, Gathers The Grass knew things that he did not know.

Not long after, a messenger came in from the village of Kicking Bird, and pulled his pony to a dusty stop outside the chief's tepee. The flap was open, so he peeked inside. Men and women stopped what they were doing and waited curiously to see what was up.

The messenger entered Au-sai-mah's beautifully decorated lodge and stayed, and the curious knew that he was being fed well, for Au-sai-mah, like many other chiefs, stayed poor because his position demanded lavish hospitality for visitors.

After awhile the messenger emerged, mounted his pony without a word to anybody, and galloped away. Nobody was surprised when Au-sai-mah appeared and announced to anybody who would care to listen that there would be a council just before sunset.

Except for Autumn Thunder, this was a council for older men and a few insignificant younger men who had little taste for war or other ambition. After the pipe was lit and passed around, Au-sai-mah stood up and began without further ceremony.

"Tay-nay-angopte has said that there would be a conference of tribes and peace commissioners the next moon at old Fort Cobb on the Washita."

There were excited noises from the *dapone*—the people without status. This might mean presents, and if there was anything the *dapone* could do, it was line up to receive presents from the white men.

It would be a big conference, said the old chief, and men would be there from the five nations.

"Who are they?" came a voice from beyond the council fire. Au-sai-mah gave the speaker a hard look that said it was not his turn to speak, then the chief proceeded to explain. "The five nations are the red white men," he said. "They come from the other side of the big river and there are many of them but somehow the white men conquered them and made them come here."

Red white men! The idea fascinated those in the tribe who may have heard of them but had never seen one.

"We must go, then," insisted the speaker in the shadows, and others agreed noisily, but Au-sai-mah raised his hands and shook his head.

"We will wait and see what the other chiefs think," he said. "Why would the white men want the five nations to be there? I will tell you. They want them to stand up and say bad things. They want the red white men to look at us and tell us what bad people we are, that we must give up our free life and be reservation people like they are, eating white man bread and drinking white man whiskey all day, getting big and fat and catching the coughing sickness and dying young without ever stealing a horse.''

''Will there be presents?'' asked another voice from the shadows.

''There could be presents. But we will not be there if the other chiefs cannot agree that we should go.''

Over the next two weeks the chiefs debated whether or not to attend the conference and finally agreed to attend if the Comanches also agreed to go. Some of the Comanche bands announced that they would go, but the Quohadi would not. The Kiowas agreed to go but said they would make the red white men wait. The Comanches agreed to do the same.

The village waited anxiously for the return of the young raiders, hoping that the agency would not come out checking to see who was around and who was not. Fortunately for them the Quakers did not like to check on their charges, afraid that if they found the warriors gone the army would go out chasing them, and the Quakers thought that killing Indians was a poor way to save their souls.

While the village waited, Autumn Thunder chafed, alone, for his friends Talia-koi, Yay-go, and Po-lan-te had gone along on the raid. He tried hunting along Red River but the game there was very poor. Too many people, he thought. Odd how when the white men ''give'' the Kiowas a reservation, there are more white men around than there ever were before the land ''belonged'' to the Kiowas.

Did that mean that when land belonged to somebody was when they had to share it? Autumn Thunder could never quite get straight this business of owning the land. Sometimes when Kiowas were raiding in Mexico, on the way down they might stop at a Texas farmhouse to ask for food, and the man in the house would tell them to get off his land. So he guessed there were different rules for when land belonged to white men and when land belonged to red men.

These things got so tangled in his mind that he decided to go to the post to find a white man to talk to about it, because nobody in the village could seem to get it straight, not even Au-sai-mah. The thought of finding a white man to talk to daunted him until Sweeney popped into his mind. When he thought about other white men, Sweeney did not seem so bad, especially once he realized that Gathers The Grass preferred him, not Sweeney.

Gathers The Grass laughed when Autumn Thunder told her he was going to visit Sweeney. "When you saw him down in Texas you wanted to kill him!" she exclaimed. "Now you want to be his friend."

"Out on the plains leading the soldiers he is my enemy. Then I remember that he is not such a bad fellow. Does he not always tell the truth?" Autumn Thunder spread his hands upward to acknowledge confusion.

"I must try to understand how the white men think," he said. "I do not believe Au-sai-mah knows how the white men think. Even Tay-nay-angopte, I do not believe he knows, though he thinks he does."

"And what makes you think you can understand them when the wise men cannot?"

"Do you not think I am wise?" he asked, surprised, because Gathers The Grass never before had mocked him.

"You are young," she said. Then she thought about the way he talked, the way he listened, the way he reasoned. "But yes, you are wise, my husband," she added.

Feathery clouds were scudding across the summer blue sky in a high plains wind when he arrived at the gate of the fort. The sentry at the gate looked at him as if he were garbage but the Kiowa sat tall on his pony and disregarded the curled lip.

"Got no food today, you beggar," said the sentry. Autumn Thunder understood most of the words, smiled, reached into his pouch and pulled out a strip of buffalo jerky.

"You hungry?" he asked as if he had misunderstood the sentry's words. The sneer turned into a look of true stomach-turning disgust. This guard may have sampled some of the Kiowa trail staple.

"Sweeney. Want to see Sweeney," said Autumn Thunder.

A sudden grin split the guard's face. "I know you!" he exclaimed. "You're the Kiowa what owns Lieutenant Sweeney. O'Doul!" he shouted to a private emerging from the guardhouse. "This here is Lieutenant Sweeney's Kiowa. Would you conduct him to the lieutenant?"

A short, stumpy Irishman walked to the gate. "If you would

kindly climb down off your animal, please, mister heathen,''
he said, counting on Autumn Thunder not to understand his
words. There he was not disappointed. The Kiowa continued
to sit straight up on his pony. O'Doul made a motion for
Autumn Thunder to dismount. ''Get down, for the love o'
God, will you?'' he said.

A look of understanding came to Autumn Thunder's face.
He came down off his pony so quickly that the little Irishman
flinched. The young warrior towered over him by four inches,
a situation not at all to the soldier's liking.

''Come on,'' he said, annoyed, and conducted him to a flat
grassy area where Sergeant Schnitzer was drilling some recruits. The lieutenant was standing with his hands clasped behind his back, rocking back and forth on his heels, watching
the recruits in their vain attempts to handle their cavalry
horses.

Autumn Thunder found himself standing on an army parade
ground surrounded by men in blue who he had fought before
and would probably fight again. It occurred to him that he had
come to ask one of these men why they were always changing
the rules. Suppose they chose to change the rules now, and
put him in chains and ship him off to Texas as they had with
Addo-eta and Set-tainte?

He was tempted to vault onto his pony and hie himself out
the gate, but he knew if he did that they would think he had
stolen something and they would chase him. He started to lead
his pony slowly toward the gate when he heard Sweeney's
voice.

''Autumn Thunder!'' came the voice, followed by a big
hand being clapped on his shoulder. ''You old horse thief!''

He knew enough English to be pleased by the fact that
Sweeney recognized his skill at stealing horses.

''Good to see you, my friend,'' said the lieutenant.

''Hello, my friend Sweeney,'' Autumn Thunder replied, although he still was not quite ready to believe that any white
man was his friend.

''You come to see me?'' Sweeney asked, with a smile on
his face that Autumn Thunder perceived as genuine.

''I need to know something,'' said the Kiowa.

''It's hard for me to understand what you're saying,'' said
the lieutenant. ''Let's go talk to Matt Leeper.''

Autumn Thunder understood little that Sweeney said but he knew Matt Leeper the interpreter and was glad he would not have to deal with the horrible language of the white man.

"Sergeant!" hollered Sweeney to Schnitzer. "Continue the drill. Autumn Thunder and I have some important things to discuss."

"Keep your hat on your head, Lieutenant," the sergeant replied. "Don't let him see your hair or he may want it for his lodge!"

Leeper was standing near Colonel Grierson's house talking to the Tonkawa scouts Standing Elk and Sharp Knife, but when he saw the lieutenant and the Kiowa approaching, he told the scouts they'd continue the talk later. Colonel Grierson had made it top priority that Leeper talk with the Kiowas and Comanches at every opportunity. "If we let them talk, and we listen, they will tell us things," he had said.

"Hello, Leeper," Autumn Thunder said so clearly that the interpreter showed his astonishment.

Sweeney laughed. "I'm afraid he doesn't know much more than that, Matt," he said. "But he wants to talk to me."

"How well do the two of you know each other?" Leeper asked, and seeing suspicion begin to cloud the Kiowa's face, he translated.

"When I was wounded in that fight down in Texas, he took me to his girlfriend's and they probably saved my life."

Leeper translated for Autumn Thunder and it became clear that Sweeney still did not know that his rescuer had nearly been his slayer.

"What's on your mind, my friend?" Sweeney asked through the interpreter.

"I come to see my friend Sweeney," the Kiowa answered.

"I see. Was there something you needed to talk to me about?"

The Kiowa thought for a moment, then he shook his head. He could not grasp the concept of owning land and was too befuddled to put his confusion into words. Besides, the smiling face was still that of a white man. He was an enemy. What am I doing trusting him? the Kiowa asked himself.

"You good man," Autumn Thunder said without the interpreter. "I come see you. I go back home now."

Sweeney understood that Autumn Thunder had come for a

purpose and had changed his mind. The lieutenant knew better than to push the issue. The young warrior would talk to him whenever he was ready.

"Is there anything you need?" Sweeney asked, through Leeper. "How about a little sack of coffee, or some sugar?"

Coffee and sugar sounded great to Autumn Thunder and he was about to smile back in gratitude but he changed his mind. He had not come to beg for goods. He was not that kind of man. "Have to go back to village now. You good man," he said.

"Come back any time," answered the big lieutenant, and walked with Autumn Thunder while the brave led his pony through the gate.

All the way back to the village Autumn Thunder was confused. He was normally a man who spoke his mind. And yet he could not talk to this white man. He could not ask this lieutenant whom he called friend why white men could demand one law for the Indian and another for the white man.

As his pony made its way west, gingerly avoiding the holes of a prairie dog town, the young warrior tried to sort out the tangles in his mind—that's what his mind was like, a tangled bridle. Patiently, slowly, he went back over events, and decided that he did not give a hoot about how white men think. And yet the tangle remained. What was it he wanted Sweeney to tell him? What can a Kiowa learn from a white soldier that he must know?

The ride back to the village was not a short one, yet such was Autumn Thunder's preoccupation that before he was aware of where he was he heard the distant sounds of a great commotion. He kicked his pony into a gallop but by the time he reached the village he realized that there was no crisis. The village was merely celebrating the return of the raiding party.

Chapter 19

That night his dreams were as tangled as his thoughts had been on the way back from Fort Sill. There were explosions. There were horses. There was Autumn Thunder killing Sweeney, then, anxiously, raising him from the dead. Set-tainte and Addo-eta were standing on the porch of a stone house at Fort Sill. Sweeney and his black soldiers slammed open the shutters of the house, fired their pistols all at once, and Set-tainte and Addo-eta fell dead, while Autumn Thunder stood beside the porch unable to warn them, though he had known what was about to happen.

He awoke in the dark, and lay listening to the strong, steady breathing of Gathers the Grass mixed with the night sounds of the plains. It was not unusual for Autumn Thunder to wake before dawn, and when he did, he always lay awake for a long while, listening to the world begin to stir. Mostly he listened for sounds that did not belong. He knew about the killer soldiers who had attacked the Cheyennes on the Washita, knew how they had killed women and children, and men with their hands held forward in surrender. It was not so long ago when this had happened. The yellow-haired officer who had led the massacre had been stationed at Fort Sill for awhile, and several southern Cheyenne survivors of the massacre had warned Gui-pah-go to watch out for that demon.

Autumn Thunder lay in the dark listening to the night sounds—listening for the sound of cavalry to come creeping in the dawn to slaughter his pregnant wife. Lying in wait like this did not put him on edge. Rather, it depressed his spirits.

Where was their future if they had to listen forever for the snakes to crawl at night?

The upper wall of the tepee began to glow with the coming of dawn. He could lay no longer. Gently he hugged Gathers The Grass, who sighed but did not wake up. His spirits were still depressed and he did not know why as he walked down to the Red River, threw off his breechclout, and plunged into the chilly waters.

An early morning wind made the river choppy but Autumn Thunder cut through the ripples with powerful strokes for about thirty yards, then he turned around and swam back to shore. The current had carried him about ten yards below where he had dropped his blanket and breechclout. He walked slowly, letting the wind dry his skin. He donned his breech-clout, wrapped his blanket around him, and stepped into his moccasins. He felt a hollow, aching feeling in the pit of his stomach. There had been a time when he did not take these early morning swims alone. He turned and looked toward the closest tepee to his own, the one that belonged to Seven Doves, the widow of Ko-yah-te.

And then it hit him like a buffalo slug. He needed to talk to Sweeney about buffalo hunters. Sweeney knew the buffalo hunters. He might have an idea of which one would most likely have killed Ko-yah-te.

Abruptly the loneliness and depression vanished. Of course! It would have taken something terribly important to make him go to Sweeney. Why did it take so long for him to realize what was troubling him? And it was then that he discovered a part of himself he had never known, yet as a Kiowa he had always known. He had had no idea of how to find Ko-yah-te's killer. Killing other white men as he found them on the plains, especially killing buffalo hunters if he could find them without their deadly long-range rifles in their hands—all that was a form of revenge, but he wanted the scalp of the precise white man who had done the deed. Failing to find a way to discover Ko-yah-te's killer, he had put such thoughts in the back of his mind.

That was the trouble. It was one thing to pretend the white man were not killing off all the buffalo. Maybe what the medicine men said was true, that white men could never kill off the buffalo. But he had no right to forget about the murder of his friend, and in trying to do so his conscience would make him pay. His conscience had sent him on a fool's errand yesterday. Today he would tell about the killing of Ko-yah-te.

But how could he tell Sweeney without letting him know that they had been down in Texas, which was unapproved behavior.

"Who gave them the right to tell us where we could go?" he said silently into the night. But he knew he would have to go to Sweeney. He might tell Sweeney half of the truth.

"You are back so soon," said Sweeney with an amused look on his face. "That could mean either that you remembered what you wanted to ask me about or that something else crossed your mind overnight."

Matt Leeper started to translate, but Autumn Thunder shook his head again and again. "I'll tell you, my friend Sweeney, that something bad happened the last snow."

"That far back?" Sweeney asked the Kiowa. "When you went to Texas?"

Leeper translated the English into Kiowa.

Autumn Thunder was silent for a moment, his face frozen in his white man mask. This "friend" was trying to trick him by getting him to admit that his people had spent the winter where they were not supposed to be. Why should this white man care? It was only an Indian that had been murdered. Autumn Thunder gave Sweeney a look of sour contempt and began to walk toward his horse. He would have gone if Matt Leeper had not spoken up.

"He has something he needs to talk to you about. When a Kiowa wants to talk, you'd best listen," he told Sweeney.

Sweeney walked over to Autumn Thunder's horse and grabbed his bridle. "Don't go," he said apologetically. "I promise I will not ask about Texas."

The three men walked over to Evans's store. Evans sometimes served breakfast at the tables in the back of the store. When Autumn Thunder smelled the bacon and eggs, his heart softened enough to sit down with Sweeney and Leeper. His body craved this white man food, so good and so rare for him to eat.

Sweeney said nothing further until the food was in front of them and Autumn Thunder was struggling to imitate Sweeney's use of knife and fork. Then he spoke, carefully; Matt Leeper translated, carefully; and Autumn Thunder listened, still suspicious.

"I just want to tell you," Sweeney said with a smile, "that I'm not mad because a bunch of Kiowas stole my horses in Texas and while we were walking home a bunch of Comanches tried to wipe us out. None of my men got hurt and I might make captain after all." Autumn Thunder found himself glad for Sweeney that none of his men got hurt, but he was puzzled by Sweeney's reference to rank because he had no knowledge of Sweeney's long, humiliating struggle for promotion in a stagnant army.

"Why do you think I did such a thing?" he asked through Leeper.

"Because last week I saw Po-lan-te riding one of those horses. I know Po-lan-te is your friend. If he was there, you were there."

"Maybe he traded for the horse," Autumn Thunder suggested.

"It does not matter, my friend. I am not mad and I won't make trouble for you. Nobody got hurt. I just wish you wouldn't steal *my* horses." He smiled. Leeper smiled. Autumn Thunder did not smile, not outside, but inside he did. The white man honestly *thought* he and Autumn Thunder were friends. "Don't steal *my* horses," he had said. "Steal somebody *else's* horses," he meant. At least he understood that horse stealing was a thing of honor for Kiowas to do.

"You came to speak to me of something," said Sweeney. "Your heart is sad, this I can tell." He leaned forward, and so did Leeper. Inside the white man house, Autumn Thunder spoke softly, and the two men did not want to misunderstand the Kiowa's words.

Autumn Thunder gave up on the fork, picked up a strip of bacon, put it in his mouth, and his face relaxed with pleasure at the strong, salty taste. "You know my friend Ko-yah-te?" he asked.

Sweeney shook his head, but Leeper described the warrior to him and Sweeney recalled who he was, a short, lean, muscular young man with the slightest beginnings of a mustache, and hair that was just a shade lighter than the normal stark black of his people. "I know him," he said.

"This winter, after a buffalo hunt, while we were breaking camp, he was killed, shot from ambush by a white man."

"How do you know it was a white man?" Sweeney asked.

Autumn Thunder produced for evidence the spent shell, and Sweeney, like Autumn Thunder, recognized it as the custom load of a buffalo hunter, not at all the kind of bullet normally used by an Indian. The warrior spread his hands and explained that he had found the shell and the shooting position in the snow a far shot away from where Ko-yah-te died.

Sweeney asked Evans to pour them some coffee. It was very good coffee, better than what the Kiowas normally received in annuities. For a moment Autumn Thunder was nearly transported by the aroma. Sweeney raised his mug and sipped it thoughtfully as Autumn Thunder told his story. When the coffee hit Sweeney's brain, he knew almost immediately that the killer had to be Tuck.

Sweeney had been the prime beneficiary of Tuck's bad run of poker luck. At the last session, clouded with good whiskey and the smoke of cheap cigars, he had broken Tuck with a full house, fours high, against Tuck's three aces. Tuck had reared up in a great roar, turned over the table, and called the whole table a bunch of cheaters, offending no one because Tuck always did that when he ran out of money at the poker table. After that he would always order drinks all around, to be paid for by the biggest winner, with Tuck promising to pay the buyer back when he returned from his next profitable buffalo hunt. He never did, but Sweeney didn't mind because he generally won the money back from Tuck, and much more, Tuck being a miserable poker player.

At that last poker session, as they righted the table, cleaned up the cards and waited for the drinks to come, Tuck had announced that, "Seein' as you boys have took my whole stake, I'm gonna have to do something I hate to do, kill buffalo in the winter time!"

Nobody said a word. Horace Jones was counting the cards to make sure they had not missed any. Schnitzer was counting his money because his stack was so close to what it was when he had started that he was curious to discover whether he was ahead or behind.

"Boys," Tuck said, "the buffalo's down below Red River, and I'm gonna kill me all of them if I have to hire a whole battalion of skinners to git their hides. Now, Lieutenant, if'n you can keep them Keeways from comin' down and takin' *my* hide, I'll be back in two-three weeks with enough money to keep you in Peruna's Tonic till the devil takes your damned soul, except this time I'm gonna get lucky and you'll be goin' home broke. Just you see that them devils don't steal your horses while you're sleepin'. I swear there ain't a sadder sight than watchin' a bunch a horse soldiers sore-footin' it into the post and knowin' that they've done given them bloody redskins good cavalry mounts to improve the breedin' of those disgustin' ponies they ride.''

With real whiskey warming his belly on this night, and a pocket full of silver dollars and greenbacks, mostly donated by old fill-an-Inside-Straight Tuck, as the poker players called him in his absence, Sweeney could not abide Tuck's big mouth without giving as good as he got.

"Why would you need us?" he asked. "I thought your hobby was killin' Indians. Why, I'd hate to deprive you of your hobby by runnin' down to Texas and killin' off every damned one of them before you get a chance to level on them with old Red-killer from a mile off. Why, you're so brave, I'll bet you never seen the eyes of a one of them before you holed them."

Tuck had just drained his glass of whiskey. There was no bottle on the table so he grabbed Jones's glass, tossed down its contents, stood up, and threw over the table again. "I guess you never learn!" he snarled at Sweeney. "You're callin' me a coward again. You remember the last time you called me a coward?''

"Seems like I nearly broke my fist on that jaw of yours and skinned my knee on your nose and scuffed the toe of my boot on your hind end!"

"Damn right you did," answered Tuck, who was becoming disoriented. "And tonight it's gonna happen to you all over again if you don't take it back."

"Well, you do love to backshoot Indians," Sweeney declared. "And you managed to miss the fightin' in the unpleasant last war. And you do your best work against a bunch of big, shaggy cows that can't shoot back. I'd say that makes you a coward. But I'll take it back if you'll let me go to bed before I get as stinkin' drunk as usual. I got to tell you all, I'm sick of gettin' drunk, especially with Tuck here—in fact, I'm downright sick.'' With that, he lurched out of the store and into the dusty road to release the contents of his stomach.

Autumn Thunder saw the sour look on Sweeney's face as the old lieutenant listened to his story, and he assumed it was a look of contempt. He stopped his story midsentence. ''I do not see why you should care about this,'' he said. ''I know how soldiers feel about Kiowas.''

The images of Tuck, Horace Jones, and Neil Evans vanished.

''You are wrong, my friend. There is nothing I'd rather do than kill the sonofabitch who killed Ko-yah-te. Because of men like that we're liable to have a full-scale Indian war on our hands and I'd rather do something that'll calm you down so you'll stop stealing my horses when me and my men are just taking a quiet little ride around north Texas.''

''Good,'' Autumn Thunder said in English. ''You help Autumn Thunder find that sumbitch and watch me kill 'im.''

Sweeney pulled at his mustache. ''Can't do that,'' he said. ''But maybe I can find out who he is and . . .'' He gave Leeper a look that he wanted the young interpreter sworn to confidence. ''Maybe I'll let you know where he is so you can get him. Maybe.''

Autumn Thunder did not smile.

''You do that, I be your friend, good friend and never steal your horses again!''

Chapter 20

Cyrus Beede was more than annoyed. His mustache fairly trembled with fury because all the Indians had arrived at Fort Cobb except the ones that had caused all the trouble.

The five great southeastern tribes were represented. So were the Delawares, the Wichitas, and the Caddoes. And the southern Cheyennes and Arapahos. Everybody in the territory who might be useful in solving the problems of the southern plains was there except the problems themselves.

In Autumn Thunder's village, the warriors were champing at the bit to go. There would be that good beef and bread, they were certain. And presents. But Au-sai-mah had been told by the chiefs of the other bands to wait, and he agreed.

When the whites held a conference, they reasoned, they did not give away food and goods out of heartfelt generosity toward the Indian. They wanted something from them. For the Kiowas to show up on time meant they were anxious to give the whites what they wanted. No, it would be good to wait. So they got started a week later than they would have had to if they wanted to arrive on time at Fort Cobb.

At Fort Sill the Kiowas came together and made their way north to Fort Cobb in one large group. Many of the men rode their finest ponies and dressed in their best clothes. When they neared Fort Cobb they went into a sort of parade formation, lances tilted upward like knights of old, their points gleaming in the sunlight.

Fully adorned, they entered the fort sitting straight up on their ponies, eyes staring ahead looking for all the world like what they thought they were, the great nation of Kiowas, mighty enough to take on all enemies and grind them into the dust of the plains. Even as they stared straight ahead, they could see the impression they were making on the soldiers, commissioners, agents, and men of the other tribes as they paraded through the gate and made a circuit of the old disheveled fort.

Having made their entrance, they now rode their ponies out of the fort and left the animals with a handful of young apprentice warriors. Then they returned to the fort on foot and circulated among the knots of men who were already there.

Au-sai-mah told Tsein-kop-te to stay near the big-mouthed Po-lan-te to shut him up if he felt like bragging to anybody about the raids he had been a part of. It was a smart move. The young brave, flushed with success, ached to tell every Cheyenne and Arapaho he met about stealing horses right out of a cavalry bivouac. But the old warrior could tell when the young man was getting ready to launch into a narration, and one stony look was enough to move Po-lan-te to silence.

Others were not so reticent. One warrior was telling anybody who would listen about Tsein-tainte's murderous feats in Texas and let slip that there were some white children being held by the various bands.

Some of the Kiowas were disappointed to find that the Cheyennes had gotten tired of waiting for them and gone home. But the Quakers were not depending upon the Cheyennes for any key role here. It was the Cherokees, the Chickasaws, the Choctaws, red men who had learned white ways, who would bring wisdom to their wild brothers.

Once the ceremonies were out of the way the following morning, a man stood up to speak—the strangest-looking man Autumn Thunder had ever seen. His skin was dark, like Autumn Thunder's, and his hair and eyes were dark, but he wore a suit—not a suit five sizes too big like the shoddy goods that were dealt out to Kiowas during the giving of annuities, but a tailored suit. The man was wearing boots, and a broadbrimmed hat like the whites wore in Texas. His hair was short, he wore no earrings, and before he spoke he pulled a watch from his vest pocket and wound it!

But he was an Indian. That Autumn Thunder knew. He was the word that meant not just Kiowas, but Comanches, Wichitas, Cheyennes, Caddoes—and these men.

The man began to speak, in English. Not stilted, stumbling English like a few of the Kiowas spoke, but English like Sweeney spoke—no, not quite—there was a different cadence, a different way with the words, yet it was the same. Autumn Thunder could make out some of the words, but not the sense of the speech, so he turned to Horace Jones, who was translating into the Comanche tongue.

"My brothers," said the Cherokee. "Many years have passed since we last fought the white man. We had fine lands to the east," he said, gesturing with his hand to that place where the sun had appeared a few hours before. "We were a powerful people. We had white man's weapons. We knew the white man's tongue. We could write our own tongue in words on paper like the white man. Some of us even prayed like the white man, to the white man's god. But the white man wanted the lands we possessed. And he was powerful. We fought with all our power, and yet he defeated us. He set us on a path to the west, across the eastern lands, and many of our people died.

"But we survived. We crossed the big river, and many other rivers too, and we came to the place he had made for us. There were some kind white men who helped us, but mostly we made a new life for ourselves. We did not turn our heads to the east, looking for white men to avenge ourselves on. We knew that killing white men would only bring more of them to kill us. We had the big river to keep them out. We thought they would stay on their side. But they did not.

"But when they came to our land, to our surprise, the white chief did not say, 'It is time for a new treaty, time to give up more lands and move west.' They told the whites who crossed the river, 'This is Cherokee land, this is Choctaw land, this is Chickasaw land. This is Creek land.' And we, the Five Nations, could take up arms to drive these bad people off our lands.

"So we know how to deal with white savages. But we do not know what to do with red savages. When we first came to Indian Territory, Osages and Kiowas would raid our farms, steal our horses and cattle. How could you do such things to your brothers? And yet it was so. We came west poor like you are. We worked hard to grow our crops, and our animals, and you would take them away from us and make us poor again.

"Now the white chiefs have offered to take you by the hand as they have taken us by the hand. They do not wish to send you on a long journey that will kill your women, your children, and your old ones, like they did to us. They wish only for you to stop raiding into Texas. If you will leave Texas alone, maybe they will leave you to raise your children in peace.

"I ask you for our sake, for your sake, to stop your killing and stealing and rape and torture. Look at us. We have a good life. We have houses that are warm in the winter and we have barns filled with food to feed us and our animals. This can be life for you and your children if you will live in peace with us, and live in peace with the white man."

The Kiowas looked at each other, puzzled, wondering who this man was to think he had the right to tell Kiowas how to live. Po-lan-te turned to Autumn Thunder. Instead of a look of anger, or betrayal, or mockery, his features drooped in gloom.

"Is that what the red white man would have us be to survive?" he asked. "Be like them? Wear tall shoes and grow a big soft belly? My heart . . ."

Autumn Thunder was stunned to see his most irrepressible warrior brother looking so sad and helpless.

"We must never be like them," he said softly, so Jones would not hear. "I will never be like them. I will join my brother Ko-yah-te first, and all the old ones too."

As the white red man droned on, Autumn Thunder thought about the last great chief of the Kiowas. To-hauson. He thought about the great battle they and the Comanches had fought against the Cheyennes long ago before they made peace. He thought about Set-tainte and his great battles so often recounted at the council fires. And Tsein-tainte, and the forty-one mules he had stolen in the dark of night from within the walls of Fort Sill. How the people would laugh every time he told of how they frightened the guards away then just took the mules without killing a single soldier.

But it was the buffalo hunts in the days when the herds were so vast that all the bands could get together, to hunt together, to feast together, to rejoice in the honor of being a

Kiowa in the days of the great Sun Dance. Now it was getting so the buffalo herds were broken up and smaller. But Autumn Thunder would not allow his shoulders to slump like Po-lan-te.

"Do not worry, my brother," he said. "We will never be like him. We will live like Kiowa men, or we will die like Kiowa men."

When the red white man had finished his speech, Au-sai-mah arose to answer. Au-sai-mah was neither Sitting Bear, who had resisted the whites without mercy until the day he died, or Kicking Bird, who always seemed to be counseling submission, like the white Indian from the east who had just spoken.

"My brother in the fine white man suit," he began, and the Kiowas laughed, as did the Comanches, who had arrived even after the Kiowas. "My brother in the white man tall shoes that make the feet cry out for a breath of air on warm days like today. Thank you for your words. Sometimes I tell my braves such words. But not today. Seeing you today, trying to be a white man, reminds me of the fish I caught from Medicine Creek long ago. I pulled the fish from the water and he danced on his tail like a man trying to walk on two legs. But soon he realized he was not a man and he flopped over and laid down breathing hard until he could breathe no longer."

The Kiowas smiled at the old story, one they had heard so many times from the wise old men.

"You said that some of your people prayed like the white man. None of the people in our village pray like the white man. The white man picks a time to pray, and builds himself a place to pray. He has a time and a place for everything. Does the Great Spirit appear only at a certain time, at a certain place? We follow the buffalo. He is sacred to us. He feeds us and clothes us and gives us so much. Do you know that many of our warriors still hunt the buffalo with the bow? Could you do the same? No, because you have taken the white man by one hand, and it takes two hands to shoot a bow.

"I tell you, my brother, we will give up the bow and arrow when the white man gives up scratching on hides." He had been standing tall and proud as he spoke, and he had the attention of all, but now he stood just a bit taller, even as he leaned toward the Cherokee delegation.

"You cannot keep us on the reservation!" he thundered. "We live by hunting the buffalo, and the buffalo do not stay on the reservation. They wander over the plains, free. On our swift ponies, free, we will find our brothers the buffalo, and we will hunt them for our food, and our clothing, and our lodges. And when we have killed enough of them, we will pray to them and thank them for giving us life.

"It is our life. It is a good life. We will not give it up."

Then he sat down, to the approving sounds of all the Indians of the west, even some of the Wichitas. The men of the Five Nations sat stolidly, as if they could have expected no more than this kind of stubbornness from their wild brothers.

But then another one of them stood up, an older man, tall, thin, still powerful, dressed not as well as the first, with strong, callused hands. He had a light complexion, but the Kiowas could still recognize from his features and his straight black hair that he was one of their eastern cousins.

He was a man who was not intimidated by his own silence. He studied the various groups seated on the ground in front of him and waited while they quieted down, quickly, because one thing the easterners and westerners shared was politeness in council, and an eagerness to hear good speakers. Then he waited a while longer, even though the silence was perfect but for the sounds of the scissortails and the buzzing of flies.

It was almost as if he were waiting for all of them to hold their breath before he would begin, and it was almost as if they let out a collective, quiet sigh of relief when he began.

"My brothers," he said. "It makes me sad that you can see only the buffalo but cannot see the emptiness. Do you not know that the buffalo are going away? Then, my brothers, what will you eat?

"The earth is a gift from God. It yields forth corn, and squash, and beans, and melons. On the other side of the river we raised great crops of these things that fed us through the worst winters and so it is for us today. In a few years, the buffalo will be gone and then come the winter, what will you eat? It would make my heart break to see you huddled in your lodges with no food because you were waiting for the buffalo that would never come again. You must learn to break up the earth and make the seeds grow, It is your only hope."

It was a short speech, a plainspoken speech, without dramatic flourishes but aimed at the hearts of the Kiowas and Comanches. His aim was true, and yet it missed its mark.

A chief of the Kiowa-Apaches rose and spoke equally briefly. The buffalo had gone before, he said, to punish the plains tribes when they misbehaved. But they had always come back. If the people just went a year or two without killing any, the mighty herds would return.

"During those years," he added. "The wild cattle in Texas will keep our lodges content through the winter."

Like most of his cohorts, Autumn Thunder was a very good listener. But it was difficult to make sense out of what he was hearing. During the winter they had looked for buffalo, and they had found buffalo, enough to get them through the winter. It seemed to him that there must be plenty of buffalo around. Could the white Indian have been lying about the buffalo? White men lied. Why shouldn't white Indians lie?

Now it was time for Lone Wolf to speak. At this time the Kiowas had no one principal chief, but Lone Wolf was the greatest of their living chiefs, and he was to be their principal speaker.

Autumn Thunder turned his attention from his own thoughts to Lone Wolf just in time to hear him tell Cyrus Beede, one of the Quaker chiefs, that the Kiowas would return the captives as well as White Horse's famous forty-one stolen mules, but only if the Washington chief extended the reservation from the Missouri River in the north to the Rio Grande in the south, removed all the troops, and brought White Bear and Big Tree back from his prison cell in Texas.

For a moment Autumn Thunder saw the answer clearly. The words of Gathers The Grass from her conversations with Sweeney made him understand. The Washington chief would never agree to such things. "Americans never give back land," Sweeney had told Gathers The Grass. "The Americans *take* land."

So there would be a fight.

Later, as the warriors were dining on beef the government had purchased from the Five Nations and the Delawares, Autumn Thunder heard Lone Wolf and Kicking Bird in heated discussion.

"They tried to get me to agree to stop raiding in Texas,"

Lone Wolf said, tearing a chunk of beef off a rib with his teeth.

Kicking Bird looked at him steadily. He knew what was coming next, and he knew that now was the time to listen, no matter how much he disliked what he heard. He had made no speeches at this council because many of his people were angry with him for being too close to the whites. Lone Wolf was doing his best to goad Kicking Bird into an argument.

"I told them we had always raided in Texas. We had a right to raid in Texas. I could see they got very mad at me. I don't care. They can eat my dung and like it."

Kicking Bird still said nothing.

"I know what you do," Lone Wolf added. "You go to your white friends and you tell them all about the bad Indians who are doing all the bad things and how sorry you are that they cannot behave. Listen to me now, my brother. We are Kiowa. We are strong. We will not be women as you would want us to be. Do not be so close to the whites or bad things will happen."

In the corner of his eye Autumn Thunder happened to catch a glimpse of Maman-ti, whom the whites called "Sky Walker." As usual, he had said nothing, but the look on his face as he stared at the silent Kicking Bird said it all.

Chapter 21

Tuck's wagons were piled so high with the hides of buffalo that he had to stop at the ranch of a livestock dealer and purchase more mules to pull the vehicles over the hills to the railroad for shipment east. He had left eastern Colorado littered with the rotting carcasses of hundreds of buffalo.

He had an old Sharps buffalo gun that he no longer cared for, having recently purchased a newer model that was custom-made for him. The old one was about worn out anyway, so he did not mind trading it to a Ute warrior for an old squaw of about forty.

He was sick of cooking for himself or eating the awful cooking of one of his skinners. In fact he was sick of doing a lot of things for himself. This woman, he thought, would be grateful to be freed from the Utes. She was a Kiowa who had been captured by the Osages on the Washita River years before, and had been given over to a Ute war party for two sturdy Indian ponies.

She had been a strong, tough woman with an unquenchable spirit before she had been left to the tender mercies of the Utes, but three years in the lodge of a vicious old Ute warrior had broken her down into a submissive, nearly toothless beast of burden.

It was the submissive part of her personality that appealed to Tuck. The succession of buffalo skinners he hired were a cantankerous, independent lot. He needed, he craved, almost constitutionally, a weak, defeated person he could kick around without fear of retaliation.

He purchased canvas and cut some lodgepoles and commanded her to construct a tepee for him to live in when he was out hunting buffalo. She raised up a pretty fair dwelling for him, kindled a fire within and began to handle the cooking chores so competently that he allowed her to sleep in the tepee with him.

Each morning she cooked his breakfast and served him. Then, while he inspected the animals, the wagons, and his guns and ammunition, she knocked down the tepee and loaded it on one of the wagons. He was so pleased by her skills that when the weather got cold, he took her under his blanket to keep him warm. Sometimes he even had sex with her and she never seemed to object.

So content was she to be away from the cruel Ute who had beaten her daily and burdened her like a pack horse that she conceived a great loyalty for this rough buffalo hunter who seemed to appreciate her homemaking skills.

In the time she lived with Tuck, life was easy compared to her life among the Utes. She was never hungry, she was seldom uncomfortable, and the men for the most part let her alone—until the day the knife of one of Tuck's mule skinners slipped while he was skinning a particularly tough old bull, slicing off half his hand.

That meant Tuck had to hire another skinner, and he chose Joe McGurk, who had a reputation as one of the best skinners on the plains. But McGurk's girlfriend had run off and married an army sergeant at Fort Riley, and that made him bitter and negative about the institutions of marriage and cohabitation.

McGurk was a sly one. He was able to tease Tuck about shacking up with a squaw without the hunter turning on him. He started carefully, but within a month of his arrival he was boldly declaring his disdain for any man who would share his blanket with an Injun woman.

Tuck swallowed the bait and wriggled on the hook.

"I ain't shacked up with her," Tuck said. "She's my cook and caretakin' woman."

"Don't try and fool me," McGurk returned. "I been around too long. I know she's your woman, and any white man who'd sleep with an Injun woman has got to be a real lowlife."

Tuck had an answer but somehow he could not get the words out. After years of bullying people to get his way, he found a man who intimidated him. Day after day McGurk kept ammering at Tuck that Indians were animals, which Tuck had always thought was so, until this woman had come along and started taking care of his life.

He wanted to kill McGurk for his nagging impertinence, but McGurk was the fastest and best skinner he had ever seen. McGurk did not know how to shut up, and Tuck simply could not stand being told again and again that "That Injun woman runs your life."

Finally after listening to one more lengthy lecture about the sins of sodomy, and how copulating with an Injun, especially an old toothless squaw, was one of the most disgusting things on God's green earth, Tuck decided that he had had enough.

So he checked the loads in his buffalo rifle, walked over to his tepee, and ducked in through the open flap. The woman was stirring a savory buffalo stew when she heard him enter.

"You ready for food now or you want later?" she asked.

"Ready for you if you want." He said nothing, just cocked his rifle, pointed it, and blew her brains all over the inside of the canvas-covered tepee.

He stood for a moment staring down at her still body, then turned and ducked out the open flap of the tepee. He walked over to one of the canvas-topped wagons where McGurk was sitting up on a pile of buffalo hides scratching his beard and wondering why some fool would wake him up by shooting his rifle so close by.

Red-faced and angry, Tuck looked hard at the skinner. "I done her," he growled. "Now if I hear another word from you about her, damned if I won't do you too!" And he walked back to his tepee to get her out of there and have some dinner.

Au-sai-mah called together the dog soldiers and told them not to let any of the young braves stray far from the village. "Settainte and Addo-eta will be released if we stay out of Texas," he told the young brave. "But if the Texans report that they have spotted any Indians raiding south, then the two chiefs will stay in prison."

For a while the young men behaved themselves. None of them wanted to be blamed if the white men decided to break their word.

Word came to the village that Kicking Bird's braves had stopped a Comanche war party on their way to Red River.

Kicking Bird himself told the Comanches he would shoot their horses if they did not turn around at once and go back to their village.

And yet for awhile it seemed that the whites might break their word. The weather was beginning to heat up and still the chiefs did not come. Po-lan-te told Au-sai-mah that if the chiefs were not delivered within the moon, he would take a party into Texas and they would bring back one scalp for every additional day of delay.

Every other day Po-lan-te was riding to Fort Sill for news and when half the summer passed without the arrival of Set-tainte and Addo-eta, it was Po-lan-te who, with some of his friends, began to vanish from the village for days at a time. They would leave very early in the morning, before others in the village were awake, and they would return very late at night.

Everybody knew what they were doing but nobody could or would stop them. Because nobody was coming home hurt the villagers knew the young men were not going south to fight, but to attack isolated homesteads. "One scalp for every day of delay," Po-lan-te had said, and there were rumors around the village that the midnight warriors were holding scalp dances elsewhere just before they returned home. There was no doubt that their horse herds were accumulating some new bloodstock.

The oaks were turning yellow along the creek banks before Set-tainte and Addo-eta came home to Fort Sill, and in return for their release the Kiowas had to agree to take up the white man's ways. They would live near the agencies and farm, they were told, and such was their desire to free their captive chiefs that Gui-pah-go, Tay-nay-angopte, and the other leaders agreed to follow the plow, although none of them liked the idea.

The Comanches had a different task. A number of their young men who had slipped across Red River to raid were still "unavailable," and some of the authorities were determined to catch them.

"We'll never find them," said Colonel Black Jack Davidson, now commanding at Fort Sill, to Indian Commissioner Smith.

The friendly Comanche chief Cheevers suggested a way out. "We may find them west of Antelope Hills," he said, and agreed to lead a group of warriors into the hills to search for them.

He chose ten braves, half of them Comanches, and half of them Kiowas, including Po-lan-te, Autumn Thunder, two Kiowas from Tay-nay-angopte's band, and a warrior named Go-tebo. A troop of cavalry went along with them, commanded by Lieutenant Lewis.

"I am not going to do this thing," Autumn Thunder told Au-sai-mah. "The Comanches are our brothers, and I will not help the white men to find them and punish them."

Au-sai-mah nodded sagely, but Autumn Thunder noticed a little smile playing on his face. "The white men have always used Indians to find other Indians," he said, struggling for a word that would describe red men and finally settling on the white man term. "They cannot find anybody without an Indian to be their eyes. Still, you should have a little faith in Cheevers. He is a good man. They will pay you money, give you a uniform, big horse, good guns. Maybe you'll have to give them back, maybe you won't. Trust Cheevers."

Autumn Thunder was ordered to the Fort Sill quartermaster, where he drew a uniform, a carbine, and fifty rounds of ammunition. This was a bewildering turnaround for the young warrior. Not so many moons ago he had been fighting against these men, now he was riding with them, in cavalry saddles on cavalry mounts, wearing the same clothes as they were. And what was so strange to him, he had not made peace with them, and yet together they were hunting down Comanche warriors whom he regarded as his brothers.

He did not like it when he was selected. He did not like it when he was enrolled. He did not like it when he drew the supplies, and he felt like an uncomfortable fool wearing pants that still had a seat in them. But Gathers The Grass told him that he looked handsome and that everything would be all right.

"You'll never have to fight your Comanche brothers," she told him. "You will see." What did Au-sai-mah and Gathers The Grass know that he did not? And yet he did not discuss the matter with them any further. Maybe he wanted to be surprised. Trust Cheevers. He barely knew Cheevers!

They had thirty days to find the renegades. If in that time they could not find them, they had better have a good reason for not finding them, or their bands would be denied rations. Autumn Thunder fretted over that. The responsibility was theirs, but Cheevers told him not to worry. "Since when did we need white man's rations to survive?" he asked. "We will get paid anyway," he said. "Then if we don't get the good, we will simply buy some food for our people from Evans the trader and hunt for the rest. You can still kill buffalo or deer, can't you?" he asked.

"Or," he added with an ironic twist, "wild cows."

As soon as they had crossed Red River, Cheevers' dispatched his Comanches well ahead of him and when they returned that night to the main group he announced to Lieutenant Lewis that his warriors had tracked the renegades to Double Mountain. If they pushed hard, he said, they could make Double Mountain by sundown tomorrow.

There was a chill in the morning air and a mist hung over a nearby creek as they headed out the following morning with good army bacon, coffee, and hard biscuits in their stomachs. Throughout the afternoon they rode like an arrow toward Double Mountain, and by the time the sun threw the shadows of the nearby peaks across the valley they were close to their goal.

Again Cheevers sent out his advance scouts. The sun was but a red memory on the horizon when they returned to Cheevers and the cavalry troop. The leader of the group of scouts spoke to Cheevers and Autumn Thunder almost laughed out loud. Only with difficulty did he hold his "white man face" when Cheevers turned to Lieutenant Lewis.

"The scouts came just in time to see the bad men leave Double Mountain and head southwest," he said. "They followed them long enough to see them make camp on the Brazos River."

"We can't follow them in the dark," said the lieutenant. "We'll have to make camp now."

"We should follow in dark," Cheevers pretended to insist.

The lieutenant sneered. "Could we find them in the dark?" he asked, skeptically.

"Maybe yes, maybe no," Cheevers answered. "But want bad to catch those men for Colonel Black Jack."

"Tomorrow," said Lewis.

Late the next afternoon the scouts returned saying the renegades had broken camp early.

"They say if only we had rode through the night we would have caught them asleep," said Cheevers.

"Do *you* think we would have caught them if we had ridden all night?" the lieutenant asked.

"For sure, for sure," Cheevers replied.

"Then we'll ride all night tonight," the lieutenant said.

"Cannot do that," said Cheevers.

"And why not?"

"Lots of rock. We're not sure which way they went from Brazos. Cannot track good by night on rock."

Autumn Thunder understood the game Cheevers was playing with the cavalry lieutenant. All the Kiowas understood. Only the soldiers did not understand. They thought that Cheevers and his scouts were merely stupid.

The next day the renegades were supposed to be on this mountain. Three days later they were said to be camped in that valley, dining on a stray cow they had killed.

The butchered cow was there all right, but the Kiowas all knew that it was their Comanche scouts who had partaken in the feast.

Autumn Thunder said nothing, not even to his fellow Kiowas, and he never cracked a smile, but as they continued south and the autumn winds began to blow a bit more chilly, he knew how this game was going to end.

The Comanche scouts had been gone for three days, and the soldiers were beginning to grumble that the scouts had taken their brand-new carbines and their fine cavalry mounts and skedaddled to join up with their renegade brothers.

Lieutenant Lewis reported their fears to Cheevers, who assured him that his men would not desert the cavalry. When they enrolled, they had promised the army that they would do a job, and a Comanche, once he has given his word, will never go back on it. Cheevers wore such a serious look as he spoke that even the skeptical lieutenant believed him, and sure enough, early the next morning, they could see the scouts approaching through the old mesquite cold and wet with morning condensation.

The scouts were sagging in their saddles. Anyone could see

that something must be wrong. When they reached the main party they dismounted wearily and reported to Cheevers. Wearing a look of keen disappointment, Cheevers walked over to the lieutenant and shook his head but did not speak.

"What? What?" asked the lieutenant, alarmed at the emotion etched morosely on the chief's usually good-natured countenance.

Cheevers just shook his head again.

"Where did they strike!" the lieutenant cried out with an edge of panic to his voice. That was all he needed, to track the warriors to the scene of a massacre.

Cheevers shook his head more briskly now. "No strike," he responded. "My men find track early and they follow. The bad men do not stop. My scouts went faster but they could see the bad men riding long strides. The big river too close and . . ." Cheevers could not continue.

"You're saying they've crossed the Rio Grande?" the lieutenant prompted.

"Must be down in Mexico by now," Cheevers said. "We try so hard to catch bad man for soldier chief Black Jack." The chief sighed and lowered his eyes.

The lieutenant slapped him on the shoulder, sending a dust cloud into the wind. "I never saw anybody try so hard," he said. "I shall tell Colonel Davidson that you all did your best. Do not worry, my friend."

Cheevers did not smile when he and Lieutenant Lewis reported back to Colonel Davidson that the renegade Comanches had eluded their clutches. The hard-bitten Davidson may have had his reservations but if he did, he wasn't saying.

A few days later a party of Comanche warriors rode into the village of Au-sai-mah. "Come on!" they shouted to Po-lan-te. "We're going to Texas!"

Po-lan-te and some of the others did not have to be told twice. Alarmed, Au-sai-mah grabbed the bridle of one of their horses.

"Why are you raiding?" he asked. "I thought you had agreed to stay on the reservation until the chiefs are returned."

"Our bands have moved back out on the plains," came the answer from the Comanches. "They are not giving us our rations anymore and there is no game around the fort. We will starve this winter if we stay close to the whites. You should think about that too.''

Autumn Thunder heard the Comanche's words and thought quickly. He had been hurt when, after the scouting party had returned to the fort, the army had simply taken back their weapons, uniforms, and horses.

In ten minutes' time he had caught his two best ponies, readied them for travel, told Gathers The Grass, in effect, not to wait up, and with three other Kiowas joined the Comanche raiding party. The young Comanche leader started to make a few remarks about "women who would let the white men put them on their knees," but Po-lan-te nudged the Comanche's pony with his own and crowded him toward the edge of the village.

"Do not get Au-sai-mah mad at you," he said, "or he will shoot your horses and then we will be going nowhere.''

Gathers The Grass stood in front of the tepee she had made when she was still more Wichita than Kiowa, holding fast to the cradleboard that contained her first child, a boy they called Deerfoot. Not long ago she would have tried to argue Autumn Thunder out of going, but now she knew better than to try, not now, not here. She just waited until she caught his eye and then shook her head slightly.

His eyes flashed sparks of warning, not of anger at her, but of his determination to strike another blow at people whose word was morning mist on a river. Outside the village he found several other Kiowas waiting, including Gui-tain and Tau-ankia. He understood why they had not come into the village. Tau-ankia was the son of Lone Wolf, who had been striving so hard to avoid direct conflict with the army, and Gui-tain was Lone Wolf's nephew. Other young Kiowa warriors were waiting in the shadows, all the sons of chiefs or other prominent Kiowas.

They all brought extra ponies but their baggage was light. Off they went like the wind, headed for Red River, headed for Texas. Autumn Thunder's heart soared. Forgotten was the month he had spent in the uniform of a cavalry private. This was life as his father had lived, as his grandfather had lived, not the life the white men would have them live.

They swept southward into Texas at an easy gallop, with a warm November wind at their cheeks and no fear in their hearts. They gave the homesteaders and the forts and the ranches a wide birth, making seventy miles a day. This was their unspoken deal with their fathers. Their destination was Mexico.

In a valley on the west fork of the Nueces River they decided to leave their spare ponies. Pago-to-goodle, who led the Kiowa contingent, turned to Autumn Thunder and Po-lan-te. "You guard the ponies," he commanded them. "We'll meet up with you later, when we get back from Mexico."

Po-lan-te's head dropped and Autumn Thunder felt his spirits plunge from its long flight. The *Onde* would command if they could, but anger surged to Autumn Thunder's throat. No! He had not come this far to guard a pony herd like an apprentice warrior. Who was this Pago-to-goodle?

To Po-lan-te's surprise, Autumn Thunder got right up into Pago-to-goodle's face. "My brother, we are going to Mexico," he said, and Po-lan-te, bucked up by Autumn Thunder's spirit, gave vent to his own temper, which was short at best. "We are not horse-herders," he said. "We are warriors. If you wanted somebody to take care of your ponies, you should have brought your little brothers."

There might have been a fight there, but the Comanche leader intervened. "This is a Comanche raid," he said. "We invited you to come along to help us kill Mexicans, not to fight among yourselves like hungry wolves over a dead deer. We can hobble the ponies and leave them in the valley. They'll still be here when we return."

Once they crossed the Rio Grande they rode roughshod over the countryside, and by the time they were headed back north fourteen scalps hung from their saddles. They were driving a herd of more than a hundred fifty horses and mules before them, and they had captured two Mexican boys.

They might have gotten away with the entire escapade had they behaved themselves on the north side of the Rio Grande. The lives of Mexicans were not held terribly valuable by Texans. But just on the Texas side of the Rio Grande, they killed a pair of Texans, and then, after they had made camp and started celebrating, one of their captives escaped and found a cavalry detachment camped in the vicinity.

Lieutenant Charles Hudson picked up some old tracks that led them to the hobbled horses, and he put two and two to-

gether. There couldn't be several mobs of Comanches raising
havoc on the border. These ponies had to belong to the ones
who had just come north across the Rio Grande, so he and his
men waited in ambush for the war party to return for their
spare animals.

It was the second week in December. Even this far south
the night winds were prophesying the coming of winter when
a messenger came to Lieutenant Hudson from Fort Clark telling him that the war party was close by, and the lieutenant
drove forward to meet them.

The rain was falling hard on the war party and the herd they
were driving when they spotted the troops in a valley two
miles away. The troopers saw them too, or at least they saw
the herd. The fun was over, Autumn Thunder thought. There
was going to be a fight, and he was not prepared to fight
cavalry.

Well, he had no choice, he thought, as the Comanches and
Kiowas dismounted and lay in wait on a ridge for the soldiers
to come up on them.

When the soldiers neared the ridge where the Comanches
and the Kiowas lay, they fanned out into a line of horsemen,
slowly moving uphill. The rain had stopped, but the hillside
was wet and slippery.

The warriors had the high ground and that encouraged them
to open up with their carbines while the soldiers were still a
quarter of a mile distant. The shots fell way short and the
troopers kept on coming. The soldiers knew the Indians' weapons well. Their horses continued their slow walk up the hill,
sometimes slipping in the mud, not approaching frontally but
to one flank until they had reached the same ridgeline. The
warriors continued to fire, but the terrain was such that the
soldiers were covered from the warriors by the contours of the
hillside as they climbed.

When the soldiers reached the top of the ridge, Autumn
Thunder saw them dismount. He had seen them do this drill
before on post, one handler for every three fighters, holding
the horses at the rear in readiness for further action. Meanwhile the dismounted troopers found cover behind rocks no
more than seventy-five yards away from the positions of Autumn Thunder and his cohorts.

From where he lay he could see the soldiers pulling cartridges from their bags and making little piles next to them. The Indians had to be careful about using up too much ammunition so their fire, while steady, was not heavy and didn't bother the soldiers very much.

Now it was guns pointed at guns, with the soldiers holding a slight advantage in numbers. They had yet to fire a shot. Autumn Thunder saw the officer, who was behind his men but still fairly well under cover, point his Colt forward, and shout, "Fire!"

Thirty-five carbines barked. The bullets thudded into the earth or *zinged* off the covering rocks, except for one that found a home in the shoulder of one of the Comanches. He let out a howl of surprise then swallowed his pain. Now both sides were firing nonstop at each other, both sides whooping and screaming, carbines popping, bullets ricocheting.

But the soldiers had better cover, more ammunition, and superior marksmanship, and even though nobody was getting hurt much, the warriors could feel that they were getting the worst of it. We are horse fighters! thought the Comanche who was leading the raid. "Let's get to the ponies!" he cried out, and the warriors vaulted from their positions and ran back over the ridge to where their ponies were tied.

Lieutenant Hudson saw his opportunity. His horses were being held in a hollow just behind their firing position. As soon as he saw the warriors leave their cover he gave the command to mount up and the horse holders brought their chargers forward. In an instant the big horses were galloping swiftly across the short space between them and the Indians. These were young warriors, many far less experienced than they pretended, and some of them panicked.

As the warriors grabbed their ponies and attempted to mount, the soldiers fired at close range and Indians began to fall. Autumn Thunder never looked back until he had leaped on the back of his pony and kicked it into a gallop. Beside him, mounting and quirting his pony, was Po-lan-te.

Autumn Thunder was lucky, Po-lan-te was not. Blood cascading from his mouth, the young Kiowa tumbled over his pony's neck and under its hooves. Disdaining the bullets that buzzed around him, Autumn Thunder dismounted and bent over his friend's body, but life had fled. All that was left was its limp vessel, face-down in the mud of south Texas.

A cavalry bullet buzzed past the left ear of Autumn Thunder. Another carved a shallow groove in his left arm. He had to leave his dead friend. His pony was running and so was he, by its side, hands on his saddle, then leaping astride the animal in full flight.

The soldiers fired again and again, forward into the scattered, fleeing warriors, several more of whom tumbled from the backs of their ponies. The spare ponies of the warriors were jumping about in a panic, frustrated from flight by their hobbled front legs. The captured herd of Mexican horses and mules took off in a body and galloped down the valley, away from the shooting.

Autumn Thunder's pony pulled hard for the top of a nearby hill. The other warriors had scattered in different directions. He turned to get a quick look down at the scene of the battle. One trooper was laboring up the hill after him. He took aim and fired a shot at the trooper, and must have nicked him because the soldier gave up his pursuit, swore loudly, and turned back down toward the valley.

Below him he could see a Kiowa afoot, limping badly, being chased by several soldiers led by the lieutenant. Autumn Thunder did not think, he reacted, galloping his pony headlong down the hill to pick up the Kiowa even though he knew his chances of getting to him before the soldiers were slim. He reloaded in full flight and fired at the horse of one of the lead riders. The horse went down, and the one behind went tumbling over him, but there were still a half dozen soldiers in pursuit.

Another Kiowa was already riding headlong toward the stranded warrior. Autumn Thunder had just finished reloading again when he realized that the man afoot was Tau-ankia, son of Gui-pah-go, and the one trying to rescue him was his cousin Gui-tain. Gui-tain reached for Tau-ankia to swing him up behind him, but the troopers were close. They fired. Tau-ankia fell in a heap, and Gui-tain tumbled from his pony and rolled to a stop beside his cousin.

This was something new for Autumn Thunder. He had never seen Kiowa or Comanche warriors routed in a pitched battle with soldiers. Now the troopers turned toward Autumn Thunder. There were too many of them and he had been working his pony hard. Quickly he turned his pony toward a downslope that put a hill between him and the troopers. His animal had a long downward glide now, while the soldiers had to either detour around the hill or go up and over it. Either way he would gain distance. He did not spare his pony. He quirted it hard and got good speed out of it for a quarter of a mile and when he looked back he was relieved that the soldiers had given up their pursuit to see if they had killed Tau-ankia and Gui-tain.

Chapter 22

For weeks word had been flying around the villages that Lone Wolf would soon be going south to recover the bones of his son and his nephew. When he did, he would be sure to leave at least as many white men lying pale and still and blood-covered. It was a measure of his status among his people that in the village of the peaceful Au-sai-mah, there were men who considered it their duty to accompany the great chief to Texas.

Autumn Thunder had every intention of going off to Texas with Gui-pah-go, but his chief, Au-sai-mah, had other ideas.

He summoned the young warrior. When he arrived in the chief's tepee he found Talia-koi already there, and so was the veteran raider, Tsein-kop-te. The flap to the tepee was closed, and Au-sai-mah lit his pipe and passed it around. Then he began to speak.

"You are like my brother," he said to Tsein-kop-te. "You have struck our enemies so many times in your life, and yet you've never let your passion for the tomahawk outweigh your wisdom."

He then turned to the two younger men. "You have no father. I have no sons. I lost my sons before you came to this earth. You are like my sons. I do not wish to lose more sons.

"Many of our warriors will go to Texas with Gui-pah-go and Maman-ti. I would like to make them stay home. But I cannot. They have no sense. Of all my fighting men, you have the most sense. If I cannot make you understand, then I know my medicine is weak and I must no longer be chief."

The two young men and Tsein-kop-te waited silently an‹
patiently for Au-sai-mah to explain.

"Birds come from Fort Sill, birds with feathers differen‹
from ours, but still birds, with stories. They say that the sol
diers know Gui-pah-go will go to Texas. They have said tha‹
when he does our villages will be naked to the long knives o
the soldiers.

"We cannot let that happen. I have spoken with chiefs o
the other bands: the Kogui, and the Kaigwa, and the Kata, an‹
the Sindiyuis. They have all said that they will keep some o
their best warriors at home because they believe that the sol
diers may attack their villages."

He paused, because he could feel Tsein-kopte's need t‹
speak.

"Au-sai-mah, my wise brother," Tsein-kop-te said. "Th‹
peace people will surely not allow the soldiers to attack."

"My birds fly to me with other words," Au-sai-mah con
tinued. "They say that the chief in Washington is calling th‹
peace people back to him. They say that he is not pleased wit‹
the peace people, and that he will make the soldier the new
chief—the angry one with the red hair on his face. We mus‹
think about our women and our children. Gui-pah-go will have
enough warriors. We need you here."

There was silence while the four men smoked and thought
These moments were among the chief's favorite times, when
men sat back and waited patiently for their thoughts to become
clear. He had seen how white men spoke before they thought.
He had told his warriors that when they were with a white
man and they wanted to know his thoughts, "If you can learn
their language, they will tell you everything. Just sit back and
look at him as if you expected him to say wise things. He will
be flattered and he will tell you everything you want to know
without you having to ask him questions. That is how they
are. They know much and yet they are foolish."

"My father," said Autumn Thunder, "our brother Po-lan-
te was killed in the fight. His soul roams the earth and begs
us to bring his body home. He longs for soldier blood to wash
away the blood he shed in Texas. How can we deny him
this?"

Au-sai-mah remained silent only long enough to be polite.
"You must deny him this, now!" he insisted, quietly but ur-

gently. "If your village were to perish while you were gone, the greatest revenge in the world could not bring back your families. You cannot afford such grief. The Kiowa must go on. You are the protectors of this village, because you are the wisest of my young warriors. You must stay home."

The silence was thicker than the smoke of the tobacco, while the old chief awaited the thoughts of his favorite warriors.

Tsein-kop-te broke the silence. "I will stay," he said.

"I will stay," said Talia-koi.

A few more moments passed.

"Autumn Thunder?" the chief asked in a voice so soft he could barely be heard.

"I will stay," said Autumn Thunder.

Not only the Kiowas were restless. The Comanches also sought revenge for warriors killed during their Texas raid. They decided the best place to find white men was Adobe Walls in the Texas panhandle, where the buffalo hunters liked to hang out. When Talia-koi and Autumn Thunder heard that their Comanche cohorts were going hunting for buffalo hunters, Au-sai-mah had to use his finest oratory to keep them home. Autumn Thunder might have gone anyway but for Gathers The Grass.

"You cannot go to fight the buffalo hunters!" she said.

"I am a Kiowa warrior. I fight whom I want to fight."

"You cannot go to fight the buffalo hunters," she repeated. She did not elaborate, but her words made him think. His wife was again with child. His son would grow up strong and brave, if he gave his family a chance to grow up. A fight against the army to save his village was one thing. A fight against the buffalo hunters could accomplish nothing.

"But they are killing all our buffalo," he said.

"No," she answered, softly but with great feeling, meaning simply that it was something he should not do. This time her passion was enough. The village must be protected.

The warm weather had arrived. The plains exploded with wildlife and prairie flowers. Autumn Thunder, Tsein-kop-te, and Talia-koi heard word of a buffalo herd two days west. Au-sai-mah judged that they could make the trip if they got

back quickly, before any of the other warriors in the village
rushed off to join Lone Wolf and Maman-ti on their revenge
raid.

They found their herd, killed several animals, loaded their
spare ponies down with buffalo meat and returned to their
village, just hours after many of the village's braves departed
for Texas with Lone Wolf.

For most of the summer, hostilities had swirled all around
them but had not touched them. But with or without Autumn
Thunder and Talia-koi, Lone Wolf's raid was about to change
the future of the Kiowas forever.

Colonel Davidson summoned Sweeney into his headquarters
on a day when the air was so hot and still that the very grass
under their feet seemed to have gone to sleep. Sweat had
dripped from his beard onto an order he was signing and
smeared the writing of the adjutant. He was blotting the paper
carefully, with a look of humiliation on his face, when Sweeney walked in, stepped to his desk, and saluted. Sweeney had
assumed that the summons was related to his belated, and surprising promotion to captain, but such was not the case.

"I seem to recall, Sweeney, that you have a special rela-
tionship with one of the Kiowas in Au-sai-mah's band," he
said.

Sweeney laughed, then remembered he was talking to the
post commander, and choked off the chuckle. "He saved my
life once and he's been tolerating me ever since," he replied.

"I don't mean the buck, I mean the squaw," said Davidson.
He mopped his face with a grayish-white handkerchief.
"Would you care to come out to the back porch here for a bit
of refreshment?"

"Nothing I'd like better, sir," he said, following his commander out to the open shade where two chairs flanked a small
table that already held two glasses and a bottle of bourbon.

"Now, about your squaw . . ."

"She's a Wichita, sir, though she is a Kiowa's woman. And
she was never 'my' squaw though there were once times I
wished she was."

"Uhh—hmm, yes. Well. You do know these people."

"Some. Matt Leeper knows them a whole lot better, and
Jones too, and others."

"Listen to me, Sweeney. We know that Lone Wolf has been down in Texas trying to bring back the bones of his whelp. And we know that he and his sidekicks have killed a few civilians down there. And would you believe those damned Quakers are trying to smuggle them back onto the reservation so we won't attack them?"

Sweeney had been drinking a little better on captain's pay—less tonic and more whiskey, but the colonel's smooth bourbon was much better than anything he customarily swallowed. Still, he almost choked on the news.

"You know, sir, I never thought they'd actually try to hide murderers from us."

"That's not all. The Cheyennes sent the interpreter McCusker to tell us that they were coming on down to clean out the post and kill us all."

"You know how some of these people get when they've been drinking," said Sweeney, draining his glass. "Surely they would not come down to tell us if they really intended to attack."

"It's not all braggadocio, Captain. There has been a lot of killing going on."

"I know, sir. My men have brought in a few bodies over the last couple of months."

"Later this afternoon I'm meeting with my staff. When I do I will announce to them that I've received orders from General Sherman taking the management of hostile Indians out of the hands of the Quakers and turning them over to us."

Sweeney lifted his eyebrows. Colonel Davidson lifted the bottle and looked at Sweeney's glass.

"Thank you sir," Sweeney said.

"But I want to be fair," the post commander declared. "I need to send somebody to Kicking Bird's camp, and the camps of the other good chiefs, and explain the change to them. 'No more refuge!' I want them to know. Either they come in and enroll now, or they'll be branded hostile and we'll fight them. We have to remind them that lately when they've been up against seasoned cavalry they haven't fared so well."

"So you want me to go out to the villages?"

"If an officer goes out to tell them, maybe they'll understand that we mean business," Davidson replied.

"If I get to tell my story before they cut out my tongue and shove it down my throat. Colonel, these people are in a bad mood.''

Davidson almost smiled at Sweeney's drastic understatement.

"Tell you what we're going to do, Captain. I'm going out myself with a troop of cavalry and a couple of interpreters. I want you to come too. We are going to the villages without warning—tomorrow—and we will enroll these devils. I want you with me to make clear to those who know you that the good old days are over. The ones who are not signed up will be considered hostile. We will hunt them down. They will know no peace, no rest, and they will be separated from their people, we will run them so hard.''

Colonel Davidson took a pull from his glass. "What do you think about that?" he asked.

"I hope that my red friends will have the sense to stay out of our way."

"That's fine, Captain. Now I have to get ready for the meeting," said the colonel. "You'll have your orders before sundown. That's all."

Sweeney was surprised at how easily the enrollments went. That did not mean everybody was enrolled. Far from it. The purpose of the enrollment was to find out which chiefs and warriors were not at home, so to speak. Also, there were a number of Kiowas and Comanches that Colonel Davidson did not wish to enroll, including the roaming Lone Wolf. These were men who had been spotted across Red River or were known to have been away from the reservation at a time bad things were happening south of Red River.

Sweeney wondered if the colonel had spies in some of the camps. He also wondered if the colonel withheld information from him because of his friendship with Autumn Thunder and Gathers The Grass. He could imagine some of the comments that went on during staff meetings.

"Oh yes, he's a good soldier but a bit of a drunk, don't you think?"

"I don't trust a man who can get along with Injuns. I guess he handles his whiskey just about as well as any Kyo-way, don't you think?"

He knew what the real problem was. The officers that got

along in this army were West Pointers, pure and simple. How else could you explain why a damned idiot like Custer was still in uniform, and a lieutenant colonel yet, while so many better men had either been sent back to civilian life, kept at low officers' rank year after year, or sometimes even forced to serve as non-commissioned officers in order to stay in the army.

He did not include himself in this group. Frankly, he agreed that he was a drunken, whoring, foul-mouthed mediocrity, and he was amazed that after nearly a decade on the frontier in faithful service they had promoted him to captain for having his horses stolen and being frightened enough to get his men home alive.

Three weeks had passed and the warriors who were still out were making it hot for the cowboys and farmers away from the fort. It wasn't really war yet, but neither was there much peace on either side of Red River.

Sweeney was settled in at Evans's store for the evening card game and health tonic when a Private Hathaway ran in and headed straight for Sweeney's table. "Better come on, Cap'n, suh," said the private. "Colonel got the Tenth Cavalry out on the parade and he wants you to come along."

That was another thing that was troubling him. He had a promotion, but he didn't have a command. It was as if the army didn't trust him to lead troops anymore.

"Where are we goin', Hathaway?"

"Anadarko, suh."

Anadarko. Wichita Agency. Kiowas were probably up there raising hell and stealing the Wichitas' rations.

He headed for his quarters, glad that he hadn't had a chance to work into the evening's supply of whiskey. He buttoned up his uniform as he ran. Inside he grabbed a hold of his equipment then headed for the stable and ordered his horse saddled. He took a quick trip to the bushes and returned, then led his mare out to the parade grounds and saluted the colonel.

"I want you with me," said Davidson. "Got a lot of inexperienced troopers and some officers not much better. You— get along well with Comanches?"

"Some of them."

"Good. Red Food's Noconee band is up in Anadarko and

I don't think he's there to tell the Wichitas and the Delawares what fine fellows they are.''

"The Noconees haven't been enrolled yet, have they?" Sweeney asked.

"Red Food has a mind of his own, that's for sure," said Davidson.

Autumn Thunder was disgusted with himself. Every young warrior he respected was spending the season south of Red River raising hell in Texas. Only a handful of young warriors stayed with the old ones to defend the women and children in the event of a white man attack.

Not only did no soldiers attack, after the first measly attempts at enrollment, he saw no soldiers out on the plains. As usual, the soldier chiefs were big talk and no action. The angry red-bearded colonel, it seemed, was no tougher than those who came before.

But word came to Au-sai-mah that the soldiers were riding to Anadarko to enroll the Noconees. Some of the Kiowa raiders heard about it and they rode back north across the river with an eye toward mischief in Anadarko. One of them was a warrior named Blue Leggings. As his party swept north, out of sight of the villages, Blue Leggings peeled off near Au-sai-mah's village and paid Autumn Thunder a nighttime visit.

"Come with us to the Wichita Agency," he insisted. "That big blowhard Pe-arua-akup-akup is up there promising that he will never give in to the whites, but we have heard that Black Jack is going up there to make a fool out of Pe-arua-akup-akup."

Autumn Thunder did not react with much emotion. "So what?" was his reply.

Blue Leggings smiled. "We are going to burn that agency down—give Pe-arua-akup-akup a chance to get his band out of there."

"How are we going to do that?" asked the skeptical Autumn Thunder.

"Come with us," Blue Leggings smiled. "And learn."

Anadarko was less than fifty miles from Fort Sill but it was ten A.M. by the time the troops arrived on a hill just south of the place. Below they could see several Indian communities, including the tepees of the Peneteka Comanches, who belonged there, and the Noconees, who did not. There were no big black smudges of smoke rising anywhere in the area. At least the war hadn't begun without them, Sweeney noted.

Davidson sent a message down to Captain Lawson, who commanded a company of infantry that did guard duty at the Wichita Agency. The note told him that if a fight started he was to cut off the retreat of the warriors so they couldn't escape from the agency.

Davidson's column then rode down into the agency and summoned Red Food. The chief would have run for the bushes, but he had to worry about his village, with its women and children, vulnerable to four heavily armed cavalry troops, so in due time he appeared, mounted, with a handful of his warriors.

With studied dignity he approached the colonel. Davidson was not a man of ceremony. Through the agency interpreter, he began at the heart of the matter.

"Red Food," he said. "I want you and your band to surrender right now."

"We will go with you, Black Jack," came the answer, "if we can keep our weapons for hunting."

The Noconee encampment where this talk was taking place was surrounded by trees and underbrush. The bushes were alive with unenrolled Kiowa warriors whose village was not nearby and who therefore were not worried about the safety of their families. They were making rude noises and telling the Comanche chief they did not want to see him on his knees to a soldier chief.

Red Food ignored them, and awaited Davidson's reply.

"Your band has not been enrolled. That makes you prisoners of war and prisoners of war must give up their weapons."

Red Food thought for a moment. "We will give up our guns," he said. "But you must let us keep our bows. The army has never asked a Comanche chief to give up his bows."

From the brush came the taunts of the Kiowas.

"Red food is a woman. He would give up his bows and arrows to the soldiers!"

"Will the colonel creep into Red Food's tent tonight?"

"Maybe the other way around."

"Come on, Pe-arua-akup-akup! There are *men* in the bushes! Don't give up. Be a man with us."

Sweeney listened to the voices coming from the woods, trying to decide if one of them could be that of Autumn Thunder. First he thought he heard him, and then he thought he did not.

Davidson turned to Sweeney. "Can you make out any of that jabber?" he asked.

"They're trying to stir him up."

"The Quakers are not running things anymore, Red Food, we are," Davidson said. "Give up your weapons and spare your—"

Before Davidson could finish his speech, the Noconee chief leaped from his pony, flapping his big red blanket. Davidson's horse reared, as did the horses of Sweeney and Woodward the adjutant. The Comanches who were with Red Food all galloped off into the underbrush.

Several troopers drew their guns, but no one gave the order to fire, and Red Food vanished into the woods.

Chapter 23

Belatedly Davidson gave the command to fire and several of the troopers fired into the underbrush just as Red Food disappeared.

"We're in for it now, boys," Davidson told Woodward and Sweeney. Almost immediately the Kiowas began shooting from the brush and more fire came from the direction of the Noconee tepees.

Captain Lawson's foot soldiers heard the firing and tried to come at the fleeing Kiowa and Comanche braves from the other side of the woods. The Comanches evaded them and rode toward the hills, but they had their villages to protect, so they didn't flee but came together and swooped down out of the hills, firing and screaming their war cries. The foot soldiers fired back, and Davidson's cavalry rode through the woods to get into the fight.

Sweeney was astonished at the quickness with which a parley had turned into a war involving hundreds of men firing as fast as they could point, reload, and point again. Before long there was so much smoke rolling across the woods and the open field that the combatants were firing blindly at each other, but Sweeney could hear the war cries behind the smoke. The cavalry had dismounted and added the massed fire of their carbines to that of the infantry. The chatter of gunfire was continual, but it was not too loud for him to hear occasional slugs whizzing by his head. He got behind the thickest tree he could find and joined Colonel Davidson and his men in firing blindly through the white smoke at the invisible riders who were firing blindly back at them.

After fifteen minutes the gunfire began to subside as the soldiers realized that they were the only ones still shooting. The cavalry remounted and moved on past the agency buildings. During the skirmish the people still in the Noconee camp had packed up the entire village and fled. Now the warriors had no village they needed to protect. From behind the buildings came more gunfire from a new group of Kiowas who did not want to be left out of the fight.

The firing increased. One soldier went down, and then another. This was the Wichita Agency. There were plenty of Wichita men and women exposed to the fire, plus a village of Peneteka Comanches who had taken no part in the battle. That was too bad. Let them keep out of the way if they could. The army's first job was to subdue the hostiles. Davidson ordered one of his troops to charge the Kiowas lurking among the buildings, The soldiers surged forward, and the Kiowas retreated across the river. Another Kiowa contingent came down from a different direction, whooping their war cries, trailing colorful streams of gingham and calico from their galloping ponies. They had looted the agency store. Davidson peeled off another troop to run down this group.

Autumn Thunder found himself with his wife's people, whom the army had forced out of their village in the south onto the Wichita Agency. Among the grass beehive huts he saw several young men arguing with the village chief and he sized up the situation immediately. Quietly, unhurriedly, he dismounted and joined the little group.

"Get away from here, Kiowa!" snapped the chief.

"Soldier Killer!" cried out one of the younger men, a name the Wichitas had conferred on Autumn Thunder when he had brought a dying Sweeney into their village. They had never bothered to change the name when Sweeney had survived. "Take us to the fight!"

"No!" cried the Wichita chief. "We are at peace with the soldiers. We will not have Kiowa wolves leading our sons to their death!"

"The soldiers will be riding through here soon," Autumn Thunder replied, calmly. "Do you think they will bother separating Kiowas and Comanches from Wichitas and Caddoes when the bullets are buzzing around their heads?"

"Always the Kiowas, bringing the white men down on us!" the chief growled.

"Always you blame the Kiowas," said Autumn Thunder. "When will you understand that the white men want *your* people dead too? To them we are all Indians." Autumn Thunder used the white man word with a sneer. "You will not save yourself by shaking in your lodges while your brothers fight your battle for you. You will only change the hour and the way your people will die."

"I do not want to listen anymore to this chatter," said one of the young men. "If you want to take us to the battle, Soldier Killer, then take us there, or you can chatter here and we will go ourselves."

Autumn Thunder gave the young warrior a hard look. Would they really follow him or were they just puffing their feathers? He would find out.

"Get your horses, men! Quickly!" There were seven of them. Every one of them immediately sprang for his weapons and pony.

The chief shook his fist. "If the white men see my young men in the fight and come looking for my village, then I will come looking for you!" he snarled.

"You are lucky I do not shoot you right here," Autumn Thunder responded, jumping on his horse. The seven young Wichitas were mounted and ready. "Stay close to me," Autumn Thunder said. "You will be all right if we stay together."

They raised a huge cloud of dust as they rode out of the village.

To escape in a hurry the Noconees had had to leave a tremendous number of their earthly possessions, including most of their food supply, much of their ammunition, buffalo robes, blankets, and weapons. Davidson saw his opportunity. He detailed a number of his men to put everything left in the Noconee village in a big pile and burn it.

"They'll feel their loss, that I can guarantee you," he said to Sweeney, without glee or sorrow, and just a trace of satisfaction. For hours after the sun went down, the blazing, sizzling fire that obliterated the Noconee village lit up the agency.

Sunday morning the Kiowas appeared on a hill and saw

hundreds of troops dug in around the agency. They had no desire to make war against the entrenched soldiers so they fired the long dry prairie grass and left the area.

The troops did not pursue. It was enough that Davidson and his men now knew who among the Kiowas and Comanches were the ones they had to bring to earth. Their own eyes, and their field glasses, brought many faces into clear focus.

Although a number of the Texas marauders had come from Au-sai-mah's village, and one or two of his braves had been sighted at Anadarko, Au-sai-mah was always so courteous to the agency people that they considered his band to be peaceful. They sent messengers to his village to tell him so. But in order to have better hunting prospects and keep his village as far away from white influences as possible, Au-sai-mah usually located farther away from Fort Sill than any other of the peaceful bands, so nobody had come out and registered them.

Au-sai-mah sent a young boy galloping to Colonel Davidson at Fort Sill. Would he please send a party out to enroll the members of his village?

Davidson sent back a message asking him to move to their old camp on Cache Creek so his adjutant wouldn't have to go so far to do the job. The boy was a smart one the soldiers called "Boy Bob" because that's what his name sounded like to them. He understood the message, climbed onto his pony, and rode on back toward his village.

It happened that Sweeney had been planning to ride out to the village to urge Au-sai-mah to bring his band in for enrollment, but at the trader's store he had overheard a lieutenant telling Horace Jones that he had seen Autumn Thunder raising hell up in Anadarko.

"I've had it in for that sonofabitch for over a year now and I'm gonna have his head on the end of my sword one way or another," the lieutenant told the interpreter.

Sweeney was convinced that there was no way Autumn Thunder or anybody else from Au-sai-mah's village could have been at Anadarko. He told Boy Bob to tell Autumn Thunder to ride out and meet him on the road west of Signal Mountain when the sun was straight overhead tomorrow.

*   *   *

Billowing white and gray clouds were tumbling in like surf the following day when Sweeney rode his mare out through the gate on the western road. With a warm fresh wind in her face, the mare felt exceptionally strong and frisky on this day, and so did Sweeney.

It occurred to him as he rode that Autumn Thunder might not meet him. They had never declared their undying friendship for each other, never did any sort of blood brother ceremony. Autumn Thunder disliked whites in general, and liked Sweeney only compared to the other whites he knew. Gathers The Grass's high opinion of the captain did very little to alter the warrior's opinion of him, Sweeney knew.

That did not matter to Sweeney, who still felt that he owed Autumn Thunder his life. He liked the young man. He couldn't help it. He was so honest and straightforward, and frankly Sweeney didn't blame him a bit for wanting to fight the white man.

He stopped on the road at the spot he had chosen for the meeting. He was a little early on purpose, because he was certain that if Autumn Thunder arrived there before him he would suspect a trap and turn right around and go home.

Out of habit he looked around in all directions. Other than a pair of circling hawks he saw no living creature. The wind was blowing the buffalo grass, bright green again from recent rains. Buffalo grass. A recent paper just arrived from St. Louis only a week old had featured an article by a Washington government worker declaring that the war with the plains Indians was almost won because the latest estimates of the plains buffalo population showed numbers to be well below the estimated number of just three years ago.

"When the buffalo are gone," the bureaucrat said, "that's when the Indians will surrender, and not before."

The clouds swept across the sky like an endless, billowing herd of buffalo, blotting out the location of the sun. Sweeney pulled out his railroad watch and saw the minute hand edging close to the hour hand at the top of the face. He looked east and watched the clouds race over Signal Mountain. He turned his head southward to the plain that led down to Red River, the Kiowa gateway to Texas.

Out of the corner of his right eye he saw movement, the lone figure of a rider on a painted pony in an effortless, leisurely gallop. Sweeney watched and marveled. There was no way to separate the movements of the rider from that of the pony. Au-sai-mah had once told Sweeney that the Kiowas were an old people but only during the last hundred and something summers had they known the horse. Watching Autumn Thunder approach with casual speed beneath the racing gray clouds, he could not imagine that this people had ever known a time in their history without the horse.

Surely then, he thought, God had created the Kiowas with the understanding among his angels that they would be fulfilled with the arrival of the horse. What then was the ultimate purpose of giving the Kiowa a century of glorious grace and beauty on horseback before the white man came and conquered and showed him that a horse was nothing next to a steam engine?

The grand dignity of the approaching rider reminded him that he had his own pride and style. Somehow he had survived this far through the day without his tonic or whiskey. His wits were pure. His pride was intact. He turned the mare in the direction of the approaching rider, erect in the saddle, reins clasped loosely in his gloved left hand, his eyes unblinking, his right hand raised in greeting.

Twenty yards away Autumn Thunder eased his pony into a slow walk, his right hand raised.

They exchanged greetings in a fairly formal way. Autumn Thunder seemed relaxed, but he approached no closer than fifteen feet, which pleased Sweeney, because a part of him distrusted Autumn Thunder as much as the Kiowa distrusted him.

By this time each of them knew enough of each other's speech, and enough Comanche, that they could speak to each other, carefully.

"I am here, Sweeney," said the Kiowa, his dark eyes fastened on the captain, and Sweeney knew that as Autumn Thunder approached him he had checked out the land around them with the utmost care.

"My friend," Sweeney said, "Lieutenant Woodward will be out tomorrow to enroll the people of your village."

"I have heard that," Autumn Thunder replied. Both waited a few moments in silence. "That is not why you wanted to make talk to me?"

Sweeney shook his head. "Were you at the fight in Anadarko?" he asked.

Suddenly the grim face of the Kiowa creased into a smile. "Is that why you came? Yes, I was there. I was visiting the men in my wife's village. They were frightened that the white men were going to attack them. I do not blame them. I think the white soldiers might have attacked them if they had found the Wichita village, don't you think?"

"I know. My friend, I come to tell you this. There are men who say they saw you at the fight. I was there and did not see you, and I know you do not lie. Do not be in the village tomorrow when the soldiers come, or you will be arrested. Take your family and go."

For just a moment Autumn Thunder's eyes softened, then the steely glint returned. The smile creases had vanished. "Maybe you are a friend, Sweeney. I tell you that we are going to go no matter what. How could I let my children live close to a white man fort and become fat loafers, begging for money to buy whiskey, being kicked around by cruel soldiers?

"I could never let my children see me live like that. Even now, Gathers The Grass is packing our things. We have many things. Many horses. Much dried meat. Some dried corn. Plenty horses. We be fine." He said this with the pride of a warrior who has looked ahead for his family.

"But if we fight and lose everything, I would still rather be free and hungry than fat and drunk at Fort Sill."

"I know that, my friend. It may be hard for awhile, but if you can keep away from the soldiers until spring, the times may change again."

"I know. White man gets mad and then the peace chiefs forgive. But I will never loaf around the fort. I may go to the mountains. I may go to Mexico. I may go to the desert. But I will never go to Fort Sill."

Sweeney felt a great sadness. He knew that Autumn Thunder was being careful. He would probably go back to his wife's village. He did not blame the Kiowa for not telling him everything.

"I will miss you and Gathers The Grass," he said. "Many a night when the owl sounded his call, I thought of you in the village, and I knew that we were not friends, and yet I knew that if I could choose a friend, I would choose you."

"I must go," said Autumn Thunder in the tone of a man who had revealed too much of himself and regretted it.

"Do not fight the whites. Stay away from them. And as long as I am here, call for me if you need help."

Autumn Thunder allowed himself one more grim, humorless smile. "White man help Indian way too much by now," he said. And then they reached out and clasped each other's right hand.

Then he was away in a graceful, ground-eating gallop. Sweeney did not immediately turn and head for home. Instead he watched as the pony and rider rode into a depression then up a gradual slope, throwing up dust on the long, straight road. Pony and rider grew smaller and smaller with the distance, teetered on the skyline against the racing storm clouds, then vanished suddenly.

Sweeney felt foolish about feeling sad. The man was just an Indian, just a momentary impediment to America's long march west. What kind of fool gives his heart to an impediment? he asked himself.

"A sentimental Irish fool," he muttered aloud, feeling more foolish as he said it.

But as he turned his mare east and kicked her into an easy trot, he felt empty and broken inside, nevertheless.

Chapter 24

To Autumn Thunder, his decision to join the bands that were fleeing west was a bolt for freedom. Had he known what the army had planned for the "hostile" bands, he might have tried to come up with a better idea.

The mastermind of the military operation that was calculated to put down red resistance along Red River was that famous no-treaty chief, Philip H. Sheridan. Sheridan was given spurious credit for the statement, "The only good Indian is a dead Indian," but just because he never said anything exactly like that didn't mean he was a member of the Red Man Benevolent Society. He planned to bring forces down on the fleeing tribes from all the major points of the compass, though it meant marching units in from Fort Concho in Texas and Fort Union, New Mexico. The five columns involved would run the free bands into the ground, harrying them and squeezing them until the children cried out for food and rest and the women cried for mercy.

Autumn Thunder, Talia-koi, Tsein-kop-te, and a young warrior named Wounded Deer, and their families, eight adults and eleven children, left the village and headed north to the Wichita Mountains, then east, to a lake near old Fort Cobb where the fleeing Kiowas and Comanches were coming together.

The group was well armed. All four of the men, and Tsein-kop-te's fifteen-year-old son, had breech-loading rifles, and two of the wives carried their husband's revolvers, just in case they were attacked by wandering Mexican or white renegades who were known to prey on any small groups that came within their reach.

In addition to the fifteen horses that carried the adults and the children old enough to ride pulled travois, and several more that carried packs, they drove a herd of about fifteen spare ponies.

Two days' travel brought them to the rendezvous area, and as they got closer and closer they became very excited. There were hundreds of lodges representing numerous Comanche, Kiowa, Kiowa-Apache, and Cheyenne bands. There was an air of anxious excitement in this temporary community. After years of letting the whites crowd in on them, years of sporadic resistance that did not make the whites go away, the time had come for them to fight for their lives.

Many of the warriors hoped for a resolution. Once they got the whites out away from the forts, on land that not even the Tonkawa scouts knew, they could fight their kind of fight. A summer of raiding and trading had armed them better than ever, and they believed that if they could just get the latest guns, then the soldiers wouldn't stand a chance against them.

When Tsein-kop-te's group arrived at the Kiowa camps there were words of welcome but no time for the socializing that was normally dear to the Kiowas' way of life. They were all business, repairing their weapons and their equipment, and seeing that their ponies were in shape for the coming ordeal. Warriors were giving their extra rifles and ammunition to those who had none, and arrows to those who still had no guns. They were consulting their medicine men for advice concerning taboos and charms, and scheduling the ceremonies that would get them ready for their ordeal. None of them doubted that they would have to fight the soldiers, and the chiefs were planning how to keep the women and children out of harm's way.

The women were tending to the food supplies, making repairs on packs and tepees. Some of them did not share their husbands' desire for the coming conflict, but few spoke out.

The Kiowa leaders were Lone Wolf and Maman-ti, the Owl Prophet whose ability to plan a battle was so uncanny that the Kiowas had great faith in his prophecies. He had announced earlier that day that not everybody would be making the trip west, and sure enough, late in the afternoon two mounted messengers from Kicking Bird arrived with news that Colonel Davidson had said that the government would forgive any

Kiowas who changed their mind and returned to the reservation for enrollment.

The people looked to Maman-ti, but he stood with his arms folded and a sour look on his face, saying nothing.

The messengers departed, quickly, and the people watched as a number of families began to tear down their tepees. The great medicine man remained silent until those families were ready to go, then he turned to the crowd that had gathered in confusion and consternation, and he spoke:

"It is good," he said, and he did not remind the people that he had predicted the event he knew they would remember. For him to remind them would be beneath the dignity of a great medicine man. "It is good that they leave us, because only the proud must stay and fight on. We need to be rid of those who have two feelings—to stay and to go.

"We must be strong. We must be watchful. And we must not surrender," he said, not as an orator would speak, but as a trusted advisor would speak face to face. His words went to their hearts and stiffened their backs. There would be no more defections.

The next morning at first light they began their flight in a long dusty caravan. At first the children were noisy with the anticipation of a long journey, but soon they picked up the mood of their elders, and then a strange silence fell over the entire vast parade, except for the footfalls and occasional whinny of the ponies and the scraping sounds of the travois as they dragged and bumped over the uneven prairie.

Many of the warriors spent the day in far-flung scouts on the flanks, ahead and behind. They knew that soldiers attacking villages did not spare women and children. This was not the confident, joyous sport of Texas raiding; this was the survival of a people, and they would not stop until they had reached Elk Creek, which was a long two days' march to the west.

But when they reached the waters of Elk Creek, neither Lone Wolf or Maman-ti felt comfortable. Their stay was short and early the next morning, the westward trek continued.

And then came the rains. Long rows of billowing black clouds arrived and disgorged their water in an electric deluge, with jagged bolts of lightning slamming into the mountain peaks and thunder rumbling back and forth through the valley and echoing down distant canyons.

The creeks took all the water they could then overflowed onto flats so wide that at times it seemed to the Kiowas that they were crossing an ocean a few inches deep. They could not deviate from their charted course because they were afraid the cavalry might be nipping at their heels. Sometimes their course took them over high ground that was wet, but at least unflooded, and then they would stop, hoping for an end to the rain that fell in sheets.

The warriors may have been fearless in battle, but the lightning came from the heavens. Why them? Why now? What had they done wrong? Had Maman-ti forgotten a necessary rite?

They asked him and he explained over the deafening rolls of thunder that the rain was covering their trail, that it took this much rain to wash out the tracks of such a great assemblage of people.

Finally, in late afternoon of the following day, the rain began to let up. There was much daylight left, but they had a large, unflooded campground surrounded by flood-washed valleys, and the pink glow to the west promised a much better tomorrow.

Autumn Thunder did not stand on ceremony. Erecting a tepee was women's work, but he wanted out of the rain. There would be no wood to kindle, but Gathers The Grass's canvas cover had kept their blankets dry. Even without a fire, Autumn Thunder and his family would be warm under a dry pile of buffalo robes.

The next day they headed southwest toward the Staked Plains. The Staked Plains is a dry, hostile place to be, but the Indians had the toughness to survive out there while the whites would struggle. Besides, deep in the Staked Plains was a huge slash in the ground known as Palo Duro Canyon. There was water there, and trees, roots and berries, and even some game. It was a place for red men, not whites.

Let the soldiers try and find them out there.

But the chiefs could not agree, not at first. Their spies reported that two different army units were prowling around on the eastern end of the Staked Plains. The big caravan went this way, they went that, waiting for more information and every day growing more apprehensive that the soldiers would find them somewhere between the Washita and Canadian rivers.

By force of will, Maman-ti finally persuaded all the chiefs to head west along the Washita, then continue into the harsh lands of the Staked Plains.

Before they could go any farther, scouts returned to the caravan with news that a wagon train of supplies guarded by a detachment of infantrymen was coming into the area from the north. There was no longer any question of trying to evade the soldiers. There was going to be a fight, and everybody knew it.

Maman-ti opened up the proper ceremonies preceding battle. The warriors painted themselves and their horses, unpacked their shields and war bonnets, and checked their weapons.

Gathers The Grass watched her husband as he made his preparations. He painted his body a solid red from his shoulders to his waist, then overlaid it with black vertical stripes. His face was a solid yellow with black stripes along his cheekbones and another black stripe down the bridge of his nose. His red body matched the red strips of cloth that streamed from his pony's mane and tail.

He wore only a single red feather in his hair. Long ago A-do-te, the medicine man of his village, had declared it taboo for him to wear more than a modest head covering, and like other Kiowas Autumn Thunder felt certain that his safety depended upon strict adherence.

He put the final touches to his facial paint with the aid of a small mirror he held in his right hand. Always, A-do-te had told him, the mirror must be held with the right hand and his face paint applied with his left. Gathers The Grass saw the bright gleam in his eyes as he made his final preparations.

How he loves the call to battle, she thought. And yet when the battle was over and he returned to his lodge, he did not spend his time boasting about his feats like other warriors did. He never talked about the battle at all. She stood back and did not offer to help him. His medicine demanded that he make all preparations for battle himself.

He walked past her as if she weren't there and ducked out the open tepee flap. Ignoring her was also part of the ritual.

She was not offended. All she felt inside was a deep sadness and fear. She did not fear battle herself. She feared for his safety, and that of their son. As soon as he was out of sight she would check his old rifle and keep it handy in case the soldiers were able to sneak up on the village and attack it while the warriors were away.

Might as well die fighting, she thought, stacking the buffalo robes in such a way that if the whites came she could hide Deerfoot beneath them. She wondered at how her life with Autumn Thunder had made her more Kiowa than Wichita.

The sky was a pale summer blue, but there was a light morning chill as a small advance group of warriors that included Autumn Thunder rode out across the plain in a strung-out file. Along a chain of low hills they looked down and spotted thirty-six wagons rumbling along in two columns, flanked by files of infantry. Ahead of the wagons rode a small group of thirteen cavalrymen.

It was infantry that the Kiowas feared most. When they had first encountered these walk soldiers many years before, they had ridden straight toward them, sensing a bloody triumph, but unlike cavalrymen, shooting their short-range carbines from jumpy, shying horses, the infantrymen got down on one knee, took aim with their long-range rifles and squeezed off deadly volleys that decimated the attacking force and scattered those who had not been shot out of their saddles.

These sons of a tribe so small that every strong arm counted did not sell their lives cheaply. They learned the range of a soldier's rifle and learned to ride just beyond, letting the blue-coats fire their weapons ineffectually at targets that on the open plains were considerably farther away than they appeared.

From the heights west of the southward moving wagon train, some of the Kiowas charged swiftly down the slope, but the brave skirmish line of cavalry rode toward the warriors, firing, and the Indians retreated, only to appear on another rise farther on down the route. Their job was not to attack, it was to keep up a sporadic running firefight that would let the main body of warriors know where the enemy was, and also keep the enemy occupied so they wouldn't have much time to think about what they were doing.

Autumn Thunder had played this game of chase and ambush before, and he thoroughly enjoyed it. It was an acting job, a handful of warriors pretending to fight, acting frustrated, making the soldiers think they were doing a wonderful job of keeping the Indians at bay.

Maman-ti and Lone Wolf had hidden most of the warriors above a ravine near the Washita. As the wagon train struggled slowly out of the ravine, Maman-ti blew on his eagle-bone whistle and the warriors were suddenly all around. The soldiers were surprised but not too surprised to take orders. As if they were on a parade ground, the foot soldiers formed two lines that met in the shape of an arrowhead in front of the wagons, while the wagons wheeled into a large circle.

Autumn Thunder watched from the heights as his cohorts swept toward the wagon train from all sides, howling and firing, testing the will of the defenders. A powerful thrill of pride swept through him at the thought that his people might achieve a quick victory, but the soldiers were up to the challenge. In spite of the heavy gunfire from both sides, only a few men were hit. The attackers could not get through the wagon corral, and so they withdrew to the hills to plan their next move.

Autumn Thunder rode around the hills surrounding the stalled wagon train until he found young Wounded Deer.

"A good day to die, my brother," he said, as they both dismounted. Neither had any intention of dying but their hearts were strong and ready for battle.

The chiefs had the men tie their horses to bushes on the higher hills behind them and settled down in the low hills, firing into the wagon corral all day long. It was boring work in the hot sun, because the veteran soldiers below had carried barrels and boxes of provisions from the wagons and lay concealed and invulnerable behind them. The continued gunfire was just to keep the pressure on. The soldiers fired back, but the warriors were experts at the art of cover and concealment, and the soldiers' fire hit only earth and sky.

Late in the afternoon Autumn Thunder saw some of the chiefs mount their ponies and ride down the reverse slope of the hill to a clump of trees. He nudged Wounded Deer, who had closed his eyes for a little catnap, and pointed down to the group of chiefs with their ornate war bonnets and fine horses.

"Looks like they're planning something," Wounded Deer

observed, turning over on his back, pulling his blanket over his eyes, and going back to sleep.

Autumn Thunder had no desire to sleep. He was primed for a fight, and thought it might come soon. Less than an hour later the chiefs rode back. Shortly Lone Wolf was on the hill with them.

"Mount your ponies!" commanded the veteran chief. "We will ride on down, but stay out of range of their rifles."

They came. Behind the wagons muscles tensed and fingers tightened on triggers as the warriors began their swift ride around the corral a couple of hundred yards away. Led by Lone Wolf, they swept in closer, in an unending revolving circle of color and noise until the soldiers began to fire, then slowly, imperceptibly, they pulled back to the edge of the range of the soldiers' rifles. The firing continued, then slackened.

Now came the show, as more and more warriors came down from the hills and joined the circle. One blue-painted warrior came in a hundred yards closer, but threw himself to the side of the pony away from the wagon corral, using his pony to shield him from the gunfire, hanging only by a hand and a foot.

"Watch this!" said Wounded Deer, whose sleepiness had left him as soon as he had vaulted onto his pony. Now, with his pony still sailing along at a good clip, he climbed up on his saddle, and stood erect while the pony continued its way around the wagons. Arms folded, back straight, eyes staring straight ahead, Wounded Deer rode around the corral in an act of such supreme impudence that he drew the fire of every rifle within the wagon corral as he rode by. Autumn Thunder marveled as he watched, and flinched when a stray shot clipped a braid from the head of his friend.

A pair of warriors who saw this feat sought to top it by loosening their breechcloths and kneeling in their saddles so that as the ponies circled the corral, their bare behinds were pointed straight at the soldiers behind the wagons. The soldiers switched their fire to these braves. But as the shadows lengthened along the Washita valley it seemed that the soldiers could not hit a thing.

A number of warriors had learned a smattering of English, particularly the profane invective peculiar to soldiers. Others knew no English but had learned Spanish invective on their raids into south Texas and Mexico. They shouted the most insulting things they could think of about what soldiers might eat, or do to each other, or to their own mothers. Some of them cried their insults in such atrocious accents that the soldiers leaned forward, desperately curious to know what was being shouted at them.

As the sun began to dip behind the rocky hills to the west, the warriors closed their circle a bit, and were rewarded by a new round of firing from the soldiers in the wagon coral. The warriors and their horses became galloping, jumping shadows, and then, circling hoofbeats, and finally, as darkness locked the scene away and the braves headed for their campfires behind the hills, ominous silence.

Autumn Thunder and Wounded Deer left their ponies in the hands of Tsein-kop-te, crawled forward, and lay still, listening in the dark. It was a moonless night and Maman-ti needed to know what the soldiers were doing. If they, or some of them, tried to escape, there must be scouts out there to bring back the news so the Kiowas would not face an empty valley the following morning.

What they heard was the sounds of tin cups scraping at the ground. The soldiers were digging cover for themselves. They would stay and fight, not try to run for it. Too bad. Autumn Thunder knew that if the whites attempted to escape under cover of darkness they would doom themselves.

An owl hooted. A coyote let out a howl. The night sounds swelled forth in full chorus. Autumn Thunder and Wounded Deer retreated to the hills, told the chiefs what they had heard, pulled their blankets close around them, and sought out a warm campfire.

Over the next few days, the Kiowas continued to besiege the wagon train, keeping up a sporadic fire at the wagon corral and receiving fire in kind, with very few casualties as a result. Sometimes warriors would ride through the corral and the newly dug trenches to show their bravery, try to demoralize the soldiers, and maybe even whack an enemy with their coup stick. After hours of staring out at nothing in the dazzling hot sun, the soldiers were so befuddled by these seemingly senseless acts of reckless individual heroism that they were too surprised to hit the leaping, dashing targets.

Then more rain came and fell on red and white alike, making everybody miserable for a day or two.

During the siege Lone Wolf continued to send out scouts to watch for other army columns, and eventually several were spotted heading in their direction. They had tarried too long. Food supplies in the villages were beginning to run low. Leaders began to have doubts that they would be able to protect their families from all the soldiers. Several more families split from the main body and headed back to Fort Sill, into captivity. Autumn Thunder still dreaded the thought of giving up the free life on the plains in exchange for a full belly on the reservation. So he was relieved to hear that Lone Wolf and Maman-ti wished to continue on to the Staked Plains, and Palo Duro Canyon.

A week after the wagon train siege had begun with such high hopes, most of the Kiowas slipped away in the middle of the night, returned to their respective villages, which were packed and ready to go, and continued their desperate flight to Palo Duro Canyon. By now the thought of that great hidden refuge glimmered like Shangri-La to the men and women of the free *Kaigwas*.

Never mind that the area was too small to support any number of people for any length of time. Never mind that it was set in the middle of a land so barren and hostile that only an Apache could thrive in it for long; Palo Duro was the place where they could breathe a free breath of sweet air without the horrible fear of white massacre or harassment.

They were too proud to imagine the whites keeping them boxed up there for long. In the mind of Lone Wolf and the heart of Maman-ti was the mystical hope, the prayer, that once they had caught their breath beyond the reach of the *Tai-bos*, they would find a way to strike them so hard that the whites would vanish and never again profane the sacred lands of the Kiowa nation.

Autumn Thunder and Wounded Deer did not immediately return to their village. They found a distant ridge where they could keep a sharp eye on the wagon train, the leader of which had finally concluded, after sending out scouting parties, that the Kiowas were gone.

"Why are we following them?" Wounded Deer asked Autumn Thunder as they watched the last wagon in the train rumble slowly past the hill from which they observed the cursing, whip-cracking teamsters urging their horses forward.

"I don't know," Autumn Thunder answered. "But there is a reason. We will soon find out."

And find out they did, when one of the wagons bumped into a pothole and not only lost a wheel but broke an axle in the process.

"There!" said Autumn Thunder quietly, pointing to the wagon, which was teetering in the middle of the road.

"So what?" said Wounded Deer. "We can't attack them. They are too many."

"Keep watching," Autumn Thunder insisted.

One of the men in the wagon had walked up to the head of the train. The two warriors watched the two men converse and then the boss of the train yelled something that was relayed down the train.

"What's going on?" asked Wounded Deer. "What are they doing?"

The wagons lined up behind the broken one began to move around it.

"They do not know our warriors have gone away," said Autumn Thunder. "They are afraid they will be attacked again, so they are leaving the broken wagon."

From the hill they watched while all the wagons except the broken one rumbled down the road and out of sight.

"All the soldiers have gone," Wounded Deer noted.

Only the two teamsters that were driving the wagon had stayed with it. They were working feverishly on the wheel and axle, pausing frequently to cast worried looks at the hills around them.

"Let's go down and take them!" insisted Wounded Deer.

"Not until they have finished fixing the wagon," Autumn Thunder replied. "We need that wagon to carry what is inside."

Now one teamster was guarding the wagon with his rifle while the other finished up the repairs. They had unhitched the horses when the wagon broke down, and now they were hitching them up again. Autumn Thunder and Wounded Deer waited while the teamsters climbed back up into the wagon seat and set the horses to straining forward. The heavily loaded wagon inched forward, then began to roll in a more or less regular manner. The repaired wheel bumped along, but it was serviceable.

"Now?" asked Wounded Deer.

"We'll take our time, approach from behind. Maybe they won't see us until we are upon them."

They approached from the rear at an easy gallop, a good half mile behind the wagon. They saw one of the men look back. Saw him tap the other one and point.

"Looks like we're going to have to fight it out with them if we want that wagon," said Wounded Deer.

Autumn Thunder agreed until he saw the two jump off the wagon, sprint forward to the horses, and begin to cut away at the traces.

"Looks like they want to run away!" Wounded Deer exclaimed. "Hurry! We have to run them down."

"Run them down?" Autumn Thunder laughed. "They're leaving four horses and a full wagon in exchange for their lives. I think that's a good trade."

"But I want their scalps!" cried Wounded Deer.

"We need their supplies more than we need their scalps." He looked at his very young friend. "Now is no time for honors," he said. "Don't you understand that our people need us to live and bring them goods to eat?" They were less than a quarter of a mile from the wagons now. Autumn Thunder whooped and his pony surged forward. The two men mounted their individual horses bareback, slapped them on the rump, and vanished down the road in a brown cloud of dust.

Autumn Thunder reached the wagon first, lifted the canvas covering, and saw barrels.

"I don't know what they are," he said, "but barrels of things are always good—food, gunpowder, whiskey."

"Ah," said Wounded Deer. "I am dry."

"We have to get rid of some things if four horses are going to pull the wagon."

They rolled a couple of barrels off the rear of the wagon and cracked one of them open with a hatchet. They did not know what was inside but it was in a green liquid that stank terribly.

"*Tai-bo* food," Wounded Deer observed. They rolled several similar looking barrels out of the wagon and worked on calming the remaining horses.

"It's all ours!" cried Wounded Deer.

"Whatever it is, it belongs to everyone. Come on, let's get that wagon moving before those men alert the soldiers," said Wounded Deer. Autumn Thunder climbed onto the wagon seat and attempted to get the horses in motion but without the lead team the remainder didn't seem to want to budge. He grabbed a whip and attempted to crack it over the heads of the animals as he had seen teamsters do, but he could not handle it.

He whooped and hollered, with no positive results. Wounded Deer rode up to the lead team and shouted in the ear of one of the animals and that finally got the animals straining forward. The wagon began to move, slowly.

Autumn Thunder's face creased into a smile that faded quickly when he looked up the road and saw a dust cloud approaching. He pointed and Wounded Deer turned in the direction of Autumn Thunder's arm.

"What should we do?" Wounded Deer asked, calmly.

"Two soldiers and two teamsters. We could ride our ponies out of here."

"Leave the wagon?"

"That wouldn't be any good," Autumn Thunder agreed, jumping down from the wagon seat onto his pony. He needed to say no more. Both men had found brand new repeating rifles in the wagon. Each one cocked his weapon and fired it into the air—both were loaded.

They kicked their ponies and sent them sprinting down the road, heading straight toward their adversaries. Stunned, the soldiers and teamsters slowed down and watched the painted warriors approach, screaming their war cries. At three hundred yards they fired their new rifles. At two hundred yards they fired again. None of the shots found flesh, but they convinced the soldiers that these Indians meant business. The wagon train had by no means sent their best men to help the teamsters. All four of the whites turned their horses and bolted down the road, with Autumn Thunder and Wounded Deer in hot pursuit, gaining with every stride, now waving tomahawks and terrifying the whites with their ululating shrieks.

The four whites reached the top of a hill and raced headlong down the other side, clinging tightly to their mounts, all riding much faster than they were accustomed. Autumn Thunder and Wounded Deer halted at the top of the hill and watched their would-be prey disappear in a cloud of dust.

"Let's get the wagon back to the village," Autumn Thunder said.

Chapter 25

Down on the Texas side of Red River due south of Fort Sill was a place that was almost but not quite a town. People like Tuck would stop there on their way to hunt the big buffalo herds in the Texas panhandle. Many of them paused at a shack with cracks in the boards so wide that they were almost windows.

Inside that shack was a pair of barrels with half a barn door laid on top of them. On one side of this improvised table stood a man in jeans and a red flannel top covered by a once-white apron. On the other side stood the hairy manhood of north Texas, buffalo hunters and skinners, unemployed cowboys, an occasional soldier on his way from one fort to another, rustlers, bums, drunks—they all came to drink Jake Ruggles's liquid bonfire.

They were fooling themselves and they knew it. Ruggles, the man in the once-white apron, served a concoction that wasn't more than one-fourth straight grain alcohol, but it was so painful going down that the customers got crooked fast just from the experience.

Besides the alcohol and the throat-grabbing alkaline water he cut it with, Ruggles's ingredients included red-hot chili peppers, rattlesnake heads, and tobacco spit fresh-gleaned from the saloon's three cuspidors every morning after the customers went home. Ruggles was so skilled at blending his ingredients that the taste of the beverage, vicious as it was, was consistent, and his customers appreciated that.

Tuck was standing in his usual place at the far end of the

half-barn door when a familiar figure moved in beside him
and slammed a heavy whiskey bottle down.

Tuck didn't have to look twice. The bottle held real bourbon. Tuck's mouth would have watered if it hadn't still been
sucking in air to numb his tongue from the pain of his last
swallow.

"Hey, Kroll," he croaked, "can I have a swaller for a
chaser?"

The bulky, bearded man in buffalo hide next to him looked
at the muddy residue at the bottom of Tuck's glass and clucked
in sympathy. "Sure," he said, pouring three fingers into
Tuck's glass.

"Obliged to ya, Kroll," gasped Tuck in a hoarse whisper.
He lifted the smooth whiskey to his lips and drank it down
quickly. He wiped off his lips with the back of his shirt.

"Thanks," he said in a clear voice. "I feel so much better."

Kroll lifted his glass and took a swallow that made his
Adam's apple bounce like a thrown cowboy.

"Sawright," he replied. "I'm celebratin'."

"Celebratin'? Celebratin' what?"

"Celebratin' gettin' out of the buffalo huntin' business.

Tuck picked up his glass and drained it down his throat,
then slammed the glass down on the barn door. Kroll was a
veteran buffalo hunter well respected in the trade. If anybody
was fated to draw his final breath staring through the telescope
sight of a buffalo rifle, it was Kroll.

"You quit? Why?" asked Tuck.

Kroll refilled Tuck's glass, then his own from the prized
bourbon bottle.

"Because I don't wanna be out there squeezin' the last drop
of buffalo blood off the plains like you just squeezed the last
drop of bourbon out of your glass. You looked so damn pathetic tiltin' back an empty glass. That's how pathetic we'll
be, bunch a scruffy old buff-killers playin' hide-and-seek in
every shadowy canyon with a few lonesome orphans moonin'
around lookin' for their herds. I tell you, Tuck, it turns a real
man's stomach!"

"Hell, Kroll, I don't give a damn about that," Tuck replied.
"Give me a thrill to be the guy that takes down the last of
them ugly critters, just like it'd give me a thrill to hole the

ast Injun runnin' free." He grabbed hold of his glass and
poured it down his throat in three huge gulps.

Kroll laughed. "Sometimes I think you ain't got the sense
of a buffalo, Tuck. It ain't the killin' that's pathetic. How
many hides did you bring in last year?"

Tuck was not about to tell Kroll or anyone else about his
business—not if his business was good, not if it was bad.

"I did all right," he said.

"Sure you did. Better'n the year before? As good as the
year before? Don't lie to me, Tuck. Gets harder and harder to
find 'em, ain't that right? Where are the big herds, Tuck?
Where are the herds that go from one horizon to another, all
around, hey? Tell you what, friend, you can be the guy in the
broken-down wagon with two skinny mules, draggin' 'round
the plains beggin' for just one more good buffalo kill, one
more good payday before you have to give it up and go to
work for a living, but I'm tellin' you, that ain't gonna be me."

He poured himself another glass of bourbon and then, point-
edly, poured Tuck a drink out of the rattlesnake rotgut bottle.

Tuck was drinking anything in any order on this day. He
tossed his head back and took a big gulp, coughed, wheezed,
teared, and spat. The bite of the cheap whiskey made him
angry.

"Tell you what, Kroll," he said. "I don't intend to quit as
long as there's a single buffalo left to hunt down, not if I have
to go back to skinnin' them myself. I like killin' buffalo. I
like comin' into a place with a wagonload or three of the prime
hides. I like gettin' good hard cash for them hides, and then I
like spendin' the cash for good things. It's a good life. Beats
plowin' a field, beats workin' in a factory, beats stoopin' in a
gold or a coal mine, beats just about anything I know of for
makin' a living. So you just quit and sell your outfit, and
maybe I'll shoot a woolly or two for you."

He took another big gulp from his glass, coughed and teared
again but did not complain. "Tell you something else," he
said. "I been killin more'n my share of them critters, and you
know it, and maybe you'd like to talk me out of going out
there and killing some buffalo that you would've killed if they
hadn't come my way first."

Kroll turned slowly toward Tuck. "You sayin' that you figure you're a better buffalo hunter than I am?" he asked. There

was no angry gleam in his eyes, only an amused twinkle.

"I'm sayin' I ain't gonna quit as long as there's a hide left out there."

Kroll filled Tuck's glass again with snakehead and filled his own with the same, but he did not drink it. He shoved his glass over to Tuck.

"Gotta push off," he said, dropping a gold eagle on the counter. It rang and spun and settled down atop the barn door. "That'll pay for the rest of that snakehead. Tuck, I hope you kill every buffalo you ever dreamed of killin'. But you won't. You're a hungry man, and there ain't enough buffalo left to quench your taste for their blood."

And he clumped out the door into the bright sunshine. Tuck turned quickly and shouted out the open door. "I'm goin' out tomorrow, Kroll, with three wagons, and when I come back they'll all be loaded down with hides, I'll betcha!"

Kroll turned and gave him a skeptical wave, then he walked off.

Tuck was in deep debt to a merchant named Tom O'Malley. In other years O'Malley would never have given credit to a man as nasty and unreliable as Tuck, but hunters were getting scarce in these parts, and he had lead and powder and provisions that he could not get rid of. Tuck, he knew, always made money on the buffalo hunt. The trick to collecting from him was to grab him right after he sold his hides, before he had a chance to drink and whore away all his money.

Last year's hunt was so sparse, and his poker playing so poor, that he had spent very little money repairing his wagons or his harnesses. He had skimped on feed for his mules and horses so their condition was only fair. Still, he found a couple of skinners desperate enough to work for food plus promised wages when they brought the hides in.

O'Malley took IOUs for the powder and lead, but when Tuck tried to buy the newest type of buffalo gun that fired a longer cartridge and mounted a more powerful scope, O'Malley drew the line.

"How do I know you'll come back this way after your hunt?" he said. "Rifle like that, everybody wants one."

"Then let me borrow a used one," Tuck said. "Damn you, gimme a rifle like that and I'm more likely to come back with the hides that'll pay you off. You wanna get paid off, don't you?''

O'Malley thought for a few moments. "Tell you what," he said. "Let me see your other rifles."

"Why?"

'' 'Cause I want to see them first, if I'm gonna sell you a new Sharps I wanna see what else you have.''

The plains were already parched. Dust from the mules was so thick that Tuck had left the wagons to his skinners and rode his horse fifty yards ahead. The skinners had never worked for him before. By the third day they were certain they were working for a crazy man because Tuck kept muttering incoherently through his scruffy beard. Every once in a while a colorful "sombitch" would emerge, but mostly the mutterings were indecipherable.

He muttered because he was angry and he was angry because once he was out on the plain he realized that Kroll was right, that discovering buffalo would be almost as difficult as discovering a lode of gold. The two wagons creaked along behind Tuck, who roamed the entire front looking for buffalo tracks.

The third day out they did find a small herd, but as if the horrible decimation of the herds had whittled them down to the fittest, they seemed to run as soon as the wagons appeared over the horizon. Tuck increased his distance ahead of the wagons to a hundred yards, then two hundred, and finally a quarter of a mile, but still the buffalo ran before he could get close enough to unwrap O'Malley's rifle.

What in hell is going on here? he thought, cursing so hard that at last the skinners could hear something coming from him that he could understand.

Finally one afternoon he spotted a tiny herd, fewer than two dozen, standing out against the dried green of a distant hill. The shape of the land was perfect, he thought. He could ride down on them and trap them against the steep hill behind them.

He turned to the wagons and gave the skinners a sign to stop. He climbed down from his horse and tied it to one of the wagons, though he was still nearly a mile away from the buffalo. He grabbed a leather cartridge box, checked out the

ammunition it held, and slung the strap over his shoulder. A
warm wind was blowing in his face, which meant that the
buffalo would not be picking up his scent. Slowly, steadily,
he walked toward the buffalo, grazing peacefully.

It was an unusual herd, one bull, seven cows, more than a
dozen calves. Was it possible that some of the calves were
orphans who had latched on to surrogate mothers after their
own had been killed? Tuck did not know enough about buffalo
calves to speculate. He did not mind such a herd. He could
concentrate on the cows. The calves would be lost without
them, and he could gun them down at his leisure.

He generally did not estimate range by precise number. His
aim was instinctive.

He set up his shooting stick, pushed it as deep into the
ground as its pointed end would allow, placed the rifle on the
fork and sighted through the scope. He began to shoot, and
the buffalo began to drop.

The kill was simple, as buffalo kills went. Two or three of the
older animals were not dead but were sufficiently weak that
they could not run off. Tuck dispatched them casually with a
pistol shot between the eyes. He saw nothing in those eyes
that made him give pause. Buffalo life meant no more to him
than the lives of Indians.

Once the animals were all dead he sat on the wagon seat,
shaded from the sun by its canvas top, and watched his skinners work. This was normally the time of day when he felt
great satisfaction that he could sit back and rest while others
doing the grueling chore of skinning the buffalo.

But he could not help thinking that these hides were a very
small return for the many days of searching out on the empty
plains. As the last carcasses yielded to the sharp knives of the
skinners, he was forced to concede that this hunt had not been
a success, that Kroll might have been right, that the creatures
were indeed disappearing.

A warm feeling of accomplishment coursed through his
veins.

As the men finished their job of staking the hides out on
the plains for drying, Tuck walked over to the more talkative
skinner, a man named Scully.

"Well, that's that," he said, disregarding the caked blood

and guts that covered the forearms of the skinner.

"What's what?" growled the skinner, and Tuck remembered that skinning buffalo often seemed to make men grumpy.

"That's about it for the buffalo."

Scully was slow, but he was not opaquely dense. He knew what Tuck was talking about but wanted to face facts even less than Tuck did. He took a huge red bandanna from beneath the wagon seat and wiped off the sweat that had been stinging his eyes for the past hour.

"Gotta be more buffalo somewhere," he said.

"Maybe," Tuck answered. "Not too many. We done a good job, me and the other hunters. When the war ended there was still big herds. Now, they're just about gone. What do you think of that?"

Although tired from the long, fruitless journey and the hot day's work in the sun, Scully could not miss the pride in the voice of Tuck. Tuck had a smile on his face, the smile of a skull.

"We done for the buffalo, we sure did. Time now we got to serious work on the Indians."

"I ain't skinnin' Injuns for you if that's what you're thinkin'," said Scully.

Chapter 26

General Sheridan had five columns of troops probing the Staked Plains in search of the fleeing Kiowas. It seemed impossible that, encumbered by their families, they could avoid them. And yet, for a time they did. Maybe it was the wandering groups of warriors that distracted the columns by leaving false trails. Maybe it was the soldiers' unfamiliarity with the area. Whatever the reason, the tough Kiowa bands were willing to suffer in order to remain free, and remain free they did. Still, with five columns tracking them, their future looked bleak.

They stopped to make camp on the creek called Elk, but warriors kept coming in reporting the approach of this column of cavalry, or that column of walking soldiers. Their pursuers seemed to have a sense of where they were and were converging on them. The Kiowas could not understand how all these white men had suddenly developed a knack for finding their way in this wilderness. They knew by now that Tonkawa scouts were guiding the soldiers, but so great was their contempt for that small nation with the overblown reputation of being *Kia-hi-piago,* or people who eat people, that they could not imagine Tonkawas being their tormentors.

They rested along Elk Creek but did not make camp. The soldiers were too close. They would be moving on as soon as the chiefs could agree on the best route to take to Palo Duro Canyon.

But they had scarcely resumed their journey when the world fell in on them in the form of another thunderstorm so dense that they might as well have been standing under a great waterfall. For a while the warriors sat atop their ponies, beneath waterlogged blankets that let as much water in as they kept out, waiting for the deluge to stop.

"Why don't we make camp?" one of the chiefs asked Maman-ti, but the holy man said his medicine was not clear. The soldiers might fool them and come through the rain with their guns blazing, just as Custer had attacked the Cheyennes on the Washita when the weather was so cold and the snow so big that the Cheyennes could not imagine anyone attacking them.

"No," he said. "When the weather clears, we will be on our ponies. That way, if the soldiers have stopped their pursuit, we can put distance between ourselves and them." His powerful personality won his point. The only problem was that the rain did not stop.

All day long the water poured down upon the Kiowas. As dark came, the people were too exhausted to put up shelters, so they collapsed where they were in the muddy puddles and hoped they would not drown in their sleep.

Gathers The Grass got out an almost-dry buffalo robe. She put a canvas cover on the ground, and she, Autumn Thunder, and Deerfoot lay down together for the warmth. They pulled the buffalo robe over them, then folded the canvas around over the buffalo robe and tried desperately to sleep. Somebody on the other side of the camp hollered that they heard the soldiers coming. In a panic people scrambled to their feet and started lashing items to their travois.

Then cooler heads announced there were no soldiers. Silently, without grumbling, they lay back down in their puddles, and Gathers The Grass repeated her bedroll routine. The rain continued to fall, but gradually sleep came to the refugees, one by one.

Autumn Thunder had just reached the point of reduced consciousness where he knew that sleep was his for the taking, when ten feet away from him he heard a child cry out. His mother reached over to comfort him and her hand wrapped around a huge, hairy tarantula. Now she cried out and suddenly the whole camp was awake, feeling around them and afraid their hands might find what they were looking for.

They did, there were huge numbers of them, marching across the soggy campground, and the Kiowas regarded their presence as a bad omen. In order to do something, they shook their blankets and robes and packed them, then climbed upon their soggy ponies and tried to grab a little rest there.

As his mind drifted in and out, Autumn Thunder considered that sleeping out in the rain while tarantulas crawled all over you was a considerably better fate than seeing your family massacred by soldiers. It was a miserable way to spend a night nevertheless, and he dreamed about Gathers The Grass's big, dry, comfortable tepee. Never did he love or appreciate her as much as he did that night, when he thought about what a pleasant, welcome, home she provided for him when he returned from a hunt or a battle.

And he knew that though many warriors took several wives, he would never hurt her by bringing another female into their home.

Dawn came pink and dry, with a divine promise of sunshine.

Silently the people stretched their stiff, aching joints, studied their water-wrinkled skin, and some of them smiled. Palo Duro Canyon was not far. They would be there later today, safe at last. Life there would be a struggle, but at least their life would belong to them, not to the agents and not the soldiers.

There were no formalities to be observed. The travois were hitched up and they simply left. A few of them laughed at the ordeal they had endured the night before. They knew that those who lived to tell the story would tell it around the night fires for many years to come.

They crossed a succession of rocky hills, over treeless land, now green but usually parched. Autumn Thunder was not with his family. As usual he was with the advance scouts, finding the route and alert for the army. It was he who arrived first at the main path that would meander down the walls of Palo Duro Canyon. He was pleased to see that others were already present and apparently safe: Cheyennes and Comanches determined to escape the soldiers scouring the plains for them.

He signaled to his fellow scouts that the way was clear, then rode back over two miles of the punished badlands to tell Lone Wolf to come on.

When the people saw him they became excited. They had

known they were getting close, now they knew that their way was clear to the sanctuary. Before the sun had moved much farther across the sky they were gazing down into the thin mist of the canyon, and then, while the scouts stayed on top to serve as lookouts, the rest of the people, single file, began their precarious journey down the narrow path that led to the floor of the canyon.

Once they made it to the bottom, Maman-ti and other seers made medicine and all agreed that the floor of the canyon was the refuge that they had been seeking. For the first time in many days life began to feel normal. The bands separated into villages and the women erected the tepees. There was good grazing along the banks of the creek, and soon the ponies were peacefully pulling at the grass, guarded by the older boys.

Some of the women went out to gather roots, while others with worn or rotted lodgepoles went out to cut new ones from the cedar trees that grew in profusion throughout much of the canyon. Others simply dropped where they were, exhausted.

Many of the Kiowas felt better because they enjoyed their villages. A lone tepee in the middle of the plains may be a shelter, but a village of tepees was truly home, even if home three days ago had been forty miles away.

Maybe in wanting to be home again, the Owl Prophet and the people were too anxious to believe that the soldiers could not find them.

The scouts remained atop the canyon for a few days, then, secure in their numbers, their position, and their belief that the *Tai-bos* would never find them, they made their way down the trail to the villages where women cooked and old man smoked and young men fished and hunted and planned future deeds that might save their people.

Colonel Ranald Mackenzie and his Fourth Cavalry were coming up from the Brazos, seeking and not finding the warriors he knew were somewhere out on the plains. Messengers came and went between his regiment and the others. At this time all of them knew that many Kiowas, Comanches, and Cheyennes were off the reservations, entire villages of them, either hunkered down in an obscure river valley, or wandering in some portion of the plains they had yet to find.

Mackenzie deduced that they were hunkered, because wandering villages leave trails that one of these columns would surely cross, and yet it had been days since any such trails had been found. The rain had done its job, just as Maman-ti had said it would. Mackenzie was pondering the problem one night in his big tent, when someone out in the dark fired several shots through the camp that buried themselves in the buffalo grass beyond.

The sergeants turned out the troops in quick order and they charged into the night. They found no warriors, though a few did hear hoofbeats fading off into the darkness. Mackenzie doubled the guard and his men settled down for a night's sleep.

He did not sleep. He called in his chief Tonkawa scout and asked him where he would go if he were a Kiowa or a Comanche. The Tonkawa suggested that Palo Duro Canyon might be just the place.

"If they go there and we find them, they'll be trapped and they know it," he told the scout, whom the whites called Tonkawa Bill.

"Maybe not," Bill answered. "Big canyon, and hard to find. Maybe they think you would not find it."

"Can you?"

"I have been there."

Mackenzie had been chasing Indians around for long enough. He did not want to chase ghosts again.

He pondered the problem for several minutes, till his sharp eye caught a picture of President Grant that his aide-de-camp hung on the wall of his tent whenever he was in the field.

"What the—" He walked over to the picture and ran his finger over the glass. There was a .40 caliber hole in the face of President Grant. Mackenzie vented an expletive or two and walked across the tent, where he found the exit hole the bullet had drilled in the canvas.

"Bill," he said through clenched teeth. "We will be up at sunrise in the morning. I want you to head straight for Palo Duro and I don't want to miss it. You sabe?"

Tonkawa Bill understood. "Many warriors plenty tough," he said.

"We will surprise them, and they will either have to surrender or risk the lives of their families."

The Tonkawa nodded and said nothing further. He was dubious. The Kiowas had bedeviled his people for many years. He regarded them with a certain awe. Even though he knew the whites had licked many other tribes, these were Kiowas, these were men. Tonkawa Bill decided that he would be very careful until he figured out just how good a soldier chief Colonel Mackenzie was.

Bill, the other Tonkawas, and the lieutenant in charge of scouts moved much faster than the colonel's unwieldy column. The Tonkawas knew where they were going. All the soldiers could do was follow the Tonkawas' trail as fast as they could. Early the following day the scouts reached the familiar rock formations that told them they were almost there. Pleased that their long scout was nearly over, they jogged their horses past the rocks and slowed them to a walk. They studied the brush carefully, sometimes found themselves staring down sheer walls, and after about an hour of diligent searching, discovered the path that led along those sheer walls down to the floor of the canyon. They entered the trail and rode several hundred yards until they arrived at a clearing from which they could look down through the haze of hundreds of tepee hearth fires, stretching down the deep valley.

"Too much Indian," the Tonkawa reported tersely to the chief of scouts, a Lieutenant Thompson.

The lieutenant shrugged his shoulders. "Too much for us," he said. "Maybe not too much for Colonel Mackenzie."

Very early the next morning, Mackenzie and his men arrived above the canyon. Mackenzie was suspicious at first. He just couldn't believe these Indians who had skillfully evaded five army columns for weeks would be so negligent as not to have guards posted to alert the people below. And yet the scouts reported that they had found no sign of lurking warriors.

"You know how these people are," said Lieutenant Thompson. "When they want something to be so, they just *wish* it. If you can find 'em right when they're wishin', and you got good men, then I believe you can beat 'em before they even know you're on 'em."

"I hope you're right, Lieutenant. Let's just take your scouts and a squad and see if we can find a trail that'll get us down below while they're still wishin','' Mackenzie replied.

If any of the Kiowas had had the ability to look through the smoke and trees to the sides of the canyon they might have seen, silhouetted against the morning blue sky, the broad-brimmed hats of Mackenzie's officers as they stared down at the tepees far below that stretched across the canyon floor.

Several scouts and troopers found a trail and rode silently as it made its way slowly downward, then abruptly stopped at the scene of an ancient rockslide. Another trail continued for only a hundred yards before it eroded into nothingness. It took nearly an hour before one of the Tonkawas remembered a very narrow trail—a goat trial, he said—and he guaranteed Mackenzie that that trail, precarious though it was, led all the way down to the canyon bottom.

Quietly the men led their horses over the path along the sheer sides. Then where the sides sloped, the path led down, and down slid the troopers and their horses, the men wondering whether death would come from a Kiowa bullet or a fall. When at last they finally reached the floor of the canyon, they formed into lines, troop by troop, and rode at a steady gallop toward the nearest cluster of tepees.

Autumn Thunder was gnawing on a tough piece of buffalo jerky and Gathers The Grass was cutting up wild vegetables for the kettle. The back of Autumn Thunder's neck was stiff because he had spent half the day before stalking a jackrabbit with a bow. Twice he had come close enough to the creature to fire an arrow at it, but each time the arrow had just grazed its hide. It had been a long time since Autumn Thunder had shot a bow.

He tilted his head far back to stretch his neck muscles and let his eyes bore through the light haze to rest on the early morning blue sky. He wondered if he would ever again see this sky from the banks of Medicine Creek.

He heard a shot, and then another down the valley. Some fortunate hunter must have flushed a deer, he thought, flexing his neck and standing up.

Then several more shots rang out. He turned and squinted in the direction of the shots but could see nothing.

What his eyes missed, his ears did not. He heard the sounds

of hoofbeats, and the scuffling of feet on the forest floor. There were shouts of panic, down the valley but drawing near. It couldn't be, but it was. The soldiers were in the valley, that had to be it! He grabbed his rifle, and his pistol, and his ammunition pouches.

"Come on!" he shouted. Gathers The Grass was already on her feet, and Deerfoot was in her arms. Other than what they carried, everything they possessed on this earth, they left. "You follow the others up the south trail!" he ordered Gathers The Grass. "I'll hang back and try to slow them down."

"No," said Gathers The Grass, frightened. "You come. You—"

"I'll be along. You know I will," he said, cocking his rifle. "Now go!"

She turned and ran, their boy in her arms. He was a big boy for his age, and she was pregnant and carrying a pack too, but she ran hard, struggling over rocks and dodging cedar trees as she headed for the steep side of the canyon.

The troops were spread out in lines across the canyon, driving the Indians before them as they charged through village after village, all completely abandoned, their tepees standing straight and tall, beautifully decorated outside and filled with their possessions inside, smoke from the hearth fires still rising from the smokeholes. There were pack horses and mules tied to trees, straining and crying out in terror at the gunfire and the cursing and the thundering hooves of the big cavalry chargers.

The troopers ignored the abandoned villages and the Kiowa pack animals and pounded on, shooting as they rode, their carbines echoing like thunder off the canyon walls, but they were firing at fleeting shadows, mostly shadows of trees and bushes that moved as they moved. The women and children were far ahead, panic-stricken, certain that the soldiers would show no mercy if they overtook them.

For the warriors, however, this was business as usual. The trees and broken ground slowed the charge; the Kiowa men slowed it further with their routine of fire and retreat, so neatly done that the troopers could scarcely see a real warrior, let alone get a good shot at one. Autumn Thunder heard his friend Talia-koi singing the song of his warrior society, saw him work the bolt of his carbine and squeeze off a shot, saw him retreat ten yards to another cedar tree, saw him load another cartridge, heard his voice sing out again. Autumn Thunder spotted the white flash of Tonkawa feathers, snapped off a shot, and retreated.

As they fell back the canyon narrowed, concentrating them to where they could direct a heavy fire on the approaching troops. They could not worry about saving ammunition for the hunt. If they could not stop the soldiers here, now, the people would have no need of future hunts.

Autumn Thunder had found good cover between a large rock and a thick cottonwood stump, and here he made his stand, loading and firing as fast as new targets appeared, mostly firing at flashes and puffs of smoke, but sometimes getting a glimpse of army blue. The sound of continual gunfire, echoing off the canyon walls, was worse than any thunderstorm, but Autumn Thunder was not listening. Nor was he thinking about Gathers The Grass fleeing up the canyon path with Deerfoot in her arms.

He was not thinking much at all. He was reacting in the way of the Kiowa warrior, first firing fast to stop the soldier charge in its tracks, then feeling the fire slacken, racing through the underbrush to a new position, hoping to outflank an unwary soldier and cut him off before he could fall back to his cohorts.

But now the firing from the front was increasing, and he knew that new troops had ridden forward and dismounted. There were too many troops to handle, but the Kiowas would not drop back until they had to. Right and left he could hear his fellow warriors keeping up a strong fire, screeching their war cries to keep up their courage.

And now the soldier gunfire was too close. He could feel the other Kiowas falling back, feel the soldier fire beginning to outflank him, and he had to fall back too. He did so without panic, first chambering a cartridge in his rifle, then, seeing close movement among the cedars to his left, pulling his revolver.

Three soldiers burst out of the cedar thicket thirty yards away. They had been firing at smoke since they had begun the attack and were thrilled by the sight of a lone Kiowa nearly in the open.

As they raised their weapons Autumn Thunder dove for a

small depression in the dirt. The three soldiers all fired their carbines, kicking up dirt and rock all around him. He took quick aim and fired one, two, three shots from his revolver. The third shot caught flesh, spinning one of the soldiers onto his back and stopping the others in their tracks. Autumn Thunder rolled to his feet and scampered into the underbrush before the soldiers could reload and aim.

Several others had joined them in the chase. Autumn Thunder was the only Kiowa they could see, and he had put one of their men on the ground. They were determined to run him down and kill him.

But Autumn Thunder was swift in his moccasins and the dismounted soldiers were slow in their cavalry boots. Quickly he melted into the cedar brush. Several of the troopers knelt and fired after him in vain, then they resumed the chase. The cedar brush slowed them down, but they plowed through it and suddenly they were in an open space. Fifty yards away, concealed in the trees and rocks, a score of Kiowas showered the troopers with bullets and arrows. Half of them went down, the other half began to retreat.

But other troopers were coming fast. The Kiowas had scored a small victory, but there were too many soldiers and too much firepower, and the warriors had their families to protect.

They scurried up the steep wooded sides of the canyon, where they joined their families, hiding among the trees and rocks, looking down upon the soldiers as they rode through the villages and rounded up the huge Kiowa horse herd. The warriors began to fire down upon the troopers. Mackenzie knew he was in a very tough spot. The canyon walls were too steep for the troopers to charge the Kiowas. But if the soldiers stayed where they were, the gunfire from above would soon be finding their targets.

Mackenzie saw that his battle was won even if he never killed another Indian. Half his men tied their horses out of sight of the Kiowas, went forward and found cover, and kept up a steady chorus of gunfire to pin the Kiowas down. Shots echoed fiercely up and down the canyon, but the man on both sides were firing into distant, covered positions, and lead found no flesh.

The rest of Mackenzie's men rode back down the valley to the villages.

Having done his part in the delaying action, Autumn Thunder dashed up the steep sloping side of the canyon in search of his wife and son. Fighting the soldiers had scarcely quickened his pulse, but now his emotions verged on the edge of panic as he failed to find his family among the women and children who were still struggling toward the top of the canyon.

At a waterfall over to his left he at last found Gathers The Grass, who had not only carried Deerfoot, but had succeeded in taking with her a large buffalo robe bundle that she had learned to keep at hand. This she called her *Tai-bo* bundle, just in case their village was attacked by the whites and they had to flee quickly.

They could go no farther along this route. The hillside was too steep and exposed. Bullets from down below were pinging off the sheer rock wall. "Over here!" he shouted above the roar of the falling water. He led them to a spot behind several large rocks. The soldiers would not be climbing this way, and he had spotted a difficult but possible route out of the canyon from where they were.

The action that counted was taking place in the villages, and Autumn Thunder and Gathers The Grass could see it all. The soldiers had pulled firebrands from the lodge fires, and now they were setting afire each tepee. From their hiding place they saw a ghastly village of fiery cones, the flames leaping upward as if the tepees were reaching out to the heavens for rescue. They knew that more than just a village was going up in flames. What they were witnessing was the death of the free Kiowa people.

The soldiers were cutting packs and saddles off the Kiowas' horses and mules and throwing them into the fires—whatever possessions of the Kiowas they found lying around the camp— saddles, blankets, clothing, food supplies, anything they could find that looked like it would burn, and some things that wouldn't—they threw onto the fiery tepees.

Around them they could hear the weeping of women and children, but both Autumn Thunder and Gathers The Grass were too keen on survival to give in to their emotions. One of the cavalry troops had rounded up the entire Kiowa horse herd and was driving the terrified, wide-eyed creatures back through the villages toward the easiest exit from the canyon. The soldiers that had been sniping at the warriors gave up and turned toward the villages to aid in their destruction.

"We must go now!" Autumn Thunder told Gathers The Grass, tearing his eyes away from the flaming villages. Quickly they scrambled up the steep path he had discovered. Gathers The Grass still lugged both Deerfoot and the big bundle. Autumn Thunder led with his rifle at the ready, because he believed that more soldiers might be waiting for them at the top of the canyon. Several other families followed them, and none of them looked down, though they could feel the heat of their burning lodges on their backs.

The wind shifted, blowing the smoke into their eyes and nostrils. Their breath came in gasps; their throats choked, and their eyes teared as they toiled toward the top of the canyon, and finally, feeling as if they were rising into the blue sky itself, they burst from the canyon onto the plateau, wheezing and spitting, their chests heaving as they struggled to suck fresh air into their lungs. Some were on their backs, some on their knees. Autumn Thunder could not stop to recover. He climbed onto the nearest large boulder, his rifle at the ready, and searched the surrounding ground for any sign of the enemy.

But all he could see was the thin grass and the rocks, occasional stunted cedar, and miles and miles of undulating emptiness. They stepped away from the canyon and left the obscene destruction behind. Others were following them, and to his right he could see people emerging from the south end of the canyon. He and Gathers The Grass moved toward the south end, where they found some of the chiefs together trying to decide what to do next.

Maman-ti looked around at his people, their heads and their hearts drooping like feathers in the rain. "We must go to the evening sun," he said. "We can survive there, the white men cannot, and they will not pursue us too far."

Others were not so sure. He had made medicine and pronounced Palo Duro Canyon safe. See what his prophecy had got them. But they were discouraged. Nobody wanted to stand up to the medicine man. Most just wanted someone to tell them what to do.

Autumn Thunder looked around at the hundreds who had escaped, many of them familiar faces from his or other villages. But Wounded Deer was not among them. Occasionally one or three lagging people continued to appear around the southern rim of the canyon. He knew that some of the young warriors were sticking close to the edge of the canyon to round up stragglers and send them around to where the survivors stood waiting to flee. Among them were a mere handful of horses and mules. The Comanches and Cheyennes who had been in the canyon had made their own escape.

Autumn Thunder walked over to Tsein-kop-te, who had a mule that did not seem overburdened. He asked the old warrior if he would load Gathers The Grass's pack on the mule. The old warrior would see to his family as they traveled west. He wanted to join the rear guard. They might be able to delay the soldiers if they pursued. Or he might be able to steal back some of their ponies.

Chapter 27

He lay amidst the brush and boulders on a little rise overlooking the main path out of the canyon. He watched several soldiers ride out of the canyon, including the soldier chief Mackenzie.

One of the soldiers carried a buffalo robe across his saddle. Autumn Thunder saw Mackenzie say something to an officer who rode beside him, and the officer said something to the soldier with the buffalo robe. The soldier dismounted, pulled the buffalo robe off his saddle, walked to the edge of the canyon, and flung the robe over the side.

Autumn Thunder understood.

More soldiers rode out of the canyon. None of them carried souvenirs. Apparently all of them had gotten the word but one—everything that belonged to the Kiowas was to be destroyed.

The herd of Indian ponies was already out on an open plain, surrounded by troopers. At first he hadn't noticed them because they were more than a mile away and mostly hidden by the contours and the rocks of the land. He decided to creep closer if he could. He thought he was as good as dead if they spotted him—these soldiers did not seem interested in taking prisoners—but the land was so broken up and he was so far from them and their attention seemed so focused on the pony herd he knew he could get fairly close without being spotted.

And it might be worth it. Indian ponies generally did not like white men and white men did not have the skill to keep the ponies from running away. There was a good chance that as the soldiers herded the animals back to the fort at least some of them would escape. The soldiers would chase them for awhile and then they would give up on them. Autumn Thunder had no doubt that he could catch one, and then he would catch more. His people needed these animals more than they needed anything else.

So he crept closer, until he had a good view of the pony herd and the soldiers herding them. Any moment they would be moving out. Had he not been so filled with anxiety over the disappearance of his friend and the sudden impoverishment of his people, Autumn Thunder might have relished watching the soldiers in their bungling attempts to herd the horses back to the reservation.

Except, he realized to his horror, they were not about to herd them anywhere!

He heard a shouted command and saw the men draw their carbines from their saddle scabbards. Another command and they lifted the carbines to their shoulders. His eyes widened in disbelief. The carbines were pointed toward the beautiful ponies, the godlike creatures that were the core of Kiowa greatness.

Another command and the men fired. Dozens of ponies went down, some of them immediately still, and some of them kicking and screaming in pain and panic.

The ponies that had not been hit went mad with fear, but most of them could go nowhere because they were in each other's way. The men reloaded as quickly as they could and fired again. More ponies went down. Smelling blood, the panic of the surviving animals increased. A handful blindly crashed through the cordon formed by the soldiers and made a dash for freedom, but a half dozen soldiers rode after them.

The escaping ponies made large targets and the range was close, but the soldiers were not great shots from the back of a bounding horse and most of the ponies were not killed immediately. They did receive painful bloody wounds that allowed the troopers to overtake them and finish them off, then the soldiers raced back to the main slaughter.

Autumn Thunder was on his knees, eyes to the sky, tears streaming down his face, his hands lifted in horror and frustration. He dug his fingernails deep into his thighs and dragged them along his skin, leaving long furrows filling with blood that oozed up through his flesh. He felt no pain through the wounds, but his soul was in agony screaming at him to do something to stop the slaughter.

He wanted to creep closer, to level his rifle at the soldiers and drop as many of them as they could. What unholy, spiritless, soulless creatures were these who could murder such wonderful animals so easily, so remorselessly!

The shooting continued. The blood and the terror of the slaughter were so great that the cavalry horses were catching the fear from the Indian ponies. Many of them were shying and bucking. The soldiers could barely lay their sights on their targets.

Still the killing went on, and Autumn Thunder felt the need to watch to the bitter end, to bear witness to the tragedy that not only ended the lives and bloodlines of the mighty Kiowa horse herd, but ended the freedom of the Kiowa nation.

Foolishly, through the tears, he pointed his rifle in the direction of the slaughter and fired. The bullet hit the sand less that a quarter of the way to where dying ponies were tumbling over the bodies of the dead and slipping on their blood in their vain efforts to escape.

From this distance it was difficult to tell one pony from another, but Autumn Thunder knew that five of the ponies and two of the mules were his and another five ponies had been his at one time or another. He had traded or given those away, but he had known them all. There were only a handful still upright now. A few of them had given up. Exhausted from running from one line of troopers to another looking for a way out, jostled by the unwounded and kicked by the dying, wide-eyed fright sucking the energy out of their bodies, they stood with their eyes glazed and heads drooping, no longer connected to the slaughter going on around them.

But most of those still left continued to surge from north to south, then back, never quite grasping that there was no way out, then finally, mercifully, tumbling onto their sides or sinking slowly to their knees and rolling into the dust.

Autumn Thunder's mind cleared enough that he remembered he had to search for Wounded Deer, and that he should make his way across the open plain back to the canyon while the soldiers were still engaged in the massacre of the Kiowa horse herd.

He raced to the edge of the canyon, found a pathway down

and half ran, half slid down the hill, oblivious to the rocks and thorns that gashed his legs. He dashed through what had been his village and did not have the time or desire to look for items the soldiers might have missed, or to agonize over the losses he and the Kiowa nation had suffered.

He remembered where he had last seen Wounded Deer. His friend was not there, nor were there any blood traces. He tried to imagine Wounded Deer's probable line of retreat, looking around as he did so. He saw no bodies from either side, and he began to hope that perhaps Wounded Deer had somehow survived.

Then he saw the thing, barely sticking out from behind a bush. The thing was a bloody, scalpless skull.

He walked over, knelt beside it, and discovered that the face had been caved in by repeated blows, either of a big rock or a rifle butt. The face was so thoroughly crushed and bloody that he could not identify the face paint, but there was no doubt in his mind, the sky-blue body paint with the yellow dots was the warpaint of his young friend and comrade in battle, Wounded Deer. Fingers were missing from his left hand. Briefly, unreasonably, he wondered if the mutilations were the work of the soldiers or their Tonkawa scouts.

For a moment, he felt so dizzy that his mind simply could not function. The dizziness gave way to despair. In one day he had lost everything. He stood up, looked away from his friend, and took a deep breath. Not everything. He had his family. He and his tough wife would see to it that their corner of the Kiowa world would survive.

He bent down, slung the body of Wounded Deer over his shoulder, and struggled up the path that led to the waterfall he had seen. Above the waterfall was a deep crevice between two large rocks. Softly he began to sing the song of the warrior society to which both he and Wounded Deer belonged. Gently he placed his friend into the crevice, then began to gather rocks and drop them until Wounded Deer was well covered and hidden forever from the sight of man. Then he got to his feet and began to climb out of the canyon.

At first he saw nobody when he reached the top of the canyon, but after he had crept north for a half mile along the canyon's edge he caught sight of the soldiers' supply train. Barely out of sight of the pony herd they had just slaughtered

he soldiers were queuing up for food. There seemed to be no
sense of urgency on their part. Having destroyed nearly everything the Kiowas owned, and putting them on foot, and knowing there were other troop columns out in the field, the white
soldier chief was content to pursue the desperate refugees at
his leisure.

When he arrived at his people's camp in a rocky valley west
of the canyon, he found them immobilized by grief and confusion. Their chiefs had made some grave errors in estimating
the ability of the white men to find and subdue them. There
were warriors missing, and women and children unaccounted
for. The people were too stunned and worn to even acknowledge him. He searched until he found Au-sai-mah and his
wife.

The old man was close to exhaustion, but he walked with
dignity among his people and exhorted them not to give up.
The future of the Kiowa nation was in their hands, he told
them, and they must be up to the task.

Autumn Thunder took his chief aside and told him that the
pony herd had been destroyed. He knew it must have been a
severe shock to the old man, but Au-sai-mah's face showed
no emotion. "Walk with me, my young brother," he said to
Autumn Thunder. "What else have you to tell me?"

"Wounded Deer is dead," the young warrior said, bitterly.
"And when I left the canyon to find you, the soldiers were
gathering to eat." He looked into the deep-set dark eyes of
his chief, who seemed to have grown very old since Autumn
Thunder had last seen him. "What are we going to do?" he
asked.

"Look around you," said Au-sai-mah. "You see the only
ones left of my people. The others have gone to other places.
It is a bad thing that they have killed our horses. And yet
look! We still have some horses. We still have some mules.
Our warriors have arms and ammunition. Those who saved
food will share. We will go to the night land where the whites
will not go.

"There was a time, in the time of our people when we had
no horses. There was a time when we were a poor and hungry
people. But we are still a strong and powerful people because
we know how to be strong and powerful. I grieve for your

brother Wounded Deer. I grieve for his mother, for his young woman, and you must tell them as soon as we are finished here. But we have lost more of our people in a winter of sickness, or a summer of raiding. We will survive, and the sun will shine again on us . . . some day.'' His last two words trailed off, not because he did not believe them, but because he did not believe that he would live to see them come true.

On his way across the village to tell Wounded Deer's mother and wife of their loss, he felt raindrops again. Why, he wondered, had there been so much rain on the dry plains these last few weeks? To drive the whites home, of course, he reasoned. Kiowas can stand anything. But no, he thought, even Kiowas cannot bear to suffer forever.

He saw his wife carrying their son, coming toward him as he walked across the camp. She peered at him intently, then embraced him. ''I must go to Little Cloud,'' he said softly in her ear. ''Do not show feelings. Not now. Not later. I will need to talk to you.''

He spotted the widow of his young friend. She was some distance away, but she had seen Autumn Thunder and was waiting for him, her arms helplessly hanging down at her sides, hoping to hear nothing but knowing better. Autumn Thunder hardened the inside of his face and walked quickly to her. As he came near, the rain began to come down harder. The people had no tepees. There were no leafy trees for shelter. No rock overhangs, no caves, no refuge of any kind for the nation that called themselves Kiowa, ''the principal people.''

Chapter 28

There were fewer than seventy people left in Au-sai-mah's band, including the children. Perhaps a dozen of them were adult warriors, and some of those were nearing the end of their useful careers.

In council they agreed that if the soldiers came, three of them would come forward on the best ponies they could scrape up and surrender themselves and their people before the soldiers could get their blood up and attack. Au-sai-mah explained that in his experience most white chiefs preferred a peaceful surrender but when they attacked, they and the soldiers often went crazy and tried to kill everybody.

Yay-go had a different idea.

"Would it not be more pleasing to the Great Spirit," he asked, "if we did not surrender? Let us send scouts out and if we see the soldiers come, let us hide the women and children and ambush the soldiers. If we win we will have horses and ammunition, maybe even wagons."

Au-sai-mah shook his head. "We do not have enough men to serve as scouts and protect our people. Even if we find the soldiers before they find us, how do we gather the scouts for the ambush when they are scattered in all directions? And even if we could, I do not believe we have enough men to defeat any group of soldiers. And if we ambush them and kill some before they kill us, they will be angry. Then when they find our women and children, they will kill them for vengeance. We want to run away from them, but if they find us, we must surrender."

Kone-bo-hone spoke up. "If we keep going to the falling

sun," he said, "are there other red people who might help us?" he asked.

There was a general murmur of disapproval among his cohorts. "Who would we go to?" one of them asked. "Our age-old enemies, the Utes? The miserable Apaches, who would kill us and enslave our children?"

Au-sai-mah spoke then. "Young men dream in their sleep at night," he said. "But an old man can dream at any time. Today after we made camp I had a short sleep, and in my sleep I dreamed that one day we had awakened to find a herd of wild horses coming through our camp. Half of them continued on but half of them stopped and lowered their heads to us while we took rawhide strips and made bridles for them.

"And the dream went on. There were enough horses for all to ride. We mounted them and rode east until we came to the Medicine Bluffs. And in the dream the buildings of the fort were still there, but they were crumbling and falling down, as if the soldiers had gone away a long time ago. I do not need a prophet to tell me the meaning of this dream. I knew before I awoke it meant that if we were patient, the white men would go."

Autumn Thunder was surprised to find himself speaking up. "Why would they go?" he asked. "They are so powerful, and there are so many of them."

"Yes," replied the chief. "But when you were young they fought against each other and many of them went someplace else. They came back because the one group of them beat the other. That time they fought for four summers. But if next time they fight for ten summers, maybe they will then leave us alone for a long time."

"Does that not mean that we must stay out and never surrender?"

"It means that we must survive. Out here, free, if we can, but if it comes down to surrender or die, then it is better to surrender, for our time will come again. Now, I will lead our people west. Some of you must go out and look for soldiers so they cannot surprise us."

It was not the soldiers who found them, but a group of traders, some of them Mexicans, some of them Navahos.

Tsein-kop-te saw them in the distance, a bizarre parade, two wagons, their dingy canvas tops billowing in the breeze, pulled by sturdy mules, and flanked by a half dozen riders of fine horses and two more riders on mules. Two of the horsemen spotted Au-sai-mah's struggling band. With a cruel tug on the reins they veered off from the line their cohorts were taking, and they rode toward the Kiowas at an easy gallop.

As they dismounted and led their horses to where Au-sai-mah walked as tall and as proud as his tired body allowed him, Tsein-kop-te turned to his chief and he said, "Au-sai-mah, have nothing to do with these men. I smell evil all over them."

The men walked over to the old chief with big smiles on their faces, hands extended. They were wearing wide sombreros, and both wore thin mustaches in the approved fashion of their people. Autumn Thunder wondered what it might look like to have a mustache like that. A few Kiowas, Set-ankia was one, could grow mustaches. He could not.

The two men started speaking in Spanish. The chief understood it well, Autumn Thunder understood a little. Tsein-kop-te understood scarcely a word.

One of them was painfully thin—thinner even than the lanky Autumn Thunder. The other was well larded and yet he looked powerful. Both wore pistol belts with revolvers.

"We heard that the soldiers stole all your horses," the fat one said, sympathetically. "Terrible thing." He shook his head sadly.

"*Gracias*," said the chief. He looked across the open space, at the wagons. "My people are hungry," he said. "Have you any food for them?"

"We do not have much," the thin one replied. "But we have a little corn flour we can let you have."

"We do not have much to give you in exchange. Maybe two buffalo robe—good buffalo robe."

The thin one put his hands up in front of him. "No, no!" he exclaimed. "My brothers have had misfortune. We have had a good summer of trading. Perhaps some day, when your days are better, we will trade with you—yes? Trade for many good buffalo robe then, and you will remember that Umberto y Luis helped you out, eh?"

"A Kiowa does not forget friendship," said the chief.

"Está bien," said the fat one. "Luis, have Carlos and Fidel bring two bags of tortilla flour."

The two men carrying the bags may have had Spanish names and worn Mexican breeches, but they were Navajos. Au-sai-mah saw that immediately. He asked Tsein-kop-te to help dole out the flour. There was not much, considering the number of mouths to be fed, and some of the families had no cookware, but in their adversity the people remained loyal to each other. Even Kone-bo-hone, who could at times be arrogant and overbearing, took his meager share and gave it to his wives to prepare for a sparse, shared, family supper.

"How did you find out about our fight with the soldiers?" Au-sai-mah asked the fat one.

"We were on our way south with goods we had traded for when we found some Cheyennes coming toward us. They had ridden their horses so hard that the *pobrecitos* could hardly move anymore. They said that the soldiers were right behind them, and would kill them if they caught them.

"We tried to tell them that we felt sorry for them, but they had only stopped long enough to tell us that they could not stop to talk, and their horses were on their way again."

"Did you see the soldiers?" Au-sai-mah asked.

"Funny thing," the fat one answered. "We didn't see anybody chasing the Cheyennes, as they had claimed, but as we traveled farther south we saw soldiers all over the country, mostly heading west, mostly looking for you, I think."

"How close are they?" said the chief.

"Not so near, not so far," answered the fat one, philosophically. "I think you'll be safe if you stay the night, but in the morning might be good if you move fast, eh?"

The people were grateful to have something in their bellies, and they were terribly tired from their long and continuing ordeal. There were no late-night council fires or warrior society meetings. Everybody was asleep quickly, even the scouts.

Several warriors dreamed that night, and in the morning all of them were anxious to recount the dreams to their cohorts when they awoke under their blankets and buffalo hides, hating to have to crawl out into the frigid morning air.

But before they could make themselves leave their warm cocoons, they heard a yell of surprise. "Everybody get up!" cried the thin voice of Tsein-kop-te. If we are quick we can catch them!"

Autumn Thunder arose from the robes he shared with Gathers The Grass and Deerfoot. He knew immediately that the few pack horses and mules they had managed to take with them had been stolen. He knew also that because of the Mexican's warnings about soldiers being close by, many of the families had left their packs near their ponies so they could load their belongings on their animals and head them south as quickly as possible.

He ran toward the space, to see what had happened to the apprentice warriors who had been assigned to guard the horses. They lay quietly, each in the middle of a red circle where the sandy ground had soaked up their blood. Their throats were cut.

"They must have fallen asleep," said Tsein-kop-te, not accusingly but sympathetically. He knew how exhausted the entire band was as a result of the relentless pursuit by the soldiers. People were running around the camp desperately, to see who else might have been killed in the middle of the night.

"Tsein-kop-te, you must lead our braves after them, quickly."

"No!" answered Autumn Thunder, sharply. "There is no time. My brother Tsein-kop-te has many winters. He can still ride. He cannot walk. I will lead."

Au-sai-mah did not argue. Neither did Tsein-kop-te. Konebo-hone, Yay-go, and Talia-koi were by his side, arms in hand. Without further conversation, Autumn Thunder broke into an easy run following the wagon tracks. He knew that on foot it would be nearly impossible to catch their tormentors, but desperation pushed them forward.

Shrewd and merciless, the Mexicans had planned their coup carefully. After they had killed the sentries, they had brazenly taken the time to load the packs on the horses and mules, within fifty yards of some of the sleeping Kiowas.

While mothers and aunts wailed for the slain boys, some of the tribesmen turned their anger on Au-sai-mah and A-do-te the medicine man. When the old chief tried to find out what supplies were left to them that might be shared, they pushed him out of the way and walked over to Tsein-kop-te.

"You are our finest warrior," they said. "You are our war chief. Au-sai-mah has had bad judgment since we left the reservation. We want to throw away Au-sai-mah. We want you to lead us. We want our ponies back. We want our lodges back. We want our land back. It is Au-sai-mah's fault that we have lost them all.''

Tsein-kop-te refused to listen. He walked right up to the warrior who was doing the most talking, and only with great difficulty did he curb his anger.

"My young brother," he said. "It is not Au-sai-mah's bad medicine, or A-do-te's bad medicine that has done all this to us. It is the white men. They are demons. I cannot do what Au-sai-mah could do. I have followed Au-sai-mah all my life. He is a great chief. He can do nothing. What could Gui-pah-go do against the whites? What could Set-tainte do against the whites? Or Addo-eta or Set-ankia?

"We have been so angry with Tay-nay-angopte because he is always trying to make us live in peace with the whites. And yet tonight his people sleep warm in their lodges on the reservation. They have their ponies, they have their kettles, and their buffalo robes and their medicine bundles. Maybe he did the right thing. And yet we all wanted to go away from the reservation. We all wanted to be free of the white men and their evil. Maybe we have come to where no Kiowa has the right answer. But I trust Au-sai-mah. What he says, I will do.''

They turned toward the old chief. Many of the women and the older men of the camp had gathered around him. One of the oldest of the men came forward to him. This was no time for ceremonies or formal councils. Fear and worry were everywhere in the camp. And yet what the old man had to say was a speech, and even the angriest of the warriors was silent while the old man spoke.

"My brother Au-sai-mah," he said. "You know that I now have to ride everywhere. It is so hard for me to walk. It could be that you will have to leave me behind. Today I wonder if you are still able to lead the people. But you have been our chief for many years, and you have always had good judgment. I want you to know that wherever you lead, I will follow, as long as I can, and if you say I must stay behind, then I will do that, for you have always been wise. I trust you.''

There were murmurs of assent, particularly from the women.

One of them, not old in years but gray-haired and toothless

from too many hard winters and too many childbirths, spoke up publicly for the first time in her life.

"What will we do now?" she asked, and then she faded back into the crowd.

The people fell silent. That was the only question that needed to be asked. Au-sai-mah thought for a few moments. But not for long. There was no time for medicine anymore, no time for ceremonies.

"We must find a place to put the slain boys," he said, to nods of agreements. "Then," he added, his voice filled with emotion, "we must go to the reservation."

"Never!" cried the older brother of Kone-bo-hone. "I will die first!" But no one else joined their indignation to his.

"My son," said Au-sai-mah, "it is not our way for the chief to make my village do as I say. You may take your family wherever you wish. Anybody who wishes to go with you can go with you. I say only that my family is going back to the Medicine Bluffs. I believe those who go with me will survive. I believe those who try to make their life out on the Staked Plains without horses will perish. Our time is precious—and, old man," he added, looking at the man who had spoken before, "we will leave nobody behind. Before we go, we must wait for our young men to return. If they do not find the wagons, they will come back discouraged. And you must keep your spirits high to cheer them up."

They waited all morning and through half the afternoon, their worry growing stronger as the sun grew higher. These four young men were their best warriors. It was a long way back to the fort, an impossible journey for people nearly bereft of horses and food.

Nightfall was near. The people despaired for the lives of the young men. How was it possible that lowly men like the two Mexicans had managed to get the best of Au-sai-mah's entire band? Was it also possible that they had wiped out their finest young men?

Gathers The Grass refused to lose faith. Carrying Deerfoot in his cradleboard, she walked away from camp, saw a nearby hill, climbed it, and found a place where she could watch for the return of Autumn Thunder and the others. The first stars were out now. The sun had surrendered to the night, leaving layers of red and gold on the western horizon. The floor of the valley below was almost completely dark when she thought she spotted movement along the trail north. She held her breath and kept her eyes fastened to the place where the movement had occurred.

There it was again. Her heart nearly burst from her breast as she made her way down the hill as fast as she dared. It never for one moment occurred to her that the source of that movement could be anyone other than the man who was her husband, her lover and her friend.

Captain James Leroy Sweeney was in the field with a small detachment from the Tenth Cavalry and a handful of Tonkawa scouts, including his old cohort Sharp Knife.

A week out from Fort Sill they were riding along a ridge northeast of Palo Duro Canyon. The scouts were spread out a mile to the left and right of the cavalry detachment, searching for signs of the Kiowas, Comanches, and Cheyennes that Colonel Davidson knew had to be roaming the Staked Plains, twisting and dodging the troop columns that were closing in on them.

It was a cool day and they had been in the saddle for hours. Sweeney had a terrible thirst and also a bit of a chill. He grabbed his canteen, the canteen on the right side of his saddle, the canteen filled with Peruna's Tonic, and took a deep swig.

Ah, good, he thought. Good on a cool day like this. The canteen was almost empty. He was glad he had stored four more canteens like this under the seat of the wagon that rumbled along with them. But he had only two left. Life would soon be getting much harder, he thought, if they didn't make it back to the post in another few days.

He caught a glimpse of a rider raising dust to his right as he galloped in.

Sharp Knife, approaching, raising more dust as he brought his pony to a halt close to Sweeney.

"Big tracks," said the Tonkawa.

"How far?" Sweeney asked.

"Just the other side of that ridge," Sharp Knife answered, pointing.

"Pierce, Curry!" he shouted. "Join me and Sharp Knife as we ride, if you will."

The four riders went off in an easy trot for a low ridge line half mile to the south.

After they crossed the ridge line, Sharp Knife rode to a spot and pointed to the ground.

Sweeney studied the tracks and grunted. "Whole village," he said grimly. "All on foot."

The Tonkawa nodded.

"How old these tracks?" Sweeney asked.

"Don't know," Sharp Knife answered. "Maybe two days."

"Headed for the reservation?" Sweeney asked. They both knew the answer.

Sweeney shrugged his shoulders. "We don't need to follow them," he said. "They can't hurt anybody."

"What then?" Sharp Knife asked.

"Let's look for a cougar that still has his teeth," said Sweeney. "And leave the old, toothless ones to the clerks back at Fort Sill."

Chapter 29

There was not enough wood out on the badlands to make a bonfire. And the past two days had brought too much tragedy for the people to want to celebrate.

Nevertheless, Au-sai-mah's band welcomed the four young warriors back like conquering heroes, both because they had feared for their safety and because they had managed to recapture some of their meager goods. Around the tiny campfire, pleased to have any food at all in their bellies, the men of the village listened to Autumn Thunder as he explained how they had finally managed to best the Mexicans.

"We were not very smart but our medicine was good," he said. "We were running so hard to catch up with them that we were not careful. Then, running through a dry creekbed, Kone-bo-hone tripped over a dead man. Farther up the creek bed were two more. Their throats had been cut. Very clean, good job. Three Navajos."

"And three more lying on their backs, shot with guns, on the bank of the dry creekbed," added Kone-bo-hone.

Au-sai-mah gave Kone-bo-hone a stern look. It was rude to interrupt a warrior in the middle of a speech, even to add helpful details.

"There were only four of them left," Autumn Thunder said. "They were not asleep. Two of them riding horses, two of them sitting in their wagons. We killed them and took our goods back with us."

Au-sai-mah was not satisfied with Autumn Thunder's explanation. White men believed that warriors were great braggarts, but he knew that Autumn Thunder had become quite

odest as he had grown up, and inclined to give the credit to
s cohorts so they would fight better when he was leading
em. Where were his details? Where was the glory?

Because of Au-sai-mah's rebuke, Kone-bo-hone had re-
ained silent. Now Au-sai-mah beckoned him to speak, and
e tall, muscular warrior was glad to oblige.

"We were all tired when we found the dead men and the
agons," he began. "We had hoped that when we found the
agons we could sneak up on them and shoot the Mexicans.
was hard for all of us to go farther, and then the Mexicans
w us and the wagons began to move. Autumn Thunder told
s to move as fast as we could to catch up, and he would run
ead and stop the wagons.

"We told him if he ran on alone the two men on the horses
ould kill him. He said that if we did not get food then the
hole village might die. It was late in the afternoon. He ran
rward, keeping to the shadows of the high rocks. The Mex-
ans did not see him at first, they were firing at us but we
ere too far away for them to hit us. Then he stopped, got on
e knee and shot a horse on one of the wagons. The other
agon got away. The two men on horseback—the fat Mexican
nd the skinny Mexican—heard the shot and turned their po-
ies and rode straight for Autumn Thunder."

Although Kone-bo-hone was speaking in a loud clear voice,
e women and children were crowding closer to the men at
e fire, so drawn were they to the story he was telling. Pleased
y the effect his story was having on his people, Kone-bo-
one paused for effect. The people waited patiently, but their
ttentive postures were telling the Kiowa warrior to get on
ith his tale.

"They were this far away from him when they began to
de," he said, pointing to a large round boulder that showed
lear in the moonlight about two hundred yards away.

"They rode straight at him. He pulled the loop on his rifle
nd cocked it, but did not shoot until they were much closer.
hey were shooting fast with their pistols. The bullets were
itting all around him but they could not hit him. He fired at
e fat one first."

Kone-bo-hone paused again. The people were all staring at
utumn Thunder.

"That fat one was the easiest to hit," Autumn Thunder said,

shrugging, as if the stares were asking him why the fat on first.

"He fell backwards off his pony and made a great dus cloud when he hit the ground. The skinny one kept comin. Kept shooting. He was not afraid. Autumn Thunder shot agai and his rifle would not shoot. He pulled out his pistol and sho three times. *Bam-bam-bam*!"

He paused again. The people leaned farther forward, as i they feared that Kone-bo-hone was still speaking and the were missing his words.

"The first two bullets missed, and then, when the skinn one was almost on top of him, he fired again and the Mexica fell to the ground. And then Autumn Thunder just jumpe aside and the pony went past."

Now the people began to murmur. They knew that Autum Thunder had unhorsed and captured the lieutenant in a fight They knew he would do great things if he lived, and here h was, doing them already. Here was a young man from one o the lower classes, on the way to becoming a great Kiow leader.

Au-sai-mah knew that the story was still incomplete.

"What about the man in the wagon?"

"He had cut the straps off dead horse. The wagon wa beginning to move again. We were still too far away. Only Autumn Thunder could stop it."

"But his rifle would not shoot," Au-sai-mah pointed out.

"First he looked for the ponies the Mexicans had been rid ing, but they had run off. With only three horses, the wagon was rolling slowly at first. Autumn Thunder ran across the open space until he was as far as that rock. He pointed to another boulder about eighty yards distant. He took aim with his pistol and shot, three more times. One of the shots hit one of the horses pulling the wagon."

Many of the people gasped with astonishment. Eighty yard, seemed an impossible shot with a pistol. Few of the warrior had modern revolvers and most of them had never hit anythin much with them.

"The horse tried to pull but it could not, and then it could not move. And then it could not stand," Kone-bo-hone con tinued. "We saw the driver jump out and start running." The Kiowa smiled. "He did not run for long. Yay-go caught him

rom behind and got first coup. I got second. Then he drew
is knife and we killed them."

The story was done. The people sat in silence, appreciating
vhat they had heard. After their terrible defeat at the hands of
he soldiers, it was good to have a victory, a young man arising
midst their tragedy, a new hero to lead them someday when
he old ones had run their race.

He stood up to speak and they leaned forward again, hoping
or heroic words.

"The two horses still with the wagon could not pull it. We
ulled supplies from the wagon and loaded them on the horses.
'hen we carried as much as we could."

What he did not want to tell them was that the other war-
iors said they were too tired to carry a big load back with
hem, but he said that they must, that the people's lives de-
ended on them. So great was his deed that none dared argue
vith them. They loaded themselves down like pack mules and
rought as much as they could back to the camp. All the way
ome Autumn Thunder praised them for their courage, though
hey knew it was his courage that had defeated the thieves.

Autumn Thunder, Au-sai-mah, and Tsein-kop-te stayed up af-
er the others went to bed and took stock of the band's pos-
essions. In spite of Autumn Thunder's heroics there was not
nuch food and ammunition for the people.

"My brother," the chief said to Tsein-kop-te, "we have so
ittle. The children will soon be hungry and we cannot stop to
unt because the soldiers are out looking for us. If they find
is they will attack us."

His pride would not permit him to ask for advice, but both
Tsein-kop-te and Autumn Thunder knew that was what he was
eeking.

Autumn Thunder had all his life looked to these two men
or guidance and wisdom, even in his early warrior years when
e believed no one had the right to tell him what to do. When
e was a child they made him feel safe. When he was older
hey made him feel understood. They had always been the
trong ones, there for him if his courage failed. But on this
night he could see the fatigue lines etched along their cheeks
and in the corners of their eyes. Their heads drooped. So did
heir spirits. Their land was gone. Federal troops were chasing

them all over the plains as if they were rabbits. They had bee
flushed from their refuge and the entire wealth of their villag
the heritage of a hundred years, had been destroyed.

They were beaten.

"Grandfathers," Autumn Thunder said. The two me
looked sharply at him. His utterance of the single word con
veyed a message. Grandfather was what the people called
man whose strength of arm was no longer what it had beer
Grandfather was a man who could dispense wisdom but wh
no longer could lead in battle. Autumn Thunder had not mean
to send that message, and the two older men certainly had no
been prepared to receive it, but they both loved the youn
man, and they had come to respect him.

They looked at him in silence, and waited for him to speak

"Ah," he said. "We must save the people, and yet we mus
save our freedom. We must do both and yet we cannot d
both. But let me tell you what I think we can do."

"We are listening," said Au-sai-mah.

"You must lead the people back to Medicine Creek. If th
soldiers catch you out here they will attack. If they find yo
standing at the gates of the fort ready to give up they will no
attack. But some of us—Kone-bo-hone, Yay-go, Talia-koi—
and our families—we can stay out."

"But what will the soldiers say when we come in withou
you?"

"Tell them that after the fight in the canyon you did no
see us anymore." He looked at his old friends with an ach
that felt like a bullet in his belly. "We will stay out, and som
day we will find a place where the people can live without th
white men's sicknesses, or his bullets, or his lies. Then w
will call for you and you will come."

The two men nodded.

"There must be young warriors to stay with you and protec
you. If all the warriors are gone, the white men might b
suspicious, and will deal hard with you. And we have learne
that our people need their men to protect them even when they
are being cared for by the peace chiefs. You must take mos
of the food but leave us most of the ammunition."

The next morning, five warriors led by Autumn Thunder stoo
with their families in the shade of the high rocks of eastern

dge of the Staked Plains, watching the departure of Au-sai-
mah and the people whom they had loved all their lives. Many
f them were their relatives—mothers, fathers, uncles, cousins.
mong the women and children there were tears, but no dem-
nstrations of grief. Those had come—and gone—three days
efore at the upper edge of Palo Duro Canyon as the tepees
urned and word of friends and loved ones killed by the sol-
iers spread around the band.

Autumn Thunder had rescued two horses from the Mexi-
ans. One went with the band, the other with Autumn Thun-
er's remnant. With one horse, how would they escape from
ie converging armies that seemed to be everywhere?

Their hearts burned like fire as they watched the great chief
u-sai-mah and his people disappear over a wavelike swell of
nd about a mile distant.

Autumn Thunder had no more time to waste. He must find
efuge.

here was a big stone corral at Fort Sill. The Kiowas were
ery fond of that corral. It reminded them of a time, only a
ouple of years back, when the great raider White Horse and
is men found his way into the corral one dark night, fright-
ned away the guards, and made off with forty-one govern-
ient mules.

The day Au-sai-mah and his band arrived at the post, gaunt,
veary, broken, but alive, the army took away their weapons.
A corporal and a handful of privates led them to the big stone
orral and, once they had entered, closed the gate behind them
nd locked it. The soldiers were not hostile, but they were
rm, and the Kiowas had all they could do to hide their fear
rom their captors.

The next day, soldiers came into the corral and told the men
o come with them. Some of the women cried out to them not
o go, that they would be killed, but Horace Jones promised
he women that this would not happen, that soon most of the
nen would be back with them.

There was a large stone building east of the fort that had
een intended as an icehouse. For some reason nobody had
ver put a roof on it so there it stood, useless, until somebody
ot the idea that it might serve as a detention center for war-
iors until they decided what to do with them. The men in Au-

sai-mah's band were led in and the door locked behind them. Inside they found warriors from other bands that had surren. dered, living in soldier tents and waiting to see what was going to happen to them. Absent were the major chiefs, said to b held in cells at the guardhouse.

Au-sai-mah spoke briefly to his men, warned them not give the soldiers an excuse to torment them, then he and Tsein. kop-te took refuge in an empty tent and there they sat, hungr and silent in the waning hours of the day. They slept an uneas sleep that night, and awakened famished at dawn. The climbed out from beneath their blankets, found a bad-smellin bucket that the men were using as a common waste repository then encountered Gotebo stomping about trying to get warm.

"Where is there water to drink and food to eat?" Tsein kop-te asked Gotebo.

"Come with me," Gotebo answered. "There are bucket of water over in that corner. As for food, it will come flyin in like eagles once the sun gets above the wall to the east."

"What does that mean?" Tsein-kop-te asked.

Gotebo laughed as if he were still free on the plains. Noth ing ever seemed to get Gotebo down for long. "You will see," he said. "Just come back here after you get water, and yo will see."

Tsein-kop-te and Au-sai-mah filled their waterskins and re turned to where Gotebo was pacing in a small area.

"Why do you stay over there?" Au-sai-mah asked.

"Too many questions," Gotebo answered. "You stay her with me," he said, "and watch the sun."

Au-sai-mah and Tsein-kop-te did as they were told. Thoug Gotebo had a reputation as a jokester, he was no clown.

"Are the soldiers taking care of our women and children?" Autumn Thunder asked Gotebo.

"Tay-nay-angopte came by to visit before you came in," said Gotebo. "He said that the women and children are bein cared for, he and Zip-ko-ete are seeing to it. But I saw th face of Maman-ti when Tay-nay-angopte came by."

Tsein-kop-te and Autumn Thunder nodded. Gotebo neede to say no more. Although the medicine man had failed at Pal Duro Canyon, many Kiowas believed that Maman-ti was sti a powerful man against his enemies, and nobody doubted tha counted Tay-nay-angop-te among his enemies.

"Ah, listen!" Gotebo smiled.

They heard the creak of a heavy wagon approaching slowly. he sun appeared over the high wall of the would-be icehouse, ut this cold morning the three warriors pulled their blankets lose to them. As the wagon crept closer, other warriors began emerge from their tents. Like ghosts in the dimly lit dawn, ey walked slowly toward the wall and waited.

The squeaking stopped, replaced by the angry cursing of vo soldiers who at that moment hated each other more than ey hated the Kiowas who necessitated their daily ritual. Au- mn Thunder heard a grunt and saw a large dark object come ying in over the wall. The Kiowas nimbly jumped backward nd the object landed with a thud on the stone floor.

Two men picked it up and were joined by several others as ey carried it away. "Whoa-haw!" said Gotebo. Beef.

Another grunt. Another huge chunk of beef, another party f warriors disappearing with it. And another. At regular in- rvals came the grunts, and the flying meat, and the thump. here was no fighting among the Kiowas for the food.

"Do not worry," said Gotebo. "There will be enough. This ne is ours," he said, leaping backwards as the meat slab nded with a juicy *splat* on the floor of their prison.

Several others joined them, including a warrior named Po- au-ah, who had once been with Tsein-kop-te on a raid against e Tonkawas in Texas. Someone kindled a fire. The warri- rs—there were seven of them to share this chunk of meat at had to last them all day—sat feeding the fire from a pile f wood that had been thrown over the wall stick by stick the ay before. Tsein-kop-te focused his eyes on the flame, then nfocused them.

Suddenly the walls of the icehouse were gone. His beloved var pony, dead and rotting on the Staked Plains, was once nore beneath him, carrying him across Red River into Texas, ne ground moving swiftly beneath him, the warm wind in his ace.

He winced as sparks leaped from the fire. Someone had hrown the beef slab on the fire, and soon they could hear the izzle of fat as the meat began to cook. "Ah," said one or wo of the warriors. The smell was good but Tsein-kop-te did ot smell it. The fat sizzling was good but Tsein-kop-te did not hear it. His mind had leaped the wall and was racing across Texas toward the Rio Grande.

Only now he was thinking that he might find something fine in Mexico to bring back to his mother who was waiting for him up on the north fork of Red River. Perhaps some silver jewelry or an embroidered dress. He wanted to see his mother smile; she smiled so seldom over the long years since the death of his father.

He barely noticed Gotebo cutting a slice of meat from the slab and handing it to him. Only when he bit into it, tasting the charred meat on the outside and the succulent juiciness of the inside, did his mind return within the high walls of the icehouse.

He looked around at the other warriors as they ate. How hungry they were! How they craved this food, as if it were all they had to think about. Like wolves, gnawing their life sustenance and concerned only with their life sustenance. He turned to old Au-sai-mah, whose eyes were nearly closed as he chewed his meat, with some difficulty, for the great chief had lost many teeth over the years.

And Po-hau-ah, chewing thoughtfully, the corners of his eyes slanting sadly downward.

And Gotebo, and the others, eating in silence, disconnected from each other.

Tsein-kop-te's mind could not leap the wall again. On this morning the reality of imprisonment hit him with the solid impact of an Osage war club. He could not finish his chunk of beef. He could barely breathe.

Chapter 30

For years Autumn Thunder had followed men—great men such as Au-sai-mah, Kicking Bird, White Bear, White Horse, Lone Wolf, and Maman-ti. He had not sought out leadership, and yet it had come to him. Other men who might have been leaders, brave young adventurers like Ko-yah-te and Hau-tau, were in the spirit world.

In fact, his people were all but gone from the plains. Kicking Bird had brought his people to the reservation long before, and now, in the wake of the terrible Palo Duro Canyon defeat, he was certain that most, if not all, of the other bands had surrendered. Only his tiny group of families remained to carry on the proud, free, Kiowa tradition. If his band died, the Kiowa people would die.

He was not afraid. Fear was an indulgence he could not afford.

There was no time to waste. As soon as Au-sai-mah's band had vanished from sight, Autumn Thunder pointed to a craggy hill beyond a rocky shelf and told the men to get their families together, that they must go immediately to a place beyond the rocks on that hill. In the late afternoon he led a single horse burdened down with their meager supplies, followed by the rest of his band, over the trackless rocks, up the hill, to a notch in the rock formation atop that hill.

Autumn Thunder told Kone-bo-hone to hold the horse while he went through the notch to see that the place beyond was safe. Kone-bo-hone did not question Autumn Thunder, he just grasped the horse's bridle and motioned for the rest of the band to halt.

Autumn Thunder knew this place, knew it would be an excellent spot to hide from the army for a night or two. He also remembered that the last time he had been here, with Ko-yah-te three summers before, the place had been full of rattlesnakes.

He found no trace of the reptiles. Something had made them leave. He motioned the people to come on.

"There must be no fire!" he insisted, as the people gathered around after they had come through the notch and found a grassy area with a creek and a cave nearly completely surrounded by a rocky formation that rose nearly fifty feet above them.

"We have no lodges. Women, do the best you can to make a camp. Take no more than the corn we need to survive tonight. Tomorrow we will try to find more food, but we cannot hunt while we are being chased by so many soldiers."

Then he called his men together. Alone none of them was a great wise man, yet together they knew much.

"We must have horses for us to survive," he said. "Where can we get horses?"

For a few moments nobody spoke. Then Yay-go stood up. Yay-go was a bulldog of a man, a little older than the rest, short but with broad shoulders and a look of iron in his eyes that belied the smile that usually played around his lips.

"Just across the river," he said, "there lives a man—part *Tai-bo*, part Witsita—sells horses sometimes to the army or to the traders. . . ."

Henry Durham stood on the front porch of his house, which perched on a hill overlooking the Red River. The day had been a good one for him. A trio of mean-eyed cowboys had awakened him from his late-morning siesta, driving a herd of horses through his gate almost up to his doorstep.

"Got you some good horseflesh!" cried one of them as Henry stepped out on the porch scratching the lice on his head and in his beard.

"Looks like a bunch of Indian ponies," he answered. "I don't believe I could get a dollar a head for them."

"Henry, I seen you get ten dollars a head for worse'n this. Come on now, open up that stiff purse of yours and we'll keep you supplied. There's lots more like these to be had and we know where to get 'em. How about it?''

Durham pretended not to be interested in the animals as they milled around the fenced-in lot in front of his home, but he had already spotted among the animals four horses considerably bigger and stronger than the scruffy Indian ponies that made up the bulk of this lot. The big horses looked scruffy too, but he saw good bones, and good movement—probably one-time cavalry horses captured and ridden by Indians until they looked like an Indian pony was supposed to look.

He didn't give the stock a second look. He wasn't interested, he said. "Get 'em off my land!" he said.

The cowboys huddled. Henry figured either they would decide to gun him down, or they would beg him to take the lot for a hundred dollars. He walked into his house for a moment and emerged with a shotgun, which he pretended to wipe clean with a cloth as he watched them muttering things to each other.

They had chosen the begging route.

"Hundred-fifty skins," one of them said, and he almost felt sorry for them, they were so pathetic. He would have been glad to pay one-fifty, but if he took their first offer they'd be suspicious.

"Where'd you get these here ponies?" he asked. "You got a bill of sale?"

"We found 'em wanderin' around in the Llano Estacado," one of them said.

"Just happened to be out there, huh?" he asked. He knew, and they knew he knew, that they were following the army around like buzzards. When the soldiers beat up on a band of Indians they were always sloppy about gathering up Indian property. These men were the scum of the earth, scavengers of plains disasters.

"Give you ninety-five—maybe . . . maybe a hunnert cause you look to need it," said Durham. He expected a big argument but what he got was another huddle.

"We figger maybe a hunnert-five?" said the leader with a pleading note to his voice.

"Tell you what, boys," he said, reaching inside for a bottle of prairie bourbon, which was just a snide name for rough north Texas moonshine. "Here's a near-full bottle of good whiskey. Hunnert and I'll throw in the bottle. If you say no, the price is a hunnert without the bottle. Now what do you say?"

"I say give us that bottle," said the leader, a short, squat, bandy-legged man with a grizzled beard and well-worn chaps.

"Fine," said Durham, reaching through the door for a box of papers.

"I'll make out a bill of sale for y'all to sign," he said.

The air wasn't exactly cool, but with the sun perched on the distant horizon, and a breeze coming in along the ridge, he felt a sense of well-being. He could get better than a hundred-fifty for the big horses alone, he knew, and another three hundred for the rest. He looked down at the river sparkling in the last rays of sunlight. A man can make a profit, he thought, go to town, buy him a bottle, buy him a whore, and be pretty happy for a few days.

He rocked on his porch and sucked on his pipe. He had started this business just five years before after failing at nearly a dozen ventures. This business was different. It was better than any gold mine he'd ever tried to work. Tomorrow a horse buyer was scheduled to appear.

He stretched his arms and took a glance at the grazing field to his left, where most of his stock would be spending the night. He and his hired hand had been working hard all day checking out the animals' hooves, culling the worst horses so they could offer a premium lot for the buyer. He could barely keep his eyes open.

Suddenly his eyes were wide open! The ponies were moving uneasily. Something was in there with them. Alarmed, he ran inside and brought out his old reliable Spencer rifle. He could see human shapes among his horses, now astride his horses. They had removed logs from the fence, and were running the ponies through the opening. They would be riding right by his house, then down the hill and across the river.

"Damn! Damn! Damn!" he cried, first checking to see that his rifle was loaded, then deciding that he had better run for his life.

He scampered out the back door of his house, past some chicken coops, and down the hill to the thick stand of cottonwoods that lined the river. Where the trees were thickest, he hid in a spot from which he could keep an eye on the raiders.

As he thought they would, they were running the herd right by his house.

No, they stopped at the house. Don't stop there! Dammit, there ain't nothing in there for savages. And for God's sake don't burn the place down! he said to himself, but even as he thought those words he could see smoke curling up around the eaves on the side of his house.

Oh damn, no! His brain screamed out as two red men burst from the door carrying things.

Tears of anger and frustration boiled in the eyes of the old half-breed trader. He could not tell what they had chosen to run off with, and he didn't care, such was his concern for his house. Get the hell out of there! he muttered under his breath. If they would leave, he might be able to come up there and stomp out the fire and save his house. But no, the two he could see were standing outside watching the place burn, and by the time they had remounted, smoke was roiling from all the front windows. Where were the rest of those devils? he asked himself.

They drove a dozen horses, including the prized big cavalry mounts, across the front lawn of the house, then down the hill toward the river.

"Aha!" he cried. "Run, you bastards, back to your damned beloved Quakers!" He watched the herd thundering northward, across the Red River, pursued by two shrieking Kiowas.

Two Kiowas! He sent a rich string of oaths toward the heavens. What's a well-oiled Spencer for if not two Kiowas? He raced up the hill to the house. Only the curtains were burning, sending up acrid clouds of smoke but the house itself had not yet caught. He grabbed a curtain, dragged it out the door and down the steps of the porch. Then back into the house he ran, grabbed the other burning curtain, and ran it into his front yard.

He ran back inside, coughing in the smoke, looking for fire or sparks and finding none. He surged through the house, from room to room. Surely they had stolen other things.

Some blankets were gone, and an old percussion cap revolver that he prized. And a half a smoked hog he had been intending to slice from for supper. His straw tick mattress had been thrown off his bed when they had taken his blankets. Under the bed was his cashbox, but they had not taken that.

Only two other things were missing—a coffee pot, and a small sack of coffee, taken off a shelf near his stove. "Those devils had to have their coffee!" he muttered, then, philosophically: "Better my coffee than my scalp." And he opened up every window and door in the house to let the smoke out and the fresh air in.

And flying north with fourteen horses, including four fine cavalry chargers, were Autumn Thunder and Yay-go. With a strong animal beneath him, thundering across the plains, Autumn Thunder felt whole again. The animals he and Yay-go were driving before them were the rebirth of the Kiowa people.

After a few days in the icehouse Tsein-kop-te was ready to go out of his mind. While most of the other warriors sat around in front of fires all day or under blankets in their tents, he wore a path walking around the perimeter of his prison, thinking about his family, nearly crazy with worry over them and obsessed with the high stone walls that seemed to be closing in on him.

Nearly every day new prisoners were coming in, leaving less room for those already there. Soon there were more than a hundred crammed into the small space, and it took the self-discipline of Kiowa warriors to keep them away from each other's throats. The daily beef rations were not increased, and even a Kiowa warrior could not subsist all day every day on fresh-cooked meat. On the fourth day the gate opened and Tsein-kop-te was summoned outside. Standing there was Kicking Bird, an old friend who had fought beside him against the Utes and other ancient enemies of the Kiowa people. Beside him was the soldier captain the Kiowas called "Autumn Thunder's lieutenant."

Tsein-kop-te was so glad to see the great Kiowa chief that he nearly embraced him. But Sweeney was there. Tsein-kop-te would not bare his feelings in front of a *Tai-bo*.

"Have you seen Au-sai-mah?" Tsein-kop-te asked. The old chief was so weak from starvation on the plains that after his band had surrendered he had been put in a wagon and driven quickly to the fort. The last thing Mckenzie wanted was for a great chief to die in his hands just when he had the Kiowas in a surrendering mood.

"He is doing all right," answered Kicking Bird. "When the colonel told me that Au-sai-mah was in the hospital, I told him he would die there, that he had a better chance to live among his own people. The colonel has good sense. He had Au-sai-mah brought to us."

"When will they let us out of the stone house?" Tsein-kop-te asked.

"You must sign a book that says you are a Kiowa and you will never fight the white men again."

Kicking Bird turned to Autumn Thunder's lieutenant and said a few *Tai-bo* words to him. Like most Kiowas outside Kicking Bird's band, Tsein-kop-te hated to hear Kicking Bird speak English to a soldier. It made them think he was keeping something from them, sucking up to the white men, raising himself above the rest.

Sweeney said a few slow words back to Kicking Bird. "Come with us," he said, leading him across the post to a building where documents were kept.

"The enrollment book, Brooks," Sweeney said to a stocky man with two chevrons on his blue sleeve. The corporal opened the book and pointed to the first empty line on the page.

"If you sign this," Sweeney said through Kicking Bird, "it means you agree never again to fight against the white men."

"Can we fight the black white men?" Tsein-kop-te asked.

"No fight nobody." Sweeney said, simply, in English. "I will show you how to make your mark."

He drew a simple "T K" to the right of the page, then pointed to where he wanted Tsein-kop-te to do it. Slowly, carefully, the Kiowa drew the two letters. Sweeney wrote beside the mark "Tsein-kop-te," in neat cursive, then wrote his name next to the writing.

"That is good, my friend."

"When do I see my wife and my grandson?" Tsein-kop-te asked.

"Now if you wish. But we could eat first."

"I want to see my grandson."

"You are hungry and their rations are small. If you eat now, then you will not eat their rations."

"Not hungry."

Sweeney knew better than to argue with a Kiowa brave who had made up his mind. They walked to the cavalry stables and Sweeney signed out a mule for Tsein-kop-te. They rode south to Cache Creek, where Kicking Bird's band was camped. The tepees stretched up and down the creek looking like half the Kiowa nation was camped there. The three men started on the north side of the village and worked their way half a mile down the creek before they finally found the remainder of Au-sai-mah's group camped together a short distance away from everybody else.

The tepees were all shabby and patched, and some of them used canvas from worn-out army tents. But as they sat on their mounts and studied the cluster of tepees, one of them seemed a little less melancholy even though it was at least as patched as the others. It had new decorative pictures on the outside, familiar stylings that told Tsein-kop-te he was home.

Tsein-kop-te jumped down off his mule and handed the reins to Sweeney. He almost, not quite started to run, but he did walk fast, straight toward his makeshift lodge.

His wife was not outside. He stuck his head inside the flap. It was quiet, but he saw within the pitifully few possessions they had left to them. He walked back to Sweeney, who was sitting patiently in his saddle, watching some of the Kiowa women stroll by and concluding that if they were young enough to be beautiful, then they were probably too young for him.

"Two days I will return with food for you to eat," said Sweeney. "But now I have duties back at the post." And he turned quickly to go, trailing the mule behind him. Tsein-kop-te watched him leave for only a moment, then he walked to the humble tepee with the sagging lodgepoles and the pretty pictures of buffalo and arrows in red and black.

Inside the tepee, away from the constricting stone walls, away from the haunted eyes of his cooped-up cohorts, away from the voices of the white soldiers, he felt a sense of peace as he waited for his wife to come home. He would sit and listen to her musical voice make sense of the horror that he had felt closing in on him from the time they had fled from the canyon to the time he saw her lodge—their lodge.

He was very hungry. During his captivity he had barely eaten enough to maintain himself. The icehouse had been a

rty place too, but he hadn't cared. Now he needed to feel
ean. He would wash himself off in the icy waters of Cache
reek before he would let his wife see him.

Once again he exited the tepee, strode along the bank of the
eek until he found a place deep enough to submerge himself.
uickly he threw his clothes off, stepped into the creek, and
asped as his body found the frigid water. He submerged him-
lf and let the swirling waters of the creek cleanse him. Then
e climbed out and dried himself quickly with his blanket and
fused to shiver though a cold wind was blowing through the
alley.

He slipped into his shirt, and his breech clout, and his leg-
ings, and his moccasins, feeling chilled but cleansed of the
th of the soldiers' prison.

He left his wet blanket to dry on the branch of a tree that
rew close to the tepee. He poked his head into the tent and
aw his wife as she kindled the hearth fire of her beautiful
pee.

In the deep part of the tepee he could see his grandson
laying with a piece of branch that had four stubs poking out
f it like the legs of a wooden pony he had once carved for
he boy. Where was that pony? Lost on the floor of Palo Duro
anyon? Dropped on the long journey home? It had not been
ost in the child's mind. The boy played with the wood with
he same care and wonder he had bestowed on the carved
vood that had so faithfully recreated the form of a Kiowa war
ony. Tsein-kop-te was so filled with emotion that he wanted
o cry. Then he thought of his daughter, and of her fine hus-
and, and of his own sons, the sons both dead in Texas raids,
he daughter of *Tai-bo* disease, her husband lost during the
ight in Palo Duro Canyon. And then he did cry silent tears
s he entered the tepee and closed the flap behind him.

Chapter 31

With three warriors beside himself to protect his tiny band, Autumn Thunder had to send them out in single scouts. The information they brought back was not reassuring. There were still at least three columns of troops roaming the land in all directions. Autumn Thunder would have to provide for food and shelter while hiding by day to stay clear of the troops.

Now, suddenly he knew the feelings that haunted all the chiefs he admired—the gut-wrenching fear that he would fail—that the white men would find him and send troops to eradicate his band. Gone were the joys of the carefree raids down into Texas and Mexico. Gone the excursions west to try their might against that of their beloved enemies the Utes. Everything was serious, everywhere was fear, not for his own life but for those of his village, and his family.

There were even nights he could not sleep. On these nights, no matter how securely hidden he felt they were, he would lay in his blankets and listen to the night sounds, listening constantly for a sound that did not belong. That was the sound that could mean the death of all the men, women, and children who trusted him to lead them safely—where?

"We must find more food for our people," he said one morning as he and Gathers The Grass were eating a sparse breakfast of dried corn and salt pork outside their lodge. "I have thought that maybe I might take Yay-go and find a ranch in Texas with some cattle we could drive across the river. If we had a few cattle with us, we would have food for awhile."

"When you raid across the river you are putting yourself in danger," she replied.

"I am not afraid of danger," he said.

"Your fears or bravery do not matter," she responded. The village must have you with us if we are to survive. And here is something else. You may remember when my mother's village was near the river. There were times the Texas lawmen would cross the river in search of Kiowas."

"They were not allowed."

"Still, they—the ones Sweeney called Rangers—they would cross over to look for Kiowas, and they said if they caught one they would take him across the river and hang him from a rope in Texas. They said they did not care about the law of the great chiefs."

Autumn Thunder nodded. "If we were strong, as we were in the days of Au-sai-mah's village, we would not fear a few Texas men coming across the river. Now, I must remember that four men to protect a village is not much, because one or two of us is always away looking for food."

"It would be better if instead of hunting, we camped along a creek and ate berries and roots that the women gathered."

"You want us to live like Wichitas and Caddoes?" he asked, scornfully.

"I want us to survive. If we can find a place like that where the white men don't go, then the hunters will leave no tracks. We only have to stay until the soldiers get tired of looking and go home."

Autumn Thunder had not thought far ahead, he had only planned from day to day to keep his people away from the soldiers. Gathers The Grass's plan was a good one.

They moved eastward until the land was a little greener, and the creeks a little wider, and the thickets a little thicker, until they found a good place to make camp. They had no lodgepoles and few buffalo hides but they did have the canvas top that Autumn Thunder had stripped from the wagon of the Mexican traders.

"We do not want tepees that rise among the tops of the trees, not now," said Autumn Thunder. Yay-go and Kone-bo-hone protested.

"That is what our people have always lived in," they complained, but Autumn Thunder was stubborn.

"We have no time to look for lodgepoles to cut," he said. "The tepee is comfortable, worthy of a strong people, but we

are not a strong people, not now, and we must hide. We wi
build little houses among the cedars and we will hide until w
know the soldiers have gone back to the fort.''

Both these warriors were older than Autumn Thunder. Bot
had known a time when they tyrannized him, as older boy
do to younger boys. But such was his force of will that the
could not erode his position of authority. He was truly th
leader of the little band. Only Gathers The Grass knew ho
he worried over the correctness of his decisions.

There were berries, mushrooms, roots, nuts, wild green:
and small birds and animals along the banks of the creek, an
there were fish to be caught, but all the warriors wanted to g
out and hunt deer or even look for buffalo to feed the peopl

''Buffalo meat makes the people strong!'' Yay-go insiste

''When you are out thinking about hunting, you are no
thinking about covering your tracks,'' Autumn Thunder in
sisted. ''We have been here for three sundowns. Our trail i
cold. We must keep it that way until the soldiers go away.''

''But you have us out watching for soldiers,'' said Talia
koi.

''We must watch for the soldiers. But you are not roamin;
as far and wide as when you hunt. You are not shooting you
rifle to announce your presence. You are covering your tracks
We must not hunt. Not now.''

They did not hunt. But the berries and roots were scarce
The fish were few and small. And the wild creatures got mos
of the nuts. The people were hungry, and the cries for gam
grew more insistent. Day after day, the people's bellies shrun
and the children cried for food that their parents could no
produce.

''We must hold out a little longer,'' Autumn Thunder tol
them. ''As soon as the soldiers leave this land we will hunt.'

And yet the soldier columns did not return to the fort. The
continued to search the plains as if they intended to study
every square foot of grass, every coulee and creekbank, every
hill and rockpile. And slowly they drew nearer.

And then one morning a breathless Yay-go came galloping
into camp.

''They are coming!'' he shouted as he vaulted from his still
running pony.

''How many?'' asked Autumn Thunder.

"Maybe nine, ten," said Yay-go.

"Maybe less?" asked Autumn Thunder, noting Yay-go's excited state, which may have caused him to see more soldiers than there were.

Yay-go shrugged.

Autumn Thunder thought a moment. His warriors were all gathered around him, awaiting his decisions.

"We cannot outrun them," he said. "We must fight, or we must surrender." He went silent again, but none of his men spoke up.

"We will see who comes," he said. "If it is a small group, then we will fight them before they get close to the camp." The warriors nodded, pleased that their leader wanted a fight. "Take us where you saw them, Yay-go. We must fight them away from the village so they will not get bloodthirsty and ride over our lodges, and kill our women and children."

They did not ride out. They wanted an ambush that would not be given away by a nickering pony. So they ran down the bank of a creek, over two swells and onto a hill above a valley where they saw the troopers, ten in all, preceded by a Tonkawa scout, studying a trail that Kone-bo-hone had not erased the day before when he had ridden out looking for attackers.

Autumn Thunder positioned his warriors on the hill and waited for the soldiers to come close enough for an ambush. But the man who led the mounted squad was an experienced old sergeant who knew his business. When his men began to approach the hill, he waved them back toward the center of the valley.

It would take some fine shooting by the Kiowas to make this ambush work.

The Kiowas worked their way along the reverse slope, trying to get closer to the soldiers before they rode out of range, but the terrain did not allow Autumn Thunder to bring them any closer without being noticed. If they did not shoot fast, the soldiers would be between them and their village and heading toward the village.

"We've got to get them now!" Autumn Thunder told them. "Maybe if we shoot straight we can drive them off."

He raised his rifle and fired, and so did the others. One horse was hit, throwing its rider. The others turned toward the sound of the rifles. To the surprise of the warriors, the soldiers began

to ride toward the hill that held the Kiowas, and then th
horses split into two groups galloping toward either side o
where the warriors lay.

Autumn Thunder realized they might be flanked and su
rounded. He waved his warriors back over the hill, but h
knew it would be impossible to escape the pursuing horseme
on the treeless plains beyond. He was about to head for th
cover of some rocks when he saw a group of riderless ponie
below being led toward them at the gallop by two riders. Th
warriors raced down the hill toward the ponies. The ride
turned out to be Gathers The Grass and Kone-bo-hone's wif
Redbird Flying.

By this time both groups of soldiers had ridden around th
hill and were each about a quarter of a mile away, coming o
fast. The warriors had a hundred yards of open ground to rac
across to reach their ponies, mount up, and flee.

But Autumn Thunder had no intention of fleeing. By spli
ting into two groups, the soldiers had lost their numerical ad
vantage for the moment. Autumn Thunder leaped on the bac
of his pony and waved the women away. He saw that on
group of soldiers was much closer than the other. That wa
the group to attack. He screamed his battle cry and urged hi
pony forward toward the closest group, followed by his war
riors, who saw what their leader saw.

Maybe the troopers were inexperienced. Maybe they wer
tired from their long ride. Or maybe they were shocked by th
sudden charge of the warriors. When they realized that th
chase was going to be a violent clash with the best light cav
alry in the world they reined up quickly and turned and ran
Three of the warriors had pistols, which they fired at clos
range, knocking one trooper out of the saddle and wounding
another cavalry horse.

The other group of soldiers was led by the old sergeant
When he saw the Kiowas attack, he raised his carbine and led
his men in hard pursuit, thinking to catch the Kiowas from th
rear as they attacked the other group. But Autumn Thunde
had assumed the sergeant would charge, so as soon as he wa
certain that he had driven off the first group, he turned to fac
the second. He raised his rifle and his men surged forward
toward the six soldiers. For a few moments the two group
galloped full tilt toward each other. Then, suddenly, the ser

ant brought his men to a halt, dismounted, handing their
orses over to two men. The other four fell to one knee and
med the muzzles of their carbines at the approaching war-
ors.

At two hundred yards, Autumn Thunder abruptly reined up.
e knew that his men could not shoot straight at such small
rgets from their ponies. If the soldiers waited until the war-
ors came close, they would not miss. He looked around and
potted a low hill directly between the soldiers and the village.
he hilltop had large rocks at the top for cover.

Autumn Thunder turned his pony toward the hill, followed
uickly by the others. His move was so sudden that it took a
w moments for the sergeant to react. The troopers were slow
imbing into their saddles. The soldiers Autumn Thunder had
riven off were rejoining their sergeant, but by the time the
ursuit was resumed Autumn Thunder had led his warriors to
e top of their hill. There they found a rock ledge that pro-
ided some cover for their ponies. The men formed a circle
ehind rocks and prepared to defend themselves.

"We will run out of ammunition if we shoot much," said
utumn Thunder. "If we hold them off until dark, we will
et away."

"What about the village?" asked Yay-go.

"By now Gathers The Grass will have them moving. We
an find them in the dark if we follow the creek downstream."

The soldiers dismounted, surrounded the warriors, and be-
an to fire at them, but the distance was so great, and the
over so good that there was little chance of anybody getting
it. The warriors had better opportunities firing downhill at
pen ground, so the soldiers had to keep their distance.

A breeze had come up, blowing dust across the valley of
parse, dried buffalo grass. The sun reached its midday zenith
s the firing began, with the soldiers firing ten rounds for every
ne fired by the Kiowas.

The shots echoed from hill to hill and into the ears of the
nxious Gathers The Grass as the women and children led
heir laden ponies along the creek bank, away from the fight.
t was never right to abandon your men in a fight, she thought,
et it was necessary because the people had to survive. There
vere not so many soldiers, she thought. The men might well
scape.

But she did not know the whole story.

As the afternoon grew late, it occurred to the sergeant th
if he waited till night, the Indians would slip away. The firi
had been going on for two hours now. The Kiowas must
low on ammunition.

So he organized a charge. They had no bugle, but he had
whistle. At the sound of the whistle the soldiers would sta
creeping up the sides of the hill, using rocks and shallow er
sion pits as cover. He knew he was risking casualties, but h
orders had been to find Indians and kill them or induce the
to surrender.

Two blasts of the whistle, he reminded them, meant that tl
men were to charge at the double quick, firing as fast as the
could. The Indians must surrender or be wiped out, he tol
his men. Mouths dry, eyes wide open, the men said they u
derstood, and fanned out around the base of the hill.

At the first blast of the whistle the soldiers all fired the
weapons and moved out. The contours of the hill were suc
that the warriors seldom had good targets to shoot at. Slowl
carefully. Whenever the soldiers found good cover the
stopped and squeezed off a round or two, then moved forwar
again.

What they did not know was that even though the Kiowa
had tried to preserve their ammunition they were almost ou
Autumn Thunder would not shoot until the soldiers were to
close to miss. If they could reduce the numbers of soldiers
little, then they had a chance in a hand-to-hand struggle. S
the soldiers fired, and the Kiowas held fast behind their rock
An occasional arrow arched out from behind the rocks, dow
the hill, but with no effect on the soldiers.

Now that the soldiers were only fifty yards away, they bega
to fire their carbines more rapidly. Scarce as their ammunitio
was, the Kiowas were forced to fire back. They knew that an
moment the troops would charge.

From his forward position the sergeant looked to the left c
him, to the right of him, and brought his whistle to his mouth
and then, out of the corner of his eye, down the hill, he saw
movement. He turned to look, and what he saw made him
smile.

Below was a long cloud of dust arising from the valley,
long column of troops—foot soldiers, cavalry—even a batter

of howitzers. Immediately he blew on his whistle, the one command he had not expected to use, one long blast that indicated his troopers should remain where they were pending further instructions.

Autumn Thunder watched the dust cloud grow for fifteen minutes before the first long column began to appear. He did not want to believe what he was seeing. First came the infantry, row on row of soldiers marching as if on dress parade, flanked by horse soldiers probing left and right. He understood that the fight was over before the four small, powerful howitzers showed up, but their arrival reminded him that the soldiers could tear his women and children apart in a distant, impersonal way if they stumbled into the path of this mighty army. The howitzers were followed by still more cavalry.

The hill-climbing soldiers stopped in their tracks and disappeared into crevices and dry creekbeds. Men in blue continued to flood into the valley below, on foot and on horseback, and now, without the sound of gunfire, Autumn Thunder could hear voices barking out commands as he had heard often on the parade ground of Fort Sill. Below him stood an army mightier than any he had ever before seen, assembled to subdue a renegade gaggle of four starving, nearly unarmed, Kiowa warriors.

"My brothers," he said quietly to the stolid men around him who were willing to throw away their lives for a gesture. "Do not fire anymore. We must see to the safety of our families."

From the right flank of the formation four figures rode forward to the base of the hill: two flag bearers, two men in officers' uniforms, and one man in civilian clothes who Autumn Thunder recognized as Matt Leeper, the agency interpreter. One of the officers held a rifle, barrel pointed upward. Affixed to the end of the barrel was a white handkerchief.

For a few moments the two unequal armies stared at each other. The west wind of the plains alone broke the silence while Autumn Thunder waited a decent, dignified interval of time before he stepped out from behind a tall rock.

One of the troopers on the hill aimed his carbine at Autumn Thunder. Disdainfully the young Kiowa pointed his finger at the soldier, then at the ground. Sheepishly the soldier looked around him and lowered his weapon.

"Autumn Thunder!" shouted Matt Leeper in fluent Kiowa. "Colonel Mackenzie wishes to talk to you."

"Let him come up," answered Autumn Thunder. "We will not harm him."

Leeper translated for the colonel, who almost smiled but did not.

"You men!" Mackenzie shouted to the soldiers who had been about to charge the top of the hill. "Come down from there and report to your company commander." Those closest to their sergeant looked to him.

"Come on, Sergeant, get them down from there, quickly!" Mackenzie urged. The men moved down off the hill. The colonel said a few words to Leeper and dismounted.

"The colonel and I will start walking up the hill and you will walk down. Where we meet, we will talk."

"I will do this," Autumn Thunder replied.

The colors stayed where they were, flapping in the stiff breeze of early autumn. The only other noise was the scraping of boots on earth and rock as the two men began their trek up the hill. Yay-go wanted to go down with Autumn Thunder, but this Autumn Thunder would not permit.

Mackenzie had long been prepared for this day. The Kiowas had given him much trouble with their marauding in Texas. He had been ready to lead a cruel, punitive final battle, but when he saw the miserable condition of the four men willing to defy thousands of armed troops for the sake of their freedom, his vindictiveness vanished.

"It is over," he said simply.

"I would rather have died from your bullets," Autumn Thunder said.

"I know," the colonel answered. He was a soldier, and he understood that Autumn Thunder was a soldier.

"Bring your men down here and lay down your weapons. That is all there is to it. The treaties cover the rest."

Autumn Thunder did not respond. He stood still, his rifle in his hands, his dark eyes fixed on the man who had conquered the Kiowa nation and made them prisoners.

Mackenzie's eyes narrowed as he waited, but he did not repeat his demand.

Autumn Thunder had to speak the right words. He could

only hope that Leeper would make his words right to the colonel.

"Mattleeper," he said. "Tell him that we will give him our guns without a fight. But he must send ten soldiers with us, and together we must go to our village. Then our families will come back to Fort Sill with you." He spoke a few more words to the interpreter.

Leeper turned to Mackenzie and explained. "They would rather fight the whole army than give up," he said. "But when the fight started their families had to flee down the river. They are afraid that if your whole army goes to get them someone will make a mistake and there will be a fight, and then their children will die."

"Will they give up all their weapons?"

"Everything but their fingernails."

"Very well. I will select ten men to go, but we will not be far behind and if there is any shooting there will be hell to pay, make sure he understands that," Mackenzie said.

The way back was long, but at least there was food. There were twenty-three people in Autumn Thunder's band, ten of them children. They were escorted the entire journey to Fort Sill by three hundred soldiers. Every night they were watched in four two-hour shifts, twenty-four soldiers per shift. Konebo-hone wanted to slip away one night but Autumn Thunder told him if he did it would go hard for the rest of them. So the soldiers had no trouble with the last free Kiowas to surrender to the army. And then, on a cool autumn afternoon, they topped a rise and saw Fort Sill in the distance.

Throughout the journey Autumn Thunder had kept his thoughts and emotions to himself, not even sharing them with Gathers The Grass. But now, the fort seemed like a prison to him. A great pain welled up in his chest and rose to a spot behind his eyes.

I am a Kiowa warrior, he told himself. They may have my body but they will never have my spirit. As they approached the post, he could see people spilling out the front gate, his people, many of whom he had known and loved all his life. He turned to those who had followed him. "Straighten your backs, my brothers and sisters," he said. "Let the soldiers see that they have not conquered that which lies within us."

But as they approached the fort, he could see that the people who came out to see them were conquered. Though he rode tall, his eyes straight ahead, his heart broke as he heard the weeping of those who stood watching them as they approached. And he knew that with his capture, the hope of the Kiowas for freedom had vanished, perhaps forever.

Chapter 32

The Kiowas at Fort Sill considered Autumn Thunder a hero, but he could not get rid of the feeling that he had bungled the chance to give his people hope for a free life on the plains. The plains were so big, he reasoned, that surely there was a place out there where the soldiers would not be able to reach them.

As for the buffalo, he felt that if the buffalo were not here, they had to be somewhere else. There was simply no way Great Spirit would permit the white men to kill all of them.

To his surprise, the soldiers did not imprison him, probably because nobody had connected his band to any killings in Texas. As they had when they were first married, Autumn Thunder and Gathers The Grass started all over again with worn out lodgepoles, and a big canvas sheet that Sweeney managed to find for them. Autumn Thunder was so depressed that during the long days of idleness he sometimes contemplated killing himself. They had taken all his band's ponies. Without ponies, with so little food, watching his people lapse into a state of melancholy indifference, he found it hard to believe that life held any purpose for him.

But in the night, Gathers The Grass came to him with a smile and a message. "Nothing lasts forever," she reminded him. "I was once a Wichita but I am a Kiowa and as a Kiowa I long for the freedom of the plains. They will not keep you penned up like this forever. Learn to speak English but think Kiowa. A good time will come again."

What she said made sense to him. He had faith in her wisdom. He began to plan for a future when he would again have ponies, provisions, a few weapons, and no Colonel Mackenzie pursuing him from all directions. Late at night, every night, he thought about all the hunts, all the raids, the places he'd been, and where they might find refuge from the white men that swarmed like locusts but surely could not swarm everywhere.

Throughout the winter the village of Kicking Bird, including Au-sai-mah's band, barely subsisted on beef from the suppliers' cattle herds, bread from the post bakery, odds and ends that friendly soldiers sometimes brought them, and roots that the women would dig along the creekbanks.

There was not really enough food but the Kiowas were used to a sparse diet in winter so they got by.

About a week after Mackenzie had brought in Autumn Thunder's bedraggled band, Captain Sweeney visited him and Gathers the Grass. He brought with him a sack of provisions and would not hear Autumn Thunder's objections.

"Do not be proud," Sweeney said. "Not now. Many of your brothers earn their living begging around the post. I know you will not sink that low. But take the help of a friend, for your family's sake, and someday I might need your help. When that happens, I hope for your friendship."

As the months passed, and the needs of the Kiowas became greater, more rules were relaxed.

One afternoon Sweeney arrived in Au-sai-mah's village on his beautiful gray mare. Trailing behind him, snapping at the rope that held her, was an Indian pony.

Autumn Thunder saw him approach. "Ah, Sweeney," he said. "You bring more bread, maybe?"

"Something better, maybe," Sweeney replied.

"This?" said the Kiowa, and a smile split his lean face. "You do this for me?"

Sweeney climbed down from his horse. "Have you thought of how you will live once you are free again?" he asked.

Autumn Thunder had been thinking quite a bit about that, but of course this was a secret he would not share with Sweeney no matter what the captain did to show his friendship.

Other people in the village had come out to gather around the two men. Ponies were scarce in Au-sai-mah's little community. This poor creature, which would have once counted for little among the immense Kiowa herd, abruptly made Autumn Thunder one of the wealthier members of his band. He didn't like the people staring hungry-eyed at the animal. He wanted to ride it—somewhere.

"We will not be free, I don't think, ever," he told Sweeney. "The white chiefs will tell us where to live. But at least . . . a pony like this . . ."

A flickering moment of gratitude pushed its way out through Autumn Thunder's severe dark eyes, then vanished. "Am I permitted to ride my pony?" he asked.

"Just stay on the reservation," Sweeney answered. "She's a bit weak, you might have to go easy on her for awhile."

"I thought the soldiers had killed all the ponies," Autumn Thunder said.

"Only at the canyon, a few other places. There were too many ponies to kill them all. They decided to sell them. The money will go to the Indians."

"Money? To us?" Autumn Thunder was astonished.

"The agency will spend it for the Indians."

"Aha!" Autumn Thunder understood. Another *Tai-bo* lie. "I thank you for the pony, Sweeney. I will go to the soldier pony house and get good soldier pony food."

"Don't feed her too much at first." Sweeney handed the rope to Autumn Thunder, turned his mare around and headed back toward the post. He needed a drink, but he had duties for the day, make-work useless duties now that nearly all the tribes were on their reservations.

Hell with the duties, he thought. He had a bottle of bourbon waiting for him in his quarters. There was still time for a swallow or two before assembly.

Autumn Thunder was very patient with the pony, whom he named Lightning because she moved so slowly he had to lead her if he was going to get anywhere. He took her up to the post and conned a sack of oats from the stable sergeant with his best poor dumb Indian routine. Indian ponies normally got by without such luxuries but this one needed help. In the old days if he had had such a pitiful animal he would not have wasted his time with her but she was the only horseflesh he possessed, and there was not much else for him to do with his time.

With so much time on their hands, the Kiowas lived on

rumors. Every Kiowa band had been brought into the reservation. The army was going to send all the Indians to a place called Florida that was hot and wet all year round; Set-tainte was going to be hanged in Texas and the rest of the chiefs would be sent to Florida.

Gradually the rumors faded and the truth began to emerge. Set-tainte was in Texas in chains and the bad Indians were going to Florida. And who would choose which ones were the bad Indians? Tay-nay-angopte! Autumn Thunder was astonished that the whites would give such power to the great peace chief of the Kiowas. Autumn Thunder thought about his raiding career. Surely he would be sent to Florida along with half the Kiowa male population, but when he went to Tay-nay-angopte to ask him, the chief smiled sadly and assured him that most of the men who would go were already being confined.

"Go back to your family, my brother, and take care of them. Your winter may not end with the coming of the warm weather." He had never seen Tay-nay-angopte looking so discouraged. He felt sorry for the great peace chief even though he felt the Kiowas would still be free people if Tay-nay-angopte had not given in so easily.

By the early spring he had built up the health of his pony to the point where he could take her for short gallops over the plains outside of the village. On one of these jaunts he found a sickly mule nibbling on some young grass shoots along Cache Creek. At first he was inclined to leave the animal there because he had heard of several of his cohorts being accused of stealing livestock. Instead he put a rope on the mule and led her straight through the front gate of Fort Sill.

He brought the mule to the duty sergeant and tried to explain that he had found the mule wandering around the reservation and that he thought it might be army property. Instead of being pleased, the duty sergeant was annoyed because he didn't want to deal with a mule nobody had even known was lost. To make things worse, the sergeant was an Italian expatriate who could barely speak English, much less Kiowa or Comanche.

When Autumn Thunder tried to say, "I found this mule down near Red River. It might belong to the army," the ser-

geant heard, "I took this mule from a family down on Red
River and now it belongs to me."

They argued for awhile, but just when the sergeant got
straightened out he said, "Don' aska me what to do wida
mule," which sounded to Autumn Thunder like, "I kick your
ass for stealin' that mule," which was what he would expect
a soldier to say to a Kiowa. He was reaching under his vest
for the butcher knife he carried in his waistband when he felt
a clap on the shoulder and found himself looking into the thin
hairy face of Horace Jones.

"Sergeant," said Jones, soothingly, "this is one good Injun
and you ought to keep on his good side. I know him since he
was a little boy and if he tells you he found this mule down
by Red River, then that's what happened."

"But I'ma tellin' you, Horsajones, we hain't lost no mules
ledly," said the sergeant.

"Then why don't you just tell my friend here to take his
mule and go home."

The sergeant nodded. "Taka you mule and hit da road,"
the sergeant said with distaste.

Jones turned to Autumn Thunder, who hadn't a notion what
the sergeant had told him.

"The mule is yours, Big Lance," said Jones, who had once
heard Sweeney call Autumn Thunder that, in a sarcastic reference to the occasion when the Kiowa had brought him in
draped over the saddle of his horse. It made him believe that
maybe Sweeney had finally figured out how he had been
wounded.

When Autumn Thunder returned to the village, Gathers The
Grass was so excited that at first she did not notice the mule.

"You hear me now, my husband," she said. "Tay-nay-
angopte told Au-sai-mah this morning that the agent was giving him permission to settle his band anywhere on the
reservation that we want!"

"We better stay close to the white man's beef," said Autumn Thunder, dryly.

"Don't you see?" she said. "We can get away from the
post and live like Kiowas again."

"We will never live like Kiowas again," Autumn Thunder
said gloomily, but he was pleased with the idea that they

would be able to move away from the post and make their own life.

On a sunny spring morning, with a warm wind stirring the leaves on the cottonwood trees, Au-sai-mah's band started northwest in a wide path that followed Cache Creek. Their numbers were fewer. Three of the older people had died during the winter, a number had decided to stay with Tay-nay-angopte's band, a few others had gone to relatives in other bands, and two young warriors had been selected by Tay-nay-angopte to go to Florida.

These two young men were former Mexican captives that had been adopted into the tribe, and everybody understood that Tay-nay-angopte had selected them to fill out a quota with the least strain on the true Kiowas. Still, the two Mexican Kiowas were well liked and some in the band were angry because it wasn't fair.

The Indian agent had commandeered several wagons to move the band up to their new home north of Mount Scott. Autumn Thunder was still the only one in the band who actually owned riding stock, which made him an important man among them. As he watched Tsein-kop-te plodding patiently beside the wagon that held his wife and his pregnant daughter, Autumn Thunder felt a pang. Tsein-kop-te was the greatest horseman he had ever seen, more graceful and skillful than his three dead friends, Hau-tau, Po-lan-te, and Ko-yah-te. He had known Tsein-kop-te since he was a child and except for the long trek back to Fort Sill after the Palo Duro disaster he had seldom seen him walk more than a hundred yards or so.

He wanted to step down and let the old warrior ride his pony, but saw the dignity with which Tsein-kop-te bore the disgrace of being afoot, and he knew that he could not make the offer.

Au-sai-mah was one of the few men who rode in the wagons with the children, the sick, and the older women. He was not riding in a wagon because he was chief, but because age and the heartbreak of captivity had broken his health.

Tsein-kop-te, Autumn Thunder, and A-do-te the medicine man had scouted out their new home on borrowed army horses two weeks before. The valley they had found was close enough to the post for them to come in on ration day and yet far enough away that there would not be too many unwelcome visitors. Colonel Davidson had insisted that they find an area where there was at least a chance to do some farming, even though the Kiowa men were determined not to farm.

How strange; only seven years before, Asa-toyeh the Comanche had guided the white soldiers to the spot they later called Fort Sill, but Tsein-kop-te's search for a village location was made with the help of a lieutenant—who the old warrior suspected went along to see that he and A-do-te did not steal the horses—and an agency man who was there to make sure that their village included bottomland along the creek. The whites thought they were saving the Kiowas from themselves. The Kiowas, on the other hand, took the white interference as a sign that they were still captive.

The journey exhausted many of them. They had had very little activity since their surrender, and their diet had been poor. When they finally arrived the following day at the site of the village, which had a beautiful long view down the valley, most of the men pronounced the site very good, wrapped their blankets around them, sat down on the new buffalo grass and told their women to put up the tepees and light the cooking fires.

The women did not complain. They unloaded the wagons and began to erect the village in the traditional circle pattern. Autumn Thunder was not as tired as the other men because he had been out riding nearly every day since Sweeney had given him the pony. He helped Gathers The Grass unload their meager possessions from the wagon, helped her erect the three lodgepoles that formed the framework of a Kiowa tepee, helped her stack the other poles around them, and let her stand on his shoulders to stretch the canvas over the framework.

He was glad to do all this, for she was well along with another child.

When the tepees were all up, shaded by the oaks and cottonwoods, on a plateau more than halfway up a hill that commanded a view of the valley, they discovered that one remaining wagon contained a side of beef wrapped in old blankets. The beef, the teamster told them, was a present from a soldier on the post.

The people were delighted but puzzled. Most of the soldiers on the post would have no more given a present to them than they would have given a present to a coyote.

Autumn Thunder was not puzzled. He knew who had donated the beef. But he still wondered why.

Chapter 33

The days grew warmer and longer, and the bottomland drie
out, and one morning Autumn Thunder awakened to th
sound of a wagon rumbling into the village.

He ducked out of the tepee and walked down the hillsid
in time to see two white men hoisting a rusted old plow fron
the wagon. Standing with his arms folded watching them wa
Tsein-kop-te. The two men were jabbering at him in Englisl
and the stubborn old warrior listened, but long ago he ha
decided that if any white man was going to communicate witl
him he was going to have to do it in Kiowa, or at least Co
manche.

Autumn Thunder walked over to the site of the one-side
conversation and listened with great dignity. The white me
were talking more slowly now, reduced to hopeful pidgin b
the old warrior's stolid silence. Soon Autumn Thunder picke
up enough fragments to understand that one of the men wa
a farmer and the agent had sent him out to teach Au-sai-mah'
Kiowas how to plow.

"Tsein-kop-te," he said. "They're here to show you how
to scratch in the dirt."

"Ah, I see," said Tsein-kopte. "Tell the man to do it so
can see how."

"Tsein-kop-te say you do and he watch," said Autum
Thunder. The farmer had brought along a mule. Now he
hitched it up to the plow and let the animal pull it down to a
level stretch of land by the creek where the soil was dry, soft
and tillable. Then he plowed a long straight row for about two
hundred feet, turned the mule and plow around, and spoke.

"Now he says for you to do it," Autumn Thunder said.

"Tell him to do it again. I will watch again," Tsein-kop-te replied. Autumn Thunder relayed the old warrior's request. The farmer nodded, pulled an empty pipe from his pocket, stuck it in his mouth, and plowed another row. The two Kiowas walked to the end of the field and waited for the farmer to finish the row.

"Now let this lazy old buzzard try a row." The farmer showed a little annoyance.

Autumn Thunder rendered the farmer's demand as literally as he could. "Tell him I'll scratch the dirt when he gets the corn to grow on top of his bald head," Tsein-kop-te answered. Autumn Thunder turned to the farmer but before he could speak, the old Kiowa tugged on his arm.

"No," he said. "Just tell him I'm too old."

By now many of the women and some of the men had come down the hill to watch. There wasn't much for them to do these days except sit around and smoke tobacco, drink coffee, and eat up their rations, which lately were sufficient because the government was issuing them on the basis of the number of people enrolled from the village, not taking into account the defections and deaths.

Not having much to do, they were pleased to have something to watch, at least. Autumn Thunder explained to the farmer that Tsein-kop-te considered himself too old to scratch the dirt.

The farmer smiled. "Are you too old?" he asked.

"I am still young," Autumn Thunder responded.

"Then why don't you try to plow a row?" the farmer asked.

"Because you have not taught me how," the Kiowa replied.

"But you were here watching while I was showing the old one."

"You were teaching the old one, not me," Autumn Thunder insisted. "And so I did not learn. Make another scratch and I will try to learn."

The farmer reddened, and growled through his beard, but he was being paid by the hour so he did not mind plowing another row, although he hated doing it for Indians. When he was through, he made a motion to Autumn Thunder with his arm as if to say, "All right, now it's your turn."

Autumn Thunder grinned, walked over to the plow, and

grabbed the handles while the farmer pulled the reins over the young Kiowa's head and behind his back. The farmer gave the mule a command and the animal began to pull. Autumn Thunder held the handles as if he had a longhorn steer by the horns. The plow went this way and that. The Kiowas who were watching laughed and whooped, then hooted when, right in the middle of the row the mule stopped and refused to move another step.

"Mule don't go," said Autumn Thunder. "Must be *Tai-bo* mule."

"Let me do!" said a big muscular woman. The farmer protested but Autumn Thunder handed the reins over to her and headed toward the lodge of Au-sai-mah.

He was saddened to see how old and sick-looking Au-sai-mah was. He was sitting up against a backrest, his eyes staring and unfocused. Autumn Thunder thought he should leave, but as he began to duck out of the tepee, Au-sai-mah said, "Do not leave, my son. I want to tell you something."

Autumn Thunder sat down by the fire and waited for the chief to speak.

"Tay-nay-angopte is dying," said the chief.

"How do you know that?" Autumn Thunder asked. "No one has come to the village with such news."

"I saw it this morning," Au-sai-mah responded in a feeble voice. "I see it now."

"Why is he dying?"

"He is being punished for picking which of his brothers should go to prison in Florida."

The tepee was silent for a few moments while the two men thought their own thoughts. And then, suddenly, Autumn Thunder understood.

"It is Maman-ti who does this thing?" he asked.

"I think yes," said the old chief.

"Tay-nay-angopte betrayed his people," Autumn Thunder said softly.

Au-sai-mah broke his stare, looked at Autumn Thunder and shook his head. "I believe that Tay-nay-angopte saved his people. Those of us who stayed out so long are weak and broken. The bands that came in early are still strong, even if they are not now free. Some day Gui-pah-go and the others will come back and there will still be real people here. That is because of Tay-nay-angopte. And now we are dying."

"You mean our band is dying?"

"Not our band," said the chief. "Me and Tay-nay-angopte. The same year you lost your father, I lost my son. You have been a son to me. You and others—but only you still live. You are the heart of this band. You must survive."

"Me? I am no chief."

"I did not say you were a chief. Chiefs must sometimes give their lives for their people. You must be one who survives."

Autumn Thunder had no idea what Au-sai-mah was talking about. Furthermore, the chief was not completely correct about what the future held. Tay-nay-angopte did die, but Au-sai-mah lived to leave his bed and walk straight among his people again. But the sickness and the captivity had done something to him. The power of his decisive leadership had waned, and as they lay about their village waiting for the next meager issue of rations, the pride and vitality of the village waned too.

The spring moved on toward summer and for a time weeds grew thick along the rows that the farmer had plowed. Nobody in the village seemed to want to do much. The army left them alone, which was surprising to them. But they had no weapons that could shoot, and warfare and hunting were what made the men real men, and consorting with real men was what made the women real women.

And then one late afternoon, Tsein-kop-te, taking a walk along one of the ridges that gave a long view of the Wichita Mountains, thought he heard the sounds of cattle. Picking up his pace, he followed a deer trail to the top of one of the hills and spotted several hundred head of cattle being driven by a handful of riders.

He ran back up the path that led back to the village, to the lodge of Autumn Thunder. "Saddle your pony and your mule," he said. "I have seen live beef." Tsein-kop-te ran back to his tepee and emerged with an ancient rifle that he had been allowed to keep because an amused lieutenant was certain that the weapon could never be fired again.

The old warrior had seen several head of cattle disappearing into a draw. With a little luck, he thought, there might be extra meat in the camp kettles the next few days.

The two men rode up the valley until they spotted the herd,

just in time to see a lone rider flush the wandering cattle from
the draw. Tsein-kop-te shook his head and prepared to turn
his mule around, but Autumn Thunder had heard things from
Sweeney and Gathers The Grass, and understood what Tsein-
kop-te could not imagine.

"Follow me," he said. "Look grim and angry and pretend
that old rifle you're carrying can still shoot."

They rode toward the rear of the herd to a man who looked
older and smarter than the rest. When they got close, Autumn
Thunder galloped his pony straight at the lone cowboy and
reined her to a halt in a showering cloud of dust and pebbles.

"This is reservation," he said. "You cannot be here," he
said.

The cowboy looked at Autumn Thunder without blinking.
For a few moments they sat staring silently at each other.
"Well now," the cowboy said. "Seems like we can make a
deal here."

The mule shambled up and stopped. Tsein-kop-te looked
cruel and angry, nervously cocking and uncocking the old rifle.

"What is deal?" Autumn Thunder asked the cowboy.

"A deal? A deal is a trade. We make trade. You let us pass.
I give you beef."

"Three beef," Autumn Thunder said.

The cowboy spat a brown stream into the dust and scratched
behind his ear, like a hound dog with a tick.

"Well, now, I don't think my boss would go for giving
three beeves just for the right to go through."

"Three beef."

The cowboy thought for a moment. "Just hold on," he said,
turned his pony and galloped away from the herd to a wagon
that was approaching. Tsein-kop-te was about to kick his mule
into motion, but Autumn Thunder stopped him.

"Wait," he said. "He'll be back."

The cowboy returned with a burlap sack. "Tell you what,"
he said. "One beef and I'll throw in three of these, just for
good will."

He reached into the sack and pulled out a jar filled with a
clear liquid. "What is that?" asked Autumn Thunder. Tsein-
kop-te reached out and took the jar from the cowboy's hand.
He unscrewed the lid and sniffed the contents. Then to Au-

tumn Thunder's surprise, the old warrior took two quick swallows, blew out his mouth, and said, "Good."

"No good!" said Autumn Thunder. "No whiskey. Three beef."

"One beef, four whiskey," Tsein-kop-te said to Autumn Thunder. He turned his grim angry look on Autumn Thunder, and the younger man knew that for him the anger was real. Until Palo Duro Canyon Autumn Thunder had looked to Tsein-kop-te as his leader in battle and had a lifetime of respect for the man, but in captivity Tsein-kop-te had changed. He had seen Tsein-kop-te drunk in those rare moments when a raid had put whiskey in their hands, but that had been long ago. Au-sai-mah had his reasons for keeping his band far away from the post, and whiskey was one of them.

"One beef, four whiskey," Autumn Thunder told the cowboy, and to his surprise the cowboy took a jar from one of his saddlebags and slipped it into the burlap sack. He handed the sack to Autumn Thunder and pointed to a small group of young cattle standing in the shade of a cottonwood tree.

"Cut yourself one of those," he said. "Any one of those, and take it, okay?"

"Good," Autumn Thunder agreed. "Need rope."

"Oh no," growled the cowboy. "You better get your own."

"Rope!" said Tsein-kop-te angrily. The hard, angry look on his face persuaded the cowboy, who rode back to the wagon and came back with a coiled lariat. Autumn Thunder rode slowly over to the cattle, dropped a loop over a young, unprotesting heifer, and led it away.

"Next time you come," he shouted to the cowboy, "three beef."

They rode back to the village without exchanging any words. Dread was creeping into Autumn Thunder's heart, slowly, like sludge. The Tsein-kop-te he had followed into battle would not have sacrificed the welfare of the village for whiskey.

Seeing the old warrior do such a thing was as big a jolt to his world as the realization that the whites had made women out of the great Kiowa nation. Once they were out of sight of the herd, up on the mountain path, he came so near to Tsein-kop-te that his pony actually bumped the mule.

"Why did you do this thing?" he asked the old warrior.

"My young brother, I cannot sleep. Tears are close to my face every day. My heart is bursting. We are a shame to our fathers. We are lost. I want to have time in my life when I do not feel broken."

Tsein-kop-te kicked at the sides of the mule and by sheer willpower worried the poor animal into a trot along the deer path. Autumn Thunder followed closely behind, leading the heifer. He was beyond words.

Tsein-kop-te cared nothing about the heifer but he clung to the sack of jars as if it were a *Tai-me*, one of the Kiowas' sacred medicine bundles. Autumn Thunder rode to the field near the creek, where Gathers The Grass had salvaged some of the land the farmer had plowed and was weeding among a tiny patch of melons. She looked up and saw her husband first, then saw the cow he was leading.

She dropped her hoe and ran to the cow.

"We will have fresh beef tonight!" he said smiling, pushing Tsein-kop-te from his mind.

"We will not!" she replied. "This animal will give our children milk and will start a herd for us."

"Kiowas kill meat!" he said. "We do not feed it."

She shook her head. "We can have our own herd of cattle like the *Tai-bos*," she insisted. "Stop thinking like an old Kiowa. Without buffalo to hunt we must raise our own buffalo to live."

He heard her words and realized that he had a choice. He could choose to die with the past like Tsein-kop-te, or live with the future, at least for a while. Gathers The Grass had already made her choice. But Autumn Thunder refused to choose. Not yet.

"We will hunt buffalo."

"You hunt buffalo. I will keep the cow."

"This beef belongs to the band," he said.

"Then I will keep the cow for the band, just as I keep the field for the band. Only two other women work this field, and they do not do much."

"You are Wichita. You know how to do this better."

She did not answer. He looked hard at her and lowered his voice. "How will you keep this beef alive?" he asked. "When the people get hungry they will want to kill it and eat it."

"Then we will move away from the band."

"Move away from Au-sai-mah? I could not do this."

"Au-sai-mah will not walk among us for many more moons," she said, her face grim, and even as she spoke they could hear voices rising from the direction of Au-sai-mah's tepee.

They stopped talking and listened. The voices were off-pitch, cracked . . . drunken.

"Tsein-kop-te," said Autumn Thunder.

"*And* Au-sai-mah," Gathers the Grass added. She resumed her hoeing. In another row little Deerfoot was trying to pull up weeds with his tiny hands.

Gathers The Grass smiled. "He is a natural farmer," she said.

Autumn Thunder grimaced. "Kiowas are not farmers."

"He is also Wichita," she smiled. "Some day, my husband, when the whites no longer feed us, you will be glad that your son is a farmer."

Autumn Thunder tied the heifer to a tree and let her feed on the buffalo grass. He told Gathers The Grass how they came to possess the heifer, and why Tsein-kop-te and Au-sai-mah were rending the air with their songs. Then, suddenly, he cut off his monologue and raised his hand. They listened. The two old Kiowas were now singing different songs, so inter-mingled that it took Autumn Thunder awhile to make out the words.

"They are singing their death songs," he said, quietly.

"Does that mean they think they will die now?" Gathers The Grass asked.

"I don't know what it means," Autumn Thunder answered. "I don't know . . . what it means."

Chapter 34

Toward the end of the summer, Gathers The Grass produced a girlchild.

"Good," was Autumn Thunder's comment. "Another farmer for this lodge," meaning that only women scratched the soil in his family.

For certain none of the men of the village showed any inclination toward joining Gathers The Grass in her garden, though she noticed several of them eyeing her melons and squashes with an appraising eye.

Late one afternoon she was out picking berries down along the creek when she heard a horrible groaning sound from the nearby bushes. She ran to the garden, grabbed her hoe, ran toward the noise, and discovered a former warrior called Kia-tah, doubled over on his knees. Next to him were the remains of an underripe watermelon.

"If you wait for the melons to ripen," she said, "you won't have to steal. I'll give them to you. And you won't get devil-in-the-belly," she said.

He flung a nasty English word in her direction.

"I will get your wife to help you," she said, but as she got closer she found that the man reeked from alcohol. "I don't know where you men are getting all that whiskey, but if your wife smells it on you she'll never let you into her lodge."

In response he threw up. "Good," she said. "You'll feel better now. You might want to wash in the creek." Kia-tah, who on this warm summer day wore only a breechclout, stumbled off toward the creek.

*   *   *

Autumn Thunder was not present during this exchange because he had gone to Fort Sill. He was determined to secure a gun one way or another. The army owed him a gun, he figured, because they had taken all his guns during the Palo Duro attack and after the surrender.

When he arrived at the post the sun was nearly straight overhead, working time for the soldiers, but Sweeney was nowhere to be seen.

The first four soldiers he talked to had no idea where he was, but the fifth was the post surgeon and he suggested that Sweeney might be found down at the post store.

He was there all right, sitting at a table by himself with half a bottle of whiskey.

His mouth formed a crooked smile when Autumn Thunder came in, and he beckoned the Kiowa to his table. "Sit, my copper-skinned friend," he said. The words went past Autumn Thunder but he sat anyway.

"See? On a captain's pay I can afford whiskey. I am rich."

Autumn Thunder knew the last three words. "Good," he said. But why, he asked, was the rich captain sitting in the trader's store in the middle of the day?

"Good you should ask that. I'm a supernumer—superernu—" He could not handle the long word that meant he no longer had a useful position on the post.

"The army is getting rid of me," he explained in simple Kiowa.

"Why? Are you a bad soldier?"

"Not that," he replied, and he tried to explain how when the government cuts the military budget a whole lot of good men have to find new jobs. Autumn Thunder did not understand it all. It was white man business and he did not ask for any more details.

"Will you stay on reservation?" Autumn Thunder asked.

Sweeney shook his head. "Going back east," he answered tersely, and Autumn Thunder was surprised to feel a stirring of emotion inside of him. He had come to like this officer, who had been the only white man with whom he had ever felt comfortable. Life would be less pleasant without him to visit on the post.

Sweeney had been drinking from a glass. Now he took the glass, which had about an inch of amber liquid at the bottom, and handed it to Autumn Thunder. Without a second thought, the Kiowa raised the glass to his lips and took a sip. The warmth felt good in his belly.

He knew that white men thought all Indians were the same: give them a drink of alcohol, and they couldn't stop. All drunks, the lot of them. "Drunk" was one English word he knew very well. But he was different. When he was much younger, not a full-fledged warrior, he had tasted rum and did not like it, so it was easy for him to stay away from it when he saw what it could do to good men.

He had only taken the glass because his friend Sweeney had offered it to him and he was sad that Sweeney would be going away.

"Sweeney," he said. "I must talk with you about something important."

Sweeney nodded his head.

"I need a rifle."

"Who you goin' after?" Sweeney asked.

"Nobody. But I need a rifle to hunt."

Sweeney tilted the bottle back and drank directly from it, then poured a little more into Autumn Thunder's glass. He nodded and slammed the bottle on the table.

"Well, what the hell is going on here!" cried a familiar, unwelcome voice. "I thought the damned Indian agent said no whiskey for redskins and here's an army officer drinkin' with a Keeway!"

"You'll keep your mouth shut about that if you want some of my very good bourbon, Tuck!" Sweeney replied, pounding the bottle on the table. "I am leaving the service and my friend and I are jus' having some farewell libation. Now, you want or don't want?"

The big buffalo hunter slapped a cloud of dust off his buckskin shirt just for effect.

"I don't usually drink with Keeways!" he said. "Usually I kill 'em. This one, for an Injun, ain't bad. I won't kill him today." He grabbed the bottle, threw his head back, and poured about half the contents down his throat.

"Woooo!" he whistled. "I sure needed a dust-cutter!" He slammed the bottle down on the table harder than Sweeney had. Sweeney poured a little more into Autumn Thunder's glass then took a couple of healthy swigs from the bottle. "To be honest," he said to the Kiowa, "I am curious to see what you do with a load o' liquor under your belt." His speech was getting thicker and a bit more aggressive. The two white men had put Autumn Thunder on his guard. But the whiskey felt good, very good.

He emptied his glass. Sweeney was his friend. These many moons of captivity had made him very sad. Sweeney made him feel better. He was a good man.

Tuck grabbed the bottle again and drank deeply from it. He had been drinking steadily from his canteen on the way to the post, and his tongue was a little looser than usual.

"The west is gettin' putty tame, least down these parts," he said to Sweeney. "Never thought I'd be drinking with you, you blue-backed sonofabitch, and I *sure* never thought I'd be drinkin' with this hear red devil or any other one of them sons o' Satan. I wasn't kiddin' about killin' Keeways. When I cain't find me buffalo to kill, why, I just up 'n' find me a Keeway."

Tuck was talking in English, and his voice was slurred, and Autumn Thunder was beginning to feel the whiskey so he wasn't sure he was hearing what he thought he was hearing.

"Bet you kill 'em from a quarter mile away with that scope o' yours like the big brave man you are," taunted Sweeney. He had enough whiskey in him that he was itching for another go with Tuck, who was strong and fairly agile, but also fairly slow. Sweeney had measured the man the last time they had fought and he was certain that he could chop him down to size again.

But Tuck was not seizing the bait. "Oh yeah!" he said, proudly. "I've drilled many a Keeway from so far away that they never knew I was there. I just pulled the trigger and all of a sudden they found themselves dead. Sure must've surprised them."

Sweeney had stopped drinking, so fascinated was he by the hunter's narrative. He took a quick look at Autumn Thunder and was relieved to see that his face was a mellow fog. The Indian wasn't following the words of the buffalo hunter, and Sweeney was glad. One thing for Sweeney to take a few swings at the bastard, he had fought drunk half the time for half his life, but if Autumn Thunder went after Tuck in his state, then Sweeney would be making a trip to Gathers The Grass with his friend's broken body draped across his saddle.

Tuck was in a positively congenial mood. "Oh yeah," he was repeating, squeezing extra pleasure out of the fact that he was making his big talk in front of a live, drunken, Kiowa warrior. "I probably killed a few of this buck's buddies that way. You ever see the way a Keeway leaps when he gets hit midsection with a slug from a Sharps .40? You ever see such a thing, Keeway?" he asked, his face so close to Autumn Thunder that the Kiowa's lungs filled with the acrid breath of the buffalo hunter.

"And not just from far away either," he added, leaning back in his chair and taking two hurried gulps from Sweeney's bottle.

"Tell you something, Sweeney, you old blue-backed son-ofabitch. I was lookin' for buffalo last year, wintertime, when I hear some shots, right? I ride to the top of the hill and there's a bunch a Keeway down below cuttin' up buffalo and packin' it away. Why, I just take out ol' Red-Killer there and put a Keeway in my sights and pull the trigger and he just flops over like an ol' buffalo cow, right? And them Keeways near him are just lookin' around like them stupid buffalo'll do sometimes when one a them suddenly drops dead next to them. I tell you, I almost forgot to skedaddle, I was laughin' so hard."

Sweeney took a quick look to see if any of this had penetrated Autumn Thunder's fog. It had. The Kiowa had not put away that much and the fog was still a little thin. Autumn Thunder leaned forward and made an effort to focus.

"You know I been around enough to have seen many o' them bucks and it suddenly dawns on me that I knew who that buck was. Bet you seen him too. The one that wore a lion claw down from his right ear?"

Autumn Thunder was out of his chair in a hurry, fumbling for his knife and missing it. Tuck was up too, reaching for his big Walker Colt. His hand found the handle in plenty of time, but Autumn Thunder was no longer a target. Sweeney had headed him off, had his shoulder to the chest of the befuddled Kiowa and was pushing him out the door of the building.

Though Autumn Thunder hadn't drunk all that much, what he had drunk had taken hold and rubbered up his limbs. He was hollering in detail what he intended to do to Tuck, but his speech was so slurred and Tuck's knowledge of the Kiowa ongue so sketchy that the hunter knew only that an Indian drinking whiskey had gone crazy.

As he rushed his friend out the door, Sweeney was trying desperately to calm him down. "Not now! Not now! He's got a gun, you don't. I'll get you a gun. I promise. You'll have your chance, but not now."

While Tuck watched, roaring with laughter, from the door of the store, Sweeney wrestled Autumn Thunder to the edge of the creek and the both of them fell into the cold water. Autumn Thunder was throwing up. But even as the contents of his stomach rushed out of him, his brain was recording forever that this one dirty, stinking, cruel devil had spent much of his life killing the sacred buffalo, and killing Kiowas, including his best friend, and it was time for his day to come.

As the cold water rushed around him and he gasped for breath, he knew for the first time since he and his people had fled broken and beaten from Palo Duro Canyon that he had a goal to pursue. He would find a way to kill Tuck if it took him the rest of his life.

He leaped upward, exploding from the surface of the creek crying his war cry. The last time Sweeney had heard that war cry was moments before he felt Autumn Thunder's lance pierce his body. Only then did he know for certain that his fine Indian friend had first tried to kill him and then decided to save his life. But when he saw the look in his friend's eyes, and the expression on his face, he knew that the Kiowa's next shaft would be aimed not at him but at the man Sweeney considered to be "the evilest bastard in the Indian nations."

While Autumn Thunder was gone, Gathers The Grass noticed a white man in rough workclothes approaching on a mule along the rough road that led into the village.

"You, squaw! Come here!" he shouted rudely at Gathers The Grass.

She ignored the rudeness.

"Where is buck?" the rider asked, in English.

"Why, is he in trouble?" said Gathers The Grass.

The rider did not even know who Gathers The Grass's husband was. He was just looking for a man, to explain that the Indian agent had sent a small herd of sheep to Au-sai-mah.

Maybe if the Kiowas did not want to farm, perhaps they coul
be sheepherders like the Navajos.

It was difficult for Gathers The Grass to get the agent's ma
to understand that if he just spoke normal English she woul
understand. He kept saying things like, "Sheep come from bi
peace chief."

"Where are sheep?" she asked.

He answered, "Where your chief?"

She didn't want to answer that one because she knew th
Au-sai-mah and Tsein-kop-te and a few of their older croni
were up on some hill or other drinking whiskey that a sergea
at Fort Sill was supplying in return for blankets, kettles, an
other items that the Kiowas desperately needed to keep for th
winter.

Finally, to her relief, she spotted Autumn Thunder ridin
down the trail that led in from Fort Sill.

Only the week before they had moved their tepee away fro
the Kiowa circle. Gathers The Grass had told other village
that her babies could not sleep because the old men kept the
awake with their drunken singing. What she did not tell Au
tumn Thunder was that she hoped to move them farther awa
later in the year so the cow would not present a temptation t
hungry villagers.

"My buck come now," she told the agent's man, and sh
waved for Autumn Thunder to come and talk.

She did not give the two men a chance to become ensnare
in a dialog neither of them would understand and which woul
probably lead to frustration, then anger, then bad blood.

"This man said that the agent has sent sheep out to th
village. Fine sheep," she told Autumn Thunder.

"Sheep." Autumn Thunder mulled over the word with dis
taste. She smelled the whiskey on his breath and sent him o
to their lodge. She would talk to the man about the sheep.

Chapter 35

Autumn Thunder awoke the following morning with a pounding headache and a floppy stomach, but his spirit was composed because he knew what he had to do.

Getting the job done was what mattered. The great camp-fires of the mighty Kiowas were forever extinguished. If he died before he accomplished his mission there would be no-body to sing of his glorious death in battle.

By the end of the morning he was feeling well enough to ride to the post to see Sweeney. Sweeney had promised him a rifle and it was terribly important that he get that rifle before his friend left the post forever.

As he rode away from the village, Autumn Thunder could hear drunken chanting beginning to arise from the lodge of Au-sai-mah. He felt sick that the men he had looked up to all his life had given up on life. He was discouraged. Only the strong belief of Gathers The Grass that one day they would be free again kept him from joining the old men in their tepee revels—that and his desire to kill Tuck, a desire that burned bright as the morning sunrise.

Before he headed south along the post road, he rode to where several of the young boys were tending the sheep.

Over the past months the Indian agent had seen fit to au-horize a dozen or so ponies for Au-sai-mah's village. He had paid a private contractor to furnish the animals, and of course the contractor had sent out the twelve most pathetic pieces of horseflesh he had on hand. The boys had hold of one of them. They had made some toy bows and were pretending that twenty-five sheep constituted a buffalo herd. The only problem

was that, try as they might, they could not urge the horse in
a run.

Not that it mattered, the sheep were not in a running mo
either. One of the youngsters climbed on the horse and urg
it into a slow, shuffling trot toward the sheep. The boy hu
over the side of the pony, leaned toward the closest shee
pulled the string of the bow and sent a notched stick in a la
arc toward the sheep. Since they had contrived to carve poin
onto their featherless arrows, the stick stung when it struc
and the woolly creature broke into a run. The other bo
whooped at the success of their cohort. The horse stood st
after its exertions, head down, chest heaving.

Autumn Thunder watched all this from a distance. Whe
the little drama had played itself out he turned his pony sout
The young sheep would not last long. Those that survived t
tender care of the boys would not live through the attentio
of hungry coyotes.

It was late afternoon when he arrived at the post. Th
crackle of gunfire in the cool afternoon air was unmistakabl
For a moment he considered turning around and headir
home. Gunfire on a soldier post always meant trouble for a
Indian no matter whom the soldiers were shooting at. Ho
could these *Tai-bos* be conquerors when they couldn't tell th
difference between a Kiowa, a Comanche, a Cheyenne, or
Wichita? Even a Wichita. He'd heard once of a man wh
killed a Wichita and they let him go when he said he thoug
the man was a Comanche who was attacking his home. Ima
ine mistaking a Wichita for a Comanche. Good thing for th
white man he did not mistake a Comanche for a Wichita.

He reined up his pony and listened for awhile. The firin
had stopped. Then it started again, all at once. Then it stoppe
again. Ah, he understood now. They were practicing on th
firing range. The soldiers could use up more ammunition i
one afternoon shooting at a dirt bank than Au-sai-mah's ban
was able to beg, steal, or trade for in an entire year. Autum
Thunder had to admit, some of them were very good shot
But the buffalo killers were the best. Especially that Tuck. H
had heard other buffalo hunters talk about Tuck.

How was he going to kill Tuck if Tuck could shoot so lor
and well? He could never shoot like Tuck. So he would hav
to find another way. As he entered through the main post ga

he smiled and waved at the guard, who smiled and waved back. Thanks to Sweeney, most of the soldiers on the post considered Autumn Thunder to be a good Injun. He was not unhappy about that. It was much easier to be a good Injun than a bad Injun around white men. So he learned to smile and say things like, "Autumn Thunder poor Injun; need oats for poor pony."

And the stable sergeant would smile back and toss him a small sack of oats. Except that when the stable sergeant wasn't there, the two-stripe man would make him sweep up the oats that had been scattered on the floor by sloppy soldiers or sloppy horses, sweep the oats and the dust and the wood splinters into a sack to feed to his pony.

"That's about the best you're gonna get from me," the two-stripe man would say, and he'd say it proudly, as if it were a very good thing to be rude to a Kiowa. Autumn Thunder imagined a time when he could have cut a man's throat for being so rude and some of his people would have said, "Autumn Thunder is a good man, so he must have had a good reason for cutting that man's throat." No matter, he had thought. Soon the pony would be a strong Indian pony and she would live on prairie grass and wouldn't need the oats.

Sweeney was out demonstrating to recruits the proper way of mounting and dismounting when Autumn Thunder caught his eye. Sweeney beckoned the Kiowa to come closer. He had chafed at the idea of being assigned a noncom's duties but then he decided that since he no longer had any captain's duties, he might as well make himself useful, but that didn't make him any less bored—and then he saw Autumn Thunder.

"Men," he announced, suddenly. "I just showed you how a trooper does it. By the numbers. And that's how you'll do it. Now I'll show you how a real horseman does it. A Kiowa doesn't go by the numbers. He just has one number: one. First he's on the ground then, one, he's on his horse, and you're standing there wondering if you really saw him mount up or did you fall asleep and miss something.

"Say, Autumn Thunder," he said. "Would you come down from your pony? I want you to meet some boys.

"Men, this here's Autumn Thunder," he said in English that Autumn Thunder did not want to strain himself to follow. "Year ago he was a real wild Indian. Take-um scalps? Several,

I'm sure, including mine, almost. Kill? Oh, he can kill all right. But he's a good man. If you don't cross him, he'll never break his word. You cross him and he can slash your throat with his knife if he's got it or his fingernails if he don't." Sweeney paused to study the effect he had on his men.

"Autumn Thunder no longer makes war on the white man. But he can still ride." He turned to the Kiowa. "My friend, would you care to mount your pony real quick and give 'er a warrior's gallop around the parade ground?"

"What for, they make a fool of me or something?"

Sweeney understood that their friendship was still limited by Autumn Thunder's suspicions about him, and his own about Autumn Thunder for that matter. He walked close to the Kiowa, out of earshot of his men, and spoke softly.

"I want to show them what they would have been up against had we not made peace last summer."

"Ah," said the Kiowa, nodding, and he gave a fierce whoop that made the young recruits flinch and all the other soldiers close by turn toward him.

He grabbed the blue *kepi* off the head of one of the privates. Quicker than one could tell it he leaped on the back of his pony, leaned forward, and the animal jumped into full gallop. He had worked hard to bring the pony back from the brink of its demise and the work had paid off.

Effortlessly the pony ate up the distance between the gawking recruits and the far side of the parade ground. He ran the horse in a straight line across their front, with him clinging to the far side of the pony all the way. To the recruits it seemed that nobody was riding the pony, and yet when he reached the end of the parade ground his body popped up onto the pony's back.

He had dropped the *kepi* halfway across the parade ground. Now he turned his pony around and galloped it back the way he came, across their front. For fifty yards he sat his pony facing backwards, arms folded. For another fifty yards he stood straight upright on his saddle. As he approached the *kepi* he dropped back into the saddle, pointed the pony just to the left of the *kepi* then, as the pony swept past, he suspended his body toward the ground, reached out his hand, grabbed the hat, and pulled himself back into an upright riding position. Then he turned his pony sharp left and galloped down the middle of the parade ground toward Sweeney's class. Just when it seemed he would run them over, and they were all out cowering in the dust, he brought the pony to a sudden stop and before the stop was complete he was on the ground, standing nose to nose with the hatless recruit, his fierce eyes drilling into the eyes of the young soldier. While the young man quailed before his burning dark gaze, Autumn Thunder slapped the *kepi* hard against his thigh. Then he waved the cloud of dust away. Only Sweeney laughed.

He placed the cap back on the head of the recruit. "You stay away from Kiowa, live a long time," he said without cracking a smile. And he slapped the recruit smartly on his back, raising another gray cloud of dust.

"That, men, is what we fought, and beat," said Sweeney. "We must have been awfully good to beat them. Treat this man with respect. Corporal, I want you to bring these men to attention and fall them out, that's all for this afternoon.

"Walk with me until we're away from everybody," he told Autumn Thunder. They walked toward the post gate, leading their horses. "You come for a gun, now didn't you?" he asked.

Autumn Thunder was glad he did not have to remind Sweeney. Some white men had to be reminded many times before they did a thing they had promised, and Kiowas thought it impolite to have to remind a man to do something he had promised.

"Gun and ammunition."

"Then after you go through the gate I want you to ride out with me."

"Why?" Autumn Thunder asked. "You got a gun hid somewhere?"

"No. Don't look, but that carbine hangin' from my saddle is what you get."

"You give me your carbine?" Autumn Thunder was overwhelmed.

"That's not my army-issue carbine," said Sweeney. "It just looks like it. Got it off a dead—it don't matter a dead what. I got it, it's mine, and it's gonna be yours. I owe you my life."

Autumn Thunder nearly laughed at that. The only time he had saved Sweeney's life was when he had intended to kill

the officer himself. Sweeney read his face. He would hav
liked to tell his friend that he had wanted to drink himself t
death, he cared for nothing, until he saw how hard a man coul
fight even when he had no chance to win. He wanted to tel
the Kiowa that Gathers The Grass was his friend but Autumn
Thunder was his teacher, and he would remember the youn
warrior for the rest of his life.

But he was sure Autumn Thunder would not understand
Kiowas were different from white men. They could not un
derstand what a white man felt inside.

They rode for about five miles south, until they came to
thick grove of oak trees. "Here is the carbine," he said, hand
ing the weapon over to Autumn Thunder. "You look dow
the barrel you will see that the weapon is almost new. An
here"—he reached into his saddlebags and took out two larg
boxes of cartridges—"is your ammunition. Don't start a wa
with them."

"Kill Tuck, hunt buffalo," said Autumn Thunder.

"It will be hard to kill Tuck," said the old captain. "B
careful or he'll kill you. As for the buffalo, it will be hard fo
you to even find them, my friend."

"So the white men say," said Autumn Thunder. "I will se
for myself soon."

When Autumn Thunder returned home he was pleased to hea
that the old men had fallen silent.

He had spent the afternoon roaming the valley in search o
cattle herds. On this day there were none, but all in all, it ha
been a good spring. No fewer than six herds had com
through. He and Tsein-kop-te had collected "rent" of eleve
head. Autumn Thunder had let Gathers The Grass pick fiv
young cows as the basis of a herd. The rest of the animal
had gone to the band, which promptly butchered and feaste
on them. Gathers The Grass had insisted that they move farthe
down the valley, but Autumn Thunder had refused. He buil
a corral on the hill near their lodge and kept them there a
night, then turned them out every day to graze along the creek
bank.

The summer had passed, the cows had fattened up, and three
of the cows were pregnant thanks to a bull they had borrowe
from a Texas rancher in exchange for passage of his herd.

But these cows, and the calves that would soon be coming, were not livestock to the people of Au-sai-mah's village. They were food on the hoof. Rations had been cut again. The same Congress that had chopped Sweeney off the army rolls for economy's sake was doing the same to the Indian Bureau's funds. It was time for the lazy Indians to get to work, they said.

The men did go to work—those who weren't spending their days in the lodge with the old men drinking booze that a Caddo trader was delivering as regularly as a milkman. Gathers The Grass had caught one of the old men trying to steal a cow from the corral. She had driven him off with her hoe. When Autumn Thunder had come home that night, she let her anger out on him.

"Kiowas!" she spat. "Look at them! The great raiders become stealers of cows from their own brothers."

"There are bad Wichitas too," he said. "Are there not?"

She nodded.

"So a bad man tried to steal a cow. We have always watched carefully the bad men in this village. Which one was he? I will go down to his lodge with my quirt and whip him in front of the whole village until he is so shamed that we will never see his face again."

"Will you?" she asked, softly, her dark eyes flashing fire he had never seen before.

"I have said I would."

"Do not say before you know," she said, and tears flowed down her face. "This bad man was no bad man, he was a good man. This lazy, drunken, lost man without a soul is Tsein-kop-te. Now will we move our lodge away from the village?"

With winter coming on, and the village hungry, he decided the time was right for a buffalo hunt. He had brought in a couple of deerskins to trade at the store for ammunition, and he was surprised to see Sweeney there. "My papers still haven't come through yet," Sweeney tried to explain to Autumn Thunder. The Kiowa could not grasp what Sweeney meant, but he nodded his head as if he understood.

"We are going to hunt buffalo, me and Kone-bo-hone and Yay-go. You come with us."

Sweeney looked down at his boots for a moment. "Have you seen any buffalo?" he asked.

"We have not looked."

Sweeney sighed. "I do not think you will find buffalo," he said.

Autumn Thunder laughed without smiling—inside. "What you think Tuck has killed all the buffalo?"

Sweeney thought for a moment, and chose his words with care. "Tuck and others like him. Yes, I think they have killed almost all the buffalo."

"We *will* find buffalo," Autumn Thunder said so defiantly that the men in the store stared at him though they did not understand the words he had spoken in Kiowa.

"I hope you do, my friend. But I cannot come because I must be here when my papers come."

"Papers?" Autumn Thunder was listening this time, and he was confused. He thought Sweeney meant cigarette papers; he knew that Sweeney smoked cigars when he smoked at all.

He returned from the post with more cartridges for his rifle and some lead and powder for a pair of old muzzle loaders that Yay-go and Kone-bo-hone had managed to scrape up during the spring.

That night the three hunters went to the lodge of A-do-te, the medicine man, who, it turned out, was visiting with Au-sai-mah and the other old ones. They were passing around a particularly nasty bottle of white whiskey and hating the taste, but still they were drinking it, for that was what they had. The three young men announced that they were going on a buffalo hunt the following morning, and that picked up the spirits of the old ones.

They decided to hold a buffalo dance right then. They went home and got their buffalo skins, those that still had them, and they kindled a fire in the middle of the circle, wrapped themselves up in the skins and moved like buffalo, and made buffalo sounds. A-do-te blew up his owlskin and tried to make medicine, but the best he could do was predict that the young men would find the buffalo to the west, in the Texas panhandle. Autumn Thunder and Kone-bo-hone knew that there was danger for them if they were found in Texas, and they didn't much believe A-do-te, who was falling asleep because that's what whiskey did to him in his declining years.

But they also thought that if there were buffalo to be found,
est to Texas was the place.

The following morning, early, they left the village. Few of
e older men were up to see them off, and most of the
ounger men could not join them, because they did not have
e arms or ponies necessary for such an undertaking. Even
ose who had a pony and a bow would not join them.

Still, the three were in very high spirits. A buffalo hunt was
omething Kiowa braves did—not farming, or tending sheep,
r loafing around their village all year-round.

On the way west, over the next three days, they pointed out
ld landmarks: here is where Ko-yah-te stalked a buck for two
ays before he found it and killed it. There is where Yay-go
nd his father chased three soldiers down the valley until one
f them fell off his horse and Yay-go's father took his scalp.

On top of that hill is where the Comanches dropped a slain
arrior in a crevice and then when they came back later the
arrior had turned into an owl who lived in a tree by the
revice and guarded his bones.

They were riding along the north bank of the prairie dog
wn fork of Red River moving slowly, when they spotted the
road tracks of a bull buffalo. They slowed their ponies to a
alk and saw close by the narrower tracks of what they
ought were three cows, and the prints of a lone calf. The
anure was fairly fresh. They moved smoothly into a fast trot,
en to a steady gallop and ate up several miles of brown-
rassy plains before Yay-go stopped his pony, eased himself
p with his knees for a better look, and pointed.

Outlined against a rocky hill stood five shaggy animals, nib-
ling quietly at the late summer grass. Slowly they approached
e buffalo. At two hundred yards they reached for their rifles.
he buffalo continued to graze. At a hundred yards, Yay-go
aised his rifle to fire, but Autumn Thunder signaled him to
rop the barrel. The buffalo did not look up and continued to
raze.

They moved still nearer. By this time the animals should
ave sensed their presence and yet they did not. Resting the
utts of their rifles on their thighs, barrels pointed skyward,
e three Kiowas walked their horses within ten yards of the
easts.

"They are not eating the grass," Kone-bo-hone noted. He

was correct. Their great heads drooping close to the ground, the five buffalo were not eating, or sniffing, or snorting, or doing anything but standing in place, seeming to stare at the earth. One of the females swished her tail. Another turned her head and cast a disinterested eye on the three warriors. The male especially showed no awareness of his surroundings.

Yay-go pointed his rifle again, and cocked his hammer.

"No!" said Autumn Thunder, sharply. "Let us find a herd."

"These five would be helpful to our village," Yay-go insisted.

"We must not," Autumn Thunder retorted with some emotion.

Kone-bo-hone looked at Autumn Thunder with surprise. "Why not?" he asked.

For a few moments Autumn Thunder thought in silence. "I don't know," he said. "But I am certain we should look for a bigger herd."

"But we have no spare horses. We cannot carry any more than these anyway."

"We must find the bigger herd." Autumn Thunder was adamant. His passion swayed Yay-go and Kone-bo-hone. They continued west along the north bank of Red River.

They found no more tracks that day, so they turned north and rode slowly for three more days. They saw no buffalo. They turned east, feeling very uneasy. It was inconceivable that they had crossed no buffalo trails whatever. Occasionally they found an old buffalo skeleton, but most of the buffalo bones on this range had long ago been scattered by the buzzards and coyotes. They left the Texas panhandle and continued east until they contacted the Washita River, then they turned south.

Their high spirits were gone. Their heads were bowed down with grief. They did not speak, but each had his own thoughts. Kone-bo-hone and Yay-go thought mostly of their early buffalo hunts with their fathers, both of them long dead, one from fever, one from a Tenth Cavalry bullet.

Autumn Thunder thought mostly of his three friends, Hautau, Ko-yah-te, and Po-lan-te. All dead so young, all gone without him. He thought about others, so many others, fathers, mothers, uncles, distant relations, cousins, so many dead of dispersed that the once-formidable village of Au-sai-mah was reduced to a handful of shoddy lodges.

"My brothers," Autumn Thunder said, gaining the immediate attention of Yay-go and Kone-bo-hone. "We are like the little herd of buffalo. We are the last of our kind. Look at us, of the whole village only three warriors with the heart to seek out and hunt the buffalo. How is it possible that they—and we—could pass so quickly from the land?"

Chapter 36

Autumn Thunder was riding in from the Valley of the Beef, as Kone-bo-hone had taken to calling the trail that the ranchers used. He thought there might be a herd coming through that day, and he would have loved to collect another calf or two for his tiny herd.

As he rode down the valley, he saw a familiar gray horse tied to a tree near his lodge. Sweeney was standing outside the lodge, his white broad-brimmed hat in his hands, talking with Gathers The Grass. He saw the white man shake hands with Deerfoot. Saw him put his face close to their new baby girl.

He rode a little closer. Sweeney heard the crunch of hooves on leaves and turned around.

"My brother Autumn Thunder," he said, raising his right hand and walking toward the Kiowa.

"My friend Sweeney," Autumn Thunder replied.

"I come to say good-bye," said Sweeney.

"Papers come to you?" Autumn Thunder asked in English, still not knowing what that meant but remembering that Sweeney needed papers to go.

"Papers come to me."

There was silence for several moments. Gathers The Grass watched with interest. She knew the two men had gotten to know each other much better in the years since she nursed Sweeney back from the edge of death. Still, it was hard for her to believe that they had bridged the huge gap that had separated them.

Without thinking, the two men walked a few steps away

rom Gathers The Grass and the children. Autumn Thunder elt an ache that he could not explain, an ache that made him hink of Ko-yah-te and yet had something to do with this captain. He wanted to say something to him, but he was Kiowa ind the captain was *Tai-bo* and when Autumn Thunder did tot know the right words to say he kept silent.

Sweeney knew that the Kiowa's silence meant something, because the Kiowa kept looking at him. But he knew of the man's great pride and would not attempt to pry open that which the Kiowa wanted to keep shut.

"I have news for you, Autumn Thunder."

Autumn Thunder did not speak, but he was ready to listen.

"Tuck bought some goods at the store yesterday and this morning he headed south, with a wagon and one skinner. You can pick up the track outside the gate. His was the only wagon to come or go today. Heavy loaded. Deep tracks. I know he'll turn west as soon as he crosses Red River. He told me he always finds buffalo at Double Mountain."

"Not this time," said Autumn Thunder, with confidence.

Sweeney nodded. So they had had their buffalo hunt, he thought. It would be a long hard winter for the Kiowas. Autumn Thunder and Gathers The Grass, he knew, would make t. He would not think about the others.

Gathers The Grass had been listening to the two men talk. Now she walked toward them, carrying the baby in one arm and holding the hand of Deerfoot. "You speaking of Tuck the buffalo hunter? Why you speak of Tuck the buffalo hunter?" Sweeney saw the agitation on her face but said nothing.

Autumn Thunder turned to his wife. "I am going to kill Tuck," he said.

She did not ask why. She knew why. Not specifically. She did not know the evil things he had done, other than hunt buffalo, but she had marked him as evil a long time ago, and resolved to keep so far out of his sight that he would not be aware that she existed.

She did not try to argue or dissuade. She found Autumn Thunder's eyes with her own and let them tell him. "I need you here. The children need you here more than Tuck needs to be dead," they said.

But his eyes said something different. They blazed with a fury that told her there was something very personal about why he had to kill Tuck. A revenge killing? Return for personal slight? She knew her man. If Autumn Thunde needed to kill Tuck, then the issue was serious. Autumn Thun der did not look for trouble, not anymore.

"Hear me, my friend," said Sweeney. "Be careful. Ther are two of them. The skinner cannot shoot, but he carries a old Army Colt and a big skinning knife. You know how fa Tuck can shoot. You must not let him see you. You must fin a place where you can get close enough to shoot him good Remember he carries the big Walker Colt. When you go, coun your chances. If they are not good, come home. There wil always be another time."

Autumn Thunder listened and said nothing. There would no be another time, he thought. If the buffalo were gone, the Tuck would soon be gone, maybe to the big *Tai-bo* crowds i St. Louis and the head chief's village in the east. How coul he ever find Tuck among all those white people? That was foolish question. He knew that he would never go to the plac where many whites lived. He would only go away from place where many whites came to.

"Do you have enough ammunition?" Sweeney asked.

Autumn Thunder shrugged his shoulders. Sweeney reache into one of his saddle bags and pulled out a box of cartridge "This should help," he said.

Then he reached down again and pulled out a .38 calibe Colt revolver. "This is almost brand-new," he said. "I didn' like the one the army gave me so I bought this one when got promoted. I won't need it back in Ohio." We got rid o all the Indians there a long time ago, he thought but did no say.

"You might need it when you go after Tuck," he added "Here's some ammunition for it."

Strong feelings welled up inside Autumn Thunder, feeling he would not have been able to communicate even if his En glish were much better. Sweeney understood.

"Say nothing about this, my friend," he said. "Just kill th bastard and don't let him kill you."

Autumn Thunder smiled.

"One more thing," said Sweeney. "The army did not bur everything the Kiowas left behind at the canyon. There is warehouse at Fort Sill where they store Indian things. I foun something of yours in the warehouse, and I brought it to you. I gave it to Gathers The Grass and she put it in your lodge.''

Autumn Thunder nodded and conversation lapsed. Even Gathers The Grass, who always knew what to say to make a stranger feel at ease, had nothing to say.

Finally Autumn Thunder asked Sweeney when he was leaving. Sweeney said he would be going east the following day.

"You have been a friend to me," Autumn Thunder said suddenly. "I will always keep . . . you here." He tapped his head. How strange, he thought. This stranger, this white man, had come into his life unwelcome, on the end of his lance, and yet it made him feel bad to believe that he would never again look upon the man's face.

There would be no ceremony, no "blood brother" drama. Autumn Thunder simply took his hand and squeezed it. "Peace to you, Sweeney. Live a long life."

Gathers The Grass knew that this was not to be her moment. But she could not forget the many days she had spent bringing Sweeney back to health. "Get a good woman," she said. "Have many children. Children good to have. Make it easier to be old."

Sweeney felt old. There was a chill in the air that made his bones ache. He hoped that once he got on the train in Atoka, he would never again have to gallop a horse across a rolling, rutted plain.

Sweeney had always told himself that he was tough. This was just a squaw and a buck, like so many he had seen in his years on the plains. In twenty years' time they would be an old fat squaw and an old fat buck. They wouldn't remember him and only rarely and briefly would they cross his mind, he told himself.

But the lie would not prevail. In the silence that followed, he felt as if he were staring at ghosts; ghosts that would haunt him forever. And he felt guilty, as if he had helped to murder them, even though they still lived and breathed in his presence.

He longed to say something to either of them that would make them remember him, something that would let them know they mattered to him. But he could not because he was too honest. He knew that once he was gone from there he would do his level best to make them not matter to him. There would be no, "I'll come back to see you some day." Certainly no "I will write a letter to Evans and when you come to the store he will read it to you." What, should he tell her that if he marries and his wife has a daughter he will name her "Gathers The Grass?"

Why, for all the Kiowa words he had learned, had he never learned to call Autumn Thunder by his Kiowa name?

Sweeney put his foot in the stirrup and swung into the saddle. He had never been graceful, but this day he seemed weary to Gathers The Grass. Autumn Thunder reached up and shook Sweeney's gloved hand, but he said nothing. Sweeney waved to Gathers The Grass and to Deerfoot. Just before he turned his face away from them forever, Gathers The Grass spoke.

"Do not forget us," she said, simply.

"Do not forget me," he said, kicking his horse gently into a walk, then again into a trot. He wanted to be gone as quickly as decently possible, so he would not have to look back. If he looked back he was afraid his heart would break.

Once he was out of sight, Gathers The Grass turned to Autumn Thunder.

"Why must you kill Tuck?" she asked.

"He killed Ko-yah-te. He killed all the buffalo."

"He may have killed Ko-yah-te. He alone did not kill all the buffalo."

He stood looking at her but did not answer.

"Do you believe that you can kill him without him killing you?" she asked. "We need you alive."

"I will not be killed," he answered. "I have been in many tough battles. I have never died."

"But your medicine was strong then. Will your medicine still be strong?"

"I have always gone to A-do-te. I cannot go to him now. But I know I will not be killed."

"Must you go alone?"

"I will be safer if I have only myself to worry about."

"When are you leaving?"

"As soon as I get my things together. Have you food for me?"

"I will have your food bag and your waterskin ready quickly. Will you take the mule?"

"No. The mule would slow me up. I want to catch him

quickly.'' He handed the reins of his pony to Gathers The Grass and walked slowly to the lodge. He pulled aside the door flap, entered, and looked around. In the semi-darkness of the tepee, his glance fell upon an object leaning against the wall beside the door. It was his lance, the one with which he had once nearly killed Sweeney. A shaft of light stabbed through the gloom from the door flap. In this light he examined the point, and found a bloodstain—Sweeney's blood.

Overhead he saw the geese moving with beautiful precision against a perfect cold blue sky. His pony felt strong beneath him. The autumn air felt cool and thick. Breathing it was like tasting a fine dinner. He felt alive enough to be five young warriors—no, ten. Behind him was his poor, feeble village with its drunken old men and young warriors with no war to fight. Ahead was the enemy. He would kill the enemy. He would plunder the enemy. He would return to the village and the village would celebrate his victory. It had always been so in the Kiowa world. It would be so now.

Just as Sweeney had told him he would, Autumn Thunder picked up the trail of Tuck's heavy wagon just outside the Fort Sill gate. There was a lone rider traveling alongside the wagon. That meant that Tuck was on the horse, and the skinner was driving the wagon. Not one but at least two men to kill. That was all right, they were only white men, not so hard to kill, if he was careful.

The sun was seeking its hole in the horizon like a prairie dog when Autumn Thunder crossed Red River. In the pale pink light he let his gaze become blurred. With him rode Hautau, and Ko-yah-te, and Po-lan-te, and Tsein-kop-te was leading them. The wind was cold in his face, but he felt warm inside surrounded by his companions.

He could not speak to them, but he thought about them. Hau-tau loved melons. Ko-yah-te loved his wife. Po-lan-te loved trouble, any kind of trouble. And Tsein-kop-te? Tsein-kop-te loved whiskey. Suddenly he did not feel the presence of his companions. Like a tumbleweed in a tornado, they were gone.

The wind was cold to his face. The sun was gone now and he had to sleep. The next day would be long and hard. In a familiar grove of cottonwoods and berry bushes he climbed

down from his pony and tied it on a long lead so it could crop
the grass. He pulled off his saddle, his packs, his waterskin
and his gun. He did not make a fire. He ate quickly, and drank
enough water to slake his thirst and no more. He wrapped
himself in a buffalo robe and two blankets, and slept a long
and dreamless sleep. Tomorrow he would kill Tuck.

Chapter 37

The following day dawned as bright and sunny as the last. The wagon made a clear, easy-to-follow trail. It must have been a heavy wagon; there were four mules pulling it and it could not have been going very fast. Still, Tuck had a good head start, so it would take some time to get close.

The new day was considerably warmer. The wind still blew in Autumn Thunder's face, but it was a mild, sunny wind, and he would have enjoyed its touch had he been on a different mission. He felt ready for the challenge. He was well armed, with a fine carbine, Sweeney's Colt, a sharp knife, a bow and seven arrows, and his lance, which had a big knife point, a nine-foot shaft, and bright ribbons streaming from it, ribbons that had been taken in the Anadarko raid by a warrior from Gui-pah-go's band. Autumn Thunder did not remember the warrior's name, but he was down in the hot country now, with Gui-pah-go, Tsen-tainte, and the others that Tay-nay-angopte had chosen for captivity, before Maman-ti had put a curse on him that made him die.

The sun was more than halfway across the sky before Autumn Thunder topped a little rise and saw the square canvas-topped wagon far ahead.

He brought his pony to a halt and backed her up until he could barely see the wagon above the horizon. To the right of the wagon was a lone horse being ridden by a tall, broad-backed man.

Tuck.

Autumn Thunder knew the route they were taking as well as he knew his own heart. For the next hour they would be riding across a broad plain, but then the plain would narrow until they entered a valley closed in by rolling grassy hills—not good hills for an ambush except for one rocky outcrop where a man could hide with a good field of fire.

He backed down behind the rise and rode south about a mile then turned west. Hidden by the roll of the plain, he would pass them quickly and in half their time he would arrive at the outcropping where he would await their arrival.

His plan was simple. The wagon driver would be the closest, most exposed target. He would pick him off, then charge across the space that separated him from Tuck, firing his pistol to keep the hunter's mount unsteady. He knew of Tuck's reputation as a deadly marksman, but he was confident that this *Tai-bo*, firing from the back of a nervous, prancing, tossing *Tai-bo* horse, could not hit a fast-moving Kiowa. No *Tai-bo* could. He and the other warriors used to talk about how they could ride among the horse soldiers and unless they were almost right up against them, the soldiers could fire at them all day long with their pistols and carbines and not hit them.

For two hours Autumn Thunder rode west at an easy gallop, turned north, and eased his pony over a hill, then down the slope to the rock outcropping. The rock outcropping was a favorite spot for Kiowa and Comanche ambushes not only because it provided good cover for shooters, but because there was a hollow right behind the rocks where a shooter could conceal his mount. He tied his pony to a bush in the hollow behind the rocks, stripped off a cotton shirt that had been given him during the last ration distribution, grabbed a piece of jerked deer meat from his food sack, and took his station behind the rocks.

While he waited he chewed on the jerky, which Gathers The Grass had packed for him. Some warriors he knew would not eat for a day before a fight because they thought that a bullet in the gut would more likely be fatal if their belly contained food. Autumn Thunder was filled with confidence. His medicine was good. He would not be killed today. He would kill Tuck. It was his mission. It was what he had been born for.

In his mind was a kind of clock, not one that divided the day into hours and minutes, but one that would tell him when to expect the appearance of his quarry. He closed his eyes and took a short nap. He awakened and drank some water. One last time he checked his carbine, his pistol, and his spare ammunition.

He was not frightened. He was ready for a fight. Now, he thought, let them come. Let them come.

They came. Not over a rise, not around a hillside. Suddenly they were there, a trick played by the sunshine and shadows. He watched them approach, carefully keeping his carbine hidden, with only a single eye exposed through a clump of brush.

Tuck was a powder barrel on a short fuse. The boom times were over—the years of two skinners, fine horses, and free spending in the frontier towns where buffalo hunters gathered. The booze; the whores with open smiles, open arms, and hungry purses; the good meals in fine hotels. Over. The buffalo were going, and he still had a wagonload of lead and powder. And so he made himself believe that out by Double Mountain, where he never failed to find a herd, he would make his last killing.

His last killing would not be the buffalo. That honor would fall to Slats Simmons, the unbathed skinner Tuck had picked up in Fort Riley right after his last two skinners had quit him.

He had been angry at them for suggesting that their kill number had been poor because Tuck had lost his talent for finding the creatures.

"I tell you," he had growled, "there's too many hunters out there. We're runnin' out of critters to kill."

"Hell!" spat Lou Cady, the skinner he had started with seven years before and who quit him every time he went out with him. "I wanna find a hunter who don't believe the buffalo are dyin' out. You'll never find a herd anymore if you don't even believe they exist."

So Slats hired on. He was the only one. It was humiliating for Tuck to have to sell one of his wagons and mule teams, and even more humiliating to find out that Slats was considered a butcher by the northwestern hunters. But no other skinners would go out with Tuck because his temper was legendary. Only Simmons had failed to get the word, which was why he had asked Tuck to advance him a few dollars because he was missing a knife from his set.

Tuck swore a horrible streak of oaths at the poor skinner

but if he wanted a skinner, he would have to spring for a knife. He hated the skinner for that, and hated him more as a month went by without Tuck giving the man a single occasion to use his knives.

He turned and glared at the stumpy, gray-bearded man who drooled tobacco juice down his chin in an unending stream that turned the top of his longjohn shirt a disgusting shade of brown. The man wore a gray slouch hat that had stains the same color. How could that possibly be? Tuck had wondered at first, but camping out one night on the way south he found that Simmons passed the time by placing his hat on the ground brim up six feet away from a large rock. He would then sit on the rock and spend an hour or so spitting long brown streams of tobacco juice into the hat.

Simmons claimed that when the juice dried it stiffened the crown of the hat. "And that's good!" he had told Tuck as if he were dispensing an item of great wisdom.

Simmons never looked left or right. He just held the reins and stared straight ahead over the backs of the mules, his eyelids sagging and his chin bobbing.

"Hey, Simmons!" Tuck called out, not because he had anything to say to the man but because he couldn't bear to see the man so relaxed and unaware driving *his* wagon.

Simmons turned to look at Tuck and opened his mouth to say something, but before he could, Tuck heard the crack of a carbine, and a gush of red blood rushed from the skinner's mouth. The impact of the bullet was enough to topple the skinner in Tuck's direction.

Tuck's horse shied as the skinner tumbled from the wagon seat.

"Damn!" cried the buffalo hunter, and suddenly over beyond the wagon he could see a lone Indian galloping hard across an open space, whooping, firing his pistol, and swinging his blanket around over his head. "Where in hell did he come from?" Tuck muttered through his beard.

Tuck's horse shied again and whinnied in panic, as Autumn Thunder closed in at a hard gallop, but Tuck did not try to fire at the Kiowa from the back of his horse. Instead he leaped off, grabbing his rifle from his scabbard, got down on one knee, and knocked Autumn Thunder out of the saddle with a single shot.

Autumn Thunder grunted as his body hit the ground and the pistol went flying. His pony had come back around and was heading toward the hill they had just descended. In desperation he reached out and caught the long lead that trailed on the ground for just such an occasion. The braided leather arrested the pony's escape midflight and jerked the Kiowa to his feet. He grabbed the pony's tail and let the animal pull him along, half running, half flying, expecting to hear another shot and feel the hot lead tearing through his body, setting it afire.

The rifle Tuck had fired to bring Autumn Thunder down was not his Sharps buffalo gun but a much lighter lever-action Winchester that he very seldom used and consequently lavished little care on. It jammed as he attempted to work the lever.

He swore loudly and reached into the mechanism to free the shell that had failed to eject. He flung the Winchester down, leaped over Simmons' dead body, onto the wagon seat and grabbed the big Sharps rifle he kept carefully rolled in an army blanket behind the seat. There was a box of ammunition he had put together himself just before they had left Fort Sill, and he grabbed it too.

The mules were skittish—the wagon jumped forward and Tuck almost fell off. He set the hand brake, jumped down and started chasing Autumn Thunder, who was struggling to mount his pony without the use of his left arm, which felt as if it were burning from his shoulder down to his elbow. Autumn Thunder looked back and saw the big man draw a bead on him. He hunched down over his pony's back and waited for the fatal shot, but in the excitement of the moment Tuck forgot that he kept his Sharps unloaded when he wasn't using it. The hammer clicked and Autumn Thunder's pony carried him up into the safety of the outcrop.

He ducked down behind the rocks, loaded his carbine, and squeezed off a shot at the kneeling Tuck. Tuck saw the smoke and snapped off a round that zinged off the boulder in front of Autumn Thunder and sent a rock chip spinning into his cheek. He felt the warm drip of blood down the side of his face. He flexed his left arm. Bloody but unbroken, hurting but not that badly hurt.

Tuck stood up and sprinted back to the wagon for cover,

leaving Autumn Thunder to ponder his next move. The Kiow
was outgunned, that was certain. But his position was muc
better. He thought about the situation, analyzed it in a wa
rior's terms.

Tuck was stuck behind a wagon in the middle of a pla
covered with long, dry grass. Autumn Thunder had the hig
ground, with room to move around behind the outcroppir
and even a covered escape route if he cared to give up a
ride away. No chance of that. His wound was a painful furrov
but the bleeding was not severe.

On the other hand, Tuck was the man with the deadly, thu
dering rifle that could kill at a quarter mile or more. Two sho
Two wounds. Autumn Thunder could not afford to let th
buffalo hunter spot him again.

From where Autumn Thunder lay, Tuck was completel
hidden, but the Kiowa knew where he was. He also knew th
sooner or later Tuck would need water. His horse was gon
but there had to be water in the wagon. If he cut the canva
and tried to climb into the wagon, even if he was stealth
Autumn Thunder might see the wagon shift. He looked at th
sky, at the sun much more than halfway across its day's jou
ney, then through the thick brush in front of him he watche
the wagon. Tuck was a man. He might well be able to hol
out until dark, and then he would be able to get into th
wagon.

He saw a shadow shift suddenly under the wagon before h
could level his carbine and shoot. The Sharps roared and
bullet thudded into the earth just in front of Autumn Thunde

Did the man have eyes that could see through bushes? No
but Autumn Thunder remembered the see-far glass that man
buffalo hunters carried on their rifles. Autumn Thunde
snapped off a shot at the shadow and he heard the buffal
hunter growl a guttural curse. It was a sound of a man sud
denly damaged, a good sound to the ear of Autumn Thunde
The hunter fired back quickly, ineffectually, high, the bulle
ricocheting off the big rock behind Autumn Thunder with
vicious, fading whine.

For a long time they waited in silence, each trying to decid
his next move, neither wishing to escape, both craving a kil
and a trophy. The sun was still an hour from the horizon; th
silence was broken by a breeze that had sprung up in the ea

and hissed through the dry grass. In the dark, Autumn Thunder thought, the buffalo hunter could not see to shoot at him. On the other hand, he could climb into the wagon for water, or even crawl off in the grass, catch his horse, and escape.

If I could set the wagon on fire, he thought.

He crawled back to where his pony stood, grabbed the bow and arrows, his cotton shirt, his fire kit, and his food pouch, and scrambled back down to the rock. He tore a strip of cloth from his shirt and wound it around an arrow. Then he reached into his food pouch and scooped up a handful of jerked meat. What he actually had was a mixture of thin smoked deer slices and crushed dried berries held together with a huge amount of congealed fat. He smeared the cotton cloth with a thick coating of the fatty substance, then repeated the effort with a second arrow.

He had no more fat left. Two chances were all he had. He arranged some dried grass in a tiny pile, struck flint and steel together, struck again, and then again. The grass would not catch. He pulled a bullet from his pouch, bit into the lead, and started twisting the cartridge until it separated. He poured the gunpowder on the grass. Then he repeated the action twice more.

Tuck's rifle cracked and a bullet flew through the bush near where Autumn thunder had been concealing himself. The bullet thunked into the earth.

He struck the flint and steel and the powder caught, then the grass caught. He held the arrow to the fire until the cloth caught with a sizzle, then he nocked the arrow, pulled it back, and from behind the rock let the arrow fly on a high arc toward the wagon. The wind caught hold of the arrow and blew it westward so it fell ten feet in front of the mules, also ten feet short. Fanned by the wind, the fire swept westward through the dry grass, and then Autumn Thunder knew he would win.

He ignited his second arrow and aimed it well east of the wagon. This time he raised his head above the rock to make certain of his aim. He saw the shadow move and he ducked, just in time to hear the bullet whiz over his head. He pulled the arrow back a little farther, aimed for a lower arc, and released the string with a *twang*. The arrow hit the long grass about twenty yards east of the wagon; when the grass flared up, and the wind caught the fire, the Kiowa could see that the wagon was right in its path.

There are men who can face many kinds of death without flinching. Bullets, arrows, flashing hooves, tomahawks, bears, cougars are all the same to these men, to whom death is an adversary to be beaten, not a force to surrender to. But even the bravest have a weakness.

Tuck was a brave man. His weakness was fire.

Autumn Thunder saw him sprint away from the wagon, as far from the fire as fast as he could. The mules, in a panic from the fire, strained at their traces but the heavy wagon, with the brake set, would not budge. Autumn Thunder laid his sights on Tuck, pulled the trigger, and saw the man's legs go out from under him. Tuck arose in a panic and continued to run, this time limping in slow motion.

Autumn Thunder did not hesitate. Loading as he ran, he sprinted out onto the plain. The fire swept rapidly, harmlessly, past the wagon, past the mules, and now Autumn Thunder had the wagon for cover, and there was Tuck, limping heavily in the long grass eighty yards away and making very slow progress. In his panic, he had dropped his rifle.

Autumn Thunder crawled out from under the wagon and slowly, deliberately, walking in a crouch out of habit, pursued his gimpy quarry. Every few yards, Tuck's pace grew slower until it seemed he could not move another step. Autumn Thunder was impatient. He picked up the pace to an easy jog, until he was fifty yards away. Then suddenly, with an evil, gap-toothed grin, Tuck turned, his big old Walker Colt in his hand and fired, once, twice, three times.

His rounds were short and well wide. With a Sharps and a telescope sight he was deadly, but with a pistol he was just another man. Now *he* was outgunned. Autumn Thunder fell to one knee, took aim, squeezed the trigger of his carbine. Tuck fell forward on his belly, but he wasn't through yet. He was afraid only of fire, not of bullets, and not of death. He climbed to his knees, pulled back the hammer of the Walker Colt, and fired again. And again. And then the hammer clicked on an empty chamber.

Autumn Thunder had reloaded but did not shoot. He ran toward the wounded buffalo hunter, watching him carefully as he reached into the pocket of his buffaloskin jacket. He pulled out a handful of bullets, but his hand was weak and shaking from his wounds and most of the bullets fell to the ground. One bullet remained in his hand, but his fingers couldn't manipulate it into the loading position and then, when they finally did, he couldn't seem to insert it into the chamber.

By the time he did, Autumn Thunder was there. He stunned Tuck with a quick rifle-butt stroke across his jaw, then, as Tuck pitched forward, glassy-eyed, he grabbed the Walker Colt and laid it aside. He looked quickly at Tuck's wounds, one that had crippled his right leg and one that had gone through his upper body and smashed his left collarbone.

Autumn Thunder always wore rawhide strips, wound three times around the biceps of each arm. It was part of his medicine.

Now he untied and unwound the strips, and used them to bind the buffalo hunter's hands behind his back, and his ankles.

Slowly Autumn Thunder walked across the plain, and up the hill to his pony. He rode it out onto the plain, dismounted, and carried the waterskin to where Tuck lay on his back, straining at his bonds, his eyes fierce and dark.

"You want water, buffalo-killer?"

"Go to hell, you filthy redskin!" was the reply. Without fire, there was no fear in the man. In clench-jawed curses he defied Autumn Thunder to do his worst.

Autumn Thunder reached into his waistband and drew out his scalping knife, a big butcher knife he had managed to keep hidden throughout his captivity.

Tuck tried to speak but he couldn't seem to remember how to form the words. So he spat a bloody stream at his Kiowa nemesis. Autumn Thunder ignored it as it flew by him. He cut open Tuck's jacket and slid it away from Tuck's body. He did the same with his shirt underneath, and his britches. The hunter now lay pale and naked in the pink twilight.

Tuck found his tongue.

"Well now, you fool," he said. "My clothes ain't no good to you now that you cut 'em off," said Tuck. Autumn Thunder ignored the remark. His knife slid into the flesh atop the hunter's head. He carved a circle around Tuck's crown, pushing the knife deep under the scalp, against his skull. The blood flowed like a red curtain and Tuck groaned but he did not cry

out, though he muttered a string of curses that Autumn Thun
der did not understand.

And now he carved a straight incision from the bottom o
Tuck's neck to his groin. Tuck wriggled and kicked and
grunted with pain as Autumn Thunder sliced the skin away
from the muscle, and pulled. Tuck had lost so much blood tha
his strength was gone. He could only kick feebly in stunned
exhaustion and watch the warrior as he tore the skin away
from his body, leaving his quivering muscles exposed like raw
meat to the sunshine. The blood flowed and spurted, covering
Autumn Thunder until it looked as if both men were mortally
wounded. As the Kiowa ripped the skin from the muscle tissue
the pain became so great that Tuck finally began to cry, then
to beg for his death.

And when at last the skin had been peeled completely from
his front torso, Autumn Thunder untied Tuck's rawhide bond
and rewound them three times around the biceps of each arm

"You can walk home now, if you like," Autumn Thunder
said, softly.

"Kill me, damn you, kill me, I'll bless your name with my
dying breath if you do!" Tuck cried.

"You don't know my name," said Autumn Thunder.

They eyed each other for awhile, the victorious Kiowa and
the dying, agonized buffalo hunter. While Tuck followed him
with his eyes, Autumn Thunder walked to his pony and took
hold of his lance. The last thing on earth Tuck beheld was a
Kiowa warrior standing over him like a giant, raising his lance
high and thrusting it through his belly, pinning him to the
earth. With a final strangled scream, the life of Tuck the buf
falo hunter came to a close.

Chapter 38

Autumn Thunder took the scalp of the skinner and left him otherwise unmutilated, sprawled on the plain, a few yards from the naked, skinned body of Tuck, noted buffalo hunter and Kiowa-killer. He hung the scalps from the frame that held the canvas top of the wagon. The scalps blew in the breeze, and dried out nicely.

He gave Fort Sill a wide birth as he drove the wagon home. It was a chore, learning to drive a four-mule team, but he had great talent for handling animals, and he mastered them.

The going was slow and gave Autumn Thunder plenty of opportunity to think of what he would do next. The death of Tuck closed a chapter in his life that began the day he had bested Sweeney in battle and then decided to let him live. Sweeney was gone now, well on his way to Atoka to take a train north to where there were no Indians.

The time had come for Autumn Thunder to make a new life where there were no soldiers. He remembered that in the days when they would ride westward to fight the Utes, they would see no white soldiers. True, the land was hard and unforgiving, but the Kiowa people could survive anywhere.

Now was the time to go. Sooner or later the white men would find Tuck's body and they would pretend he was a good man so they could punish an Indian for killing him. Sooner or later someone would wonder how Autumn Thunder had managed to get a wagon and a mule team. Sooner or later, if he did not break out, Autumn Thunder would be rotting in prison down in the hot country.

So when he arrived in the village, he went to the tepees of

Kone-bo-hone, Talia-koi, and Yay-go and told them it was time for them to go. He had a wagon full of weapons and ammunition, animals for them and their families to ride, even a few cows to drive along with them.

The men were still young and full of adventure, and they were bored. Guns? they asked, their eyes eager. Ponies? Mules? When do we go?

Tonight, he told them.

He told Gathers The Grass the same, and got no argument from her. She did point out that there was no sense taking a wagon full of lead when it would be necessary to transport the women and children. He was reluctant to leave any ammunition behind, but she convinced him to leave some.

They agreed to tell only one person before they left, and Autumn Thunder chose Tsein-kop-te to be that person. Three hours before dawn, while the others were preparing to leave, Autumn Thunder awakened his old friend with a gentle tap on the shoulder. He pointed to the door flap and the two men left the lodge. He explained to the old warrior that some of them were leaving.

"Why do you tell me and not Au-sai-mah?" he asked. "Au-sai-mah is village chief. He is the one who should be told."

"Au-sai-mah would try to make us stay. He would say that the people need us."

"Au-sai-mah is very wise," Tsein-kop-te answered. "He would be right."

Autumn Thunder shook his head. "Au-sai-mah would be wrong. You have seen what is happening to us. The old men stay drunk. The young men wait for their rations and have nothing to do. The women shout at their men that they are lazy good-for-nothings. The children are not taught to hunt because there is no game. They are not taught to fight because they have nothing left to fight with. The white men try to teach them useless things."

Tsein-kop-te stood staring at Autumn Thunder, looking ashamed, also realizing that his mouth felt dry.

"I wish I could go with you," he said. "I am too old."

"You must stay, even if you would go," Autumn Thunder replied. "I want you to tell the people that if we find a good place to live that is away from the white people, a place where we can live the way we were meant to live, then we will send somebody back to them, to take them to us."

Tsein-kop-te nodded his head. "It is good," he said. "Will give them hope."

"I hope to give them life," Autumn Thunder replied. "Tell them we will find a place for our people if we have to ride all the way into the setting sun."

Autumn Thunder had left the wagon hidden in a cedar thicket a half mile away from the village. Now, quietly, he and the others loaded the wagon with all the food they had and filled every container they had with water, which they also stowed in the wagon. Next they loaded the children, and mounted every horse and mule they had. They had none to spare. Whoever did not have a mount rode in the wagon.

When the sun was still two hours below the eastern horizon, he flapped his reins and the mules began to move. By the time the first light of dawn lay pale on the plain, the refugees had ridden beyond the hills neighboring Fort Sill. Autumn Thunder's three cohorts were patrolling in all directions but they saw not a soul. And then, two hours after sunup, the clouds began to gather and a cold rain began to fall.

Yay-go came to Autumn Thunder with a cloud on his face darker than those in the sky.

"What kind of omen is this?" he asked. "A cold rain our very first day out?"

"It is good medicine, my brother," Autumn Thunder answered, thinking of the medicine man, Maman-ti, and hoping he proved to be a better prophet. "This good hard rain will cover our trail. By the time they find out we are gone they will have no idea what direction we have taken."

"But you told Tsein-kop-te."

Autumn Thunder smiled. "I told him we were going. I did not tell him where or by what trail. Still, I am worried that the soldiers will catch us, bring us back to the fort, and send us down to the prison in the hot country. If they ever put me behind walls, I will kill myself."

At the end of the first day Autumn Thunder found a grove of cottonwoods that grew along a small creek. The rain had stopped. The night was mild and the air had a wonderful smell to it. "No tepees tonight," he said. "If anybody is out looking for us, I don't want them to see our lodges.

So the children slept in the wagon and the men and wome made ready to sleep on old buffalo skins piled on the groun

"Do you think anybody is out looking for us?" Yay-g asked.

"I think nobody outside Au-sai-mah's village knows we ar gone. And they will not tell."

"But we should know if we are being followed," Yay-g insisted, stubbornly.

"We will know," said Autumn Thunder. "We have not ye traveled so far. I will ride back tonight and see if anybody i following us. They will have to guess. The rain has washe away our trail."

He saddled his pony and rode eastward in a careful trot ove the slippery grass. The clouds had cleared and the stars wer brilliant. The moon was so bright that he could see long dis tances. What he could not see, he could hear. The plains wer as they should be. When he stopped to listen, as he did ever few miles, the night sounds were as they should be. Halfwa back to the fort, after less than two hours on the back of hi pony, he felt that there was no need to continue. They ha made a clean break. They were so few, and the *Tai-bos* wer so careless, that by the time they found some of the enrolle Kiowas were missing, Autumn Thunder would be on the othe side of the Staked Plains. Let them look for their lost Indian at the bottom of Palo Duro Canyon. All they would find woul be ghosts.

He got back in time to grab a few hours of sleep then, befor dawn, they were moving west again, slowly, inexorably. Lik a white man's wagon train.

The fifth day out dawned misty, promising more rain. Talia koi peered through the mists and saw them then, the vague curved bodies, the great woolly heads, hundreds of them thousands of them, filling the valley far ahead. He urged hi mule into a trot to where Autumn Thunder was sitting on hi pony, trying to decide on the route for the rest of the day.

"Can you see them?" Talia-koi asked, pointing toward the valley that opened up in the northwest.

Autumn Thunder squinted and followed Talia-koi's finger "See what?"

"The buffalo!" Talia-koi replied. "See!" He crooked hi

elbow and straightened his arm twice, insistently, as if to urge Autumn Thunder's vision through the mists, to the mighty animals that had been the source the Kiowas' greatness.

"Oh, them," Autumn Thunder said. "I saw them yesterday morning. I rode to them, but they were not there. They are not for us to kill. They are only for us to follow. Now. Maybe where they stop, there is where we should stop."

The mist was fading. Talia-koi's eyes could no longer see the buffalo. "They were there," he said. "I know they were there."

Autumn Thunder nodded. "Only to show us the way, my brother," he said, and he turned his pony toward where Talia-koi had seen the buffalo vanish. Autumn Thunder looked back at the wagon and those riding mules and ponies on either side of it. Beyond the wagon, toward the east, the mist had closed in behind them. He could only hope that someday the mist would open up once again, and his people would follow them westward, that once again they would raise their tepees for miles beneath the cottonwoods along the banks of some great western river.

Valley of the Greasy Grass, June 1876

When Stephanie walked outside, the hazy morning fog was just beginning to lift, revealing that she had overslept considerably. Waving to Red Bead, whose lodge stood next to theirs, she began to walk toward the rushing hum of the river when suddenly a warrior came splashing across the water, riding hell-bent into the center of the Cheyenne camp, yelling excitedly and waving his rifle in the air. Her heart froze as she mentally translated his cries into English:

"The Blue Coats are attacking!"

Stephanie dropped her water bucket and dashed back to her lodge. Everywhere around her chaos erupted as mothers called out for their children and babies wailed in fright. Young children stood by, their eyes round with fear. Two girls began gathering the smaller children together in a protective huddle while the boys looked to their elder brothers, hoping for the chance to use their toy weapons. Men rushed into their lodges in search of their bows and guns, shouting orders to their families.

Stephanie reached Red Bead, who remained calm amid the pandemonium, calling out for several boys to put down their small game bows and enter their lodges. Disappointed, they obeyed. "What are we to do?" Stephanie asked the older woman.

Before Red Bead could reply, Chase galloped into the center of the circle of lodges and leaped from Thunderbolt's back. He had with him half a dozen of the horses from their herd including the big dun. "Where are the children?" he demanded.

"Still asleep—or at least they were," Stephanie replied.

"Get them up and pack some food and water quickly. I've brought horses. Can you handle the dun?"

"Yes, but—"

"Our scouts say the soldiers will be here soon," he interrupted her. "I want you well out of the line of fire by then."

Red Bead nodded, checking the position of the sun in the hazy sky. "Plenty time." She entered her lodge and quickly set to work.

Stephanie did not budge. "How many soldiers are there? Surely their leader can't hope to attack a camp of this size unless he has several thousand men."

"We don't know their strength yet or even who it is—could be Crook or Terry, but I'd bet it's Custer, riding hell-bent through fog all morning with no advance reconnaissance to tell him how badly outnumbered he'll be."

Icy fingers of dread squeezed her heart. "What are you going to do, Chase?" *He'll have to fight.*

"See you to safety, then join my uncle and the rest of our warriors."

Stephanie pressed her hand on his naked chest, stopping him. "Chase, they could kill you."

He stroked her cheek and held her. "I don't plan to die today," he said simply. "Now, let's get Smooth Stone and Tiny Dancer. I want to be certain you're well away from the fighting. The soldiers will come from across the river. Elk Bull wants the women to camp on the benchlands far to the west, out of harm's way."

They entered the lodge where the children were awake, sitting wide-eyed on their pallets. At a glance it was obvious that they were badly frightened. They had already suffered so many tragic losses in their brief lifetimes. Stephanie prayed there would be no more this day. "You must pack your things quickly. We are moving west to the benchlands with the other families," she said calmly.

Tiny Dancer ran to her but Smooth Stone looked at Chase expectantly. "I heard the crier say Blue Coats were attacking."

"They're on their way, yes," Chase replied.

"I will fight them beside you. You will be proud of me," the boy said boldly, reaching for his small bow and quiver.

"Listen well, Smooth Stone, for I give you a very important duty." At once the child paused and looked up at him. "You must protect your sister and foster mother and Aunt Red Bead. Some warriors must see that they get safely to the benchlands. Will you do this thing for me?"

The boy swallowed manfully, disappointed that he could not join the battle with his hero but not surprised for he knew he was yet small and unproven. He had been entrusted with the women of their family. That was an honor for which he would endeavor to be worthy. "I will do as you say," he replied solemnly.

Chase hugged the boy. "I am proud of you, Smooth Stone." Then he took Tiny Dancer from Stephanie's arms and held her for a moment to calm her trembling. Setting her down he said, "It will be all right. Gather your belongings and do as your foster mother says." She nodded gravely.

Stephanie and Chase looked at each other as the children obediently began to pick up their simple possessions. "I must go. You know what to do. Elk Bull and some of the other older warriors are waiting at the edge of camp."

"We'll hurry, Chase." There was so much she longed to say, but she could not find the words.

He pulled her into his arms for a swift kiss, just as the sharp crack of rifle fire echoed up the valley from the south. At once he released her. "They're coming at the Cheyenne camp first! No time to waste," he said, scooping up Tiny Dancer and thrusting her into Stephanie's arms as the child clutched her doll tightly to her chest.

Smooth Stone led them out of the lodge looking over his shoulder to be certain Stephanie followed. Chase lifted the boy onto a small pinto, then handed Tiny Dancer up. Red Bead, laden with two large packs, emerged from her lodge. Chase took the items from his aunt and helped her onto a gentle old mare, then handed her one of the packs. Stephanie waited beside the dun, holding the reins of the spare horses. There had been no time to pack their belongings. She had heard stories around the forts about whole villages set to the torch. Visions of the charred ruins of a whole winter's hard work flashed before her eyes. *It isn't fair!*

Everywhere horses were churning up thick dust as youths rode in with their family mounts and women began to load the ponies with belongings. Dogs barked excitedly, adding to the melee. The shouts of angry warriors blended with the wails of babies. Ominously the sharp report of distant gunfire and the loud yips of embattled Cheyenne and Lakota rolled up the valley floor.

Once his family was safely en route across the valley, Chase turned Thunderbolt to the south, headed toward the battle. By the time he arrived the warriors had driven the attacking soldiers from their horses. The Blue Coats were dug in along the river in a dense stand of timber from which they fired desultory shots. The warriors, too, had mostly dismounted and were returning fire from behind rocks and bushes. There seemed to be more than ample defenders to keep the troops pinned down.

Judging from the number of rounds fired, there could surely be no more than a couple of hundred soldiers in the trees. Where were the rest? Remembering Custer's tactics at Washita, splitting his command and attacking from several sides at once, Chase grew worried. Then he saw the rising plumes of dust to the east, northerly along the steep ridge across the river which was rent by two deep ravines. It would take only moments for soldiers to pour out of them and across the shallow ford in the river.

The nearest of all the combined camps was that of the Cheyenne, most of whom were engaged in fighting the entrenched soldiers to the south. Turning Thunderbolt around, he headed back up the valley toward the Lakota camp where the chiefs readied their men. If this was Custer, Chase had learned a thing or two about how they must fight the Long Hair. As he urged the big black forward, he prayed not all of General Terry's forces were converging on them, especially any coming from the west where the noncombatants had sought sanctuary. But he knew bluebellies never considered the old, the women or the children exempt from slaughter.

When he reached the central Lakota camp, which was scattered several miles along the twisting riverbank, he saw the same pandemonium he'd witnessed earlier with the Cheyenne. Wasting no time, he searched for the young war chiefs among Sitting Bull's men. Spying Gall, one of the most influential chiefs, Chase headed toward the Lakota, a man who had listened with respect when he spoke in council.

"My warriors bring word of many more Long Knives beyond the ridge," Gall said without preamble, pointing to the east. "What of those who attacked from the south?"

"They are being held down but I fear many more come from the east. They will ride through the coulee there."

Gall nodded. "My warriors ready themselves to stop that. I have already sent some down to the edge of the water to lie in wait in the bushes.

"What of Crazy Horse?" Chase knew the young war chief mistrusted him because of his white blood, yet Crazy Horse was the most brilliant tactician among all the Lakota.

"He gathers his warriors to the north of here. There are many of them and they can strike quickly wherever they are needed. He has said to tell you he is grateful for the many-bullet rifles you brought us. Now more than ever they will be needed."

Chase had brought Henry and Winchester repeaters as gifts from his band. The loot had been taken from raids on stages and supply trains last summer. "I am only glad my brothers have the weapons this day," he replied. "I think these Blue Coats are led by the Long Hair, Custer. He would split his command this way. We must learn how many soldiers he has and where he has sent them. If they ride down on us from the north or worst of all, the west, our women and children will be in terrible danger."

"Come. You should tell this thing to Crazy Horse and see what he will do. I will lead my warriors across the river to the coulee and stop the Blue Coats there."

Chase nodded, knowing he would stand a better chance of having the Lakota war chief listen because of his gifts than he would have before last night. Just then the sound of a bugle blowing a charge rolled across the open river. Gall yelled for his warriors to follow him and vaulted onto his horse. Quickly the dust churned up from the hundreds of ponies filled the air as the Hunkpapa charged toward the river with his warriors.

Chase kneed Thunderbolt, guiding him through the melee of people toward Crazy Horse's camp. Some warriors still adorned themselves for battle while others rushed back for fresh horses. Women returned to seize more belongings left

behind in the first dash to get the children to safety. In a few
moments he spied the great war chief, mounted on a splendid
piebald stallion, and made his way toward him.

Crazy Horse was a young man with fiercely imposing features. Although not particularly tall by Cheyenne standards,
he sat on his horse with arrogant grace, calling out commands
with the cool aplomb of a West Point veteran. His keen brown
eyes were set deep in a wide flat face with high cheekbones
and surprisingly well-defined eyebrows below a shallow forehead. His heavy hair was stretched tightly from a center part
into two thick braids adorned with eagle feathers. A deeply
grooved mouth with wide thin lips set in a flat line gave his
face a perpetually austere appearance. He inclined his head to
Chase when the Cheyenne reined in beside him. Chase quickly
outlined his fears.

Crazy Horse took it all in, weighing the White Wolf's
words. Then the slightest hint of a smile touched his mouth.
"I, too, am going to attack from behind." He pointed northward to a shallow ford in the river across to the east where
the steep bluffs sloped off.

"We will go around the hills and circle the Blue Coats."
He made a sweeping motion, curving his arm in an arc. "No
one will escape . . ."

The sun was at its full summer zenith. Chase reckoned the
date to be late in June although he had no way to accurately
count the days. Waves of blistering heat pounded down on
him as he rode through the scene of carnage, intensifying his
building sense of horror. In the past five years he had seen
bloody battlefields, but nothing ever of this magnitude. Although the victorious Lakota and Cheyenne did not know it
they had utterly annihilated the command of George Arms-
trong Custer, the infamous Long Hair. Chase recognized what
remained of the regimental flags and other insignia.

The battlefield stretched nearly three miles across the ridge
and ravines of the Valley of the Greasy Grass. Everywhere
bodies lay sprawled grotesquely in death, some scalped of
their hair, others of their beards. Paper money, bright green
against the brown dusty earth, fluttered in the wind, tossed
away by the Indians, who saw no value in the 7th's last pay
roll. Rather they took the gaudy uniforms of the officers

proudly donning jackets with gold braid and trousers with yellow stripes, even though the tall Horse Indian's arms and legs were usually too long for the clothes to fit. A group gathered around a stripped soldier, marveling at the large eagle tattooed across his chest, never having seen "war paint" on a white man before.

The 7th's horses were rounded up. The saddles would be given to the women and old men. Cartridge belts and guns were also sought after prizes, as were tobacco and coffee. Here and there other items were taken, the whiskey flasks being especially popular with some of the young warriors. Field glasses were another valuable prize, but pocket watches and compasses frightened the Indians. One youth pulled a ticking watch from the pocket of a soldier and held it to his ear, exclaiming, "It is alive!" Then he tossed it away, fearful of the White Eyes medicine.

Chase could only guess how many soldiers had died in the senseless attack but the numbers were staggering—probably several hundred. He had seen Custer's body, shot in both head and heart, lying up on the ridge surrounded by his troops. The blaze in those zealous pale blue eyes had been extinguished forever, yet Chase found no comfort in the sight. The Indians had not recognized the Long Hair, for he had cut his hair before this campaign. Chase did not tell anyone who he was. What use was there now? The greatest tragedy of the day was not Custer's death, but the death it would bring to the Lakota and Cheyenne. The 7th Cavalry's destruction would be enough to bring white vengeance down on the victors, who had paid a high price already. Dozens of Lakota and Cheyenne had perished. Now their women came to claim the bodies, slashing their arms in mourning as the slain warriors were carried away for burial. He knew by nightfall the sky would blaze brightly as the lodges and possessions of the dead were burned.

There would be no celebration after such a costly battle, but Chase knew his people had no idea what this unexpected victory would cost them. He did. Generals Terry and Crook would not be all that far behind Custer. Once Sheridan learned of the death of his favorite young officer, he would move heaven and earth to destroy those who had killed him. There would be no place on earth they could hide.

I must get Stevie out of here before it's too late.

He had put off the melancholy thought during the hours the battle had raged, fighting with Gall's Lakota in the narrow ravine where soldiers fired down on them from the heights until the numerically superior Indians climbed around and encircled them. If not for the repeating rifles he had brought in such numbers, the bluebellies might yet have cut through and ridden across the valley to destroy their families. As it was, a small force of troopers—the first to attack the Cheyenne from the south—still held out in the timber, having been reinforced later in the course of the battle. Once Custer's main force was destroyed, Chase had wished to fight no more. Some Indians continued to keep the troopers pinned down, and had run off all their horses, but would wait to rush them until their ammunition ran out. Enough warriors had already died this day.

Chase knew what he must do.

THE ENDLESS SKY
**by Shirl Henke—look
for it in January from
St. Martin's Paperbacks!**

THE TRAIL DRIVE SERIES
by Ralph Compton

From St. Martin's Paperbacks

The only riches Texas had left after the Civil War were five million maverick longhorns and the brains, brawn and boldness to drive them north to where the money was. Now, Ralph Compton brings this violent and magnificent time to life in an extraordinary epic series based on the history-blazing trail drives.

THE GOODNIGHT TRAIL (BOOK 1)
_____ 92815-7 $5.99 U.S./$7.99 Can.
THE WESTERN TRAIL (BOOK 2)
_____ 92901-3 $5.99 U.S./$7.99 Can.
THE CHISOLM TRAIL (BOOK 3)
_____ 92953-6 $5.99 U.S./$7.99 Can.
THE BANDERA TRAIL (BOOK 4)
_____ 95143-4 $5.50 U.S./$6.50 Can.
THE CALIFORNIA TRAIL (BOOK 5)
_____ 95169-8 $5.99 U.S./$7.99 Can.
THE SHAWNEE TRAIL (BOOK 6)
_____ 95241-4 $5.99 U.S./$7.99 Can.
THE VIRGINIA CITY TRAIL (BOOK 7)
_____ 95306-2 $5.50 U.S./$6.50 Can.
THE DODGE CITY TRAIL (BOOK 8)
_____ 95380-1 $5.99 U.S./$7.99 Can.
THE OREGON TRAIL (BOOK 9)
_____ 95547-2 $5.99 U.S./$7.99 Can.
THE SANTA FE TRAIL (BOOK 10)
_____ 96296-7 $5.99 U.S./$7.99 Can.

TERRY C. JOHNSTON

THE PLAINSMEN

THE BOLD WESTERN SERIES FROM ST. MARTIN'S PAPERBACKS

COLLECT THE ENTIRE SERIES!

SIOUX DAWN (Book 1)
92732-0 _____$5.99 U.S. _____$7.99 CAN.

RED CLOUD'S REVENGE (Book 2)
92733-9 _____$5.99 U.S. _____$6.99 CAN.

THE STALKERS (Book 3)
92963-3 _____$5.99 U.S. _____$7.99 CAN.

BLACK SUN (Book 4)
92465-8 _____$5.99 U.S. _____$6.99 CAN.

DEVIL'S BACKBONE (Book 5)
92574-3 _____$5.99 U.S. _____$6.99 CAN.

SHADOW RIDERS (Book 6)
92597-2 _____$5.99 U.S. _____$6.99 CAN.

DYING THUNDER (Book 7)
92834-3 _____$5.99 U.S. _____$6.99 CAN.

BLOOD SONG (Book 8)
92921-8 _____$5.99 U.S. _____$6.99 CAN.